KU-323-927

INVINCIBLE

By Troy Denning

INVINCIBLE

TROY DENNING

arrow books

Published in the United Kingdom by Arrow Books in 2009

1 3 5 7 9 10 8 6 4 2

First published in the United Kingdom in 2008 by Century

Arrow Books
The Random House Group Limited
20 Vauxhall Bridge Road, London SW1V 2SA

www.rbooks.co.uk
www.starwars.com

Addresses for companies within The Random House Group Limited can be found at:
www.randomhouse.co.uk

The Random House Group Limited Reg. No. 954009

A CIP catalogue record for this book
is available from the British Library

ISBN 9780099491187

The Random House Group Limited supports The Forest Stewardship Council (FSC), the
leading international forest certification organisation. All our titles that are printed on
Greenpeace approved FSC certified paper carry the FSC logo.
Our paper procurement policy can be found at:
www.rbooks.co.uk/environment

Mixed Sources
Product group from well-managed
forests and other controlled sources
www.fsc.org Cert no. TT-COC-2139
© 1996 Forest Stewardship Council

Printed and bound in the United Kingdom by
CPI Bookmarque, Croydon, CR0 4TD

For my parents
Robert and Jane Denning
and the rescue dogs
of the
Longears Ranch

acknowledgments

Many people contributed to this book in ways large and small. I would like to thank them all, especially the following: Andria Hayday for her support, critiques, and many fine suggestions; James Luceno, Leland Chee, Howard Roffman, Amy Gary, Pablo Hidalgo, and Keith Clayton for their valuable contributions during our brainstorming sessions; Shelly Shapiro and Sue Rostoni for their many wonderful ideas, for their patience and insight, and especially for being so much fun to work with; my fellow writers, Aaron Allston and Karen Traviss, for all their hard work and their myriad other contributions to this book and the series; Laura Jorstad, for her careful copyediting under pressure (with my apologies); all the people at Lucasfilm and Del Rey who make writing *Star Wars* so much fun; and, finally, George Lucas for letting us take his galaxy in this exciting new direction.

Most of the jokes at the start of each chapter came from one of my favorite *Star Wars* collections, Kevin J. Anderson and Rebecca Moesta's *Young Jedi Knights* series. Jokes were also contributed by Andria Hayday and Sue Rostoni.

THE STAR WARS NOVELS TIMELINE

1020 YEARS BEFORE
STAR WARS: A New Hope

Darth Bane: Path of Destruction
Darth Bane: Rule of Two

33 YEARS BEFORE
STAR WARS: A New Hope

Darth Maul: Saboteur*

32.5 *YEARS BEFORE STAR WARS: A New Hope*

Cloak of Deception
Darth Maul: Shadow Hunter

32 *YEARS BEFORE STAR WARS: A New Hope*

STAR WARS: EPISODE I
THE PHANTOM MENACE

29 *YEARS BEFORE STAR WARS: A New Hope*

Rogue Planet

27 *YEARS BEFORE STAR WARS: A New Hope*

Outbound Flight

22.5 *YEARS BEFORE STAR WARS: A New Hope*

The Approaching Storm

22 *YEARS BEFORE STAR WARS: A New Hope*

STAR WARS: EPISODE II
ATTACK OF THE CLONES

Republic Commando: Hard
Contact

21.5 *YEARS BEFORE STAR WARS: A New Hope*

Shatterpoint

21 *YEARS BEFORE STAR WARS: A New Hope*

The Cestus Deception
The Hive*
Republic Commando: Triple Zero
Republic Commando: True Colors

20 *YEARS BEFORE STAR WARS: A New Hope*

MedStar I: Battle Surgeons
MedStar II: Jedi Healer

19.5 *YEARS BEFORE STAR WARS: A New Hope*

Jedi Trial
Yoda: Dark Rendezvous

19 *YEARS BEFORE STAR WARS: A New Hope*

Labyrinth of Evil

STAR WARS: EPISODE III
REVENGE OF THE SITH

Dark Lord: The Rise of Darth
Vader

Coruscant Nights I: Jedi Twilight

10–0 *YEARS BEFORE STAR WARS: A New Hope*

The Han Solo Trilogy:
The Paradise Snare
The Hutt Gambit
Rebel Dawn

5–2 *YEARS BEFORE STAR WARS: A New Hope*

*The Adventures of Lando
Calrissian*

The Han Solo Adventures

STAR WARS: A New Hope
YEAR 0

Death Star

STAR WARS: EPISODE IV
A NEW HOPE

0–3 *YEARS AFTER STAR WARS: A New Hope*

Tales from the Mos Eisley
Cantina
Allegiance
Galaxies: The Ruins
of Dantooine
Splinter of the Mind's Eye

3 *YEARS AFTER STAR WARS: A New Hope*

STAR WARS: EPISODE V
THE EMPIRE STRIKES BACK

Tales of the Bounty Hunters

3.5 *YEARS AFTER STAR WARS: A New Hope*

Shadows of the Empire

4 *YEARS AFTER STAR WARS: A New Hope*

STAR WARS: EPISODE VI
RETURN OF THE JEDI

Tales from Jabba's Palace
Tales from the Empire
Tales from the New Republic

The Bounty Hunter Wars:
The Mandalorian Armor
Slave Ship
Hard Merchandise

The Truce at Bakura

6.5-7.5 YEARS AFTER
STAR WARS: A New Hope

X-Wing:
Rogue Squadron
Wedge's Gamble
The Krytos Trap
The Bacta War
Wraith Squadron
Iron Fist
Solo Command

8 *YEARS AFTER STAR WARS: A New Hope*

The Courtship of Princess Leia
A Forest Apart*
Tatooine Ghost

9 *YEARS AFTER STAR WARS: A New Hope*

The Thrawn Trilogy:
Heir to the Empire
Dark Force Rising
The Last Command

X-Wing: Isard's Revenge

11 *YEARS AFTER STAR WARS: A New Hope*

The Jedi Academy Trilogy:
Jedi Search
Dark Apprentice
Champions of the Force

I, Jedi

12-13 *YEARS AFTER STAR WARS: A New Hope*

Children of the Jedi
Darksaber
Planet of Twilight
X-Wing: Starfighters of Adumar

14 *YEARS AFTER STAR WARS: A New Hope*

The Crystal Star

16-17 *YEARS AFTER STAR WARS: A New Hope*

The Black Fleet Crisis Trilogy:
Before the Storm
Shield of Lies
Tyrant's Test

17 *YEARS AFTER STAR WARS: A New Hope*

The New Rebellion

18 *YEARS AFTER STAR WARS: A New Hope*

The Corellian Trilogy:
Ambush at Corellia
Assault at Selonia
Showdown at Centerpoint

19 *YEARS AFTER STAR WARS: A New Hope*

The Hand of Thrawn Duology:
Specter of the Past
Vision of the Future

22 *YEARS AFTER STAR WARS: A New Hope*

Fool's Bargain*
Survivor's Quest

25 YEARS AFTER
STAR WARS: A New Hope

Boba Fett: A Practical Man*

The New Jedi Order:
Vector Prime
Dark Tide I: Onslaught
Dark Tide II: Ruin
Agents of Chaos I: Hero's Trial
Agents of Chaos II: Jedi Eclipse
Balance Point
Recovery*
Edge of Victory I: Conquest
Edge of Victory II: Rebirth
Star by Star
Dark Journey
Enemy Lines I: Rebel Dream
Enemy Lines II: Rebel Stand
Traitor
Destiny's Way
Ylesia*
Force Heretic I: Remnant
Force Heretic II: Refugee
Force Heretic III: Reunion
The Final Prophecy
The Unifying Force

35 *YEARS AFTER STAR WARS: A New Hope*

The Dark Nest Trilogy:
The Joiner King
The Unseen Queen
The Swarm War

40 YEARS AFTER
STAR WARS: A New Hope

Legacy of the Force:
Betrayal
Bloodlines
Tempest
Exile
Sacrifice
Inferno
Fury
Revelation
Invincible

*An ebook novella

dramatis personae

Ben Skywalker; Jedi Knight (human male)

Boba Fett; Mandalorian bounty hunter, *Mand'alor* (human male)

Darth Caedus (formerly Jacen Solo); Sith Lord (human male)

Han Solo; captain, *Millennium Falcon* (human male)

Jagged Fel; Jedi support pilot (human male)

Jaina Solo; Jedi Knight (human female)

Leia Organa Solo; Jedi Knight (human female)

Lon Shevu; captain, Galactic Alliance Guard (human male)

Luke Skywalker; Jedi Grand Master (human male)

Mirta Gev; Mandalorian bounty hunter (human female)

Prince Isolder; father to the Hapan Queen Mother (human male)

Saba Sebatyne; Jedi Master (Barabel female)

Tahiri Veila; Sith apprentice (human female)

Taryn Zel; Hapan security operative (human female)

Tenel Ka; Hapan Queen Mother (human female)

Trista Zel; Hapan security operative (human female)

Zekk; Jedi Knight (human male)

prologue

A LONG TIME AGO . . .

Jaina Solo sits alone in the cold, her knees drawn tight to her chest and her arms wrapped around her legs to conserve body heat. She is fourteen, and she hasn't slept in days because her captors flood her cell with harsh bright light at odd intervals. She has never been so hungry, and her body aches from the daily beatings her tormentors call "training." She knows what they are trying to take from her, and she refuses to surrender it. But she is alone and frightened and in more pain than she has ever before endured, and her will is a strand of spider silk holding a crystal chandelier. One more beating, one more sleepless rest period, one more hour spent shivering on a bare durasteel bunk, and she may drop that chandelier. And that scares her more than dying, because it means submitting to her fear, embracing her anger . . . because it means turning to the dark side.

Then the place in her heart that belongs to her brother begins to warm, and she knows Jacen is thinking of her. She pictures him sitting in his own cell in another spoke of the space station, his brown hair wavy and tousled, his jaw clenched with earnest resolve, and the warm place in her heart starts to grow. She stops shivering, her hunger fades, and her fear turns to resolve.

This is the gift of their twin bond: that neither Jaina nor Jacen is ever truly alone. They share a connection through the Force that will always sustain them. When one grows weak, the other strengthens. When one hurts, the other soothes. It is a bond that cannot be broken by any power in the galaxy, as much a part of them as the Force itself.

So Jaina puts aside her despair and turns her thoughts to escape, because when she and Jacen work together, nothing is impossible. They are on a space station, so they are going to have to steal a spacecraft. They will have to find a way to deactivate the hangar's containment field, perhaps through sabotage or by forging a launch authorization. And that means they are going to need some time before the guards realize they're gone—especially since they have to free their friend Lowbacca before fleeing.

The only way to tell time in the cell is to count heartbeats, and Jaina is too busy planning to do that. So when Jacen's place in her heart begins to grow larger and more full, she has no idea how much time has passed. But she has felt the sensation thousands of times before, and she knows what it means: her brother is coming.

Jaina's pulse begins to pound with excitement, and soon she can feel Jacen's pulse pounding to the same rhythm. He is very close now, coming down the corridor outside her cell—and she cannot sense any other presences accompanying him. She doesn't want him to know how frightened she has been—or how close she has come to breaking—so she begins a Jedi breathing exercise to calm herself.

Then she feels him stop two cells away.

Not there, dummy, *Jaina thinks.* Keep coming.

There is a flutter in Jaina's heart as Jacen grows confused, and she worries that her brother is about to open the wrong cell and ruin their escape. She reaches out to him in the Force, trying to physically pull him toward her, and soon the control pad outside her cell door begins to click.

Jaina breathes a sigh of relief, then folds her arms across her chest and leans back against the wall. She knows this is going to take awhile, because Jacen is really bad with machinery.

Somehow, though, he deactivates the alarm before he unlocks the cell, then manages to unlock the cell without activating the intercom to the control center. Finally, the door hisses open, and Jaina sees her twin brother standing outside, smirking at her with a replica of their father's famous lopsided grin.

"Hi, Jaina," he says. "I don't suppose you'd like to—"

"What took you so long?" Jaina demands, interrupting her brother's fun. He is always making jokes and wisecracks, and they are always lame. "I've been waiting for you."

She slips off her bunk and steps through the door past him, then looks down the corridor in both directions, searching for guards or other signs of trouble. Jacen isn't much better at planning than fixing machinery, so—however he managed to get this far—there is a good chance that the guards are on to him by now.

But the famous Solo luck seems to be with him today, and Jaina sees nothing but the closed doors of other cells. She would like to free the other captives, but she knows better than to try. Their wills have already been broken, and one of them would be sure to alert the guards. So Jaina simply closes her own door and leans closer to Jacen.

"What now?" she asks. "Have you figured out where Lowbacca is?"

Jacen flushes, then drops his gaze to the floor. "Not yet," he admits. "I was sort of hoping you might have a plan."

Jaina smiles. "Of course I do," she says. "Didn't I say I've been waiting?"

chapter one

What do you call the person who brings dinner to a rancor? The appetizer!

   —Jacen Solo, age 14, Jedi academy on Yavin 4

The tunnel descending into Nickel One's transportation warrens was typically Verpine: square, straight, and lined with so many tubes, ducts, and conduits that it was impossible to see native rock. It was also crazy-clean in that maybe-the-hive-mother-has-a-problem kind of way, with a spotless smoke-blue floor and gleaming aquamarine pipe—work which made it virtually identical to the rest of the passages Jaina had seen while touring the asteroid's defenses. Even with her Force abilities, she found it impossible to tell exactly where she and Boba Fett were inside the insect colony . . . and whether they had any chance of rejoining the Mandalorian garrison commandos before stormtroopers began landing.

It was three weeks after the battle of Fondor, and—following a series of threats and overtures from all sides of the Galactic Civil War—the Verpine had invited the Mandalorians to establish a base on Nickel One to deter anyone who might think of forcing the issue. Obviously, the deterrent hadn't worked. Just a standard hour earlier, Jaina and Fett had been inspecting the asteroid's defenses when an Imperial Remnant flotilla had unexpectedly arrived from hyperspace and made a feint toward the primary loading docks. Half an hour later, a full planetary invasion fleet had arrived and pounded Nickel One's surface defenses into slag and dust. Soon the actual troop-drop would begin, and even the Verpine entertained no hopes of repelling it. The only question was where the Imperials would land first.

An urgent drone rose ahead, and the bitter taint of Verpine alarm pheromones grew thick in the tunnel's muggy air. The guide—a thick-limbed insect with the spiked carahide and heavy mandibles of the soldier caste—started to walk faster, and Jaina began to worry that a swarm of frenzied warriors would mistake her and Fett for the enemy. When Fett's hand drifted toward his holstered blaster, she knew she wasn't the only one concerned.

Still, she didn't dare suggest that their guide comm ahead to remind his fellow Verpine that she and Fett were on the hive's side. She knew how Fett would view such an obvious precaution—and maybe he was right. Maybe any appearance of weakness *was* a weakness.

Jaina had been training with the legendary bounty hunter for just a little more than a standard month, but she had come to know him well. At times, she could almost read his mind. When the Remnant flotilla had feinted toward the loading docks, she had predicted that he would pretend to fall for the ruse . . . and watched him send a wing of *Bes'uliike* out to "drive off" the enemy. When the actual invasion fleet had arrived, she had guessed that Fett would counterpunch hard. In fact, he had convinced Nickel One's High Coordinator to hurl her entire starfighter force at the Remnant's flagship, the *Dominion,* and the Super Star Destroyer had quickly become a flaming hulk.

Now, with the asteroid's capture a virtual certainty, Jaina knew Fett would not meet the invaders on the surface. He would opt for a far bloodier strategy, attacking them in the narrow access tunnels that led down from the air locks, making them pay in lives for every meter they advanced.

And Jaina knew that her training had just come to an end, because Boba Fett would not risk her—the tool of his vengeance against his daughter's killer—in a battle he could not win. As soon as they passed a hangar with a serviceable starfighter still inside, he would cut Jaina loose and tell her to go hunt down her twin brother.

What Jaina did not know was whether she was ready. She could fight any three men in Keldabe and be the only one left standing. She could splat a dyeball on Fett's armor anywhere she wanted. She could outfly Mandalore's best pilots in any vessel they chose, and shoot down an entire squadron in elite combat simulations.

None of that meant she was good enough to bring down a Sith Lord.

And she had to be. If Mara had been frightened enough of her brother's transformation to attempt killing him, then it was up to Jaina to finish the job. Jacen—or Darth Caedus, as he called himself now—had to be stopped—for Mara and Ben and Luke, for her parents and Tenel Ka and Allana, for Kashyyyk and Fondor and the rest of the galaxy.

But was she ready?

After a few moments of descent, the alarm pheromones grew so thick that Jaina's eyes started to burn, and the Force sizzled with the excitement and outrage of thousands of insectoids. The drone ahead blossomed into a dull roar, and then the tunnel opened into the worst pedjam she had ever seen. Swarms of thick-limbed Verpine with spiked carahide and ryyk-sized mandibles were pouring into the main transportation depot, climbing over one another or using their shatter rifles like plow blades as they crowded into the cavern from a dozen different directions.

Jaina and Fett's escort pushed into the writhing mass and

was immediately shoved first one way, then the other. Soon he became almost indistinguishable from the rest of the Verpine mass—even to Jaina, who, as a former Killik Joiner, could tell the insects apart far better than most humans. She grabbed hold of the guide's ammunition belt and held tight, using the Force to shoulder aside any warrior who tried to slip between them.

When they had made no appreciable progress after fifteen seconds, Fett butted his way to the guide's side. "At this rate, the Imperials are going to be inside before I can post my men. Is there another way to the command bunker?"

The guide rocked his tubular head, thinking, then blinked his bulbous eyes. "We might be able to cross the surface—"

"Forget it," Fett said.

There was no need to explain his reluctance—not to Jaina. With an invasion fleet bombarding Nickel One and an armada of assault shuttles about to descend on the surface, trying to cross fifty kilometers of asteroid in a dust-crawler was a long shot—and Fett always played the odds, especially when it came to risking his life.

"You've got clearance from the High Coordinator," Fett said. "Tell 'em to make a hole."

"I *am*," the guide replied. His voice was surprisingly thin and reedy for a being nearly the size of a Wookiee, most likely because it was so seldom used. Verpine usually "talked" using biologically generated radio waves, resorting to sound only when speaking to other species. "But the enemy has launched its first swarm of assault shuttles, and a thousand other combat directors and several battle coordinators are also demanding the right-of-way. We *all* have priority one clearance from Her Maternellence."

"I thought your kind was supposed to be organized," Fett growled. He pointed across the vault toward a loading area that Jaina could barely see through the swarm of huge insects ahead. "That our tube?"

"Yes—DownYellow Express FiftySeat," the guide said. "But they are running low on passenger capsules, so we may need to switch—"

"So we need to get there first," Fett growled.

He squared his shoulders and started to shove ahead, but Jaina had anticipated his impatience and was already using the Force to hold him back. "Ladies first," she said, gliding past. "Now that you're a Head of State, you might want to learn some manners."

She began to use the Force to clear a path, her hand moving back and forth ever so slightly as she sent Verpine warriors tottering aside or stumbling to sudden halts. Fett grunted and followed close on her heels, with their guide— Osos Niskooen—peering over both their shoulders in astonishment.

A couple of rib-battering minutes later, they emerged from the swarm onto a yellow loading platform and found themselves teetering above a two-meter drop into a transportation tube. At the bottom, Jaina could see translucent waves of energy sweeping along a raised repulsor rail, carrying a steady stream of dust, stone, and refuse at speeds in excess of two hundred kilometers an hour.

The Verpine behind them continued to press forward, and now Jaina found herself holding the swarm back with the Force as a long durasteel capsule shot out of the adjacent tunnel and whooshed to a stop in front of the loading area. The capsule opened along its full length, the entire upper quarter sliding upward. Jaina got a brief glimpse of two rows of inward-facing seats before Verpine soldiers began to literally spill into the capsule.

"Come on, Jedi."

Fett grabbed her and jumped into the writhing mass, elbowing and kicking alongside the rest of the passengers as he fought for a place. Jaina used the Force to keep a small area around them clear until a loud hiss sounded above their heads and the door slid closed. An instant later the capsule shot down the transport tube and the entire mass of occupants was thrown toward the rear of the passenger compartment.

As the capsule reached full speed, the Verpine quickly began to untangle themselves. Despite the loading chaos, everyone seemed to have a seat. Jaina and Fett sat across from a soldier she thought she recognized as their guide.

"Niskooen?" she asked.

"Correct," the insect replied. "Most humans have as much trouble distinguishing our scents as we do yours."

"She's had practice," Fett said, turning his helmet toward Niskooen. "So what's the situation topside?"

Niskooen fell silent for a moment as he consulted with his fellow Verpine, then said, "Our surface batteries have taken a heavy toll, and the enemy's first assault shuttles are starting to land. Their whiteshells are beginning to debark."

"I could guess that much," Fett grumbled. "I mean *where*? Which air locks?"

Niskooen was quiet for a moment, then reported, "No air locks. The initial mass is swarming HighGround Rocky-Plain TwentyKilometer Left."

Fett turned to Jaina. "The next time I do a base inspection, remind me to bring my own communications officer—or better yet, not to get caught in a surprise attack at all."

"Like you'd listen to a Jedi," Jaina retorted. She turned to Niskooen. "Isn't that landing zone near your fusion plant's exhaust ports? Twenty kilometers down the left side of the asteroid?"

"Correct," Niskooen said. "We assume that's how they intend to enter the hive."

Fett's alarm suddenly grew as sharp in the Force as the Verpine's pheromones were in the air. "They won't *enter*."

Niskooen's antennae straightened. "You think they hope to sabotage our primary power supply?"

"Hope isn't the way I'd put it," Fett said. He began to murmur into his helmet mike, trying to issue orders directly to the commando company he had stationed on Nickel One as a symbol of Mandalore's commitment to its mutual-aid treaty with the Verpine. After a minute, he gave up trying to get a direct signal and turned back to Niskooen. "Can you relay a message to Moburi?"

"I can reach Commando Moburi through my hive mates," Niskooen replied. "There are still capsules coming behind us."

"Tell Moburi that he's in command until I get there," Fett said. "And that it may be awhile. The power grid is about to blow."

Fett's declaration sent a clatter of dismay through the capsule, but none of the Verpine questioned his certainty. First, when it came to killing and fighting, his reputation was unmatched. Second, insects of the soldier caste were too disciplined to question the pronouncement of a superior—even a superior from another swarm. And they probably knew that he was right, anyway. Eliminating the power plant would bring Nickel One's transportation to a screeching halt, and limiting an enemy's mobility was always a good idea.

Fett turned to Jaina. "What do your Jedi instincts tell you about this attack?"

"That someone wants the Verpine munitions industry for themselves," Jaina replied. "But you don't need Jedi instincts to know that. Verpine manufacturing is nearly self-contained, which makes it a tempting target; the Verpine have been supplying all sides since day one of the war, which makes them everyone's enemy; and they're unaligned, which makes them ripe for the picking."

"They're aligned with *us*." There was some bristle in

Fett's voice, but Jaina could feel in the Force that there was no real irritation—he knew as well as she did that Mandalore was suddenly playing out of its league. "But who is the someone behind this? The Moffs I *didn't* kill already? Or did your brother send them?"

Jaina thought for a minute, then shrugged. "My gut tells me it's too early for Jacen to have the Moffs under control—but he is full of surprises."

Fett's helmet remained fixed on Jaina. "Not for you, I hope," he said. "Not anymore."

"The only surprise will be if there are no surprises," she replied. "But I have a few of my own now, too."

"Good answer."

Then he looked away, and Jaina could feel him gathering his resolve. Here it came.

"Listen, Solo," Fett began. "This isn't your fight. When we get to the command bunker, I want you to grab a Bessie and slip out of here."

"To where?" Jaina asked, pretending to be surprised. "To Mandalore to fetch Beviin?"

Fett's helmet swung back toward Jaina. "Beviin knows—or at least he will by the time you could get there."

"Then . . . oh," Jaina said, still acting. *Never let them know that you know,* especially when they might be your enemy one day. She paused for a moment, then asked, "Am I ready?"

"Why are you asking me?"

"You've killed more Jedi than I have."

Three seconds passed before Fett answered. "Not like your brother. Not anyone that powerful." His viewplate slid from Jaina back to Niskooen. "What's happening with the whiteshells?"

"They've penetrated our positions around the exhaust vents and—"

The Verpine's answer came to a halt when the capsule

went dark, dropped to the tunnel floor, and began to buck, bounce, and knell as it clanged down the passage. Jaina felt herself starting to fly forward and used the Force to stick herself in place—then instantly regretted it as big spiny insect bodies began to slam into her from behind.

Fett's sleeve lamp came on three meters away, swirling and blinking as he tumbled forward with the other passengers. Jaina pulled her knees to her chest and tucked her chin, making herself small, and felt a sharp pang as something creased the durasteel wall behind her. A terrific screech sounded from the front of the cabin, followed by a rush of dank air and an enormous clang from the ceiling at the rear of the capsule.

Then the noise stopped, and the Force began to churn with rolling waves of pain. Jaina snatched a glow rod off her belt and shined it toward the front of the passenger cabin, where she could just make out the glow of Fett's sleeve lamp buried beneath a couple of meters of crooked insect limbs and cracked thoraxes. The front of the capsule was gaping open where the bottom of the nose had been torn away, and the iron smell of insect blood was thick in the air.

"Fett?" Jaina started forward—and made it about halfway to the front of the cabin before she was stopped by an impenetrable tangle of thrashing insect parts. "You hurt?"

The light at the bottom of the heap remained stationary.

"Fett?" When there was still no answer, she began to clamber over the jumble of insects. Ignoring their pained squeals and dodging their angry mandible snaps, she called to him using a diminutive—one that she had never heard anyone but Goran Beviin use. *"Bob'ika?"*

The light suddenly swung in her direction. "You must have thought I was dead," Fett said. "So I'll forgive that—once."

"Sorry." Jaina laughed, then felt instantly guilty. The injured warriors around her were insects, but they felt real pain—as a former Killik Joiner, she understood that better than most. "Just checking."

"Come on." Fett's light turned toward the nose of the capsule, then began to move toward the gash. In its ambient glow, she could see that the self-contained body glove beneath his armor had been ripped in half a dozen places; a large flap was hanging down beneath the bottom rim of his helmet. "We need to get going."

"Right." Jaina didn't bother to ask about helping the wounded. Compassion was a weakness, and she knew better than to show a weakness in front of Boba Fett—especially a *jetiise* weakness. "Meet you outside."

She slipped off the body heap, then ignited her lightsaber and started to cut through the side of the capsule. By the time she had finished, Fett was standing a few meters down the tunnel, gathering up the Verpine who could still fight.

Ten of the fifty warriors the capsule had once held were now standing near him. An equal number lay dead or still inside the capsule, and the remainder were slumped or curled along the tunnel walls, being looked after by a pair of soldiers who were still functional but limping too badly to march.

"Niskooen?" she asked.

Fett shot a glance at the warriors gathered around him. "Any of you Niskooen?"

"Niskooen's thorax split open," replied one of the soldiers standing with Fett. "He is no more."

Fett grunted in acknowledgment, then tipped his helmet back to look up into the speaker's face. "What's your name, soldier?"

"Ss'ess," the Verpine replied. "Combat Director Ss'ess."

"Well, Combat Director Ss'ess, you're with us now." Fett pointed at the rest of the able-bodied soldiers. "So are they. Got it?"

Ss'ess clacked his mandibles.

"Good." Fett turned and started down the tunnel, not bothering to avoid the repulsor rail. Obviously, it was no longer a danger to anyone. "How far is the command bunker from here?"

"We're almost there," Ss'ess replied, starting after him. "It's only ten kilometers."

"Ten k's? Great." Fett broke into a gentle run, and Jaina noticed he was trying to hide a limp. "I was wondering how I'd get my exercise today."

"Don't you want a situation report?" Ss'ess asked, loping along behind him.

"We know the situation," Jaina said. The repulsor rail was too narrow to take more than one runner at a time and the tunnel walls curved up a sharp slope, so she was forced to fall in behind Ss'ess. "The Imps blew your power plant, and enemy assault shuttles are landing everywhere. Unfortunately, your artificial gravity has its own energy supply, so we're going to have a long walk to wherever the battle starts."

Ss'ess looked back, his antennae raised in astonishment. "Did you see that in the Force?"

"Yeah—Jedi see everything," Fett said. "It's what makes 'em so irritating. Let me know when the whiteshells start blowing air locks."

Fett fell silent and continued to lead the way up the tunnel, breathing into his helmet rather than removing it and allowing anyone to see how hard he was working. Jaina imagined him wishing that he hadn't left his jetpacks aboard his ship and smiled. He might be her mentor—for now—but he had delivered her father to Jabba the Hutt frozen in carbonite, so it was nice to see him suffer just a little. Besides, given that her brother was the one who had tortured his daughter to death, she suspected that Fett felt much the same about her.

They had been running for nearly an hour when the tunnel branched up and down. Fett stopped and pretended to study his options while he caught his breath, then turned to shine his lamp in Ss'ess's face. "Which way?"

"Either. If we go up, we will pass the LongCrater Dust-Lake ThirtyKilometer Top air lock." Ss'ess looked down the descending tube, probably more to get Fett's lamp out of his eyes than to indicate direction. "This way, we will go through Client Hangar Two where your *Bes'uliike*—"

Ss'ess was interrupted by the clatter of stone collapsing in the upper passage. All the Verpine jumped and swung their long necks toward the sound, but Fett casually turned to look up the tunnel, no doubt scanning it with his helmet's built-in sensors.

Jaina merely reached out with the Force, trying to get some idea of the number and nature of whoever had breached the passage. She sensed nothing but a vague danger, amorphous and elusive.

Without looking away from the tunnel, Fett asked, "Ss'ess, didn't I tell you to let me know when the stormtroopers started blowing air locks?"

"And I will," Ss'ess replied. "When it happens."

Now Fett's helmet swung back around. "They haven't blown any air locks?" he demanded. "Not a single one?"

"Not one," Ss'ess confirmed. "You said to tell you when the whiteshells started. One is a start. I would have told you."

Jaina felt exasperation boiling off Fett like a steam cloud. *"Di'kut!"* he said, using one of the few Mandalorian words she had heard him use without Mirta's prompting. "Before you and your buggies die, I need you to relay a message to Moburi."

"We're going to die?" Ss'ess sounded more surprised than frightened. "How do you know?"

"Did I say something to make you think there's time to

explain?" Fett demanded. "Focus, Ss'ess. You don't have long."

Jaina understood. If the stormtroopers weren't blowing the air locks, it was because they wanted to keep the asteroid's ventilation system sealed—and that could mean only one thing.

"Gas!"

"Don't sound so surprised, Jedi. It makes you look bad." Fett pulled an emergency breath mask from his equipment belt, then turned back to Ss'ess. "Tell Moburi to fall back to Client Hangar Two with everyone who can make it."

"You're breaking our contract?" Ss'ess gasped. "Boba *Fett*?"

"No." Fett raised his helmet high enough to push the breath mask through the torn body glove and up under his visor. "We're running out of time, Ss'ess."

When Ss'ess's antennae remained flat against his cheeks, Jaina explained, "There will be air scrubbers and hazmat suits in the hangar. He's just trying to keep his men alive to counterattack."

"I could use a few of you guys, too," Fett said to Ss'ess. "Too bad you don't have a photon's chance in a black hole of lasting that long. You going to relay that message before you die?"

"Yes." Ss'ess's antennae swung away from his cheeks. "Thank you for your candor."

A faint siffling began to whisper down the tunnel from which the clatter had come.

Fett glanced toward the sound, then turned back and pointed at Jaina's equipment belt. "Guess you weren't much of a student after all," he said. "No breath mask?"

"Sure, I've got one," Jaina said. "Just don't need it."

Fett cocked his helmet to one side. "This I've got to see."

"Be my guest."

Jaina would have liked to avoid showing this particular

trick to any Mandalorian—and especially to Boba Fett—but the only way to keep the technique secret was to let the Verpine die. She knew what a Mandalorian would have done—but she was still a Jedi, and she wanted to stay one.

The siffling continued to grow louder. Jaina shined her glow rod up the tunnel and saw a glittering cloud of vapor drifting—no, pushing—down the passage. She raised her palm and began to pull the Force through herself, using it to push the dank air up the transport tube. The sound sharpened into a high-pitched buzz; then the cloud stopped advancing and began to glitter even more brightly.

Jaina's stomach rolled with surprise. She felt Fett's eyes watching her and unfurrowed her brow—too late to fool him, she knew, but at least the lecture on revealing surprise would only be perfunctory. She pulled harder on the Force, drawing it through herself faster and pushing more air up the tunnel. The buzzing deepened to a drone, and a pearly glow rose within the cloud's heart.

"Haven't seen that before." The comment was muffled by Fett's breath mask, but not nearly enough to conceal the amusement in his voice. "So what's it do, exactly?"

Jaina bit back a sharp retort and pushed even harder, forcing so much air up the passage that her robes began to ruffle in the breeze. The drone rose rapidly in pitch, then suddenly ceased as the cloud flew apart in a blinding flash.

There followed a moment of stunned silence as Jaina and the others tried to blink the dazzle out of their eyes. Then, as her vision began to return, so did the siffle, fainter than before, but also somehow more urgent. She shined her glow rod up the passage and saw that the eruption had sprayed the glittering cloud onto the floor and walls—not the ceiling—in the form of a silver film.

And that film was sliding down the tunnel, coming fast and shaping itself into a dozen gleaming arrows, each pointed at one of the beings in Fett's makeshift fighting squad.

Fett pulled his breath mask from beneath his visor. "Neat trick." He took a T-21 borrowed from the Nickel One armory—he'd left his EE-3 aboard the ship, thinking he wouldn't need it on an inspection tour—off his back and pulled the actuating knob. "But I think you just made it mad."

Fett opened fire with the repeating blaster, and the Verpine followed his lead with their shatter rifles, all shooting at the arrows approaching them. The mag-pellets were no more effective than the blaster bolts, simply blunting the tip until the arrow reshaped itself into a fork or a trident or half a dozen blobs and continued forward.

Jaina had no idea what the stuff was—and it was coming too fast to waste time wondering. When she could not think of a Force technique that would be more effective than what Fett and the Verpine were doing, she simply activated her lightsaber and squatted, laying the blade as flat as she could and using it like a broom to keep the stuff burned away from her.

The film divided and moved around her, staying out of reach until it had her completely encircled, then swept in from all sides. She launched herself into a Force flip, arcing over Fett's head into the tunnel that led down toward Client Hangar Two. She came down facing back up the passage.

Fett's boots and greaves were already covered in dull, creeping silver, and Jaina could see that some of it had slipped through a rip in the ankle seam. Behind him, Ss'ess and his soldiers had finally panicked and turned to spring down the tunnel, but the film was sliding after them, and it was obvious they wouldn't be able to stay ahead of it.

Jaina pointed at Fett's feet. "Boba, you've—"

"You, too." Fett gestured at her lightsaber hand. "Your arm."

Jaina looked down and saw a silver stain spreading

down her sleeve onto her wrist and hand. She deactivated her blade and flipped her arm down, but it was like trying to shake off a tattoo.

"Fierfek!" Jaina felt herself growing angry; she had not spent the last five standard weeks trading bruises with the most notorious killer in the galaxy to have it end here. She had to survive long enough to go after her brother. "Any idea what it is?"

"What difference does it make?" Fett asked. "It's probably going to kill us—I already feel it starting to burn."

"Acid, then." Jaina pulled a canister of neutralizer from her equipment belt and popped off the cap, then felt her own hand begin to tingle—not burn. She looked over to see Fett holding a green stim-shot hypo, but doing nothing except looking at his feet. "You said *burn*!"

"Maybe it should have been sting." Fett continued to look at his feet. "What's the difference?"

Jaina started to tell him the difference was whether to use a neutralizer or a countertoxin—and that a stim-shot was the wrong thing to use no matter what—but realized that Fett's retort had been based on something else entirely. The silver film on his greaves and boots was dissolving and falling away.

Then the tingling on Jaina's hand and wrist faded. The silver stain decayed into a dingy powder, leaving her flesh slightly reddened but otherwise undamaged. She used the Force to concentrate her awareness on the area, searching for any hidden damage, and felt nothing worse than a mild sunburn.

The Verpine were not faring so well. They had only made it a few meters down the tunnel before being overtaken by the film, and now the passage was filled with staccato clattering and the fading squeals of dying insects.

Jaina looked to Fett. "How are *you* feeling?"

He shined his sleeve lamp down the passage. Ss'ess and

the rest of the Verpine lay on the floor beneath powdery coatings of gray. Most were writhing in the final throes of a death seizure, but some already lay motionless, with dark blood seeping from their eyes and thorax spiracles.

"Lucky," Fett said. "That happens sometimes."

He turned away from Ss'ess and the others, then brushed past and started down the passage at a run again. Ignoring the implied order to follow, Jaina pulled her medpac from her belt and went to squat beside Ss'ess, where she began to burn detailed Force impressions of his symptoms into her memory. It took another ten steps before Fett finally decided to stop and turn around.

"You're not trying to save him?" Fett asked. "Tell me we've done better than that with—".

"Just trying to find out if your message got through to Moburi." As Jaina said this, she experienced a faint sense of guilt and failure beneath Ss'ess's pain. "It didn't."

Fett shrugged. "He'll be there."

"If you say so." Jaina didn't bother to hide her doubt. It was going to be difficult enough for her and Fett to reach the hangar ahead of the Imperials, and *they* didn't have orders telling them to put up a stiff resistance. "But if it's all the same, I'm not counting on it."

She used a swab to collect some dust and blood from Ss'ess's body, then—using a Force suggestion to put him to sleep—gave him a single pat on the shoulder and stood.

"I can tell you what that stuff is," Fett said, waiting as she sealed the swab inside a sample tube. "Nano."

"It won't hurt to run some tests," Jaina said, joining him. "Better to be sure."

"I *am* sure." Fett started to run again. "It's the Imperial style—they probably got the idea from the stuff your dad found on Woteba back when you were kissing bugs."

"They weren't bugs," Jaina said, restraining the urge to Force-slap him upside the head. "Killiks are—"

"So you *were* kissing 'em?" Fett asked. "I always thought that part was just—"

Jaina Force-shoved him into the wall—hard—then pushed him down the tunnel at a run. "You shouldn't waste your breath, old man," she said. "You've got a contract to keep."

Fett laughed and picked up the pace. "Anger is weakness, Jedi," he said. "And try to keep up. We've still got five kilometers to go."

In the course of the next thirty minutes, they passed at least two hundred dead Verpine. Some lay near crashed capsules, badly mangled but curled into peaceful little balls by the companions who had left them there. Most of the others were sprawled where they had fallen, twisted into painful-looking shapes and coated in the same gray powder that had been left on Ss'ess and the others after the silver film overtook them.

But a few scattered corpses—all from either the technician or labor caste—appeared to have died of more typical wounds, mostly blaster burns and grenade detonations. None of them had any sign of the gray powder that had coated the dead soldiers. Jaina didn't bother pointing out the ramifications to Fett; she was certain that he could see them as clearly as she did—and would find them just as unnerving.

If the Remnant had engineered a weapon to kill only the Verpine soldier caste, they clearly intended to get the munitions plants running again soon. Within a matter of days, the entire military industry of the Roche system would be supplying the Remnant—and therefore Jacen—with some of the finest weaponry in the galaxy.

Jaina was still trying to digest this unpleasant realization when the fear and anger of a battle began to ripple through the Force from somewhere not too far ahead. All the presences felt human to her, and one or two of them were even vaguely familiar. They had found Fett's Mandalorians—in the middle of a battle. With the Force, she pulled Fett to a stop, then used hand signals to communicate what she sensed.

Fett nodded and took a couple of seconds to arm his entire weapons array. Then they shut off their lights and began to creep up opposite sides of the tunnel, Fett using his helmet's infrared sensors to navigate in the darkness, Jaina relying on the Force. They hadn't gone far when the battle began to assault their nostrils. This was not the typical smell of blaster-scorched flesh and spilled entrails, but the kind of odor that came out when a repair crew tore the patches off a combat vessel that had survived a nasty turbolaser barrage—the acrid reek of flash-melted metal and incinerated bodies.

After moving just twenty meters in two careful minutes, Jaina sensed the tunnel opening up ahead, no doubt at the Client Hangar Two loading platform. She could feel a dozen angry Mandalorians about thirty meters ahead, crouching in the transport tube at the opposite end of the platform. Scattered around one side, arrayed in a large crescent across a vast space that had to be the entry to the hangar—if not the hangar itself—she sensed about two dozen disciplined presences. Stormtroopers, she assumed.

Fett began to murmur into his helmet mike . . . then ducked as a colored flash came crackling out of the darkness and blasted a head-sized crater from the tunnel wall. Instantly he began to return fire, pouring blaster bolts toward his unseen attacker, and the loading platform grew bright with crisscrossing lines of color. In the strobing light, Jaina glimpsed half a dozen Mandalorian bodies ahead, lying below the loading platform at the bottom of the transportation tube. Their *beskar'gam* appeared to be more or less intact—but so badly discolored and deformed that it looked like they'd taken laser cannon blasts square to their chest plates.

Fett yelled something she couldn't make out over the wail of so many blaster rifles, then crouched and charged into the transportation tube, sticking his weapon arm up over the loading platform to return fire. A blaster bolt caught his T-21 in the cooling module, blowing the weapon apart and sending it flying in three different directions. A second bolt ricocheted off the inside of Fett's vambrace, flinging his arm straight up above the edge of the platform, where a third bolt burned through his palm and blew out the back of his gauntlet, spinning him around and dropping him flat to the dead repulsor rail.

These were not her mother's stormtroopers, Jaina realized. These guys could *shoot*. She ignited her lightsaber and charged after Fett, simultaneously batting blaster bolts back toward her attackers and using the Force to push Fett along the rail so he wouldn't become a stationary target.

Then the hair rose on the back of her neck, and she had the sense that someone very dangerous was focusing on her. She thought for a second it might be her brother—but realized she would have been dead by the time she sensed *him* watching. She dived for the repulsor rail, catching Fett square in the back as he came up holding a BlasTech S330 he had taken from one of his dead mercenaries.

They slammed down flat, Fett cursing inside his helmet and trying to throw her off, Jaina using the Force to keep them pinned until whatever she had sensed . . .

. . . crashed against the back wall, lighting up the transportation tube like a nova burst to life. The blast seared the left side of her face and filled her nose with the sulfurous smell of melted stone, scorched cloth, and singed hair. Jaina glanced over and saw a half-meter ball of crackling, boiling *white* still burrowing into the tunnel wall, stone pouring from the hole in a bright liquid stream.

Fett finally squirmed out from beneath her and spun around on his knee, still cursing and oblivious to the thumb-sized hole that had been burned through his hand. If he noticed that he was now kneeling on the warped chest plate of a helmetless mercenary, or that the man's face was as red and puffy as that of someone who had been steamed alive, he showed no sign.

"Not what I had in mind, Jedi." He nearly had to shout to make himself heard above the scream and crackle of the battle. "When I said cover me, I meant with a *blaster*."

"My mistake," Jaina replied wryly.

She was about to add that it wouldn't happen again when a dozen Mandalorians came running up from the other end of the loading platform. The leader, a tall broad-shouldered fellow armored in red and black, was crouching low and keeping a careful watch on a chrono he carried in his hand. Everyone else was returning Imperial fire, only half crouching behind the platform's cover and relying on their *beskar'gam* to deflect enemy fire while they picked off stormtroopers.

The leader dropped to a knee beside Fett. "Good to see you, boss." He displayed the chrono, which was counting down by seconds. "We've got nine seconds till they hit us again."

"Good to see you, too, Moburi." Fett's helmet swung in Jaina's direction, shooting her a glance she was fairly sure would have been smug had she been able to see beneath his viewplate, then looked back to Moburi. "Plasma cannon?"

"Just a gun," Moburi corrected. "That's why—"

"Where?" Jaina poked her head up, but she was so blinded by the flurry of blaster bolts that she could not pinpoint anyone's location—much less the plasma gun's. "Just one?"

"One's enough," Moburi said.

Jaina glanced at the chrono in his hand and saw that it was down to six seconds. She didn't have time to explain— not if she was going to take out that gun before it fired again.

"Where?"

Moburi glanced at Fett, who looked at Jaina and shook his head. "No way. I'm not going to—"

"You're not." Jaina knew what Fett was going to say, that he wasn't going to risk the tool of his vengeance against her brother—and she understood why. Assassins didn't make it to Fett's age by taking chances they could avoid. But Jaina also knew that she was going to have to take a lot of chances to bring Jacen down—that from the moment she began her hunt, she would be assuming far greater risks than facing down a few dozen crackshot stormtroopers. "Cover!"

Jaina reignited her lightsaber, then Force-sprang out of the tube and into an evasive somersault.

Behind her Fett yelled, "Fierfek!" then, "Go, go, go!"

By the time she came down again she was halfway across the loading platform, a dozen Mandalorians charging out of the darkness behind her. She landed in a near trance, her pulse racing with battle exhilaration, her lightsaber whirling by instinct, her mind focused on discovering the location of the plasma gunner. It was impossible to see anything in the darkness behind the strobing crescent of color that marked the stormtroopers' skirmish line. But Jaina knew that was where her target would be, defended by the rest of his squad, tucked behind hard cover with nothing visible but his muzzle and sniper sight.

And he would be up high. The plasma ball had been at face level while she was in the bottom of the transportation tube, which meant the sniper had been shooting down at them.

Behind her, a Mando grunted in anguish as a lucky blaster bolt found a seam in his armor; a concussion grenade detonated off to her right and sent chunks of white armor spraying everywhere. Jaina felt her lightsaber catch a trio of powerful bolts, then saw the fiery dashes return to send a stormtrooper and his G-8 power blaster flying in opposite directions. She spun through the resulting gap in the enemy line, dancing left, then right to slice through a white-armored shoulder and send a boxy helmet and its contents tumbling away.

And that was when she sensed the plasma gunner's focus returning. It wasn't as strong this time, probably because it was centered on someone else, and she wouldn't have noticed it at all if she hadn't been searching for it. But she could feel the sniper preparing to fire again, somewhere ahead, above . . . and *right*.

Jaina smiled, more in satisfaction than bloodlust, and rushed into the darkness. Extending her Force awareness high along the wall and ceiling of the loading vault, she sensed a human presence. Two presences—sniper and spotter, hiding on an observation balcony high above the battle. She did not reach for a blaster or a glow rod or try to leap up to their hiding place. She just *grabbed* and pulled, using the Force to jerk them both forward.

The sniper and his partner almost certainly yelled or cried out as they flew from their firing post, but the sound was inaudible beneath the booming crackle of a plasma discharge. An orb of silver brilliance came arcing down from the balcony, followed by two dark-armored figures and their gun. Then the energy ball crashed into an overturned service cart, creating a cannon-sized detonation that illuminated the entire vault for a full two seconds.

Jaina glimpsed stormtroopers staggering, running, and somersaulting away from the explosion. Then the Mandalorians were on the skirmish line, felling enemies with blaster, boot, and blade. She sensed danger on her left and turned to see, in the flickering gleam of her lightsaber, a trooper stumbling away backward, shaking but still pointing an E-18 in her direction. She gestured him forward with her free hand, using the Force to pull him onto her lightsaber before he could open fire.

The blade burned a three-centimeter hole in his chest plate and sank through. A pained gurgle escaped his helmet comm, and the blaster rifle slipped from his grasp to land on Jaina's boots. She deactivated her lightsaber then heard footsteps behind her and spun around, reactivating and striking in the same instant.

The attack landed but did not slice, the blade sliding along a *beskar* neck guard to burn a dark furrow into Fett's green armor. Jaina gasped in surprise, but managed to stifle the apology—*regret is a weakness*—that rose automatically to her lips.

"Take that as a lesson," she said instead. "Never sneak up on a Jedi."

"Didn't know you *could* sneak up on a Jedi," Fett retorted. "Thanks for the tip."

Jaina deactivated her lightsaber, more aware than Fett realized that they weren't really joking. There were a lot of things he didn't seem to know about Jedi, one of them being that Jedi weren't just good eavesdroppers, they were the *best*. So when Admiral Daala—no fan of Jedi herself—had boarded the *Bloodfin* at Fondor and asked to meet with Fett, Jaina had made it her business to be on the deck below, where she could use the Force to listen in on what passed between the two Jedi-haters. It had been no surprise to hear them dreaming of the day when the galaxy was rid of Sith and Jedi alike—and that included Jaina. She had no illusions about that.

But Jaina was content to let Fett think she didn't know just how serious he was, that she actually bought the fatherly-affection act he sometimes put on for her. She expanded her Force awareness to include the entire loading area, noting the diminished blasterfire and retreating battle sounds, and decided it would be safe to activate her glow rod.

"Looks like everything's under control," she said, starting toward the fallen sniper team and their plasma gun. "Sometimes the Jedi way *is* better."

"Faster, anyway." Fett knelt to check the sniper team and, discovering that the spotter was still breathing, put a blaster bolt through the fellow's head. "Not necessarily better."

Jaina recoiled from the cold-blooded killing of the wounded trooper, but recalled the Mandalorian whom she had heard grunting earlier and knew that Fett would be thinking of his own losses, not those of his enemy. She wanted to ask how many men he had lost during the charge but knew better than to betray her interest.

Fett stood and started forward, motioning for Jaina to follow. When they came to a huge archway opening into the depths of Client Hangar Two, he pointed into the darkness.

"There should still be a couple of full-spec Bessies in there, fueled and ready to go," he said. "Consider one of 'em yours. I'll put it on your account."

Jaina stopped at his side. "So this is it, then."

"I guess so," Fett said. "I've seen you fly. You shouldn't have any trouble slipping out of here."

Jaina paused. "What about you? You know you can't stop the invasion."

She felt Fett smile inside his helmet. "You worried about me, Jedi?"

"Not really," Jaina said. "But I do want to keep track of you."

Fett snorted. "We both know you're going to be too busy for that," he said. "I'll be fine. There's a *Tra'kad* in there, too. We just have to prepare some things for our return."

Jaina cocked her brow. "You're coming back?"

"Of course," Fett said. "I gave my word."

"In that case, may the Force be with you," Jaina said. "You're going to need it."

"Not as much as you." Fett cocked his head, listening to a report, then said, "Time for me to get moving. Good luck, kid."

For a moment, Jaina was silent. That was exactly the kind of thing her father, Han Solo, would have said.

Finally, she asked, "How much do you think I'll need? Luck, I mean?"

Fett shrugged and pretended to look over his shoulder; then his wounded hand shot forward—just as Jaina had known it would. She blocked down, then slipped inside his guard, shouldering him backward and sweeping his front foot from beneath him.

Fett landed in a crash of armor and curses, but chuckled from inside his helmet. "Well, I've taught you everything you need to know."

"But not everything you know," Jaina surmised.

Fett looked up at her for a moment, then said, "You don't have that long." He extended a hand for Jaina to help him up. "And there's no need."

Jaina ignored the hand and stepped back, then asked, "No need for *you*?"

"Right." Fett sighed and lowered his hand. "Either way, I get my revenge."

"Either way?" Jaina narrowed her eyes, then realized what he was saying. She wasn't surprised, but she was hurt—maybe only a little, but she *was* hurt. "If I don't kill my brother—"

"Your brother kills you." Fett hopped to his feet as lightly as any unarmored Jedi apprentice, then added, "Some things are worse than death. I know that better than anyone, except for maybe Sintas—and Han Solo. Send your father my sympathies."

Jaina studied Fett for a moment, trying to remind herself that she had gone to him, that he had given her exactly what she asked for—and she still found herself getting angry.

Finally, she said, "Dad's right about you. The Kaminoans did use rancor drool to fill your veins."

Fett laughed. "Smart barve, your dad." He spun on his heel and started down the access corridor at a jog. "No wonder he's so hard to kill."

chapter two

Hey, Jaina—do you know why TIE fighters scream in space? Because they miss their mother ship!

                —Jacen Solo, age 14, Jedi academy on Yavin 4

This deep in the Transitory Mists, there were no stars to relieve the night's gloom, no constellations to make the black skies seem less alien. The vista outside the viewport was an inky fog of light-swallowing gases that never thinned and never lifted—and never failed to leave spacegazers feeling a little lost and alone.

The Jedi had retreated to the abandoned mining world of Shedu Maad to hide from Jacen, and ever since joining them here, Jaina had been wondering whether this dark corner of the galaxy would become their tomb. Like most good refuges, it felt safe and secure . . . and that was an illusion. After the trouble the Jedi had caused at Fondor, Jacen would be searching for their secret base with every resource he could spare—and this time, he would give them no time to evacuate. He would have a strike force waiting to pounce the instant he had any idea where they were.

Their only hope was to get him first.

The Jedi would never leave Shedu Maad alive—not unless they hunted down and killed Jacen before he hunted *them* down. Jaina knew that in her heart.

But could she convince the Masters?

Several of them were gathered around a table behind her,

holding an impromptu war council with Luke, Jagged Fel, and her father and mother—the renowned Han and Leia Solo. Not for the first time in her life, Jaina wondered whether she could ever live up to her parents' legend, how she could possibly impact the galaxy as they had during their long and illustrious lives.

". . . and are we sure Jacen *sent* them?" Corran Horn was asking. "The Remnant is still an independent government."

Not wishing to involve herself in the conversation until she was invited—or at least until the time was right—Jaina kept her back to the table and continued to stare out the viewport.

"This might have been the Moffs' play," Corran continued.

"Could be," said Jaina's father . . . *Han Solo*. In this context—in the company of so many other greats, trying to plan a response to her brother's latest outrages—it felt wrong to even think of her parents as *Mom* and *Dad*. They were bigger than that, along with her uncle Luke, the most legendary of the many legends sitting at that table. "Maybe all Fett did was streamline their decision-making process."

Nobody laughed. During the wildly confused Battle of Fondor, nearly a quarter of the Remnant's Moffs had been executed by Boba Fett and his Mandalorians aboard Admiral Pellaeon's flagship, the *Bloodfin*. Most coalition intelligence agencies had concluded that the survivors would fall into a bitter power struggle and scurry home to protect their turf. But Luke and the Jedi Council had realized that, *somehow,* the only Moffs who had been trapped aboard when Fett arrived were those who had been a problem during Pellaeon's reign. The rest had managed to escape and rejoin the main body of the Remnant's fleet—again, *somehow.*

The Masters had concluded that those *somehows* were the doing of Pellaeon's aide, Vitor Reige. They had also realized that a shrewd leader such as Pellaeon would have made provisions to ensure a smooth succession of power after his death. Unfortunately for the Verpine—and the Jedi coalition—it appeared they had been right.

After a long pause in the conversation, Luke said, "I don't think it matters whose idea it was to enslave the Verpine. If Jacen doesn't control the Remnant already, he soon will."

There followed another silence during which no one disagreed. Then Kenth Hamner said, "Which means he's reaching the tipping point. Once he has full control of the Remnant's fleets, he'll be able to project more power than all of his enemies combined."

"We could always accept Admiral Niathal's offer to assume supreme command of all coalition forces," Kyp Durron said, his tone clearly mocking. "That would give us, what, another dozen hulls?"

"At least," Kenth said, joining the others at the table in a bitter chuckle. "And all she wants in return is to negate our nonaggression pact with the entire Confederation."

The laughter trailed away into dumbfounded silence, until Jaina's mom—*Princess Leia*—said, "All the same, I'd suggest the Council phrase its rejection as politely as possible. It's never good to alienate a potential ally, no matter how inconsequential they may seem at the time."

"Thank you for the reminder, Leia," Kenth said. "I *will* be careful with my phrasing."

"In the meantime, we'll just have to sign up the Chiss Ascendancy," Kyp said. Jaina could not tell from his tone whether he was still joking or actually believed there was any chance of such an alliance happening. "Then, if we can get the Corporate Sector—"

"Forget the Ascendancy," Jag interrupted. "You won't involve Csilla in this. Even if the Nine Ruling Families *would* take sides against the Imperial Remnant, they won't get involved with Jedi problems."

"Still stinging from Tenupe?" Han asked.

"That, and the Jedi habit of telling interstellar governments how to run their sovereign territory," Jag replied. "No offense meant, of course."

"Not much taken," Corran assured him. "At least there's no question about the coalition's situation."

"No question at all," said Leia. Her voice was dignified and calm, but the Force was smoldering with her frustration. Just days before the Remnant invasion, she and Han had failed to persuade the Verpine to withdraw from their treaty with Mandalore and join the Jedi coalition instead. "I believe the term is *borked*."

"Sorry, Luke," Han said. There was a bitter edge to his voice that Jaina suspected only she and her mother would recognize as a personal sense of failure. "We told Siskili what you've been seeing when you look into the future. But the Verpine's mutual-aid deal with Mandalore was exclusive, and he was too afraid of Fett to break it."

"Nor would Fett let them modify it," Leia added.

"Buckethead skulo!" Saba spat. "Does Boba Fett think one world of dirt-comberz is the match of thousandz? Mandalore has been hunting too far up the chain, and now the whole jungle will suffer."

"Fett does what works for Fett," Han replied. "The rest of us can suck entropy."

"That's not true anymore," Jaina said, turning from the viewport.

The décor of the makeshift conference room could only be described as mining-complex salvage, with age-yellowed sturdiplas furniture and poured plastoid walls the color of dust. The sliding door at the far end of the small chamber—it had probably been a break room when the mine was still in operation—remained open because of a corroded actuator arm that had not been serviced in centuries.

Most of the war council sat on benches beside a long dining table that had probably once been some color other than stained amber. Their cloaks were fastened tight against the chill of a not-quite-repaired environmental control unit. Only Luke wasn't seated, standing on the near side of the table with his back to the others, gazing out the same viewport through which Jaina had been looking. Judging by the casual acceptance of this position by everyone else at the table, it had not been unusual of late.

"Fett has a family now," Jaina continued, "and he has Mandalore. He still cares about his word, too."

"Then I guess this war has accomplished something," Leia replied bitterly. She was dressed in a white robe that was only a few shades lighter than the gray wisps now running through her hair. "Boba Fett has grown as a person. And here I was wishing the kriffing war had never started."

"I'm not defending him," Jaina replied. She could see the sad pain swimming just beneath the surface of her mother's brown eyes, and was not surprised to find that it only served to make her appear more regal than ever. "I'm just saying he has more vulnerabilities now, and we should remember that. Of all the things I learned training with Boba Fett, the most important were these two: he isn't a good guy, and he'll never be our friend."

This drew a crooked, deep-wrinkled smile from her father. "I always said you were our smart one."

He was seated next to Leia, who sat on a stool at the end of the table—very much her own woman, but still *with* Han, as always. It was a stark contrast with Fett's fifty years of loneliness, and Jaina found herself glancing at Jagged Fel's square jaw and squarer shoulders, hoping she would survive long enough to someday have what her parents did.

Then Jag caught her looking at him, and his grim frown was replaced by a passably warm smile. Jaina glanced away without returning the gesture, telling herself that she had only been looking in Jag's direction because Zekk wasn't present, that she wasn't ready to think about choosing *anyone* until she had finished with Jacen.

And to do *that*, she needed to win the support of the Jedi Council. The first step was to convince Luke and the others that the Jedi had to challenge Jacen no matter *how* strong he was; that they did not dare hide in the Transitory Mists until they could find some way to shift the balance of power back in their favor.

Jaina stepped to the corner of the table closest to her parents. "If I may, I'd like to express an opinion."

Leia turned toward her with an air of attentiveness, but everyone else seemed taken aback. Her father's jaw fell, Jag's gaze grew even more penetrating, and the brows of several Masters rose in shock. During her tenure as a Jedi Knight, Jaina had hardly cultivated the reputation of someone who followed proper procedure.

"You're requesting permission to talk to us?" Kyp asked. For once, his brown hair was neatly trimmed at his collar, his face was clean-shaven, and his blue robe had only a few wrinkles. *"Jaina Solo?"*

"That's right." Jaina checked her posture, drawing herself up straight and formal. "I think it's important."

Kyp whistled in disbelief, then looked to Han. "I don't know what Fett did to her, but I'll help you hunt him down."

"Come on," Jaina complained. "Can't a girl learn from her mistakes? I just want to do this right."

"Then by all means, proceed," Kenth said. He placed both hands flat on the table and glanced around at the others. "Unless there are objections?"

Saba snorted. "This one did not realize you had such a good sense of humor, Master Hamner." She let out a long siss of Barabel laughter, her forked tongue flickering between her pebbled lips. "Who would not want to hear *this*?"

Jaina was fairly sure she could name two people at the table who were not going to like what she intended to propose, but she nodded her thanks and began.

"It's obvious that we have no hope of actually stopping the takeover of the Verpine munitions industry," she began. "By the time I left the system, the Remnant had already captured Nickel One and most of the other important hives. With the advantage of their aerosol weapon, it's clear that they'll have the rest before the coalition can mount any sort of response."

"*If* we can mount a response," agreed Corran. "Most of our partners' fleets are already engaged near their own sectors, and they're not going to pull out to defend an unaligned system—especially when that system has been selling arms to all three sides."

"That doesn't mean we can afford to ignore the Roche system," Kenth objected. "Once Jacen has control of those munitions factories, the war is over."

"Not necessarily," Jaina said. She could not allow the Jedi to slip into a defensive frame of mind. She had to keep them focused on going *after* the enemy. "If Jacen can't get the munitions to his navies, it doesn't do him any good to control the factories."

"You think we should forget the Verpine?" Kyp asked.

"Not *forget*," Jaina corrected. "But the Mandalorians are the ones who have the mutual-aid agreement. All I'm suggesting is that we let them honor their contract and leave the asteroid fighting to Fett. In the meantime, we'll concentrate on what's important to us and—"

"Raid the supply train," Kenth finished. "Classic guerrilla tactics—for which we happen to be perfectly positioned."

"Exactly," Jaina said. "We make them choose between defending their munitions convoys against a concentrated StealthX campaign, and keeping their fleet in the Roche system to protect their new munitions factories against a Mandalorian counterattack. They don't have enough hulls to do both missions well, so I'm betting they'll want to protect their new factories."

"And that leaves the Jedi free to demolish their freighter capacity," Jag said. "How many cargo vessels do they have?"

"Um . . . there wasn't a lot of time to count," Jaina admitted. She could have kicked him for jumping to details *now*, before she had a chance to talk about the other half of her plan, but that was Jag—focused, careful, and alert. "And I wasn't thinking *demolish*. More like, um, *appropriate*."

"You mean *steal*," her father said, smirking in pride. "I like it. It shows your Solo blood."

"This one likez it also," Saba said. "There will be fewer pointlesz killz this way."

"Yeah, that, too," Han said. He winked at Leia. "But mostly I'm looking forward to playing pirate again."

"All you had to do was ask," Leia replied sweetly. "I'm always happy to clap you in leg irons, flyboy."

"Okaaaay," Jaina said, feeling herself blush. "We really don't need to hear more—at least *I* don't."

A chuckle ran around the table, then Kenth, all business as usual, brought the discussion back to strategy.

"I think we've all heard enough to agree this is an idea worth exploring," he said. "We can refine our tactics when we have a better idea of their shipping capacity, but fundamentally this plan makes sense. We're just about directly between the Roche system and the Core, so we can knock out their convoys almost at will. And when they do decide to come after us, we can fade into the Mists and take them by ambush. Master Skywalker?"

Luke nodded without turning around, and Jaina congratulated herself for achieving the first part of her plan.

Now all she had left were parts two and three—the hard ones.

Luke's gaze shifted from the darkness outside to Jaina's reflection. "Now—Jaina, why don't you tell us what's really on your mind?"

Jaina nodded, then summoned to mind the speech she had been rehearsing about how the coalition couldn't win the war through military might alone; their only real hope was to dismantle the enemy command structure from the top down.

But then she glanced in her parents' direction and saw the pain lurking in the depths of her mother's brown eyes, and how her father seemed to have aged ten years in the weeks she had been gone, and she knew she couldn't do that to them. It would be more honest to just come out and say it, to simply tell them about the awful decision she had made not so long ago, looking out over the beautiful Kelita valley with a forgotten Jedi general.

"Mom and Dad, I'm sorry for this." As Jaina spoke, she did not take her eyes from her parents. "But I think we have to go after Jacen. I think it's our duty."

Their eyes grew instantly glassy. Her mother's lip began to tremble, and her father's face grew red and grief-furrowed, but they did not look away.

Neither did they speak. It was Saba Sebatyne who asked, "*Go after?* What do you mean by *go after*? Arrest? Capture?" She ruffled her scales in disapproval. "This one knowz you have been training with Boba Fett, but that has not worked before."

Jaina shifted her attention to the Barabel. "I know, and it cost us some good people." She glanced around the table at the other Masters. "I mean eliminate. I mean hunt down and kill."

Not too surprisingly, it was her father who responded first. "*No.*" Instead of looking at Jaina or anyone else, he stared at the table and just shook his head. "That's *not*

Jacen. Jacen died in the war against the Yuuzhan Vong, just like Anakin did."

Jaina frowned, wondering how badly she had misjudged the impact her decision would have on Han Solo. "Dad, Jacen didn't die," she said. "He escaped with Vergere and—"

Her mother grabbed her arm, silencing her with a short squeeze. "Jaina, we haven't lost touch with reality. We're just saying that the man you're talking about *isn't* our Jacen."

"Jacen was a hero." Han's voice was as harsh as forge fumes. "He killed Onimi and won the war with the Yuuzhan Vong, and then he died of his wounds." He stopped talking for a moment, drawing in a loud breath and seeming to gather his strength, then finally looked up at Jaina with more anger and despair in his eyes than she recalled seeing, even when Chewbacca died. "Caedus is just the monster who stepped into the hollow shell that was left behind . . . and if anyone here is capable of taking him out, I'll gladly arm the detonator."

Jaina did not know how to react to the raw hatred in his voice, perhaps because she had not allowed her own anger to play a part in her decision—because she had decided *dispassionately* that it was appropriate to put a blaster bolt through her twin brother's head.

So Jaina merely nodded and reached over to take his forearm. "Okay, Dad . . . *Caedus* must die. We have to hunt him down and kill him."

Jaina had not used Jacen's Sith name earlier because she could not allow herself to pretend that she was thinking these things about someone other than her own brother—because when the time came, she knew it would not be Darth Caedus she saw in her sniper sight, but her brother, Jacen Solo, and if she wasn't ready to kill *him,* then she would be the one who died.

Jaina shifted her attention to Leia. "Mom?"

Her mother's eyes grew distant and unreadable; then she merely looked at the table and nodded. "That's not Jacen," she said. "And even if it was, I don't think we'd have any choice."

Luke finally turned away from the viewport. With sunken eyes and hollow cheeks, he looked like he had not slept in many nights. But there was also an eerie tranquillity about him that seemed both frightening and vaguely reassuring, as though he had been staring out that viewport for days, waiting for just this moment.

"Thank you," he said, and Jaina knew she had accomplished the second step of her plan. Now all she had to do was convince them *she* should be the one to send. "I've been wondering when someone else was going to come to the same conclusion."

"Then you approve?" While Kenth's voice was condemning, there was something in it that did not sound quite sincere to Jaina—as though he secretly agreed with Luke's decision, but felt the argument had to be made for form's sake. "*Assassinating* a Head of State?"

"I doubt we'll be fortunate enough to get away with simple assassination," Luke replied. "But yes. For some time now, it's been clear to me that our survival—and civilization's well-being—depends on ridding the galaxy of Darth Caedus."

Corran shook his head. "There are a lot of legitimate ways to be rid of Ja—" He caught himself and stopped, casting an apologetic look toward the Solos. Again, there was something missing from his tone, and Jaina had the sense that while he was sincere in what he was saying, he already knew that this was an argument he had no chance of winning. "To remove Caedus from power. Assassination isn't one of them. It would make us no different from him."

"We have *tried* arrest, and we have tried politicz," Saba replied. "And we have failed because we refuse to see the truth: Caedus remainz in power because he never balkz at the kill. If we wish to remove him, neither can we."

Kyp nodded in agreement. "That's right. Caedus won't be taken alive . . . and if we try, we'll be the ones who end up dead." He turned to Luke. "But if you've already decided we have to do this, why wait until Jaina brings it up?"

"To tell the truth, I was worried that my judgment might be clouded by a desire for vengeance." Luke glanced in Jaina's direction, and a look of genuine relief came to his eyes. "So I wanted to hear someone else say it first."

Jaina's heart sank. It was beginning to sound like Luke intended to go after Caedus himself, and she could not decide whether to feel betrayed or confused. She had no hope of convincing anyone—maybe not even herself—that she was more capable of slaying her brother than Luke. But what of the vision he had experienced on Mon Calamari, when he had promoted her to Jedi Knight? Hadn't he foreseen that she would be the Sword of the Jedi, always leading the fight against enemies of the Order?

Then Jaina had a terrible thought: perhaps the vision had not referred to what *was,* but to what was *to be*— perhaps she would become the Sword after the current one fell.

"I'm going with you," Jaina said. When she saw a look of disappointment flash across his face, she realized that she had reverted to the old Jaina—the Jaina who pronounced instead of offered—and amended her approach. "I mean, I'd like to help."

Luke surprised her with a sad smile. "There's nothing I'd like better, Jaina," he said, "but I'm afraid that won't be possible."

"Do you mind if I ask why not?" Jaina knew by Luke's tone that she would not get him to change his mind, but she intended to keep fighting until after the battle was over . . . something else she had learned from the Mandalorians.

"You're going to need support, and I *have* been preparing."

"I know you have," Luke said. "But I'm not going to need support because *I* can't kill Caedus."

There was a short silence while everyone contemplated this startling statement. Then Saba Sebatyne began to siss.

"Master Skywalker," she said, "you are alwayz making jokes at such strange timez."

"I don't think he's joking," Han said. He turned toward Luke. "Look, buddy, if this is about our feelings—"

"Han, it's not." Luke met the gazes of both of Jaina's parents, then said, "To tell the truth, I've been looking forward to running him down."

Jaina winced inside, and not just for herself. Her parents had told her that Luke claimed to hold only himself and Caedus responsible for Mara's death—that he had not let slip one bitter remark or asked a single pointed question. But all the Solos realized how difficult it must be for him not to blame the parents for the crimes of the child. It would only be natural to blame them for raising a monster, to wonder how they could have gotten it so wrong. So if Luke had finally let slip a vengeful remark, Jaina knew her parents would be willing to overlook this one moment of human imperfection—as would Jaina, had she not understood what he was really saying.

"You've been looking forward to it a little *too* much?" she asked. "Is that what you mean?"

"Exactly." Luke's gaze slid away from the table. "Every future that begins with me going after Caedus ends in darkness. I know I'm the only one who can be sure of stopping him, but no matter how I envision it, it always leads to darkness."

"Because you want it too much," Kyp said. "You said yourself that your judgment was clouded by vengefulness. If you could purify yourself, maybe go to Dagobah and meditate—"

"It is not Master Skywalker'z judgment that is clouded," Saba said. "It is *him*."

"What?" Han demanded. "He's not allowed to get mad when someone kills his wife?"

"This one does not think it is anger that cloudz him," Saba replied. "This one thinkz it is what he did to Lumiya."

"I think the word you're looking for is *taints*, Master Sebatyne," said Leia. "You're saying that killing Lumiya in vengeance tainted him with the dark side."

"Yes." Saba glanced in Luke's direction, then lowered her chin in apology. "This one fearz that if you go after Caedus, no matter how the hunt beginz, it must end in vengeance. That is why you can see nothing but darknesz down that path."

"And *this* one believes you're right," Luke replied. "Thank you for your honesty, Master Sebatyne. It's only one of the reasons I value your friendship."

Saba lifted her chin again. "It is only this one's duty."

She paused and began to glance around the table at the other Masters, and Jaina knew that the Barabel was trying to decide whether any of the other Masters were better prepared than she was to hunt down a Sith Lord.

Before Saba could act, Jaina stepped to her uncle's side. "Let *me* go."

"You?" This came from the other end of the table, where Corran sat looking surprised and worried. "You're only a Jedi Knight."

"So is Jacen," Jaina replied, relying on a technicality—but knowing that it would work in her favor if anybody tried to argue that a Jedi Knight wasn't powerful enough to confront Caedus. "I know that you Masters—and several Jedi Knights—are more skilled in both Force and lightsaber than I am. But I'm his twin sister. I'll have advantages no one else will."

"What kind of advantages?" Kenth asked.

Relieved to discover that she was actually being taken seriously, Jaina turned to address the table—and tried not to look toward her parents, whom she could feel beaming fear and dismay into the Force like a nova ejecting its gas shell.

"First, I've been preparing with the Mandalorians," she said. "He'll expect me to fight like a Jedi, and I won't."

"It'll take more than Fett tricks," Corran said doubtfully. "Caedus has plenty of his own—and *he* won't fight like a Jedi, either."

"I know," Jaina said. "But it will trouble him that it's *me* coming after him. We know from debriefing Allana how misunderstood he feels, how betrayed he feels because we've all chosen to stand against him. It won't protect me in a fight, but I *can* use it against him in other ways."

"And he won't use your feelings against *you*?" Kyp asked. "He's your brother, and you still love him. I can feel that."

"I still love him," Jaina admitted. "But that *won't* make me hesitate—not even for a nanosecond."

Then support arrived from an unexpected quarter.

"And there's the whole Sword of the Jedi vision Luke had when he made Jaina a Jedi Knight." His voice was cracking, but Han Solo didn't falter as he spoke—and he didn't balk. "That's got to mean something."

Jaina's heart beat an extra time in surprise, and she looked over to see her parents shining approval at her through tear-filled eyes.

"You understand Force visions better than I do," Jag said from the other end of the table. "But I suspect that doesn't guarantee her survival."

"Jagged, the Force *never* guarantees," Leia replied. "That doesn't mean you can ignore it."

"Thanks, Mom," Jaina said, sufficiently recovered from her shock to react. "You, too, Dad. Your support means a lot."

"It better," Han said. "Because you're not doing this without us. Got it?"

Jaina was too surprised to react instantly, though she knew she shouldn't have been. *Of course* her parents would want to be her support team; their feelings about Jacen had to be as strong as her own, and they would want him stopped just as much as she did. And Jaina knew better than to think she would have any chance of keeping them away when she was placing herself in this kind of danger—her mother might have had the strength to let her go after her brother alone, but not her father. He was going to be watching her tail whether she wanted him there or not.

Besides, if it was going to trouble Jacen to know that it was his sister hunting him, then it would trouble him even more to have all three Solos after him. It would hurt *anyone* to discover that his entire family was determined to kill him.

Finally, Jaina nodded. "Okay, got—" She choked on the lump in her throat and paused, hit hard by the realization that she would be placing the entire Solo family in harm's way—and that it was possible, maybe even *likely*, that none of them would survive the chain of events she was setting in motion. She looked at both her parents and nodded again. "Got it—and thanks."

"Do not assume too much, Jedi Solo," Saba warned sternly. "Your parentz' support does not mean you have *ourz*. You said you wanted to do this right. Why?"

Jaina gulped away the lump that was still in her throat and thought for a minute, then turned to Saba. "Because I need Jedi resources?"

Her honesty drew an appreciative laugh. She waited for it to fade, then continued, "And because I want to eliminate Darth Caedus—not replace him. If *I* go after him without sanction, I'll be just another murderer—like him."

"But if we send you," Kenth concluded, "you're a soldier."

"Close enough," Jaina said. She would have said executioner, but soldier *did* feel better. "This isn't about me, or even Mara or Allana. It's not about anything that Caedus has *done*—it's about what he's *going* to do, and that makes this a lot bigger than I am. If I don't have the Council's blessing, then I won't even try it."

Saba blinked twice in what was either approval or surprise—even after dozens of missions with Tesar, Jaina still couldn't read Barabels well enough to tell which—then steepled her taloned fingers, propped her elbows on the table, and turned to Luke.

"Perhapz we should send more unruly young Jedi Knightz to Boba Fett for training," she said. "If the one before us is any example, he has a gift for teaching them their place in the pack."

Luke smiled, but did not laugh. "Then you agree that she's ready?"

Saba took a moment to gather nods from the other Masters present, then turned back to Luke and inclined her own head. "It seemz you were right, yes." She turned back to Jaina. "You have the sanction of the Masterz. What else do you need from us?"

Jaina's relief did not blind her to the implications of what Saba had just said. "*Were* right?" she asked. "The Masters have *already* been discussing this option?"

"Of course," said Kyp. "We're Jedi Masters. Anticipate is what we do."

"Every day, it growz more clear to us that this fight will be won or lost in the mystic realm, not the physical," Saba added. "And the Force has named you Sword of the Jedi. We would have been foolz not to discusz your request."

"Even before I made it—that's the creepy part." Jaina turned to Luke. "You *knew* I was going to ask for the Council's sanction, didn't you?"

"I've seen some things that have led me to expect it, yes." A note of distress in Luke's voice suggested that not all those futures turned out well. "I apologize for not being more direct, but we had to be sure you were ready."

"So this was a test," Jaina said, turning toward Kenth and Corran. "Your reservations about killing Caedus—"

"Have already been discussed at length in your absence," Kenth assured her. "We just wanted to be sure everyone present appreciated our reluctance in granting this sanction."

Jaina frowned, trying to read through the multiple layers of the Master's meaning. "Are you saying that if I *can* bring Caedus in alive, I should try?"

"And get yourself and the rest of your family killed?" Kenth responded. "Absolutely not."

"A couple of us had been holding out hope that Master Skywalker would be able to pursue a less drastic course," Corran explained. He glanced in Luke's direction. "We didn't realize that wasn't an option."

"I'm sorry about that," Luke said. "But I didn't want that to influence your decision."

"And you didn't want us to know what you were seeing in your own future," Kenth surmised, "in case Jaina wasn't ready."

"I never doubted she would be, Master Hamner." Luke turned to Jaina. "Ben will accompany you to Coruscant."

"*Ben?*" It was Han who asked the question, but only because Jaina had been slowed by the cold lump of fear that had formed in her stomach. "Luke, that's got to be your worst idea since apprenticing yourself to Palpatine's clone. You *do* know we may not be coming back from this?"

"I know that Ben is a Jedi Knight," Luke said. "And that Jaina will need his connections inside the Galactic Alliance Guard to get to Caedus. Anything else I know is irrelevant to my decision."

Luke folded his hands behind his back and turned

toward the darkness outside, then caught Jaina's gaze in the viewport reflection.

"I'm afraid your brother is already expecting someone to come after him," Luke said. "I'll be doing everything I can to keep him from seeing that it's you."

chapter three

He had made a few mistakes. Caedus could see that now.

He had fallen to the same temptation all Sith did, had cut himself off from everything he loved—his family, his lover, even his daughter—to avoid being distracted by their betrayals. He could see now how blinding himself to his pain had also blinded him to his duty, how he had begun to think only of himself, of *his* plans, of *his* destiny . . . of *his* galaxy.

Self-absorption.

That was the downfall of the Sith, always. He had studied the lives of the ancients—such greats as Naga Sadow, Freedon Nadd, Exar Kun—and he knew that they always made the same mistake, that sooner or later they always forgot that they existed to serve the galaxy, and came to believe that the galaxy existed to serve *them*.

And Caedus had stepped into the same trap. He had forgotten why he was doing all this, the reason that he had picked up a lightsaber in the first place and the reason that he had given himself over to the Sith, the reason that he had taken sole control of the Galactic Alliance.

To *serve*.

Caedus had forgotten because he was weak. After Allana had betrayed him by sneaking off the *Anakin Solo* with his parents, his pain had become a distraction. He had been unable to think, to plan, to command, to read the future . . . to *lead*. So he had shut away his feelings for Allana, had convinced himself that he was not really doing this for her and the trillions of younglings like her, that he was doing this for destiny—for *his* destiny.

It had all been a lie. Even after what Allana had done, Caedus still loved her. He was her father, and he would always love her, no matter how much she hurt him. He had been wrong to try to escape that. Caedus needed to hold on to that love *whatever* it cost him, to cling to that love even as it tore his heart apart.

Because that was how Sith stayed strong. They *needed* pain to keep the Balance, to remind them they were still human. And they needed it so they would not forget the pain they were inflicting on others. To make the galaxy safer, *everyone* had to suffer—even Sith Lords.

And so there would be no angry outbursts when he confronted the Moffs over their unauthorized adventures, no demonstration killings, no Force chokings or threats to have his fleets attack theirs, no intimidation of any sort. There would be no consequences at all, for how were they to know of the worrisome things he had been seeing in his Force visions lately—the Mandalorian maniacs and the burning asteroids, his uncle's inescapable gaze—if he failed to *tell* them? Whether blunder or master stroke, the taking of the Roche system was as much his doing as the Moffs', Caedus saw now, and he was beyond punishing others for his mistakes. Starting today, Darth Caedus was going to rule not through anger or fear or even bribery, but as every true Sith Lord should, through patience and love and . . . pain.

Caedus finally crested the winding pedramp he had been ascending and found himself looking down a long tubular tunnel coated in the gray-yellow foamcrete the Verpine reserved for their royal warrens. At the far end—guarding one of the shiny new *beskar*-alloy blast hatches that had done absolutely nothing to stop the Remnant's aerosol attack—stood a squad of white-armored stormtroopers. Their gray-striped shoulder plates identified them as members of the Imperial Elite Guard, and the two tripod-mounted E-Webs set along the walls suggested they were serious about preventing unauthorized access to the chamber beyond.

The stormtroopers were still turning in his direction, no doubt trying to decide whether the single black-clad figure striding toward them was anything to be alarmed about, when Caedus raised a gloved hand and made a grasping motion. The squad leader raised his own hand as though returning the greeting—then was knocked off his feet as both E-Web supply cables tore free of the power generators and came flying down the corridor with weapon and tripod bouncing along behind them.

The remainder of the squad swiftly moved to firing positions, dropping to a knee in the middle of the corridor or pressing themselves against the tunnel wall, and brought their blaster rifles to their shoulders. Caedus sent a surge of Force energy sizzling down the corridor, reducing the electronic opticals inside their helmets to a blizzard of static. They opened fire anyway, but most of the bolts went wide, and those that did not, Caedus deflected with the occasional flick of a hand.

He was still ten paces away when the squad leader pulled his helmet off and, bringing his weapon to bear, began yelling for the others to do the same. Caedus raised his arm, catching the leader's bolts on his palm and deflecting them harmlessly down the tunnel. As the second and third man prepared to open fire, he flicked a finger toward the leader's blaster and sent it spinning into them. It slammed the second man into the wall and knocked the third's weapon from his hands.

Caedus summoned the leader forward with two fingers,

using the Force to bring the astonished soldier flying into his grasp.

"I have no intention of harming anyone beyond that door," Caedus said, making his voice deep and commanding. "But I have no time to waste, so I won't hesitate to kill *you* or your men. I trust that won't be necessary?"

The sergeant's eyes bulged as though his throat were actually being squeezed shut—which it was not—and his face paled to the color of his armor.

"N-n-no, sir. N-not at all." The sergeant motioned for his men to lower their weapons. "S-s-sorry."

"No apologies necessary, Sergeant," Caedus said. "Obviously, you haven't been informed of the new chain of command."

Caedus set the sergeant's boots back on the tunnel floor, then turned to look at each of the others in the squad. He made it appear that he was requiring each man to look into his yellow eyes, but actually he was Force-probing their emotions, looking for any hint of anger or resentment that suggested there might be a hero in the group. He was down to the last two when he sensed a fist of resolve tightening inside one.

"Don't do it, trooper," he said. "There aren't enough good soldiers in the Alliance as it is."

The fist of resolve immediately began to loosen, but the trooper wasn't too surprised to say, "With all due respect, *Colonel,* we're *not* Alliance soldiers."

"Not yet." Caedus gave him a warm smile and turned toward the blast hatch, presenting his back to the entire squad. "My escorts will be along shortly. Don't start a firefight with them."

When he felt the squad leader motion the hero and everyone else to lower their weapons, Caedus nodded his approval without turning around. Then he circled his hand in front of the blast door, using the Force to send a surge of energy through its internal circuitry until a series of sharp clicks announced that the locking mechanisms had re-tracted. A moment later, a loud hiss sounded from inside the heavy hatch, and it slid aside into the wall.

Caedus stepped through without hesitation and found himself looking down on a sunken conference pit where a couple dozen Imperial Moffs—most of the survivors of the slaughter aboard the *Bloodfin*—were rising to their feet, some reaching for their sidearms and others looking for a place to take cover. Across from them, a small swarm of in-sectoid administrators from other Verpine hives squatted on their haunches, their shiny heads cocked in confusion and their mandibles spread wide in an instinctive threat display.

"No, please." Caedus extended his arms toward the Moffs and motioned for them to return to their seats—using the Force to compel obedience. "Don't get up on my account."

The Moffs dropped almost as one. Most landed in the chairs they had been occupying, but a couple missed and landed on the floor. Several of the aides standing behind the Moffs' chairs were pointing hold-out blasters in his direc-tion, looking to their superiors for some hint as to whether they should open fire or stand down. Caedus swept his arm up and sent them all flying out of the conference pit onto the surrounding service floor.

"I'm afraid this will be a confidential conversation," he said. "Leave us."

When the aides did not instantly obey, he gestured at one of those who had been pointing a blaster at him and sent the man tumbling out the hatch.

"*Now.*"

The remainder of the aides scrambled for the door, many without bothering to stand. Caedus watched them go, his attention divided between them and the Moffs, ready to pin motionless anyone who even thought about raising a weapon. Once the aides were gone, a simple glance was all it took to send the Verpine administrators scuttling after them, leaving him and the Moffs alone with a single huge Verpine with age-silvered eyebulbs and a translucent patch on her thorax where the carahide was growing thin. She showed no inclination to rise from her position at the far end of the conference table, where she lay stretched along a heavily cushioned throne pedestal.

"Jacen Solo, where will the hives ever gather the wealth to settle our account?" The Verpine spoke in an ancient, thrumming voice that seemed to resonate from the very bottom of her long abdomen. As the High Coordinator of the Roche system's capital asteroid, she was effectively the hive mother and chief executive officer of her entire civilization, outranking even the Verpine's public face, Speaker Sass Sikili. "First, you rescue us from the Ancient Ones, and now you come with your fleet to send away the whiteshells. Welcome."

"Thank you, Your Maternellence. But the name now is Caedus. *Darth* Caedus."

The hive mother inclined her head. "We have heard you went through a metamorphosis. It is hard to believe you were just a larva when you saved us before." She unfolded an age-curved arm and gestured at the Moffs. "The hives will be happily rid of these wasps. Proceed."

"I wish it were that simple," Caedus said. He turned his attention to the Moffs, who were studying him with expressions ranging from impatience to annoyance, depending on whether they were brave, astute, or just plain foolhardy. "But you're misinterpreting our presence. My fleet and I aren't here to *free* the Roche system—we're here to *hold* it."

It was difficult to tell who was more outraged, the mandible-clacking hive mother or the grumbling Moffs. Caedus raised his hand and—when that failed to produce quiet—used the Force to muffle the clamor.

As soon as he could be sure of making himself heard

again, he said, "This will be best for everyone. The conquest of the Roche system has given it a significance far beyond the value of its munitions factories."

The hive mother raised her thorax off her couch and demanded, "What significance? The hives are neutral! We have nothing to do with your war."

"You have been selling munitions to all sides—and profiting handsomely," interrupted a combat-trim Moff with close-cropped gray hair. "That makes you a legitimate target."

"Moff Lecersen makes a good point," Caedus said. "And I *did* warn you that the Mandalorians lacked the strength to protect you." Before the hive mother could argue, he turned to Lecersen. "But the Moff Council should have consulted with me before acting. There have been indications in the Force all along that this invasion would be a mistake."

"Because you want the Roche munitions factories for yourself?" scoffed a youthful Moff.

Caedus recognized him from intelligence holos as Voryam Bhao. With his honey-colored complexion, curly black hair, and a sneering upper lip just begging to be ripped off his face, he looked even younger than the twenty-three standard years listed in his file.

"Spare us your dark prophecies, *Colonel* Solo," Bhao continued boldly. "Everyone at this table sees what you're trying to do."

The bile began to rise in Caedus's throat, but he reminded himself of his resolution and resisted the urge to snap the young Moff's neck—as he had Lieutenant Tebut's not so long ago.

Instead, he said in a calm, durasteel voice, "You really should listen more carefully, Moff Bhao." He made a dipping motion with his index finger, and Bhao's head sank toward the table as though he were bowing. "It's Caedus now. *Darth* Caedus."

If Bhao's older peers were amused, they did not show it—not even in the Force. They simply glared at Caedus, and another of the Moffs—this one a round-faced man with a roll of red neck-flab hanging over the collar of his buttoned tunic—shook his head in open disapproval.

"We are all aware that you are very powerful in the Force, Darth Caedus," he said. "But you seem to be forgetting that *we* are quite powerful in our own right. If not for us, that catastrophe at Fondor would have been the end of you *and* the Galactic Alliance."

"Nor do we need to *consult* with you about anything," Moff Lecersen added. "The last I checked, the Empire was an *ally* of the Galactic Alliance, not its territory. We don't need your permission to conduct our operations . . . and we surely don't need your fleets to hold what we take."

Caedus brought his anger under control by reminding himself that he *deserved* such a rebuke. He had not failed at Fondor because of Niathal's treachery, or his admirals' lack of boldness, or even because of Daala's surprise attack. He had failed because of his own blindness, because he had allowed his anguish over Allana's betrayal to make him arrogant and selfish and vindictive.

And then, once his thinking had cleared, he began to see how the situation must look to someone who did not have the Force. To someone who could not look into the future and see Luke hunting him down, or see Mandalorian maniacs bursting from walls and asteroids burning as bright as stars, Caedus's assertion might be hard to believe. Without such foresight, it might be easy to convince oneself that this lonely cluster of rocks could not be as important as all that—that the balance of an interstellar war could never hinge on what was about to happen *here*.

After a moment's silence, Caedus said, "You don't believe me." His tone was more disappointed than angry. "You think this is about spoils."

Lecersen exchanged suspicious glances with several of

the other Moffs, then asked, "You don't really expect us to believe you came out here to *protect* us, do you?"

Caedus had to stifle a laugh. While he hadn't been thinking of it in those terms, he realized that was *exactly* what he was doing here—protecting the Moffs and their crucial fleets.

"I suppose that *does* sound absurd." Realizing that only events themselves would convince the Moffs of his sincerity, Caedus turned and started toward the exit. "The truth so often does."

Ben had heard officials from the Reconstruction Authority speak of Monument Plaza as their crowning achievement— a fitting finale to the agency's commission as the rebuilder of galactic civilization. Their technicians had spent three years sonichipping a two-meter crust of Yuuzhan Vong yorik coral off the classic Old Republic architecture that surrounded the square, and their artisans had dedicated *five* years to replicating—with original methods and materials— the thousands of ancient statues that had given the plaza its name.

Even KnobHead, the outcropping of bare mountaintop that was one of the only places on Coruscant where one could touch actual planetary surface, had been rescued: a team of RA geologists had spent more than a year scrubbing away a blanket of stone-dissolving lichen that may or may not have been a Yuuzhan Vong terraforming device. By the RA's own very loud proclamation, the project was a stellar success, one more example of the job it had done restoring the galaxy to its pre–Yuuzhan Vong glory.

What Ben *saw,* however, was a vast durasteel square teeming with bored tourists and loitering office workers, strewn with litter and badly in need of a cleansing rain. The smog-pearled sky was kept blissfully free of air traffic by a no-fly security zone, and the only possible location for an observation post was inside the monuments themselves, all of which were surrounded by softly rumbling rivers of sightseers that would render even the most sophisticated eavesdropping equipment useless. In short, what Ben saw was the perfect place to avoid being seen without being obvious about it, a seething mass of life so vast that even GAG could not identify every being it contained.

No wonder Lon Shevu liked to meet his informants here.

Ben found one of Shevu's favorite statues—a gray monolith depicting a droid mechanic—and sat on one end of the empty viewing bench. A hologram of an attractive female Sullustan rose out of the plaza decking and began to explain that *Devoted Technician* was both the newest and largest monument in the plaza, a fitting tribute to the billions of dedicated beings who had worked so hard under the Reconstruction Authority to rebuild the galaxy after the war against the Yuuzhan Vong.

The hologram continued, spewing a self-congratulatory stream of propaganda about the remarkable job the RA had done with limited resources in a very difficult political climate. If Ben had not had more important things to think about—like why the hairs on his neck were standing erect when he *knew* he hadn't been followed from the Mizobon Spaceport—he would have been bored to yawns.

Ben had experienced that same sensation a thousand times since he had left the *Sweet Time*—the much-modified KDY space yacht the strike team was using as its base of operations. He reached out in the Force, searching for anyone who might be watching him. Lon Shevu might be a GAG captain himself, but anyone who caught him talking to Ben would instantly realize that Shevu was also a spy, a traitor who wanted to bring Caedus down as much as Ben did—well, *almost* as much. Caedus hadn't murdered Shevu's mother, after all.

Ben *was* being watched, of course. Aunt Leia and his cousin Jaina were both in the crowd, serving as his backups but keeping their distance to avoid drawing attention to him or Shevu. And he could sense about a dozen young females keeping a furtive eye on him, overly interested but bearing no hint of harmful intentions—probably just admiring the Arkanian wardrobe that Aunt Leia had chosen as part of his nobleman's disguise. There were also several presences that felt watchful but not focused, no doubt just plainclothes security agents looking for nervous demeanor, irrational conduct, or any of a thousand other behaviors that usually betrayed terrorist attacks in the making.

What Ben did *not* sense was any curiosity or suspicion directed his way, no hint that he would be bringing danger along when he made contact with Shevu. Reassured, he rose and made his way to the opposite corner of the monument.

Shevu was standing behind a viewing bench, posing as a tourist. He wore the now meaningless uniform of the Reconstruction Authority Space Patrol, and he was using a small vidcam to record another hologram, this one narrated by an attractive Falleen female. His hair was tinted gray, and he was wearing a false goatee beard in the same color. In fact, he looked so much like a retired RASP pilot that, despite his familiar Force presence, Ben wasn't quite sure he had the right man.

Or maybe it was the changes that *weren't* part of Shevu's disguise that were throwing Ben off—the sunken eyes and ashen complexion, and the worry lines that seemed to have appeared from nowhere. Ben stopped half a step in front of him and a little off to the side, pretending to be interested in the same hologram. It *was* a bit more interesting than the last one. The Falleen was explaining how the Reconstruction Authority had liberated the Maltorian mining belt from the notorious pirate captain Three-Eye.

Shevu surprised him by speaking first. "That's not quite how it really happened, you know," he said. "I could tell you about Three-Eye, if you're interested."

Ben casually turned and found Shevu smiling at him

from behind his vidcam—but also holding his brow cocked in concern and curiosity.

"So you were there, sir?" Ben asked, still playing the role of the polite young noble.

Shevu shook his head. "I'm acquainted with some people who were. The way I heard it, the fighting was over by the time we arrived. Three-Eye was actually handed over to us by a pair of Jedi Knights." He lowered his vidcam and looked directly at Ben. "Jedi have a funny way of doing that—just appearing when nobody expects them."

"I'm sure they have their reasons," Ben said. "Did you serve with RASP long, sir?"

"The whole ten years," Shevu said. "Time of my life."

When Shevu did not suggest a snack or lunch as a prelude to going somewhere they could talk more freely, Ben realized his friend was also worried about their security. He extended his Force awareness again, and this time he *did* feel a pair of focused presences—but they were focused on Shevu, not him. The watchers could have been a GAG backup team, of course—but Ben doubted it. Shevu came here to meet informants, and a careful spymaster did not risk his assets by allowing a backup team to see them. If someone had Shevu under surveillance, it was because they suspected him of treason.

Ben's first instinct was to take his friend and flee, but that would be a stupid move. Even if they could fight their way out of the plaza, Shevu's defection would be considered a security emergency. By the time they reached the *Sweet Time* at Mizobon, GAG would have a full-scale "recovery" effort under way, with every spaceport on the planet sealed tight and whole divisions of GAG troopers scouring every cranny within a hundred kilometers of the plaza.

Ben finally identified Shevu's watchers, a narrow-snouted Rodian couple about thirty meters away. They were pressing suction-tipped fingers to each other's green cheeks, running a vidcam, and generally trying too hard to look like a couple on holiday. Ben began to subtly flick his fingers in their direction, sending a steady stream of surveillance-negating Force flashes toward the vidcam.

Once Ben felt certain that the Rodians' recording equipment was useless, he turned back to Shevu.

"Do you know what happened to him—Three-Eye, I mean?" Ben asked, continuing to speak obliquely but coming directly to the point. If he and Shevu were at risk, it was best to get done and get gone. "I have some friends who might like to meet him. I'm sure you would find it worthwhile to help us."

Shevu's brow shot up. "How worthwhile?"

"We could make you a very happy man in a very short time," Ben replied. "As a matter of fact, we're making preparations for a meeting with him now."

The look that came to Shevu's face was equal parts surprise and fear. For an instant, Ben thought that he had been misreading his friend all along—that either Shevu did not want to be involved in moving against Caedus so directly, or he had been Caedus's double agent from the beginning.

Then Shevu smiled. "There's no telling how long it would take to put you in touch face-to-face," he said. "But I *can* tell you where to find him. Would that be worth something to you?"

Ben nodded. "Probably. How much depends on how hard it would be for us to arrange a meeting."

"Should be easier than on Coruscant," Shevu replied. "I hear that Three-Eye's new gang has been causing problems on Nickel One. The last I heard, he was on his way to bring them into line."

"Are you sure?" Ben asked. Two different intelligence services—Hapan and Wookiee—had confirmed that the *Anakin Solo* was in its hangar at Crix Base above Coruscant. "We've heard that his space yacht is still in its moorings."

"Security precaution," Shevu replied. "He crossed some

Bothans awhile back, and it's become advisable for him to travel in something a little less conspicuous. He's definitely gone to Nickel One."

"Nickel One?" Ben repeated. Suddenly, the Remnant's easy conquest of the Roche system seemed more convenient than alarming. Asteroids were small places, and if the Jedi acted quickly, they would be able to slip a strike team into place before the Imperials had a chance to debug their security operation. He reached for a credit chip. "That should be worth something to us. How about . . ."

Ben let the sentence trail off as he felt Jaina reaching out to him in the Force, warning that trouble was on the way. He looked past Shevu and saw the Rodian couple coming, their hands slipping into the pockets of their outer tunics.

"Ten thousand?" Shevu asked, misinterpreting Ben's sudden silence and still trying to maintain cover. "It's not easy to come by that kind of information, and if Three-Eye ever finds out—"

"Seccer!" Ben yelled, using the galaxywide slang for a public security officer. He hit Shevu in both shoulders, but harder in the right so that he would be spun around and see the approaching Rodians. "*Dead* seccer!"

Hoping to make it appear that he was resisting arrest—and that Shevu was therefore not involved in anything disloyal to Caedus or GAG—Ben drew his hold-out blaster and fired past his friend's head. The first bolt came close enough to raise a heat welt along Shevu's jaw and make it appear the effort to kill had been sincere. The other three shots were not so close, scattering the crowd and sending the two Rodians diving for safety.

"*Sorry!*" Ben hissed, leaning close to Shevu's head. "I think they were watching *you*. Maybe you should come—"

Shevu elbowed him in the ribs, lifting him off his feet and drawing a real grunt of pain.

"*No. You go!*" Shevu spun around, simultaneously

reaching for his blaster and clutching at Ben's cloak lapel. "*Make it look*—aaargh!"

The order ended in a surprised scream as Ben clamped a hand over Shevu's wrist and pivoted away, sending his friend into a flying somersault that ended with him lying flat on his back.

"*See ya!*" Ben whispered. "*Good luck!*"

He put a couple of blaster bolts through the loose cloth of Shevu's tunic for good measure, then turned to run.

He found himself staring down a hundred-meter aisle that seemed to be spontaneously opening in front of a woman sprinting through the crowd toward him. Dressed in a dark cloak and black GAG armor, she had blond hair, a lightsaber hilt in her hand, and a dozen GAG commandos following close on her heels.

"Oh, *kriff*!" Ben said. "That's Tahiri!"

The rising whine of repulsorlift cooling fans began to howl over the plaza, and Ben looked up to see a flight of GAG-black troopsleds sweeping down from the milky sky.

"*Go!*" Shevu ordered. "Make this count!"

Ben obeyed instantly, charging into a mass of beings slowly pressing away from the Reconstruction Authority monument in an effort to escape the fight about to erupt in their midst. Assuming Shevu would be close behind him, he began to use the Force to clear a path ahead, at the same time tearing away the wig and heavy robes of his Arkanian disguise.

Ben was traveling in the opposite direction from Jaina and Aunt Leia, trying to protect the mission by moving the action away from his backup team. When the odds got this bad, it was better to split up and avoid getting your partners captured or killed as well. That way, at least there would be someone left to file the report.

The crowd broke into screams as energy bolts began to zing back and forth across the square behind him, and that's when Ben realized Shevu wasn't with him. He stopped and spun around, but all he could see was the constant flash of blasterfire flickering through the wall of panicked tourists backing toward him.

Ben tore the finger socks—part of his disguise—from his hands and started to push back toward the fight, then remembered the last thing Shevu had said to him before sending him off. *Make this count.* If Ben rushed back there now, he would be doing just the opposite, robbing Shevu's sacrifice of meaning—and in all likelihood *still* failing to save him.

Leaving his lightsaber to hang on the belt beneath his tunic, Ben pulled the comlink from his pocket. He allowed the press of the crowd to push him slowly backward, away from what now sounded more like a tapcaf fight than a shootout, determined to *make this count* and *then* go back for his friend.

He did not open a direct channel to the *Sweet Time.* That would give GAG eavesdropping droids the few precious seconds they needed to trace his signal and identify the rest of his team. Instead, he recorded a quick message describing what he had learned about Caedus's location, ending with a report of Shevu's capture and, most likely, his own. He formatted it for a five-millisecond burst transmission that would be too fast to track, then opened the channel to the *Sweet Time* . . . and felt a cold prickle of danger sense race down his spine.

A familiar female voice sounded a pace behind him. "Don't transmit it, Ben. I won't hesitate to kill you."

"You just *did.*"

Ben depressed the TRANSMIT button, then tossed the comlink into the air and reached for his lightsaber—only to find Tahiri's hand already there.

"Bad idea," she said.

Ben spun toward the hand, bringing an arm up and smashing his elbow into the side of her head. He started to tell her she talked too much, then heard the *snap-hiss* of an igniting lightsaber and realized he had just made the same mistake.

A line of scalding pain erupted across his lower back, and he saw the bright glow of Tahiri's blade tip shining beside and a little behind him. When his body did not fall to the plaza deck in two pieces, he guessed that he was still alive and continued his spin, bringing his hand around in a reverse knife-hand strike that *would* have caught her just below the ear and almost certainly knocked her unconscious—had she not blocked.

As Ben's head snapped back, he caught a glimpse of scarred brow and blond hair, then felt his teeth biting through his tongue and his feet flying out from beneath him and realized Tahiri had caught him beneath the chin with a fist or an elbow or a hydraulic hammer, and it hardly mattered which because all he could feel was the inescapable darkness of a black hole drawing him down into the singularity of unconsciousness, into helplessness, defeat, and death.

Ben refused to go. He lashed out in the Force, grabbing at the last place he had seen Tahiri, pulling with all his might and feeling . . . feeling *something* give, feeling something like legs or ankles or feet come flying toward him, then hearing Tahiri scream in anger or pain or maybe just surprise.

A sharp clang echoed through the plaza decking as her armor hit, and the darkness started to retreat from Ben's head. He sensed Tahiri lying at his feet, just as flat on the deck as he was. She swore, profaning Ben's dead mother and promising to make him pay for *making this so hard*, then he saw his lightsaber lying on the durasteel not far from his hand—surrounded by a dozen pairs of black boots, but still within his Force grasp.

Ben reached out in the Force. Half a dozen troopers cried out in astonishment as the weapon banged off their boots, spinning and tumbling through the thicket of shins and ankles to arrive in his hand *upside down,* with the emitter nozzle pointed straight into his eye.

Tahiri's voice sounded from a meter beyond his feet. "I've had it with this kreetle!"

Ben flipped the lightsaber around and sat up. Tahiri was sitting up now, too, looking straight toward him. Her face was slimmer and more lined than he remembered it, but still as beautiful as ever, framed by a halo of flowing golden hair and marred only by the three diagonal scars on her brow and the fury in her eyes.

"Put him out," Tahiri ordered. *"Now!"*

Ben ignited his lightsaber, and *that* was when he saw—finally—the black wall of GAG troopers arrayed around him in a ring, all pointing blaster rifles in his direction. He gave himself over to the Force and felt himself springing to his feet, his blade moving to block, then heard it bat *one-twothree* blaster bolts aside before a flurry of hot punches caught him square in the back. His body exploded into paralyzing pain, and the electric darkness rose up to swallow him again.

chapter four

*How many stormtroopers does it take to change a glow panel?
Two: one to change it, and one to blast him, then take credit for the
work.*

—Jacen Solo, age 14

By the time Jaina pushed through to the front of the crowd,
Tahiri and her troopers were clamping Ben into the GAG
Doomsled, fitting his wrists and ankles with electromagnetic bands that would keep his limbs firmly affixed to his
durasteel seat. His head had already been enclosed inside a
full-faced "blinder" helmet—basically a durasteel bucket
with no viewplate, secured to the ceiling by a short chain.

Ben had fled *away* from his backup. Jaina knew her
young cousin had only been trying to preserve mission security, that he had followed textbook procedure when facing overwhelming odds—but that was GAG thinking. *Jedi*
stuck together. They trusted one another to do the impossible, and when they found themselves in trouble, they did
not make it harder for their partners to extract them by
running in the opposite direction.

Across the compartment from Ben, Shevu lay stretched
over several seats, his wrists and ankles already magclamped
to the durasteel. He wasn't wearing a blinder helmet—the
chain was too short to reach someone lying prone—and he
was cursing and screaming as an MD droid tended to a
blaster wound he had suffered, abrasion-cleaning it without the benefit of a numbing agent.

All this was being done with the Doomsled's detention

compartment open to full view, so the public could see the stern efficiency with which GAG dispatched traitors to the Alliance. Good government was transparent, after all.

But there was also another reason, Jaina knew. Ben remained in full view so his backup team would feel encouraged to attempt an ill-advised rescue. There was simply no other reason a Sith apprentice and a full GAG security detail would take ten minutes to secure a pair of semiconscious prisoners—or wait for a Doomsled to arrive in the first place. Standard procedure was to whisk prisoners away instantly, both to maximize their confusion and to minimize any chance that they would be rescued—or silenced—by unconstrained colleagues.

Jaina realized all that, recognized an obvious setup when she saw one, and it meant nothing to her . . . because she *wasn't* losing Ben. She wasn't putting her uncle through that kind of anguish, and she wasn't giving her brother another shot at their cousin. Ben had stepped too far into the light to fall again, and Jaina knew that he would let himself be tortured to death before turning dark—and knowing Caedus, that might be exactly what happened.

Jaina saw the black streak of a vidlog droid zipping down the line of bystanders toward her, creating a record of onlookers that would be analyzed frame by frame back at headquarters. She was disguised as an Elomin office girl, but her mask-flattened nose and fake skull-horns would not fool a GAG facial-recognition servobrain. She used a Force flash to disrupt the vidlogger's optics, then slipped back into the crowd. Of course, the Force flash itself would confirm that Ben had had a Jedi backup—but Tahiri certainly knew that much already. At least now she wouldn't know exactly *which* Jedi it had been.

Once Jaina was sufficiently hidden in the crowd, she made her way to within a few meters of a sultry Codru-Ji female who had males of all species stealing furtive glances. The woman's outfit—a daring mini-vest-and-clingpant combo—was part of a hide-in-plain-sight strategy, the kind of thing that anyone who knew the stately Leia Organa Solo would be shocked to see her wearing. Even more shocking, at least to Jaina, was the throng of admirers that her mother could still attract . . . and she felt fairly certain that the prosthetics and makeup did not have all that much to do with it.

Jaina caught her mother's eye, then flicked her gaze toward one of the medwagons that had arrived to gather the GAG casualties Ben and Shevu had left scattered across the plaza. Leia nodded and shot a flirty smile at a red-skinned Devaronian who had been dipping his brow horns in her direction, then sent a teasing brow flash toward a blue-faced Duros whose red eyes had remained fixed on her for a good five seconds. She put on a sad little pout and waved good-bye to both, then started to work her way through the crowd toward the medwagon Jaina had indicated.

They met at the circle of gawkers surrounding the vehicle. Jaina kept her eyes on the two Rodians being loaded into the patient compartment by MD droids, but her attention was on her mother.

"You've got half the males in the plaza standing on their tongues," she whispered. "I hope Dad doesn't know how you act when you're dressed like that."

"Of course he knows," Leia replied. "He *loves* it when I dress like this."

Jaina tried not to imagine her father leering at her mother in that outfit and failed miserably. "Thanks for that picture. I knew there was a reason I don't travel with you guys much."

Leia chuckled. "You ought to—maybe you'd learn to dial down the gravity setting a little," she said. "You need to give your alter ego room to play in these situations. That's the best way to make it work for you."

"*Really?*" Jaina wondered why her mother would think

her "alter ego" was an uptight secretary from an emotion-
ally restrained species. "I look forward to hearing more
about your theory later. In the meantime . . ."

Jaina gestured at the medwagon, where the second Rodian's gurney was being magclamped to the floor, opposite
his companion. From what she could sense through the
Force, both agents were in pain, but completely stable and
far from death.

"Shall we?"

Leia eyed the medwagon, then said, "You know we
don't stand a chance, right?"

"I know that it's *Ben.*"

Leia let out a huge sigh of relief. "I was *hoping* you'd say
that."

She stepped across the intangible line of control that a
pair of Coruscant Security officers had created by the simple fact of their presence. Ignoring them, she started
toward the medwagon's patient compartment, wailing and
whimpering and in general doing a pretty credible job of
looking like a vac-brain glitter girl on the verge of hyster-
ics.

"*Webbbbi!*" she screamed. "*What* happened?"

The two security officers sprang after her, both raising
stun sticks and yelling dire warnings to stop.

"It's okay," Jaina said, also crossing the line of control
and coming up behind the two officers. "She's with *me.*"

Force commands only worked on weak-minded individ-
uals, which Jaina felt sure had to include most of the beings
serving her brother. These two were no exception. They
stopped almost in their tracks and turned around, their
shoulders already sagging in an unconscious gesture of
subservience.

Still, an Elomin secretary in a high-necked sheath was far
from the uniformed superior they had been expecting.
They frowned and glanced at each other, then the older
of the two—an anvil-headed Arcona with deep cracks in

the flesh around his green eyes—extended a long-taloned hand.

"Credentials, please."

"I'm undercover." Jaina gestured with her hand, giving the Arcona something to focus on other than the mesmerizing tone of her voice. "I have no credentials."

The Arcona's gray brow knitted into a deep furrow. "She's undercover," he said. "She has no credentials."

"So?" asked his companion, a handsome human with bright white teeth and what looked like a two-day growth of beard stubble. "That just means she's GAG. Leave her alone."

"Good thinking," Jaina said to the human. "And you don't need to file a report about this. We're undercover."

Now the human frowned, and she realized that she might have overplayed her hand. "No report? Sergeant Qade will have our heads."

"No, he won't." Jaina leaned in close, then lowered her voice so that the two officers had to lean down to hear her. "Who do you think we're investigating?"

The cracks around the Arcona's eyes suddenly widened into red stripes of raw flesh, and the human's white teeth vanished behind his pale lips.

"*Qade?*" he gasped. "I don't believe it!"

Jaina leaned in even closer. "Does that mean you're unwilling to cooperate, Officer . . ." She paused until she sensed the man's name rising to the top of his mind, then finished, "Tobyl?"

Tobyl's eyes widened, and he stood up straight. "Not me!" he said. "Er, I mean, we never saw you." He turned to the Arcona. "Right, Jat'ho?"

The Arcona simply looked away and stepped back toward the line of control, threatening to arrest a hapless Falleen couple who had done nothing wrong.

"Good," Jaina said. "A note of commendation will be placed in your file."

Tobyl smiled. "Thanks. After my last review, I could use—"

"Not *those* files," Jaina said. "*Ours.*"

Tobyl's smile turned to an expression of dismay. "GAG has a file on me?"

Jaina frowned. "Come now, Officer," she said. "You *know* I can't tell you that."

She stepped past Tobyl and continued toward the medwagon, where her mother had already deactivated both MD droids and was closing the doors of the patient compartment. Jaina went directly to the front of the blocky medwagon and used the Force to deactivate the security circuit on the pilot's hatch, then stood back as the door swung up to reveal an operator's compartment nearly as packed with controls and gauges as a starfighter's cockpit— though with nearly a meter of empty space separating two thickly padded safety seats, it was far roomier.

A surprised Bith looked out from the pilot's seat, his lidless eyes bulging in alarm. "What are you doing?" He reached up to pull the hatch closed. "Get back! You're not author—"

"Officer Tobyl will explain." Jaina caught his arm, then slapped the quick-release latch on his crash webbing and pulled him out of the seat. "These patients are my responsibility now."

"What?" The Bith tried to return to the pilot's seat, only to find Jaina's hand in the middle of his chest, sending him stumbling back toward the control line. "Who do you think you—"

"*Officer Tobyl will explain.*"

Jaina hopped into the pilot's seat, pulling the hatch closed in the same motion, and engaged the repulsorlifts. The medwagon lurched into the air with a shrill whine and sent dozens of bystanders scrambling out of its path. She held back on the throttle under the pretense of giving them time to clear a lane, but she was also peering over their heads in the direction of Ben's Doomsled, watching as it streaked across the plaza toward the rectangular maw of the Arakyd Towers ThroughPass.

Jaina activated the routing screen on the instrument panel and saw the logo of the Borsk Fey'lya Center across the top. Below that was a schematic of Monument Plaza and the surrounding area, with a series of blinking red arrows running out through the TravRat Gap and up into the Four-Thousand Skylane. She turned in the direction indicated by the screen's waypoint dot, and found herself looking at a dark stripe of emptiness about an eighth of the way around the plaza from where Ben was headed.

The patient compartment access panel opened, filling the operator's area with the stinging smell of disinfectant and antiseptic. Leia came forward, now minus the extra set of Codru-Ji arms but wearing the belt and equipment that had been stowed inside them. She had also donned a tan robe, but continued to wear the wig and face makeup that had completed her disguise.

"What are you doing?" Leia pointed across the plaza toward the Doomsled, which was just vanishing down the black mouth of the Arakyd Towers ThroughPass. "That way!"

"Can't," Jaina said. "We have to make this run look legitimate, at least until we're out of the plaza."

"Who cares about legitimate?" Leia demanded. "I'm not letting Ben out of—"

"*They* care." Jaina pointed through the upper canopy, where the dark rectangles of half a dozen troopsleds were still circling the plaza. "And they've got auto blasters."

Leia glanced up at the black rectangles, then let her breath out in frustration. "Stang. They probably *would* notice."

"Once we're clear of the surveillance umbrella, we won't have any trouble finding Ben," Jaina assured her mother.

"We *know* where Tahiri's taking him, and that Doomsled sticks out like a Gamorrean at a state banquet."

"Good point." Leia began to tap the routing screen keypad. "We should be able to catch up at Big Snarl. After that, we can take them somewhere in Galactic City."

Jaina slipped the medwagon into the narrow chasm between the transparisteel monolith of the Traveler's Palace and the octagonal cylinder of the Curat Commercial Center. A transparisteel safety wall flashed past beneath them, marking the end of the plaza decking, and suddenly they were traveling over a band of dark nothingness barely ten meters wide and so deep that it took a kilometer just to reach the murk.

Jaina counted to three to make certain they had passed beyond view of the troopsleds still circling Monument Plaza, then shoved the throttle forward. The medwagon shot past so close to the Palace's guest rooms that she could see the eyes of some occupants widen with astonishment, and a pair of loud crashes sounded from the rear of the medwagon as the two MD droids tumbled against the doors.

"What about our patients?" she asked.

"They should be okay as long as the droids don't land on them," Leia said. "They're strapped in, and their gurneys are magclamped to the floor."

"Mom, I'm not worried about their health," Jaina said. "I want to be sure *we're* secure."

"Oh." Jaina felt her mother's gaze on her, not necessarily disapproving, but certainly evaluating. "They won't be giving us any trouble, Jaina. They're sedated."

Jaina sighed. "Look, I'm not suggesting you blast them in their sleep. Just be sure this isn't part of Tahiri's setup."

A wave of relief rolled through the Force. "Of course." Leia slipped out of her seat and turned toward the access panel. "For a moment, I was worried you'd learned a little *too* much from Fett."

"Well, I *did* learn not to underestimate my enemy," Jaina replied. They reached the end of the TravRat Gap and shot out between two levels of perpendicular traffic. "Hold on!"

She banked hard and dropped toward the leftbound lane, leaving her mother momentarily weightless, and another series of crashes sounded from the rear of the medwagon—this time from up near the ceiling. She felt Leia exert herself in the Force, then glimpsed her settling onto the floor again.

As the medwagon neared the skylane level, an air taxi shot up ahead of them, the furry little pilot flashing his front incisors and making a rude gesture. To avoid a collision, Jaina had to bring the medwagon's nose up sharply, then ease off the repulsorlifts and more or less hull-flop into the traffic lane. The MDs banged to the floor, shaking the whole medwagon, and Leia let out a grunt as she struggled to stay standing.

"You *are* your father's daughter!" she complained. "What do you think I am, a why-vee?"

"Not my fault," Jaina replied. "Squib air taxi."

"You dislocated my knees to avoid hitting a *Squib*?" Leia asked. "What, you didn't want to scratch our paint?"

Leia retreated into the patient compartment and began to bang around, securing the Rodians to their gurneys and magclamping the MDs to the floor. Jaina decided not to activate the medwagon's blue emergency beacon. That would only necessitate a three-level climb into the emergency lanes, where finding the Doomsled would be next to impossible. Besides, it was going to be hard enough to sneak up on Tahiri without advertising their arrival with a flashing light.

Jaina checked the traffic screen, rotating each cam through its full angle of view, but she found no signs of pursuit. In fact, the only hint of GAG at all was a single troopsled crossing two lanes overhead on its way back to headquarters.

Jaina didn't trust anything this easy.

Leia came back through the access panel with the miniature signal scanner from her equipment belt in hand.

"Our patients were starting to come around already," she reported. She began to run the scanner over the interior of the pilot's cabin, working from the top down, paying special attention to the light and overhead instrument panels where an eavesdropping bug or tracking device was most likely to be located. "I gave them a little something extra to fix that problem."

Leia scanned the seats and instrument panels next, then dropped to the floor and checked even the rudder pedals beneath Jaina's feet. By the time she had finished, a maelstrom of traffic had appeared at the end of their skylane, with speeder vehicles of every type zipping past in a blur of dark streaks and glowing ribbons.

"Big Snarl coming up," Jaina reported. Big Snarl was one of the countless ventilation chimneys that helped draw hot, humid air up out of Coruscant's lower levels; its role as a traffic interchange was only a secondary function. "And it looks really charged."

Fully aware of the dangers of entering a traffic vortex unsecured, Leia returned to her seat and began to strap in, and it occurred to Jaina how strange it felt to be an infiltrator *here*. Coruscant was the planet that always came to mind when she imagined a safe place to rest, the home that she was always fighting to defend. The steady drone of traffic that echoed through its duracrete canyons was as familiar to her as her own voice, and its endless panorama of skyscrapers would always make her feel like she was gazing out the viewport in her parents' living room.

Now her own brother had made it hostile territory.

They reached the end of the skylane, and Jaina swung the medwagon into a steep bank as she followed a Soro-

Suub Touristar sightseeing van into the vortex. Through the viewing bubble, she glimpsed arms, tentacles, and prehensile tails flying up in alarm as the van entered the unpredictable air currents. Then her seat slammed up beneath her, and she found herself struggling to retain control as the medwagon slipped, rolled, and pitched around the vast ventilation chimney that was the Big Snarl.

"There's Ben!" Leia pointed about a quarter of the way around the vortex, at a steep downward angle. "Looks like they're heading for the Pipe."

"The GeeCee?" The Galactic City SpeedPipe was a private speeder tunnel that shot under Galactic City diagonally, cutting an hour-long trip to fifteen minutes . . . for a price. To keep traffic light, the one-way toll was a hundred credits. "Any escorts?"

"There are a couple of troopsleds ahead, but they're still high—probably taking the skylanes back." Leia paused for a moment, then said, "They're making this easy on us. You couldn't ask for a better place to take down an unescorted Doomsled than the SpeedPipe."

"Yeah, *too* easy." Jaina began to work the medwagon over to the descent lanes on the interior ring of the vortex. "And, like Fett says, when something's too easy, something—"

"—stinks," Leia finished. "He stole that line from your father, you know."

Jaina smiled. "I think there are a lot of things Fett learned from Dad," she said. "That's probably why he carries a grudge."

"That, and the Sarlacc's pit," Leia said. "But Fett had the pit coming."

"No argument here." Jaina thought of Fett's wife, Sintas, and all those years alone because Fett had needed his revenge more than he needed her, of Ailyn growing up hating her father, of Fett spending the rest of his life alone—

three lives wasted because of his pride. *And he probably deserves a couple more decades, too.*

Finally, they reached the inner rings of the vortex. Jaina lowered their nose and began to spiral toward the Speed-Pipe along with the rest of the traffic. Her mother pulled and armed her blaster, then pressed her forehead to the viewport on her side of the wagon and peered down the chimney.

"What's the holdup?" Leia demanded. "Worried you'll lose your speeder license again?"

"Lose my *what*?" Jaina asked. She got the joke an instant later and chuckled, though she also understood what her mother was really saying: *Stop poking around in traffic and catch that Doomsled* now. "We'd be tipping our hand."

"Jaina, we don't *have* a hand," Leia said. "The Speed-Pipe's a trao*aaa*—!"

The sentence ended in a startled cry as Jaina rolled them toward Leia and let the medwagon slide sideways into the center of the chimney, where traffic laws and heavy updrafts kept the eye of the Snarl free of vehicles. The yoke started to jump and shudder as they were caught by the fierce winds, then a steady stream of trash—rumpled flimsiplast, discarded clothing, the occasional hawk-bat—came at them like ground flak. Jaina dropped their nose again and poured on the throttle, and the whole vehicle began to lurch as it powered its way downward.

A couple of jaw-clenching moments later, Jaina spotted the Doomsled four levels below, still at least half a kilometer above the brightly lit entrance to the SpeedPipe. She picked a cutoff angle and swung their nose around—then heard a faint, muffled voice coming from the rear patient compartment.

"Activate, activate, activate!"

Jaina glanced over to find her mother looking at *her* with a puzzled expression.

"Was that . . . *Tahiri*?" Jaina asked.

"You heard it, too." Leia frowned and started to turn toward the access panel—then her eyes flashed with sudden comprehension. "The Rodians!"

Leia released her safety webbing and jumped up, using the Force to keep her balance in the diving, bucking medwagon as she clambered up into the patient compartment. Jaina started to ask what was so worrying about the Rodians when she remembered that her mother had been forced to give them another shot of anesthesia . . . because whatever the MDs had given them was wearing off. Perhaps the original dose had been meant to last only a few minutes—just long enough to trick a pair of Jedi hijackers into believing their "patients" were not a threat?

A soft hiss began to sound beneath the instrument panel, and Jaina knew she had guessed correctly. "Gas!"

Jaina did not inhale after shouting the warning, did not even *think* about trying to pull down a quick breath before the gas filled the compartment. She simply pressed her tongue up against the roof of her mouth and concentrated on not *wanting* to breathe, on using her Jedi discipline to convince her mind that she did not *need* air.

A few hundred meters below, not far from a disk of bright light surrounded by the blue spiral-arrow logo of the Galactic City SpeedPipe Concern, a hangar door opened. Jaina reached out to her mother in the Force, passing along a silent warning, and was relieved to feel a conscious presence.

A line of armored aircars slid out of the hangar, causing a chain of minor accidents as they shot across seventy lanes of traffic and began to ascend the center of the chimney. The aircars were all GAG black, with a trio of thrust nozzles flaring from their tails and a single cannon protruding from a small turret on their roofs.

Funny how even a human Jedi could hold her breath for four or five minutes underwater without much effort . . .

but try to do the same thing in air, and her body began to fight her after less than a minute, to demand what it could feel available just a skin's thickness away.

Jaina craned her neck around, looking over her shoulder through the medwagon's upper canopy, and saw troopsleds dropping into the eye of the Snarl from all directions. Trapped. No place to go, so she kept going down.

Her head began to swim, but not from oxygen deprivation. Too early for that. Probably coma gas—sneaky stuff. Didn't even have to breathe, just let it get into your nose. Absorbed through the nasal passages.

Vision dark around the edges. Jaina snapped the lightsaber off her belt, jammed the emitter against the side hatch. Thumbed the activation button on and off. Acrid smell of melted metal, then a piercing whistle. Rushing air.

Didn't help. Darkness still closing in, losing battle to hold breath. Doomsled the only thing Jaina can see, turning toward a bright blur. SpeedPipe entrance.

Chin dropping . . . going . . . going . . . Reach out in Force. Mom still alert, worried not frightened . . . gone.

Darkness.

Came back to the shrill whistle of rushing air, bright flashes blossoming all around. Dizzy, but grogginess lifting fast. Cool breath filling her lungs, something warm and synthetic-smelling clamped over her mouth and nose.

Detonations booming through the medwagon, bouncing Jaina against her safety restraints . . . not just detonations. G forces. Two hands in front of her, not hers, jerking the steering yoke side-to-side, up and down.

The hands were attached to a pair of arms attached to an unfamiliar woman in a tan Jedi robe. The lower part of her face was hidden by a breath mask, but above that she had the long barbed ears and upward-slanting eyebrows of a Codru-Ji female; still, there was something wrong with the eyes themselves. They were too big and round, and they

were a rich deep brown that Jaina recognized as the color
of her mother's.

And then Jaina recalled that her mother had been disguised as a Codru-Ji in Monument Plaza. The whole mess
came back to her, Ben's capture and their pursuit into the
Big Snarl, trying to catch the Doomsled before it disappeared into the . . .

. . . big white disk ahead, surrounded by a spiraling
arrow of blue light. The Galactic City SpeedPipe. Leia was
taking them in after Ben.

Something about that bothered Jaina.

Leia juked when she should have jinked, and a deafening
bang rang out from the patient compartment. The medwagon swung into a sideslip, tail threatening to overtake
the nose, and began to drop toward the busy traffic lanes
below. Jaina glimpsed the bubble-topped wedge of a can-
noncar pouring colored bolts of energy toward them, and
then she remembered the problem with going into the
SpeedPipe after Ben.

Tahiri.

A line of cannon bolts streaked along the pilot's hatch,
pinging and sizzling along the outer skin. The GAG gunners were good—almost good enough to make it look like
they were really trying to shoot the Jedi down. But the
medwagon was a big soft target at such close range, and
Jaina had fired enough blaster cannons to know that even
average gunners could have reduced it to so much fluttering jetsam within a few seconds. Now that there was no
question of catching the Doomsled outside the SpeedPipe,
Tahiri and her GAG cohorts had returned to the original
plan and were trying to trap Ben's backup team in a carefully controlled environment with no escape routes.

Leia brought the medwagon under control barely a
dozen meters above the closest traffic lane, then raised the
nose back toward the luminous white mouth of the Speed-
Pipe.

"Mom, wait!" Jaina grabbed the yoke, but did not try to change course while her mother was still steering. "We can't go in there!"

Leia did not yield control. *"Wad?"* Her voice was so muffled by the breath mask that it was difficult to understand even that single word. "We hab to! Ben's in there!"

"Along with a few hundred GAG troops, I'll bet." Jaina gently began to pull on the yoke, and her mother reluctantly yielded control. "It's a trap, remember?"

"So?" Leia replied. "We still have to try."

"We *can't*." Jaina began to juke and jink like she was in an X-wing, still continuing more or less in the direction of the SpeedPipe but keeping her eye on the traffic lanes below, looking for a small gap coming their way. "Tahiri *planned* this. She had this medwagon rigged and *waiting*."

Leia glared into the SpeedPipe with a furrowed brow. "You think she knew Ben was coming?"

"I think she's known for a while that Shevu has been spying for Ben," Jaina said. "And I think she's been sitting on Shevu, just waiting to pick up Ben *and* his backup team."

Leia sank into her chair but kept staring into the rapidly swelling brilliance of the SpeedPipe. *"How?"* she asked. "No one knew about Shevu but a handful of Masters. Who would betray us?"

Jaina continued to watch the traffic lanes below. "Good question." She thought back to the windswept turf near Fenn Shysa's memorial on Mandalore, recalling a conversation with Fett—a conversation in which she had unwisely shared the recording Shevu had made of Jacen's confession to killing Mara. Fett never broke his word, and he had said that he knew how to keep a secret. But *knowing* how to keep a secret was not exactly *promising* to do it. "We'll figure that out when we get back to base."

Leia looked over, tears welling in her upslanted eyes. "So you're just going to leave Ben here?"

"We can't get him back, Mom." Jaina spotted the traffic gap she had been looking for and began to line the medwagon up on an interception vector. "Not now. It's time to cut our losses and move on."

That was something else Jaina had learned from Fett—not to buck impossible odds—and she hated him for it. It was not, after all, the Solo way.

The traffic gap started to disappear under the medwagon's front passenger's-side corner. Jaina dropped their nose and cut power to the repulsorlifts, and they shot through the opening like a falling star.

The cannon fire died away almost instantly, and a curving ribbon of lights appeared ahead and began to swell rapidly as the medwagon dropped toward the next traffic level. Jaina returned power to the repulsorlifts and dropped into a lane, becoming just one of an endless stream of vehicles descending into the shadows of Coruscant's undercity.

If Leia noticed that they had escaped their pursuers, she did not show it. She simply slumped in her seat and stared out into the growing gloom.

"I don't think I can do it," she said, shaking her head. "How can I tell Luke that we lost his son?"

chapter five

How long does Uncle Luke need to sleep? One Jedi night!
—Jacen Solo, age 14

Jaina and her parents did not make it back to the secret Jedi base on Shedu Maad. The *Sweet Time* had barely entered Hapan space before the Mist Patrol intercepted them with rendezvous instructions. Now here they were, in the launch hangar of a Hapan Battle Dragon, just one short hyperspace jump away from their target.

With some very sad news.

After a moment of looking, Jaina spotted Luke at the far end of the StealthX line, a tiny black-robed form standing with R2-D2 at the brink of the launching deck. He was still as a statue, hands clasped behind his back, head tilted slightly forward as he stared out through the containment field into the fire-flecked velvet of deep space.

"There he is." Jaina pointed and started forward, circling behind a long line of Wookiee-piloted Owool fighters to avoid disrupting operations on the ready deck. "I'm really not looking forward to this."

"Then why'd you find him?" her father asked, coming alongside her. "I'd have been okay with putting this off for a while . . . like, until we figured a way to fix it."

"We can't fix *this,* Han," Leia said. She came up on his far side and took his hand, leaving C-3PO to clump along behind. "No one can."

"And it's not like we're telling him something he hasn't already sensed through the Force," Jaina said. "But he needs to know how it happened—and not just because it's Ben."

"Yeah, I know." Han sighed. He glanced over at the bustling preparations on the ready deck. "He needs to know that someone close to him is a traitor."

They passed behind the last of the Owools and started past a squadron of Skipray 24r Blastboats. A modernized version of the venerable Series 12, the Series 24 was slightly larger and deadlier than its predecessor. And the r-model was especially lethal—a pure ship-killer. Designed as a hit-and-run fleet raider, it was equipped with an advanced targeting computer, the latest jamming package, double-sized ammunition bays, and two overpowered sublight drives.

As they passed behind the squadron, Jaina was surprised to notice that most of the pilots and crews were, well, too *plain* to be Hapans. And many were still wearing military flight suits bearing the unit patches from various branches of the GA military.

As Jaina and her parents walked past, several crewmen interrupted their preflight checklists to turn and gape. Well accustomed to being gawked at in public, none of the Solos was offended. But Jaina did notice that instead of flashing the warm smile that had made her the darling of billions, her mother pretended not to notice the stares. Her father responded with his usual lopsided grin, but somehow it looked more sheepish than cocky.

Suddenly, Jaina understood how much guilt her parents felt over what their son had become . . . over what he was doing to the galaxy. On the trip back from Coruscant, she had overheard them talking about their sense of failure, asking each other in a dozen ways how they could have missed what was happening with Jacen, whether they had let slip some moment when they could have steered him back into the light. She had dismissed their conversation as the natural emotions any parent would feel when a child turned bad. But now she realized it was more than regret they had been discussing—it was *responsibility*. They were serving as her support team not only because they loved *her*, but because they felt it was their duty to stop her brother before he destroyed the galaxy.

Jaina didn't know why that surprised her. They had started risking their lives to save the galaxy long before she was born—and for reasons a lot less personal.

They finally passed the last of the Skiprays and left the commotion of the ready deck behind. As they started across the relatively narrow expanse of the launching deck, Jaina began to take calming breaths, struggling to keep her mind clear and her chest from clenching up. It had been her call to leave Ben in GAG's custody, and it had been the right decision. She knew that. But being right wasn't going to make it any easier to look Luke in the eye and report that *she* had been the one who insisted his son be abandoned.

They were still five paces away when R2-D2 spun his dome around to tweedle a greeting.

Then Luke spoke without turning to face them. "It wasn't your fault." There was no disappointment or displeasure in his voice, only concern. "I knew Ben would be captured. I knew it before I sent you."

All three of the Solos stopped cold, forcing C-3PO to step around them before he continued forward. "I beg your pardon, Master Luke," he said. "I must have misunderstood you. Did you just say that you *expected* Ben to be captured?"

"Not expected." Luke turned, revealing a face so ashen and haggard that Jaina almost gasped out loud. His eyes were a pair of black holes, seeming to swallow every ray of light that came near, and the wrinkles around his mouth were so deep and long that he looked like a Bith. "*Knew.* I saw it in the future."

"*Before* you sent us?" Leia demanded. Her shock had given way to anger, and Jaina had the feeling that her mother was strongly considering Force-blasting Luke off the edge of the launching deck. "And you didn't warn us?"

"I couldn't," Luke said. "It would have changed the outcome."

"That's the point," Han said, stepping so close that Jaina reached out to grab his arm. He jerked free, then jabbed a finger toward Luke's chest. "I don't know what kind of spacesick got hold of you, but that's my *nephew* you set up."

"I know, Han," Luke said, and Jaina could feel his heart breaking. "He's also a Jedi Knight, and it had to be done. I'm sorry I couldn't tell you, but that would have changed how you reacted."

Leia's boiling temper ebbed to a simmer. "I hope you can explain *now*," she said. "And it had better be good, because I'm beginning to worry that my son isn't the only one in this family who's gone to the dark side."

Luke's face twitched as though he had been slapped. But he nodded as though he had been expecting this reaction, and suddenly Jaina realized why her uncle hadn't warned them about what he had foreseen.

"You did it to protect me," she said, stepping forward. "You didn't tell us because it would have betrayed something to Jacen."

"That's right," Luke said. "He would have realized that I'm using visions of the future to plot strategy, and he would have started to grow suspicious of what *he* was seeing."

Leia's brow shot up. "You're altering Caedus's visions?"

"It's . . . more like jamming," Luke said. "When I meditate on the future, I'm focusing so hard on Caedus that when *he* looks into the future, I keep showing up."

"Sounds like altering to me," Han said. "If you were just jamming, Caedus would know it. But you're fixing it so he sees you instead of the real future."

"Not exactly," Luke said. "Remember, the future is always in motion. Caedus sees what *might* happen—if I were there instead of Jaina."

Han frowned and ran a hand over his brow. "My head hurts."

"It's not that hard to understand," Jaina said. She turned to Luke. "You're influencing what Caedus sees by focusing on him in your meditations—"

"Then forcing the future to move along a different course by not acting in accordance with your visions," Leia finished.

"To an extent," Luke said. "But it's a balancing act. I try to stay close enough to what I've seen to prevent Caedus from realizing that I'm trying to mask something."

"That something being *me*," Jaina said.

"Right," Luke answered. "I stay as close as I can to the future we're seeing without actually fighting Caedus—at least, not physically."

"I must say, that seems quite wise," C-3PO said. "The last time you two fought, you were forced to spend your nights in the bacta tank for an entire week."

"I don't think that's why Luke let Ben be captured, Threepio." Leia looked into the dark holes beneath Luke's brow, then demanded, "What are you seeing? What scares you *that* much?"

Luke looked away, studying the ready deck as though the answer were down there somewhere. "I'm not sure," he said. "There's a shadow in the future. And the farther I look, the darker it grows."

"*Caedus.*" Han spoke the name as though it were a curse. "No mystery there."

"He's part of it," Luke said, "the seed—though exactly how remains hidden to me."

"But the darkness doesn't go away when you kill Caedus," Jaina surmised.

Luke nodded and looked away. "That's right."

"You *lose?*" Han asked, incredulous. "Tell me you're kidding."

Luke swallowed and forced himself to meet Han's eyes, and Jaina could feel something like . . . *shame* in the Force.

"It's worse," Luke said. "I *win.*"

As usual, it was Jaina's mother who understood first. "Oh," she said simply. Her hand went to her mouth, then she reached for his arm. "Luke, I'm sorry. What I said earlier, about going to the dark side, I didn't mean . . ."

"I know." Luke smiled and patted her hand, but there was too much darkness in his eyes to tell whether the smile was genuine. "But it's true. If I had any doubts about it before, my visions have only confirmed what Saba suggested on Shedu Maad—I *have* been tainted by killing Lumiya in vengeance. I can't go after Caedus without becoming the same as Caedus."

"Which is where I come in," Jaina said. It gave her no satisfaction. In fact, she was beginning to feel like a holopiece in a dejarik match between her uncle and her brother—one that would determine not only *their* destiny, but that of trillions. And she wasn't even a player in the game, just a monnok being moved through dimensions she did not comprehend. "Does that mean you can see whether—"

"I *can't,*" Luke interrupted. "I'm trying to keep you hidden from Caedus's visions, which means I can't see you, either."

"Good—I really don't want to know anyway," Jaina

said, noting that Luke had misunderstood her question—and misread the immediate future. She only hoped her brother would show the same weakness when she attacked him. "I was asking about Ben."

Luke looked a bit embarrassed, then shook his head. "That's not clear yet. I've seen many possibilities."

They were silent for a moment. Then Leia asked, "What can we do to swing those possibilities in Ben's favor?"

"Nothing." Jaina kept her gaze fixed on Luke as she spoke, both awed and frightened by the resolve that gave him the courage to risk his only son like this. In his own way, he was as calculating and ruthless as Fett—but guided by the strength of his inner convictions. It made him so much more . . . *dangerous*. "We can't influence the future without giving away what Uncle Luke is doing—and that would give away *me*."

"That's right," Luke said. "The best thing you can do for Ben is complete your mission. Get Caedus—soon."

Han and Leia exchanged glances, then Han said, "That's our plan." He glanced back at the preparations on the ready deck, then added, "Just so I'm clear on this—there is no spy on the Council. Caedus saw Ben in a vision—one you saw, too—and *that's* how Tahiri knew Ben would be on Coruscant?"

Luke nodded. "In Monument Plaza, by the *Devoted Technician*," he said. "If I saw Ben there, then so could Caedus. The only thing I don't understand is why Caedus wasn't there himself."

Jaina saw her parents shoot concerned glances toward each other. Her mother said, "Probably because he's on Nickel One."

Luke's eyes flashed with sudden comprehension . . . and alarm. "Caedus is in the Roche system?" he asked. "You're *sure*?"

"It's what Shevu told Ben," Leia said. "But if Caedus

knew Ben was coming, maybe he's been feeding Shevu phony intel."

"No." Luke's gaze began to turn inward. "It explains too much."

"Yeah?" Han asked. "Like what?"

"For one thing, the reason the Fourth Fleet is guarding every munitions convoy we target." Luke turned back toward the hangar mouth, staring across space toward the Roche system. "Caedus is *there*. That's why they always know which convoy we're going to hit."

Leia glanced back toward the massive preparations on the ready deck. "Which means he's probably foreseen *this* raid, too," she said. "He already knows you're coming to Nickel One."

"Probably," Luke said.

"So you're going to call it off, right?" Han asked. "You can't go in there with him just waiting for you."

"If we don't, he'll figure out what I've been doing to him," Luke said. "And then he'll see who's *really* coming for him."

Jaina began to feel raw and guilty inside. She was going to need every possible advantage to take down her brother, but sacrificing all of those lives just to mask her identity did not feel right. The truth was, it felt terribly wrong.

"Uncle Luke, there has to be some way to avoid this."

"There *isn't*." Luke pivoted around and glared down on her with eyes that suddenly looked like a pair of suns blazing up from a dark well. "And it's not your responsibility to worry about those lives. It's mine—*mine*, Jedi Solo. Is that clear?"

"Yes, Master," Jaina said. His voice was so hard and cold that she had to will herself not to cringe away from it, and she realized she was going to have to take a different tack if she hoped to talk him out of sending these pilots on a suicide run. "I just meant maybe there's some way to modify that plan. And anything I can do to help—"

"There is, Jedi Solo." Luke's voice was softer now, with just enough humor in it to suggest that he realized Jaina had not given up. "You can go get yourself fitted for a dropsuit."

"A *dropsuit*?" Han asked. "If you're thinking of shooting my daughter out a torpedo tube—"

"Dad—"

"—in the middle of a battle—"

"*Dad*." Jaina grabbed her father's arm—and was instantly shaken off.

"—you're crazy!" Han finished.

Jaina waited an instant to be sure her father was done ranting, her thoughts flying a kilometer a second as she began to see what her uncle was planning. "Dad, it just might work."

Han scowled at her. "You're crazy, too."

"I'm a Solo," Jaina said, shrugging. "But I *was* just on an inspection tour of Nickel One's defenses with Boba Fett. I know the layout pretty well."

Her father's scowl only deepened. "That won't do you any good if you get blasted to atoms on the way down."

"Han." Leia took his arm—and did not release it when he tried to pull free. "What are you *really* worried about?"

The fire drained from his eyes in an instant, and Jaina knew what he was *not* going to say: that now that they were talking about a solid plan—about *really* sending her after her brother—he was scared to death he was going to lose her . . . as he had lost Anakin and Jacen.

"I just think we need a better plan," Han said.

"Han Solo, demanding a better plan?" Leia rolled her eyes. "Look around. Who do you think you're fooling?"

R2-D2 gave a short whistle, though Jaina couldn't tell whether he was trying to support her mother or father.

"No one," Han admitted. "I just don't like throwing Jaina into an operation at the last minute."

"Han, that's the best way," Luke said. He gave Han's shoulder a reassuring squeeze. "It's the only way to make sure Caedus doesn't see her coming."

Han sighed, then glanced over at Jaina. "You really think you can get to him down there?"

Jaina nodded. "I inspected Nickel One's defenses less than a week ago," she said. "How many times are we going to be this lucky?"

Han closed his eyes for a moment, then finally nodded. "Okay, let's do it."

"Good." Luke looked over his shoulder, out into space, and a glint of comprehension came to his face, as though he finally understood something that had been puzzling him for some time. He remained silent for a moment, then activated his comlink. "Master Horn, please have the Owools stand down."

"The Owools?" came Corran's confused reply. "*Just* the Owools?"

"That's correct," Luke replied. "All other elements of the mission will launch as planned."

There was a long, doubtful pause, and even Jaina found herself wondering if her uncle knew what he was doing. Space raids looked simple at first glance—pop out of hyperspace, blow something up, then escape back into hyperspace. But the truth was that they were one of the trickiest missions a small force could undertake. They relied on several different kinds of combat craft working together in a carefully choreographed dance of dazzle and destruction, and no one element could be removed without placing the others at terrible risk.

Finally, Corran said, "I don't understand, Master Skywalker. What are the blastboats going to do about a fighter escort?"

Luke turned back toward the mouth of the hangar, once more focusing his attention on the black depths of space.

"That won't be a problem, Master Horn," he said. "Our escorts will be waiting for us at Nickel One."

chapter six

*Do you know why the bantha crossed the Dune Sea? To get to the
other side!*

—Jacen Solo, age 14

A wall of turbolaser strikes erupted ahead, momentarily
concealing the gray nugget of Nickel One behind a curtain
of boiling color. Jaina's heart raced, as it always did when
she was forced to sit idle during the opening stages of a battle, but she calmed herself by remembering that her uncle's
attack plan was as good as it was simple. The blastboats
would strike at the Remnant Star Destroyer *Harbinger*.
When the enemy sent its starfighters to engage them, the
Jedi StealthXs would slip in and destroy the loading docks.
During the confusion, Jaina would drop onto the asteroid,
sneak inside, and hunt down her brother.

Simple. Uncomplicated. Straightforward.

Except for the fact that unescorted runs at Star Destroyers were suicide missions. And the blastboats certainly
wouldn't be receiving any help from Verpine Stingers. The
Remnant's aerosol weapon had wiped out the Verpine soldier caste across the entire asteroid belt. Jaina didn't understand why her uncle had insisted on leaving the Owools
behind—or why he had been so mysterious about his reasons. She felt sure it involved the strange duel of Force visions he was waging with her brother. Obviously, there
were things he couldn't reveal without messing up his plan,
but it would have been nice if he'd just said that.

The blastboat began to shudder rhythmically as Jaina's mother and Saba Sebatyne opened up with the laser cannons. Luke's hands flew over the defense systems console, adjusting shields and deploying countermeasures. R2-D2 was plugged into the comm system behind him, monitoring squadron communications and coordinating with other astromechs to avoid duplicating attacks. C-3PO sat in the co-pilot's seat, struggling to filter the blast static out of the sensors. Han Solo, of course, was in the pilot's seat, doing what he did best: dodging Imperial turbolaser fire.

Only Jaina, kneeling on the deck at the back of the blast-boat's cramped passenger cabin, was not involved. Trapped in a bulky dropsuit that was as much a weapons system as it was protection against the cold vacuum of space, she could do nothing but wait . . . and remember the time she and Jacen had been tricked into fighting each other as young teenagers. Their captors at the Shadow Academy had cloaked them both in holographic images and pitted them against each other with live lightsabers, but they had both sensed a trap and held back just enough to avoid landing any dangerous blows.

Still, it was risky to recall such moments. As much as her brother might regret having to fight her now—might even wish there was a way to avoid it—he would not hold back this time. He would not even hesitate. He would simply try to kill her in the fastest, safest way possible, and if Jaina so much as thought twice before doing the same, that second thought would be the last one she ever had.

Tiny blue tongues of ion efflux began to pour out from the thin shell of Remnant capital ships surrounding the asteroid. Even with its fleets spread across the entire asteroid belt—and the GA's Fourth Fleet escorting its munitions convoys—the Remnant was being careful to keep Nickel One well defended.

"Stay awake back there!" her father called. The blast-boat jumped and shuddered even more as he began to dodge through the thickest part of the turbolaser barrage. "We've got Starhunters coming."

A cluck of reptilian delight sounded through the floor grate covering the belly turret. The Remnant Starhunter was the modern version of the classic TIE interceptor, with shields and heavy armament that made it far more dangerous than its predecessor. To a Barabel, of course, that only meant it was more fun to kill.

C-3PO did not share Saba's enthusiasm. "It's hardly something to celebrate, Master Sebatyne," the droid said. "Our escorts haven't arrived yet. May I suggest we postpone our attack run?"

R2-D2 emitted a derogatory whistle.

"I will not be quiet," C-3PO replied. "I'm the sensor officer. It's my duty to report malfunctions in the plan."

"Thank you, Threepio, but the plan hasn't malfunctioned," Luke said. "Our escorts are here. They've been waiting for quite some time."

Jaina lifted her brow at this news, but did not dare expand her Force awareness to see if he was right. She was concentrating on keeping her presence hidden, and the technique—the same one Caedus had taught Ben, and which Ben had then taught to her and his father—was too new to her to risk splitting her concentration.

After turning knobs and adjusting glide switches for a moment, C-3PO announced, "I'm sorry, Master Skywalker, but you appear to be mistaken. The only starfighters our sensors show belong to the enemy."

"Do the sensors show our StealthXs?" Luke asked.

"Of course not," C-3PO replied. "But I hardly see how the StealthXs can be *our* escorts when we're supposed to be *their* diversion."

"As much as I hate to admit it," Han said, "laserbrain's got a point."

Luke smiled and turned toward the cockpit, but before he could say the *trust me* that Jaina had sensed coming,

R2-D2 tweedled for attention and flashed a message across the pilot's display.

"*Who?*" Han exclaimed. He slammed the yoke hard to port, sending the blastboat into a barrel roll, and the hull rang as it was slammed by the shock wave of a nearby turbolaser strike. "Are you kidding?"

R2-D2 trilled an impatient reply.

"All right—just asking," Han said defensively. "Put him on the speaker."

A moment later, the familiar voice of Boba Fett filled the blastboat cabin. "Are you barvy? What happened to your escort?"

Han glanced at Luke in the canopy reflection and raised a questioning brow. When he received nothing but a blank expression in return, he scowled and said to Fett, "We, uh, thought you guys might want to volunteer, I guess."

Now it was Fett's turn to be surprised. "*Solo?* Last I heard, you were on Coruscant with—"

"You hear a lot of things you shouldn't, Fett," Luke interrupted. "Very soon, I'm going to be interested in learning how that happens."

"I could say the same," Fett replied. "But I already found those bugs Jaina left at Beviin's farm."

"If you found them, they weren't Jaina's," Luke replied smoothly. "In the meantime, we're kind of busy here, and I'd rather you didn't get in the way."

Jaina was surprised that the conversation was still being held over a hailing channel, which meant that Remnant eavesdroppers would be listening to every word—and matching voiceprints to records in their intelligence files.

After a moment of silence, Fett said, "So that's the way it is. Either we cover your run, or we watch those Starhunters blast your Skippers apart before they even get close to the target."

The smirk that crept across Luke's mouth was more sad

than satisfied. "There are no free rides, *Mand'alor.* You know that."

Luke paused there, leaving unspoken a threat that only he and Fett seemed to comprehend, and Jaina slowly began to realize why her uncle was holding this conversation on an unscrambled channel. He *wanted* her brother to know who was up here—to know that Luke Skywalker and Boba Fett were teaming up to come after him.

"We're in," Fett finally said. "Tell your gunners not to shoot anything dark, fast, and pretty."

"What are you worried about?" Han asked. "The way I hear it, those new Bessies of yours fly through novas."

"*Han!*" Leia had to shout to make herself heard above the chuffing of her laser cannons. "Be nice to the Mandalore. We need his toys."

"Sorry," Han said, apologizing more to Leia than Fett. "No worries, Fett. Our gunners don't have any practice shooting down *pretty* fighters."

"Funny," Fett said. "I'll laugh when I get a minute."

A loud siss rose through the floor grate that covered the belly turret. "This one did not know Mandalorianz possessed humor," Saba said. "This one is looking forward to hunting with them!"

"Don't get used to it, Jedi," Fett said. "It's a onetime deal."

R2-D2 opened an encrypted channel to Fett's fighter and set up a tactical comm net that would allow the Mandalorians and blastboats to coordinate with each other. Dozens of charcoal-gray wedges began to slide into position around the squadron, tipping the odds a bit back toward the raiders. Within a few moments, they were all dodging through the barrage together, not quite flying like a well-trained squadron but at least avoiding collisions and bouncing no more than the occasional cannon bolt off one another's shields.

Once their own blastboat had settled into a comfortable

rhythm with its *Bes'uliik* escorts, Jaina said, "You guys aren't doing this."

No one was rude enough to pretend they didn't know what she was talking about. Her father simply glanced at her reflection in the canopy and said, "Kind of late to change your mind, sweetie."

"I'm *not* changing my mind." Jaina pulled at the front collar of her dropsuit, holding it away from her neck in the hope of getting a little extra ventilation. "I just didn't sign on to make a decoy of my whole family."

"So what *did* you think Luke meant by *hold Caedus's attention*?" Her mother paused to fire another burst. "Beam down the latest episode of *BattleSun Odyssey*?"

"I didn't think he meant paint a target on your blastboat." Jaina directed the rest of her objection directly to Luke. "You *know* Caedus is waiting for you."

"Better us than you," her father said, giving Luke no chance to answer. "What's wrong, kid? You think we're too old for this?"

The blastboat dropped into a long wild spiral, and suddenly the forward canopy was streaked with cannon bolts and missile trails, all fanning outward from the tiny white wedge of the Imperial II Star Destroyer *Harbinger*.

"Now you have dragged us all into the dungpit!" Saba yelled up. "Never call your father old."

"I didn't," Jaina protested. Behind the *Harbinger*, she began to make out the lumpy black shadow of Nickel One's dark side. "And you don't have to be old to be crazy."

"What's wrong with crazy?" her father protested. "Crazy has gotten me out of—"

"Jaina, you're not the only one who's afraid for her family," Luke said, using the Force to speak over her father. "But you *are* the only one who's allowing her attachments to interfere with her judgment."

The lights flickered as Starhunter cannon bolts began to

test the blastboat's shields. Leia cursed and Saba sissed, then both turrets began to whine and chuff as the pair returned fire. Jaina was left feeling a little foolish and a little self-centered. Until that moment, she had been thinking only of her fear for her parents and uncle. It had not even occurred to her to think of how terrifying this must be for everyone else—or of how hard it must be for Luke to be *here,* while Ben was being held in a GAG prison, how hard it must be for her parents to be ferrying her to an all-too-likely death.

The blastboat lurched as a concussion missile detonated nearby. C-3PO began to quote their odds of survival, then Han cursed and threatened to flip the droid's circuit breaker, and Jaina realized that things were going pretty much as usual.

"Sorry, everyone." Realizing it wouldn't be long before they reached the drop zone, Jaina picked up her helmet—a full-view bubble model—and thumbed open the locking tabs. "Just feeling guilty about taking the easy job, I guess."

An amused siss sounded over the chuffing of Saba's cannons, and her father glanced away from his flying long enough to catch her gaze in the canopy reflection.

"No problem, sweetheart," he said. "And don't worry about us. We'll be fine. Just—"

"*Trust me,*" Jaina said. "I know."

Both of her parents laughed, though their voices were a bit sad and brittle.

"Don't lose your focus down there," her mother called from the upper turret. "You do what you have to, then come back to us safe."

"I will, Mom," Jaina said. "And you do the same."

Her father rolled the blastboat up on its side to let a flurry of cannon bolts go flying past its belly; then the dark wedge of a *Bes'uliik* dropped in to cut off the attack. Jaina saw a flurry of cannon bolts bouncing off its *beskar* hull.

The Mandalorian pilot returned fire an instant later, and his fighter was haloed by the orange glow of an exploding Starhunter.

Jaina lowered her helmet over her head, then Luke left his seat to come back and help her arm the dropsuit's weapons array and check her suit seals.

As he worked, Luke put his head close to hers so his voice would be audible inside the helmet. "You told me you could do this." His voice was muffled, but understandable. "That means more than just facing your brother. It means trusting us to do our jobs."

"I know," Jaina said, thinking of what Luke had put at risk to get her here. "I'm sorry you had to let Ben get captured. I don't know what I was thinking—"

"It's okay." Luke raised a hand to silence her. "Ben is the one who made me promise to treat him like any other Jedi. I think he could sense how vulnerable I am to my attachments."

Jaina thought she could see where this was going. "Master Skywalker, I understand. I really do."

Luke studied her for a moment, then said, "I hope so, because you can't let your emotions control you. Down that path lies defeat, torture, death . . . maybe worse."

"Worse?" It took Jaina a moment to understand what her uncle meant, for she had never considered the possibility that Jacen would attempt to corrupt *her*. "Don't worry. The way things have gone between us, I'm pretty sure I'm the last person Caedus would want to turn."

"*Caedus* won't," Luke warned her. "Be wary of yourself, of your own emotions."

Jaina scowled inside her helmet. "Have you seen something I should know about?"

"You *do* know about it," Luke replied evenly. "And if you react the way you did a minute ago, your emotions will betray you—love as much as hatred. Allow neither to control you."

"I'll keep that in mind," Jaina said. "I promise."

Luke studied her for a moment, then nodded. "Good. I'm counting on it."

He activated the dropsuit's life-support system, then disconnected her from the blastboat's air circulators and opened the hatch at the rear of the passenger's cabin. Jaina retrieved her sniper weapon—a QuietSnipe pellet accelerator with a telescoping barrel—then carefully backed into the little air lock.

Once she was inside, Luke asked, "Want to hear a joke?"

Jaina frowned. "A joke?"

"That's right, Jaina—a joke," Luke said. "Why is a droid mechanic never lonely?"

"Because he's always making new friends," Jaina answered, chuckling despite herself. The joke was terrible, but it had been one of Jacen's favorites back on Yavin 4. "Don't tell me those things keep popping into *your* head, too?"

An enigmatic smile crossed Luke's lips. "It's not wrong to mourn your brother's loss, Jaina—just don't forget who he is now." He pressed his head to her helmet. "May the Force be with you."

Before she could reply in kind, he stepped back and returned to his station. Jaina spent the next two minutes peering up the narrow aisle, watching the battle over her father's shoulder. The *Harbinger* grew from the length of her hand to the length of her arm in the forward canopy, and its shields began to glow with golden circles of dispersal energy. *Bes'uliike* and Starhunters alike flashed past almost too quickly to identify, occasionally bursting into blue fireballs as they were caught by a line of cannon bolts.

Utterly isolated inside the dropsuit—her comm unit was deactivated and her Force awareness dampened to maintain her concealment—Jaina passed the time by meditating on the coming battle . . . and on the fears that still plagued her. Death was a big one, of course, and if it came, Caedus was unlikely to make it easy.

But even that fear paled compared with the concern Jaina felt for her parents, the knowledge of how crushed they would be if she were killed—and how sad it would be for them even if she killed Caedus and managed to survive herself. Where they were finding the strength to deliver her to this asteroid, she did not know. Then again, she had *never* understood where their strength came from, how anyone could endure so much trial and tragedy in one lifetime and always emerge stronger and more in love than before.

After a minute or so, Jaina noticed that fewer Starhunters were flashing past the canopy, and there did not seem to be as many horizontal strands in the web of cannon fire between the blastboat and the *Harbinger*. It was impossible to see exactly what was happening from inside the cramped air lock, but Jaina guessed that the StealthXs had started their run. If everything was going according to plan, the Remnant would be pulling Starhunters away from the blastboat assault in a doomed effort to defend the asteroid's crucial loading facilities.

The *Harbinger* was so large now that it completely filled the forward canopy, and its shields were rippling and sparkling as they struggled to dissipate the energy being poured into them. Her father's hand rose into view and made a fist, signaling Jaina to prepare for the drop. She acknowledged the order by repeating the signal. Then, as she pulled the hatch closed, she touched the glove of her free hand to her faceplate and turned its palm toward him and her mother, throwing them what she hoped would not be her last kiss.

Jaina sealed the inner hatch, then entered the safety override code into the floor hatch's control panel. She felt the blastboat turn so sharply that the inertial compensators could not quite counteract the g forces, and then the status light in the ceiling changed from red to amber.

Jaina positioned herself dead center on the floor hatch

and made sure her QuietSnipe and lightsaber were mag-clamped tight to her suit. Then she tucked her elbows tight against her ribs and tried not to think about what might happen to her—and the blastboat—if the drop did not go perfectly.

The status light never changed to green, at least not that Jaina saw. She just heard a loud pop against her helmet, then her stomach jumped, and the inexorable hand of a pressure imbalance shot her into space. Her helmet's blast-tinting darkened as the brilliant glow of the blastboat's ion engines shot past—then darkened again as two more sets of ion engines followed.

Jaina checked the heads-up display inside her visor—and felt her heart stick in her throat. A pair of blue Starhunter symbols were coming up underneath her parents' blast-boat, and Saba's turret had been turned forward to prevent her from hitting the cannon barrels as she ejected.

Her right arm came up almost of its own accord. Luke's admonitions were still fresh in her mind, but with a free shot like that, the Starhunters could take out her entire family. Jaina fixed her left eye on the lead fighter and blinked twice.

Its symbol turned red, and she said, "Fire one."

Her arm shuddered as a mini missile streaked from the dropsuit's sleeve launcher. The Starhunters opened fire on the blastboat, burning enough bolts into its shields to make its symbol turn yellow. Jaina fixed her eye on the second craft.

Before she could get a lock, the Starhunters detected her missile and stopped firing. They began to jink wildly, but the distances were too small, reaction time nil. The missile entered the target's left engine and detonated.

The explosion did not happen all at once. The engine simply flickered out, then a yellow spark shot from its exhaust nozzle and extended itself into a red tongue of flame. The Starhunter's canopy flew off, but before the pilot could eject, the red tongue turned orange and blossomed into the full-sized fireball of an exploding starfighter.

By then, the surviving Starhunter had passed beyond the range of her mini missiles, and Jaina's only choice was to trust her family to take care of themselves. She hit her thrusters, then started toward the shadowy mass of Nickel One's dark side.

Between flashes of turbolaser fire, Jaina could already see brilliant domes of light rising from the surface of Nickel One: Jedi shadow bombs, reducing Verpine loading docks to slag and pebbles. Near the middle of the asteroid, a triangular cluster of still-glowing craters marked the ruins of the Knob Nose Transfer Facility. It was located less than a kilometer from the primary command bunker—where her brother would almost certainly be. She locked in the Knob Nose coordinates and began to angle toward the glow, trying to ignore both the terrible sadness she felt at the prospect of success—and the sickening fear that she would fail.

That was when a tiny blue halo appeared in the corner of her vision, winking in and out of view as turbolaser bolts flashed past, growing a little larger each time she saw it. She checked her heads-up display and saw a single Starhunter approaching from the direction her parents had gone, moving slow and sweeping its face back and forth to maximize its sensor sensitivity.

Jaina shut down her thrusters and nonessential systems, trying to make herself as difficult to detect as possible. She could think of only one reason a pilot would approach that slowly in the middle of a battle—and it wasn't to search for a fellow pilot's remains. Somebody had ordered him to find the source of the mysterious mini missile that had killed his wingmate.

The blue halo continued to approach, its dark heart assuming the shape of a bent-winged ball. Jaina primed the blaster cannon in the dropsuit's left arm and tried to ignore the guilty hollow in her stomach. She had done exactly what Luke had warned her against, and now she was in danger of being discovered even before she reached the surface of the asteroid.

But what should she have done? The day she could watch a starfighter blast her family back to atoms would be the day Luke needed to send someone to hunt *her* down.

The Starhunter was close enough now to make out its ball-shaped cockpit and solar array panels. The pilot still seemed to be searching, sweeping slowly back and forth, and Jaina began to hope he would pass without spotting her. If she could remain undetected, maybe his superiors would attribute the mysterious missile to the fog of war and focus their attention elsewhere.

Maybe.

The Starhunter turned directly toward Jaina, so close now that she could see the stripes of passing turbolaser bolts reflected in the pilot's black goggles. She remained as motionless as was possible when floating weightless, hoping that he was looking in some other direction—but ready to open fire the instant she saw a cannon tip swivel in her direction.

The Starhunter swiveled away, and Jaina let out a sigh of relief. With a little luck, Caedus would never even hear of the other fighter's unexplained destruction, and she would not have to spend the rest of the mission wondering if he was waiting in ambush for *her.*

Then a turbolaser bolt flashed past only a dozen meters behind Jaina, lighting her silhouette, and the pilot's head snapped around. She used the Force to rip a power cable away from the shield generator on the Starhunter's left wing brace, then opened fire on the right brace and blasted the communications array into a spray of hot shrapnel.

The pilot reacted instantly, opening fire even as he spun his starfighter back toward Jaina. She hit her thrusters, trying to get in between his solar arrays where he would not be able to target her, but was not quite fast enough. A streak of red heat flashed past her shoulder so close that she felt its warmth even inside her dropsuit.

A failure alarm chimed inside Jaina's helmet. In the next instant, she crashed through a solar array wing and found herself tumbling wildly out of control. The Starhunter shot out from under her and started a steep climb, no doubt looping back to attack. Then she was spun around toward the near end of the asteroid, where the *Harbinger* was belching flame and bodies through half a dozen hull breaches and still continuing to pour turbolaser fire after its fleeing attackers.

Jaina checked the damage display inside her faceplate and discovered that the feed line to her right-side maneuvering jets had been cut. She ordered the dropsuit's computer brain to shut down the line, then quickly brought herself more or less under control . . . and saw the Starhunter coming out of its loop directly ahead, just a few degrees from being able to bring its weapons to bear.

Jaina dived under the Starhunter and began a sloppy corkscrew toward the surface of the asteroid. There was no question of outrunning the starfighter—or, with her right-side maneuvering jets disabled, of outflying him. But at least she could give him something else to worry about as he targeted her.

Streaks of cannon fire began to stab past her all too soon, darkening the blast-tinting in her faceplate then bursting into tiny cups of flame as they struck the asteroid five kilometers below. She locked her thrusters on maximum and snapped her lightsaber off its magclamp—then found herself flying blind as a cannon bolt hit something critical on the asteroid and triggered a secondary explosion that sent flames spraying up at least a kilometer above the surface.

Jaina pulled up, swinging her boots around beneath her. The dropsuit's tiny inertial compensator screamed in protest and let the g forces rise high enough to dim her vision. When she could see again, cannon bolts were flashing past all around and the dark ball of the Starhunter's cockpit was swelling in front of her.

She dropped her arm and activated her lightsaber in the same instant, then glimpsed the startled pilot pushing his yoke forward as his starfighter streaked into the glowing blade.

Because the blade was pure energy, there was no true impact. Instead, Jaina saw the tip touch the cockpit, then felt a small shock wave slam into her dropsuit. It sent her tumbling, only a few meters above the Starhunter's tail of superheated ions.

Damage alarms began to chime inside her helmet again. She deactivated the lightsaber and slapped it back into its magclamp, then brought herself under control. By the time she had turned back toward the Starhunter, it was just a distant coil of efflux, spiraling down toward the asteroid.

After a few deep breaths to calm herself, she checked her damage report. Her air scrubbers had been disabled—knocked free of their mountings, most likely. With no way to repair them and only fifteen minutes of good air left, Jaina began her own descent, following the damaged starfighter toward the center of the asteroid.

She felt sure she had destroyed the Starhunter's comm array before the pilot could report seeing her. Whether that would work in her favor, she had no idea. His superiors might decide that both craft had simply been lost to StealthXs, or they might realize that something else had taken the pair out. She could only hope for the best—and be alert for the worst.

As the Starhunter neared the surface of the asteroid—not far from Jaina's primary landing zone near the Knob Nose Transfer Facility—a torrent of flames shot up to engulf it. Had she not seen a similar detonation just a few moments earlier, she might have believed that she was just seeing things wrong, that the starfighter had actually crashed *before* the explosion.

But Jaina knew better. As the Starhunter had neared the surface, the blast had erupted *beneath* it—and that could only mean one thing: cluster mines.

Now with just twelve minutes' air left, Jaina did not have much time to reach her secondary landing zone—but she turned toward the far end of the asteroid anyway. Cluster mines and dropsuits did not mix, and that made her wonder whether it had been the Moffs or her brother who had foreseen the wisdom of trapping the area around the command center.

Jaina had just started to debate the answer when the arrow-shaped silhouette of a blastboat came streaking down from space, dodging wildly and laying cannon fire with an accuracy that betrayed its two Jedi gunners. It was being escorted by a whole wing of dark, pretty wedges—Fett's *Bes'uliike*—and a pair of flying boxes that could only be Mandalorian *Tra'kads*.

A cold knot of fear formed inside Jaina's chest. She didn't need the Force to know that Luke, Saba, and her parents were in the blastboat, preparing to grab Caedus's attention by attacking the command bunker directly. Her first instinct was to warn them off—but her brother would be inside the bunker, as alert to any alarm she sent through the Force as Remnant eavesdroppers would be to a comm transmission. To caution them was to betray her presence—and her mission.

The blastboat passed overhead, waggling its wings just enough to make Jaina wonder if her father had seen her. She didn't want to watch, but she couldn't turn away. This had to be the moment her uncle had warned her about, the moment when she resisted her emotions and trusted her parents as they were trusting her.

The blastboat continued toward the command bunker, weaving and dodging as the surface gunners concentrated their fire. The *Bes'uliike* came close on its tail, loosing missiles and pouring cannon fire into enemy weapons emplacements. The two *Tra'kads* stayed high but close, using the *Bes'uliike* like shields. Jaina was puzzled by their presence, until she recalled a comment Fett had made about them being good insertion craft for commandos. Clearly, the Mandalorians intended to honor their mutual-aid treaty with the Verpine.

When cluster mines did not start detonating, Jaina began to hope she had been wrong about what she had seen—or that her uncle had disabled them with some Force technique she had not even realized he possessed.

Then the first spray of flame and shrapnel erupted beneath a *Bes'uliik,* not so much tearing through its *beskar* hull as simply splitting it open, and the annihilation began. Jaina watched in horror as detonation after detonation shot up, sometimes engulfing the starfighters so completely that they just ceased to exist, sometimes hurling them away in spinning whorls of fire.

Her parents' blastboat continued toward its target, picking its way as though her father knew where every mine was hidden, dodging away just before a neighboring *Bes'uliik* triggered a detonation.

As it passed deeper into the conflagration, Jaina began to wonder how much of this her uncle had foreseen—whether he had known about the minefield all along, or had just sensed that something terrible might happen to the escort squadron. It didn't matter. Either answer explained why he had ordered the Owools to stay behind, and either answer made conning the Mandalorians into taking their place an act of ruthless manipulation. When it came to cold calculation, Fett was so far out of his league that Jaina almost felt sorry for him.

Almost.

The detonations began to come so fast and furious that it looked like Mustafar had cracked open. One of the

Tra'kads got caught in a column of flame and vanished in a white flash. The other banked away and started in Jaina's direction, dropping toward the asteroid surface and trailing smoke, flame, and bodies. Trying not to wonder how many of the friends she had made during her time on Mandalore had just died—and hoping Mirta Gev was not among them—she continued to watch until the minefield finally began to expend itself and she could see her parents' blastboat circling around for an attack run.

Now that the inferno was dying down, they were diving straight at the command bunker, pounding it with cannon fire and missiles. Following close behind were the ten *Bes'uliike* that had survived the detonations, still flying cover for the blastboat—but, Jaina suspected, none too happy about it.

Boba Fett was no idiot. He would understand how Luke had taken advantage of him, and—while he never betrayed his word—this would be the last time he ever gave it to a Jedi.

And that was just as well. Working with your enemies was a good way to take a blaster bolt in the ear. Jaina swung back around and started toward the Knob Nose Transfer Facility. A lot of Mandalorians had lost their lives clearing her primary landing zone, and she wasn't going to waste their sacrifice.

chapter seven

What's the difference between an AT-AT and a stormtrooper on foot? One is an Imperial Walker and the other is a walking Imperial!

—Jacen Solo, age 14

After an awkward single-thruster landing and a short-but-taxing hike to her penetration point, Jaina lay on the dropsuit's belly, reconnoitering the surrounding area. To her left, the crater-pocked surface of Nickel One extended barely a kilometer before plunging away into star-dappled void. To her right, it broadened into a sweeping panorama of boulder ridges and powder lakes that stretched for dozens of kilometers before vanishing beneath the blue-flecked curtain of space. Directly ahead, at the base of a steep slope, sat the bantha-sized cylinder of a FlakBlaster Ten.

The artillery piece was pumping hard with all eight barrels, spitting dashes of white-hot neurodium plasma out over the ridges and powder lakes to Jaina's right. Its target was a cloud of distant blue specks flittering a few hundred meters above the silver plain, no doubt Jaina's family and the Mandalorians continuing to attack the command bunker.

On the opposite side of the gun emplacement lay the air lock Jaina needed, a triangular hatch located in a shallow cave-hangar. Unfortunately, the gun crew had positioned their weapon just meters in front of the hangar entrance, so there was no way to reach the air lock without going through them.

This was the part Jaina did not like about being a Jedi. She had grown up knowing stormtroopers only as enemies, had even fought a few of them as an adolescent. But she was old enough now to realize that being stormtroopers didn't make them evil, or corrupt, or even wrong. It made them a lot like her—just soldiers trying to do their duty, serving a cause they probably believed to be a good one.

And Jaina was going to kill all twelve of them—not because they were shooting at her parents, or even because she needed to reach the air lock behind them. She was going to do it because if she didn't, they would report her infiltration and ruin her mission. She was going to kill them for the most dispassionate of all reasons: because it was *necessary.*

It made her wonder how different she was from her brother, really. Perhaps she and Caedus were just soldiers in the ancient war between Sith and Jedi. Jaina would have liked to believe that, because then she could pretend this was just something demanded by the war instead of a choice *she* had made out of hatred for what her brother had become.

But Jacen had been a Jedi once. Now he was a Sith. That made him a traitor, and didn't traitors *deserve* to be hated? They were breakers of vows, betrayers of trusts . . . corrupters of the innocent and murderers of their beloved. Killing them was more than necessary. It was a duty, an act of deterrence and military preclusion, but also of outrage and reprisal, and *that* made it personal.

A burst of orange flashed at the far edge of the asteroid, and Jaina looked across the dusty plain to find the blue flicker of a blastboat being chased skyward by a funnel-shaped cloud of flame, vapor, and tumbling specks. Having seen similar eruptions more times than she cared to remember, she guessed that the assault on the command bunker had actually overloaded the shields and shattered the observation dome. If *that* did not fix Caedus's attention on Luke and her parents, nothing would.

Jaina snapped her lightsaber off its magclamp and turned back to the doomed gun crew. She had only about six minutes of good air left—half that if she exerted herself in a fight—so that ruled out any thought of waiting until she could just slip past. She would have to take them all out before they could report what was happening—ideally, before they *realized* what was happening.

Twelve stormtroopers, one Jedi assassin in a damaged dropsuit, three seconds to do the job. No problem.

Jaina primed the mini cannon in the dropsuit's left arm, then focused her attention on the dust caps dangling from thin cords at the ends of the FlakBlaster's emitter nozzles. They were probably the simplest technology on the weapon, just shrinlasti socks designed to seal out dirt, moisture, and anything else that might get down the barrels during storage or transport. But they were also electrical nonconductors— to prevent static buildup—which meant the magnetic sleeves that encased the plasma packets as they raced up the barrel would disintegrate on contact.

Confident that Caedus would be too busy worrying about Luke and her parents to sense what she was doing, Jaina used the Force to grab three dust caps—all she could control at once—and slip them over their emitter nozzles.

The gun commander cocked his helmet and just seemed to stare at the barrel ends in disbelief. The gas chief and his tank changer spun away and dived for cover, distracting the master engineer, who turned toward *them* instead of keeping his attention fixed on the output gauges and barrel monitors that might have saved them all.

The master engineer was still turning when the first plasma packets reached the dust caps. The three emitter nozzles vanished in an eye-blistering flash; then the plasma packets already ascending the barrels also began to disintegrate, triggering a chain of ever-growing secondary explosions that engulfed the gun in milliseconds. The entire gun crew disappeared beneath a boiling dome of white fire.

A couple of seconds later the FlakBlaster's defensive shields finally came down. What looked like a miniature solar flare went arcing out over the asteroid . . . then liquefied gas began to boil from damaged neurodium canisters, expanding into a thick, emerald fog.

Jaina sprang down into the fog, using the Force to descend the slope in a single leap. She landed a few meters behind the ring of jagged, blue-glowing metal that had once been the FlakBlaster. Knowing that any survivors would be inside the hangar, where the power master and his assistant had positioned their fusion core, she raced into the hangar—and collided headlong with a stormtrooper rushing out to aid his companions.

Being the smaller one, Jaina found herself accelerating backward with the stomach-churning abruptness possible solely in low gravity. Fortunately, she was the only one expecting a fight, so she had time to reach out with the Force and pull the stormtrooper along. He was so surprised and confused that he did not reach for his blaster holster until he was chest-plate-to-chest-plate with Jaina, and by then she had the hilt of her lightsaber jammed against his ribs. She ignited the blade and stirred it around to be certain of a quick kill.

The life left him in a red puff of decompression. Jaina rolled him away from her, then used her still-functional left-side maneuvering jet to bring herself under control. A pair of armored figures emerged from the hangar entrance, looking like armored ghosts as they came rushing through the fog carrying medkits and emergency life-support packs. Jaina raised her arm and ran a line of cannon bolts across their faceplates, reducing their helmets to balls of red mist before they had any hope of reporting her presence.

When no more crew emerged from the hangar, Jaina extended her Force awareness just far enough to confirm that there were no survivors, then quickly shut it down again. She was probably being somewhat overcautious, but after hearing Ben describe some of the things Caedus could do with the Force, she saw no reason to take chances.

Trying not to think about the death she had just wrought, Jaina slipped into the hangar and went straight to the air lock. Of course, there was a security pad in the center of the hatch. Despite her scrubber problem, she resisted the temptation to retrieve the magnetic key from the gun commander. That would create a record of the door opening *after* the explosion had killed him. Instead, she removed an automatic lock slicer from her belt and affixed it to the security pad.

A red flash announced that it had made contact with the security system. Leaving it there to do its work, Jaina returned to the fusion core and reversed the sensor feeds on the cooling valves, then disabled all eight safety shutoffs. The core temperature began to climb slowly. She slid the output switch to three-quarters, which would allow her about five minutes to clear the area before the reactor blew and destroyed all evidence of her attack on the gun emplacement.

By the time Jaina returned to the hatch, the automated slicer was flashing double green to indicate that it had defeated the security system and erased all traces of the breach. She returned the slicer to her equipment belt, then opened the hatch, stepped into the air lock—and felt her spine tingling beneath someone's gaze. Jaina leapt to one side of the air lock and slapped the SECURE pad, *then* spun around.

Through the closing hatch, she glimpsed a line of figures entering the hangar. Armored in colorful Mandalorian *beskar'gam,* they were moving quickly but cautiously, covering one another as they crossed the threshold, then shining their sleeve lamps into every dark corner to ensure there were no stormtroopers hiding in ambush.

The smart thing would have been to let the hatch close and jam the controls, leaving the entire squad to die when the fusion core overheated. That was what Fett would have done, and probably most of the Mandalorians in the squad as well. But Jaina could not let herself become quite *that* ruthless. The Mandalorians were hardly allies, but they weren't foes yet, either, and that meant she couldn't go around killing them because their presence happened to be inconvenient.

Besides, the leader was a female in familiar yellow-orange armor with gold sigils. And—assuming Jaina was the lucky one who walked away from the fight with her brother—the last thing she wanted was to have Boba Fett after her for letting his granddaughter die.

An orange beacon flashed on Jaina's head-up display, warning her that her air scrubbers had failed. Now she was rebreathing her own exhalations. Instantly, she began to feel a little queasy, but she suspected the sensation was more psychological than physical. Even filled with air that she had already breathed once, the dropsuit contained enough oxygen to keep her conscious for two or three more minutes.

Jaina reopened the hatch and waved an admonishing finger at the two commandos who swung their blasters toward her, then used hand signals to explain that the fusion core was rigged to blow. The Mandalorians gave up their search, and the first three crowded into the air lock.

As they waited for the chamber to pressurize, an anger verging on harmful intent began to boil into the Force. Jaina pretended not to notice and simply stared at the commando across from her, a broad-shouldered titan in a red helmet and black armor. Jaina was pretty sure he was Vatok Tawr, a talented fighter as quick as he was strong, with a ready smile and a quiet manner that seemed at odds with his rawboned cheeks and fist-flattened nose. She had trained against him several times.

The green glow of the equal-pressure light finally filled the air lock chamber, not a moment too soon for Jaina. Her head was starting to feel light, and she had to fight her own involuntary reflexes to keep from breathing too fast. She slapped the control pad and stepped through the internal hatch first, presenting her back to the Mandalorians as she opened her faceplate for a moment and gulped down several sweet breaths of dank, musty air.

Beyond the hatchway was a small marshaling vestibule where groups could assemble before and after they had passed through the air lock. Jaina Force-flashed the vidcam monitoring the area, then—knowing that the entire area would be obliterated when the fusion core detonated—simply blasted the security cam apart. As it dribbled to the floor in pieces, she crossed the vestibule and peered down a long, straight tunnel that descended toward the heart of the asteroid. It remained as empty as her inspection tour with Fett had led her to expect.

Jaina turned back to find Mirta and a Mandalorian male she did not know—at least judging by his blue helmet and *beskar'gam*—standing shoulder-to-shoulder behind her. Their G-10 power blasters were not pointed *at* her, but they weren't really pointed anywhere else, either. Vatok stood behind them, towering over the pair almost like a Wookiee.

"I'm surprised you warned us," Mirta said. "That's not too bright, after what your uncle pulled up there."

"You don't like the door charge, don't crash the party," Jaina said. "We didn't invite you."

"But you knew we were coming," the third Mandalorian said. "And you set us up."

"And Fett knew *we* were coming," Jaina said. She spread the bulky arms of her dropsuit in a sort of shrug. "Galaxy's a cold place, Blue. Get used to it."

A snicker sounded inside Vatok's helmet, and Jaina instantly felt an aura of general hostility radiate outward from Blue. She made a mental note to keep him where she could see him, then turned back to Mirta.

"What are you doing here, anyway?" she asked. "I *know* Fett didn't send you to help me."

"How bad you want to die, Jedi?" Blue asked. "Keep asking questions—"

"It's okay, Roegr." Mirta disconnected her helmet from its vac suit connectors, then took it off and ran a gloved hand through her curly brown hair. "Jedi Solo is going to be helping us with the Moffs."

Jaina cocked her brow. "Sorry to disappoint you, but I have other plans this trip."

"Plans can be adjusted." This from Vatok. "We're down two-thirds of our strike team. A *Mando*-trained Jedi might take a little sting out of that."

Jaina's heart sank. Two-thirds of the strike team; that was probably twelve or fifteen Mandalorians—some of them people she likely knew. Then a sad thought occurred to her, and she turned back to Mirta.

"Ghes?" she asked.

Mirta's eyes turned glassy, and she quickly slipped her helmet back on.

"He'll make it," she said, "if there's enough left of our *Tra'kad* to get past the Imperials."

"There will be," Jaina assured her. It had been less than a month since she had been on Mandalore drinking at the wedding of Mirta Gev and Ghes Orade, and she had never seen two people so much in love—aside from her parents, of course. "You can't stop a *Tra'kad*."

"*Really?*" Roegr retorted. "Tell that to my brother."

Jaina went from feeling sorry for Mirta to remembering that compassion was a weakness—and one she could not allow *any* of the Mandalorians to prey upon.

"I'm sorry for your loss, Roegr." Jaina turned back to

Mirta. "But let's just settle for staying out of each other's way. I'm *not* going to help you take out the Moffs."

"Actually," Mirta said, "you *are*."

She reached for her equipment pouch—and found her hand suddenly frozen in midair by the Force.

"You really don't think I'm going to let you pull a thermal detonator, do you?" Jaina asked. "That trick's as old as my mother."

"I'm just trying to show you something," Mirta said. "Something that will make you *want* to help us."

"I really doubt that's possible." When Jaina sensed no dishonesty in Mirta's presence, she released her Force grasp and said, "But go ahead and try."

"You Jedi." Mirta pulled a small vidreceiver from her pouch, then activated it and punched in a few codes. After a moment, she smiled and turned the vidreceiver so Jaina could see it. "Always underestimating Mandalorians."

The display was small, the image it showed even smaller, and it took Jaina a moment to make out what she was seeing. Even then, she did not quite believe her eyes.

The screen showed one of the smooth-polished cells that passed for VIP quarters in Nickel One. Seated in the corner, slumped in a large flowform chair with one hand raised toward his brow and his yellow eyes focused vacantly on the floor, was the brooding, dark-cloaked figure of her brother.

Darth Caedus—alone, deep in meditation, and vulnerable.

Jaina understood almost instantly. "The preparations!" She looked up at Mirta. "That's what Fett was doing when I left—tapping into the surveillance system."

"Not *tapping*." There was a note of jolly good humor to Vatok's correction. "*Taking*."

Mirta continued to hold the vidreceiver, allowing Jaina to study the image as long as she liked. It was hard to believe it might be so easy—that all she had to do was watch her brother's cell until he was meditating or sleeping or doing any of a dozen other things that would leave him vulnerable.

And of course, it would never be quite that easy. Her brother would feel her coming, or sense that he was in danger, or just change locations unexpectedly.

But it was a start.

"Okay," Jaina said, "maybe I *do* want to help you. But we have to do it my way, or you're on your own."

"As long as your way includes killing the Moffs, sure," replied Mirta. "We don't mind following a Jedi Knight. They used to make good generals, after all."

Jaina didn't believe her, of course—but it was good enough for now.

chapter eight

Hey, Tenel Ka—you know why wampas have such long arms? Because their hands are so far from their face!

—Jacen Solo, age 14

Even with a comm feed into Nickel One's surveillance system and help from the Verpine resistance network, the trip down from the surface had been one nerve-racking dash after another. Jaina and the Mandalorians were literally steaming sweat into the closed confines of their makeshift observation post inside the Data Assimilation Chamber, and the air inside had grown as muggy as it was sour. The Verpine technicians kept coming over to ask the humans to stop perspiring so heavily, explaining that the extra humidity would soon begin to wreak havoc with the delicate circuitry of the VerpiTron cyberbrains that were streaming updates to the giant holodisplays out in the Strategic Planning Forum.

When that happened, Jaina knew, Mirta would strike whether or not they knew Caedus's location. Nearly the entire Moff Council was gathered in the Strategic Planning Forum, discussing the imminent arrival of the fleets of Admirals Daala and Niathal, and no Mandalorian would let pass an opportunity to eliminate so many targets at once.

Jaina finished scrolling through the feeds on her borrowed vidreceiver, then shook her head in disgust. There had been no sign of her brother in any of the monitored chambers, no hint that he had even passed down one of the asteroid's spotless tunnels. Nickel One's security system had simply lost track of him.

Jaina glanced over and found an image of the Strategic Planning Forum on the display of Mirta's vidreceiver. Most of the small screen was filled with an image of the holodisplays the Moffs were studying, so that the room looked like a tiny yellow dot—representing the system's sun—surrounded by an inner ring of floating stones—the Roche asteroid field, depicted far larger than true scale. In front of the hologram, twenty speck-sized humans sat clustered together near the bottom of a dozen rows of theater-style seating.

"Hear anything useful?" Jaina asked.

"Plenty," Mirta said, removing the soundplug from her ear. "Just nothing that's going to help us find your brother."

She disconnected the vidreceiver's audio jack, and human voices began to spill from the speaker, surprisingly clear and resonant.

". . . should have listened to Caedus after all," a deep, refined voice was saying. "It certainly seems he was correct about this 'conquest.' We're lucky that suicide run on the *Dominion* only killed two of us—"

"*Very* lucky," added a raspy-voiced jokester, "considering the two Moffs we lost."

The interruption drew a round of hearty laughter, then Refined Voice continued, "Yes, I suppose every catastrophe has its positive side. But now we've lost the *Harbinger* as well, and with the Hapans, Daala, and Niathal all converging on us, that certainly won't be the last Star Destroyer we lose."

"Caedus's intelligence was better than ours *this time*," replied a durasteel-voiced man. "I'll give you that. But that hardly means we should present him with the *dozens* of Star Destroyers we have in the Roche system. Even if we were inclined to turn the Empire over to the bad seed of a

common spicerunner and his gutter-crawling Princess—
which I sincerely hope we're *not*—"

A chorus of amused snorts confirmed that the Moffs
were not.

"—Caedus has hardly proven himself worthy of our
confidence. That mess at Fondor was very nearly the Alliance's undoing."

"Hear, hear!" boomed a thick-tongued Moff. "Caedus is
no Palpatine, *I* can tell you that."

"Yes, yes, Jowar," said Refined Voice. "We're all aware
that you served on the Emperor's personal staff as a young
officer."

"And he's not likely to let us forget it," added Raspy
Jokester.

This drew a few polite chuckles, then Refined Voice continued, "But I *hope* everyone here realizes that if Caedus
hadn't brought the Fourth Fleet along, we'd actually be
outnumbered right now."

"True," agreed Durasteel Voice. "And doesn't that betray a certain naïveté? A wiser man would not have
brought in the Fourth until we were *already* outnumbered.
He might well have been in a position to dictate terms to
us, rather than the reverse."

Mirta thumbed the volume down, then said, "That's the
gist of what they've been talking about. Most of them seem
to like the idea of joining with the Galactic Alliance to
form a New Empire, but only if it's under *their* control."

"Not that it matters *what* they decide," added Vatok,
looming over Jaina and Mirta in his black *beskar'gam,*
"seeing as how they're all going to be dead in five minutes."

"*Five* minutes?" Jaina looked from Vatok back to Mirta,
then understood—Mirta had already given the go-order
over her helmet comm. "You gave the order?"

Mirta tipped her helmet in acknowledgment. "How long
do you expect us to wait?" She glanced back at the big cy-

berbrains, where two Verpine technicians were monitoring systems displays and casting fretful looks back toward Jaina and her sweaty Mandalorian companions. "If those VerpiTrons go, so does our element of surprise."

"If we attack without knowing where Caedus is," Jaina countered, "*we* may be the ones who get surprised. There's a reason we can't find him on the security system, and it's not because he's using the refresher."

"You're saying he might know we're here?" Mirta asked.

"I'm saying he definitely knows *you're* here," Jaina said. "He can feel your presences in the Force—and if he hasn't told the Moffs, there's a reason."

Mirta and the other Mandalorians were silent for a moment, then Vatok asked, "He's setting up the Moffs for us?"

Jaina shook her head. "Whatever he's doing, it's not for you," she said. "Maybe he's thinking that with the Moffs gone, he can seize their fleets. Or maybe he's using them to draw *you* out—that's what I'd bet on."

"Or maybe the Jedi just wants to take out her brother first," said Roegr, the blue-armored man whose own brother had perished in the first *Tra'kad*. "Nice try, *aruetii*, but we're not buying."

Jaina looked to Mirta. "You know me," she said. "I'm *not* making this up."

"Wouldn't matter if you were," Mirta replied. "We're here to kill the Moffs, and we're *not* going to get a better shot at them."

"That wasn't our deal."

"Sure it was," Mirta said. "You're in charge—as long as we attack *now*."

Jaina sighed and looked at the floor. If she was right about her brother's intentions, she could use the Mandalorian attack to her advantage—she knew that. But she wouldn't be able to kill a Sith Lord *and* save Mirta's life. She knew that, too.

Vatok nudged her elbow with his. "What's wrong, *jetii*?" he asked. "Afraid of your brother?"

"Actually, yes." Jaina took the QuietSnipe off her back, then looked toward a small hatch in the center of the room's curved wall. "I'll be in the projection booth—but don't expect covering fire until Caedus goes down."

"Just like a Jedi—any excuse to stay out of the fighting," Roegr said. A grunt of disgust sounded inside his blue helmet, and he started toward the exit on the far side of the cyberbrains. "Let's go do this. I'm getting hot."

Mirta's saffron helmet turned after him, and Jaina could sense that her friend was about to say something sharp. She caught the Mandalorian by her arm.

"His opinion means nothing to me," Jaina said. "Stay focused."

Mirta continued to look after Roegr for a moment, then nodded. "You're right," she said. "Sorry we couldn't do this your way."

"Me, too," Jaina said. "May the Force be with you out there."

Mirta snorted through her golden faceplate. "Yeah—*that's* going to help a Mandalorian." She slapped Jaina on the side of the shoulder. "Shoot straight and run fast. We'll see you when it's done."

She said something into her helmet and started after Roegr. Four of her commandos started after her, but Vatok remained behind. He pulled off his helmet and looked down at her, his blond beard and hair plastered flat by sweat.

"You really think he's waiting for us?" he asked.

"I can't *sense* it," Jaina said. "But yes, that's what I think."

"And it scares you?"

Jaina nodded. "It does."

A twinkle came to Vatok's eye, and he flashed her a smile every bit as mischievous as any she had ever seen from her father. "That's what I was hoping."

Jaina cocked her brow. "Yeah?"

"Yeah," he said. "Did you think I kept coming back to Beviin's barn because I like bruises?"

"Frankly," Jaina said, "I did."

Vatok looked surprised for an instant; then his smile returned. "And you liked giving them." He shook his head, then put his helmet back on and turned to leave. "What did I expect from a *jetii*?"

Jaina laughed. "I liked fighting you, too, Vatok," she said. "You were my favorite."

Vatok turned back. "You mean that?"

"Sure," Jaina said. She hadn't realized he was growing so fond of her; it seemed a lifetime ago—since before Mara's death—that she had paid any attention to that sort of thing. "Even better than Fett."

"You better not be making fun of me." Vatok's tone was only about half joking. "I'm the sensitive type, you know."

"A sensitive Mandalorian? No such thing," Jaina retorted. "But I'm telling the truth. Fett's an old man. It's like bruising your father."

Vatok laughed and started toward the door. "I'm going to tell him you said that, you know."

"I hope you do," Jaina said. Silently, she added, *Because it means you came back alive.* "Shoot straight and run fast."

This stopped the big Mandalorian in his tracks. His helmet turned back toward her, and she could sense that his mood had swung toward the serious.

"What is it?" she asked. "Don't tell me that's something Mandalorians only say to women?"

"Only to *assassins,*" Vatok corrected. "To commandos, you say, *Die proud.*"

"Sorry—*jetiise* ignorance," Jaina said. "But please— *don't.*"

Vatok chuckled. "Okay, since you asked so nicely." He started toward the door again. "May the Force be with you, Jedi."

This time Vatok didn't look back, leaving Jaina alone with her fears, wondering not only whether he and Mirta and the rest of the Mandalorians were headed to their deaths, but whether she might be, as well. Even Luke did not know the full of extent of Caedus's powers, and Jaina had no illusions about being her brother's equal in terms of Force strength. If it came down to a straight Force battle, she would die. It was that simple.

But her fears ran deeper than just dying. She knew her parents too well to think her death would destroy them or ravage their marriage—but it *would* crush them, and she could not bear to imagine the craziness they might under-take in a grief-fueled quest for vengeance. And the risks of actually succeeding were even greater. Jaina's best chance of success lay in ambush, but she did not imagine for a mo-ment that she could kill her own brother in cold blood and remain untainted by the dark side.

All that assumed, of course, that when Jaina looked into her brother's yellow eyes, she *could* pull the trigger—that she did not lose her resolve. She extended the barrel of her QuietSnipe and slipped a magazine of pellets into the feeder, then summoned one of the cyberbrain technicians over to the projection booth. The Verpine resistance network— consisting of roughly the entire insectoid population of the Roche system—had already explained to Jaina and the Mandalorians that this booth housed only part of the pro-jection equipment. Similar booths were located on the two flanking walls, and there was one in the floor below the hologram. Inside each booth were two Imperials—a member of the stormtrooper Elite Guard, and a holopro-jectionist.

"Call the guard out for me," Jaina whispered.

The Verpine lowered his long snout. "Why?"

"So I can take him down quietly," Jaina said. "We don't want to alarm the Moffs, do we?"

"I mean why should the resistance help *you*?" the insectoid asked. "The Verpine do not have a mutual-aid treaty with the Jedi."

Jaina grated her teeth, recalling how exacting insectoid minds tended to be—and wondering if she had been this annoying as a Killik Joiner.

"The Jedi don't require treaties," she explained. "We help where help is needed. But if the Verpine don't *need* help . . ."

She began to break down the QuietSnipe.

"Wait." The Verpine punched a code into the security pad on the triangular hatch, then called inside, "Trooper Aitch-Four-Forty-nine-Dash-Bee-Seven, there may be a security breach you should check."

"Again?" came the electronic-voiced reply.

Potential security breaches were the standard excuses that the Verpine technician and labor castes had been using—under the pretense of full cooperation—to lure stormtroopers aside as Jaina and the Mandalorians penetrated the depths of the asteroid.

"What is it this time?" the trooper asked, coming toward the door. "Strange pheromones? An open hatch? Someone's pet mynock on the loose?"

The technician waited until the stormtrooper was coming through the hatchway before answering.

"I'm not sure." He looked toward Jaina. "It might be a Jedi."

"A *what*?"

The trooper turned to look, leaving Jaina with no choice but to push the barrel of her QuietSnipe up under his jawline and pull the trigger. There was a barely audible *krafuut* as the mag-pellet accelerated up the barrel and into his brain. A red spray shot from beneath the stormtrooper's helmet, and he stumbled back toward the nearest VerpiTron, dying even before his feet had stopped moving.

The technician cried out and leapt after the trooper, pulling him away from the delicate cyberbrain and to the floor in a loud, plastoid clatter.

Jaina frowned down at the Verpine. "That wasn't much of a diversion."

The technician blinked up at her. "You wanted him to look the other way?" he asked. "Why didn't you say so?"

Before Jaina could reply, a female voice called from inside the booth. "Aitch? What's going on out there?"

Jaina stepped through the hatchway into a large durasteel booth packed with softly humming holoprojection equipment. At the front of the cramped little chamber, a projectionist in a brown Imperial uniform was standing in front of a chest-high control board, peering through a panel of one-way transparisteel. Her small hands were splayed wide over an array of knobs and glide switches designed for long-fingered Verpine technicians, flying back and forth as she struggled to maintain the crispness of the holoimages out in the Strategic Planning Forum.

When her stormtrooper companion did not answer, she turned away from the transparisteel panel, at the same time calling, *"Aitch?"*

Jaina was already leaping.

Unfortunately, she could not use the Force for fear of alerting her brother to her presence, so it took a couple of bounds to reach the front of the booth. The projectionist's eyes grew wide, and her hand darted toward the blaster pistol hanging from her belt—which was what saved her life.

Jaina reached the woman just as the blaster pistol cleared its holster and quickly pushed it down. A single bolt *ping*ed off the floor and began to bounce around inside the projection equipment, triggering a succession of hisses, clinks, and pops that left no doubt about the damage being done.

Jaina cursed under her breath, then slammed a side hammerfist into her attacker's jaw hinge, catching the nerve bundle just under the ear. The projectionist fell instantly unconscious and dropped to the floor in a heap. Jaina used plasticuffs to bind her at the wrists and ankles, then smashed the emitter nozzle of the woman's blaster pistol against the floor and tossed it aside.

By the time she had finished, acrid smoke filled the air, and the sounds coming from the holoprojectors had grown even more loud and exotic—long descending whistles, low raspings, sharp bangs. Jaina peered through the one-way panel and saw many of the images in the hologram starting to break up. Down in the forum's front seats, a cluster of twenty men dressed in medal-heavy Imperial uniforms were scowling up at the display. They did not appear to have any aides with them, but a detail of stormtroopers in the gray armor of the Remnant's Elite Guard were stationed a dozen meters away, on the small apron area between the forum's uppermost seats and the exit doors.

There was, of course, no sign of Darth Caedus.

The projectionist's comlink began to chirp for attention. Jaina checked the name tag on the woman's uniform, then pulled the comlink from her breast pocket and opened the channel.

"Sangi here," she said, deliberately putting a little shrillness into her response in an attempt to divert attention from any obvious differences in their voices. "Just having a little problem."

"What *kind* of problem?" demanded a tinny male voice. "And give me a proper report, Ensign. We have good reasons for these protocols, you know."

"Of course, uh, Lieutenant," Jaina replied, taking an educated guess. "It's nothing serious, just blew a couple of—"

"*Lieutenant?*" the man interrupted.

"Sorry—Lieutenant Commander," Jaina said, taking another guess. "We just blew a couple of capacitors. Everything should be back online in a minute."

"Very well," the voice said, and Jaina knew she had guessed wrong. Had she been right, there would have been another lecture about completeness, perhaps even a request for an authentication code. "Carry on."

"You bet."

Jaina dropped the comlink on the floor and crushed it beneath her boot heel. Sangi's commander already knew where she was, but at least this way the communications team would not be able to activate the comlink remotely and eavesdrop on what she was doing. She closed the hatch at the back of the booth, locking it from the inside so any Remnant security personnel coming after her would have to cut their way into the booth . . . then heard a muffled chain of thuds as the Mandalorians began their assault on the Moffs.

Jaina extended the barrel of her QuietSnipe and went to the projection aperture in the center of the booth's front wall. Unlike the transparisteel panel through which the projectionist had been watching the holograms, the aperture was just an empty hole through which the holoprojector beam could pass without suffering any image degradation.

Or through which a mag-pellet could pass without being deflected.

By the time Jaina had reached the projection aperture, most of the Elite Guard lay more or less helpless on the floor. Many were obviously dead, their bodies torn apart by the detonite explosions with which the Mandalorians had opened their initial assault. Others were too wounded or too blast-shocked to fight, some holding their arms over gaping holes in their stomach armor, others banging charred limb-stumps on the floor. A few were sitting upright with their arms hanging at their sides or resting in their laps, their faceplates fixed on the ruptured doors at the back of the room, as though they could not see or hear or weren't even aware of the seven maniacs in brightly colored *beskar'gam* charging out of the smoke.

At least two dozen guards had escaped the carnage of the initial assault, and now they were retreating toward the front seats. As soon as they saw the Mandalorians, they began to fire up toward the apron with their repeating blasters, slowing the onslaught but hardly stopping it. Their hits merely knocked the Mandalorians off their feet without penetrating their *beskar'gam,* and a second later the Mandos would be up and coming again.

Unfortunately, time was something the attackers did not have. Even *beskar'gam* was no match for sheer numbers, and it would be only a minute—perhaps a matter of *seconds*—before stormtroopers began to pour through the doors behind them. Jaina was in a perfect position to tip the balance by opening fire and clearing a lane down to where the Moffs had taken cover in the forum's lower seats.

The trouble was, helping the Mandalorians meant revealing her presence to Caedus, and *that* meant reducing her own chances of success to almost nothing. She knew what Fett would do in her place . . . and in this case he was right. The Mandalorians had their mission and Jaina had hers.

The only thing that caused Jaina doubt was the lack of her brother's actual presence. She could think of a hundred reasons he might be hiding from Nickel One's security cams, but the only ones that made sense right now had to do with the Mandalorians. Either he intended to ambush them, or Vatok had been right about him setting up the Moffs for assassination.

Jaina watched with strained patience as a string of bolts finally slipped beneath the bottom edge of a Mandalorian helmet and sent it tumbling away, the head inside trailing curls of smoke and blood. The fellow's companions were too disciplined to look or even acknowledge the reminder of their own mortality, but the assault did stall for just an instant.

No strangers to battle themselves, the troopers of the Elite Guard sensed the minuscule shift in momentum and immediately changed tactics, concentrating their fire on the most exposed Mandos. A torrent of fiery beams drove a brown-armored Mandalorian to the stairs, where he lay thrashing and cooking inside his armor until a lucky bolt finally found a seam and put him out of his misery.

With only five enemies remaining, the Elite Guard started to advance back toward the upper rows of seats, literally pushing their foes ahead of them with blaster bolts. Another Mandalorian went down, a melt hole opening in his breastplate when he made the mistake of presenting the same side of his armor to the Imperials for too long.

The Mandalorians finally gave up their charge and dived for cover between the seats. Eager to press their advantage, the Elite Guard began to race upward, stepping from seat-top to seat-top and blowing apart whole rows in their attempts to get at their enemies. Jaina saw Mirta glance up toward her hiding place and began to wonder if there was any sense in remaining concealed. At this rate, the Mandalorians were going to be killed without any help from her brother.

Down in the lower seats, the Moffs had apparently reached a similar conclusion. They began to show their heads, shouting encouragement and orders—usually conflicting—to their bodyguards. And that was what Mirta had been waiting for. Four grenades flew up from behind the seats.

Explosives weren't necessarily the most accurate or certain way to kill someone, but they *were* alarming. About half the Elite Guard turned to dive for cover before it grew apparent that the grenades were arcing over their heads down toward the Moffs. Some actually turned to watch, while others let their fire stray as they instinctively ducked or dodged.

Several meters from where the grenades had originated, Mirta and Roegr came over the seats firing and leaping across rows. Three Imperials went down with scorch holes in their armor before they could react, and two more fell to the floor, still spinning when they turned to fire—and were rewarded with bolts through the faceplates.

Then, when the remaining guards turned toward the two bounding commandos, Vatok and the last Mandalorian popped up from where the grenades had originated. They began to lay covering fire, catching half a dozen Imperials square in the back, bringing the odds close enough to even that Mirta and Roegr were almost assured of reaching the Moffs in one piece.

But Jaina was far more interested in the grenades. Instead of detonating in the midst of the Moffs, they seemed to catch a nonexistent wind and drift through the deteriorating hologram toward her projection booth. She could think of only one explanation for such an odd flight.

Caedus. He was coming to the Moff's defense. Did that mean he was using the Moffs to draw the Mandalorians out—or the Mandalorians to draw *her* out?

The battle sounds out in the forum seemed to fade as Jaina's pulse began to pound in her ears. The grenades were coming in her direction, under her brother's control. Convinced she knew what that meant—*terrified* she knew—she lowered her QuietSnipe and reached out to the grenades in the Force . . . then felt them drop away.

They detonated outside the booth, somewhere a few meters below. The floor shook beneath her feet, and a blinding curtain of light and flame shot up in front of the image aperture. The sound of Jaina's pulse pounding in her ears changed to sharp banging, and the acrid smell of detonite and smoke scorched her nostrils.

Then a lightsaber *snap-hiss*ed to life out in the forum and began to whine and whir through a deflection pattern. Still, Jaina did not quite grasp that she had been mistaken—that the approaching grenades had not been a sign of her brother's omniscience, merely a coincidence of timing and location—until she began to hear the *cheee-chew* of blaster bolts being deflected by Caedus's blade.

Jaina quickly shut herself off from the Force and returned to the aperture, the QuietSnipe raised to her shoulder and her finger on the trigger. Her brother was just dancing out of the yellow ball of the holographic sun, a dark-cloaked figure with no helmet and yellow eyes, weaving baskets of crimson light as he spun through the holographic asteroids, batting bolts of blaster energy back toward alarmed Mandalorians and confused bodyguards alike.

Jaina braced the barrel of the QuietSnipe on the edge of the image aperture. But Caedus—she could not bear to think of him as her brother, not at that moment—was moving too wildly and quickly to give her a clean shot. She would have to wait until he engaged someone and slowed down.

Mirta Gev was the first of the original combatants to recover from the shock of his arrival. A bouncing figure in yellow-orange armor only a few rows from her targets, she turned her G-10 power blaster on a round-faced Moff with a ruddy complexion and three chins, and a smoke hole the size of Jaina's fist erupted from the man's back.

Caedus came out of a spin looking in Mirta's direction. She sailed meters into the air, flipping upside down and crashing into a ceiling corner on the far side of the chamber, then dropping four meters to the floor. She landed on the crown of her helmet in a metallic crash audible even above the battle and folded in two, and she did not move again.

Jaina forced herself not to feel the sentiments rising inside her, the rage and shock and sorrow. *Emotion is a weakness*. It would not save the living, she reminded herself, and it could not bring the dead back to life. She returned her attention to Caedus and saw the Moffs cowering in the seats behind him, returning the Mandalorians' fire with underpowered hold-out blasters and T-21s taken from their fallen bodyguards.

Caedus himself was driving a boot into Roegr's blue breastplate, sending him tumbling backward over a row of seats. Jaina set the QuietSnipe's sight on the back of the Sith's head and squeezed the trigger—then saw a gray helmet spurt blood when a bodyguard stepped between her and her target. He fell toward Caedus, smashing him in the small of his back and nearly knocking him over the seats after Roegr.

Caedus righted himself with the Force and came around with his lightsaber sweeping low, his yellow eyes blazing with anger as he sliced through the bodyguard's helmet. Jaina adjusted her aim—then barely prevented herself from squeezing the trigger when a streak of blue armor came leaping over the seats to block her shot, the curved blade of a *beskad* flashing at Caedus's neck.

Roegr never had a chance. Caedus simply spun inside the attack, staggering his assailant with a Force-driven elbow to the helmet. Knowing the folly of trying to track a whirling target—especially without the Force to aid her—Jaina kept her eye on her sniper sight and waited for him to move into the shot.

But Caedus slipped in the opposite direction, dragging his blade across the Mandalorian's faceplate, then pulling it back across the breastplate. The slashes would have cut through normal armor like a plasma torch through plastoid, but all they did to Roegr's blue *beskar'gam* was burn a couple of deep furrows.

Still, good armor was hardly a match for the speed and power of a Sith Lord. By the time Roegr recovered from the elbow strike and tried to bring his *beskad* up again, Caedus was already trapping the Mandalorian's sword arm in an elbow lock. Continuing to spin—and denying Jaina a viable target—he deactivated his lightsaber and cocked his arm back for a pommel strike.

Then Caedus did a peculiar thing. He paused for an instant, glowering at the Mandalorian's blue armor as though offended by its color. Jaina saw the chance for a difficult oblique shot past Roegr's helmet and swung the Quiet-Snipe over.

Caedus brought the pommel of his lightsaber down, striking the breastplate not all that hard, not quite in the center . . . and *shattering* it. The *beskar* didn't burst apart or send shards flying, or do anything remotely explosive. It just crumbled away from the vacproof underliner, leaving Roegr faceplate-to-chin with his soon-to-be killer.

Jaina was too disciplined to let her shock distract her, but she *was* shocked. *Beskar'gam* was some of the toughest armor in the galaxy, able to deflect blaster bolts and lightsaber strikes with little more than a scorch mark, and her brother had just destroyed a piece with a *tap*. Had he mastered the shatterpoint?

The academy Archives claimed that it was a lost and rare art, the ability to perceive points of weakness where a small amount of precisely applied force would unlock the unseen structures that bound together even the most indestructible materials and situations. The great Jedi Master Mace Windu, who had died in the Clone Wars, had been known to possess the gift. He had been the last.

Until Caedus.

Growing more frightened than ever by the magnitude of her brother's powers—and therefore even *more* resolved to stop him—Jaina set her front sight on Caedus's ear and fired a burst of three pellets . . . just as Caedus flipped his lightsaber around and thumbed the activation switch.

The blade ignited inside Roegr's chest, splitting him open

at the sternum. The tip extended up through his neck and hit the back of his helmet, failing to penetrate the tough *beskar* and snapping his head back into the path of Jaina's first mag-pellet. The third pellet whispered past, barely a centimeter behind Caedus's unprotected head, and punched a hole through a seat.

But the *second* pellet, the one that didn't miss, caught Caedus in the shoulder and sent him spinning. With Roegr's sword arm still trapped in an elbow lock, he pulled the Mandalorian around with him, and Jaina's next burst of mag-pellets slammed into the blue plate still affixed to the dead man's back. The impact tipped the balance, driving Caedus over a row of seats and out of sight down on the floor.

Jaina continued to fire, her mag-pellets tearing seats apart as she swept the barrel back and forth. Either the Moffs and their bodyguards did not know where the attack on Caedus was coming from or they did not care—which was hardly a surprise. Half a dozen Moffs lay strewn over seats with gaping scorch holes where their medals or eyes or ears used to be, and the four bodyguards left to protect the survivors were clearly not up to the job. Vatok and the other surviving Mandalorian were working their way down toward the lower seats, taking turns moving and covering—and reducing the number of Moffs and bodyguards by one each as Jaina watched.

The QuietSnipe finally ran out of mag-pellets. Jaina ducked out of the image aperture and rolled to one side, ejecting the empty magazine and wondering whether she could possibly have taken Caedus out so easily.

She had her answer an instant later when a fork of Force lightning danced through the aperture and shattered the lens of the holoprojector. Jaina slipped a fresh magazine into her QuietSnipe and continued to roll until she reached the control board where the projectionist had been standing.

The Force lightning ceased, but Jaina did not make the mistake of returning to the aperture through which she had fired the first time. Instead, she poked her head up above the control board and looked through the viewing panel out into the forum seats.

Caedus was on his feet again, dancing back and forth, his wounded arm hanging limp at his side, wielding his lightsaber one-handed and still deflecting everything that Vatok and the other Mandalorian were pouring down toward the Moffs.

Jaina started to step back to her original firing position—then noticed a trio of blaster barrels scattered across the lower seats, pointing up toward the aperture. Clearly, someone had taken control of the situation down there—and she had the sinking feeling that it was her brother.

She pulled her lightsaber off her belt and jammed the emitter nozzle against the one-way viewing panel above the control board. Out in the forum, she saw Caedus look toward the second Mandalorian. The man suddenly stopped firing and grabbed for his throat, scratching at the bottom rim of his helmet as though he believed that was what had crushed his larynx.

Jaina thumbed her lightsaber's activation switch, and the blade snapped to life, burning a thumb-sized hole through the one-way transparisteel in front of her. The three blaster barrels she had spotted a moment earlier swung toward the blade's glow and began to pour sizzling bolts of energy into the viewing panel. Jaina ignored the attacks and worked her blade in a circle, enlarging the hole into a suitable firing port.

By the time she had finished, Vatok was the last Mandalorian remaining, only a few paces from Caedus and the Moffs, and his attacks were being deflected without going anywhere near their targets. Jaina wanted to yell at him to stop, to turn and run, but even had there been time to pull her comlink and open a channel, she knew her words would have been futile. Vatok would never flee while his companions lay dead on the field of battle; nor would Caedus allow him that option.

Jaina was looking at a dead man. She knew that, knew that even if she killed her brother, she would not save her friend. She pushed the barrel of her QuietSnipe through the hole she had made and pulled the trigger. But this time, Caedus was not surprised. He spun away even as she opened fire, leaping in close to engage Vatok hand-to-hand, deftly placing the big Mandalorian between Jaina and himself.

Jaina did what Fett would have done—what Vatok himself would have done—and continued to fire, doing her best to direct her pellets past his shoulders into Caedus . . . and failing. Even without the bodyguards' blaster bolts streaming up to blind her as they ricocheted off the exterior of her viewing panel, half her pellets were driving dents into Vatok's back plate, and the rest were sailing harmlessly past to destroy seats.

Though Vatok still had two good arms and Caedus had only one, it was all he could do to defend himself—and Jaina suspected that was only because her brother needed to keep using Vatok as a shield. The Mandalorian tried to slam the butt of his blaster into Caedus's head—only to have the lightsaber slice it in half. He drove a knee into the ribs on Caedus's vulnerable side—only to meet a Force block that sent him stumbling back into a burst of mag-pellets from Jaina. He caught a lightsaber strike on his *beskar* vambrace, then tried to drop an iron-gloved fist across the bridge of Caedus's nose—only to find himself striking at empty air when his foe was already ducking away and driving him back with a shoulder to the midsection.

Nor could Jaina do anything to help. Her brother seemed to anticipate every adjustment she made, swinging Vatok around to block her line of sight when she tried to slide a burst of pellets past the Mandalorian's flank, dancing aside when she streamed fire straight into his back in an effort to push him forward and bowl Caedus over.

Then, three seconds and a hundred pellets later, Jaina ran out of ammunition again.

Before she had even pulled the barrel out of her makeshift firing port, Caedus had Force-hurled Vatok down between the seats and was driving his lightsaber down toward the Mandalorian's head. Even without the scream, Jaina would have known her friend was dead.

chapter nine

Which side of an Ewok has the most fur? The outside!
—Jacen Solo, age 14

It looked like the stars just kept exploding. There would be a few moments of tranquillity when the blue-flecked curtain of space hung outside the blastboat canopy, as still and stunning as the first time Han had sat in a pilot's seat. His chest would go hollow with awe at the vast beauty before him, and he would be struck by what a gift his life had been, by how much his famous Solo luck had brought him—the freedom to wander an entire galaxy at will, a real live Princess for a wife, and children who had made him proud . . . *almost* all the time.

Then the swirling ion trail of a starfighter would come corkscrewing out of the dark, or the luminous halo of an approaching frigate would drift into view. Boiling balls of fire would erupt ahead, like stars going nova. The blastboat would chug when Leia and Saba returned fire, and a bright, shrinking disk might flare away as Luke launched a concussion missile. R2-D2 would scroll a tactical update across the pilot's display, C-3PO would declare their imminent doom, and Han would slam the yoke to one side, diving away into the shelter of the star-dappled void.

But this time, the proximity alarm broke out squawking, and crooked snakes of color began to jump across space in front of the cockpit canopy. Blue rings of ion glow formed in the dancing iridescence ahead and swelled into the back-lit forms of an arriving war fleet. Almost instantly, columns of turbolaser fire began to streak back and forth between the newcomers and the disorganized Remnant flotilla that had been trying for hours to chase off the Jedi raiding force.

Han pointed their nose straight at the heart of the arriving fleet, trying to run parallel to the fiery torrent rather than ducking out before he had some sense of the newcomers' gunnery patterns. Despite his efforts, one bolt flashed past close enough to rock the blastboat sideways and darken the canopy blast-tinting. The shield generator sizzled with strain, and the cabin filled with the caustic scent of melting circuitry.

Han cursed, then checked his tactical display and saw that not just one, but *two* fleets were arriving: a mixed bag of Galactic Alliance defectors clustered around Cha Nia-thal's *Ocean,* and a flotilla of old Empire-era Star Destroyers and *Scimitar*-class frigates led by Daala's renowned *Chimaera.*

"The Conniver Sisters One and Two," Han commented. "Who invited *them*?"

"I wasn't aware that battles *required* invitations," C-3PO said, reaching for the blastboat's comm controls. "But we should certainly extend a gracious welcome."

"You're asking me to lie?" Han asked. "No way."

"I'm afraid I don't understand, Captain Solo," C-3PO replied. "We are in desperate need of relief, and they clearly appear to be taking our side."

"The only side those two take is their *own*," Han said. "They're just here because they smell blood and want to see what they can pick off for themselves."

"Nevertheless, they are shooting at our enemies instead of us, which is the very definition of *ally* in nearly six thousand galactic cultures," C-3PO noted. "Might I suggest that now would be an excellent time to broaden your horizons?"

"No."

The intensifying brilliance of an oncoming turbolaser strike flared before Han's eyes. He pushed the yoke forward, then slammed into his shoulder restraints as the bolt skipped off their shields and bounced the blastboat downward. The generators failed with an earsplitting *thraaawkk,* and acrid yellow fumes began to pour out of the recirculation vents.

R2-D2 let out a long stream of beeps and tweedles, and damage reports began to scroll across the pilot's display. Their shields were only down until Luke could bring the backups online, but a coolant line had sprung a leak—that explained the acrid fumes—and their fusion core was about to start overheating.

"You see?" C-3PO asked. "Even Artoo is frightened, and that never happens. We should definitely request an escape vector and let them take over the fight."

"Not going to happen, Goldenrod." Han spotted a flight of XJs and antique TIEs streaming away from the two fleets and dropped into their transit lane, then swung back toward Nickel One. "Not while my daughter is still down there in that rock."

The frigate that had been pursuing them most recently hung in the distance, a little above their plane of orientation, a knobby-ended cylinder trailing a long, curving tail of ions as it turned away from the oncoming fleets. Beyond it floated Nickel One itself, an inky-black nugget visible only in the sense that its dark mass blotted out the stars beyond. Swarming around the asteroid were the flickering pinpoints of perhaps a hundred vessels: the Remnant's scattered flotilla rushing to regroup and defend their conquest.

Two-thirds of those flickering pinpoints were probably

Starhunters or other small combat craft, which meant that the Remnant would be slightly outnumbered—at least until the Alliance's Fourth Fleet returned from its escort duty to support them. Unlike the Third Fleet, which had lost nearly a quarter of its strength to Niathal's call for desertion at Fondor, the Fighting Fourth remained at nearly full strength. It would be more than a match for Niathal and Daala—especially under the capable command of Gavin Darklighter.

Not being privy to Alliance military plans—or to the level of Darklighter's commitment to his Darth-in-chief—Han had no idea how long it would take the Fourth to arrive. But he knew that once it did, getting through to extract Jaina would be impossible, even for him.

And he wasn't about to let that happen. He was already so frightened for her that he could feel his heart shaking—and so sad about her mission that he hadn't eaten anything but nutripills in a week. The thought of letting her be trapped down there after she finished her mission was more than he could bear . . . and he didn't need the Force to know he wasn't the only one who felt that way.

Han opened a channel to the squadron's number two blastboat. "Jag, you there?"

"This is Dry Ice, receiving you crisp and clean," came Jagged Fel's always proper reply. "Proceed."

"We're going in," Han said. "You coming?"

Before Jag could reply, Leia's voice came over the cockpit speaker. "Going in *where*, Han?"

"You know where," Han replied.

"But she hasn't sent the extraction code," Leia objected. "We don't even know which rendezvous point."

"And if we wait to find out, it won't matter," Han replied. "Unless you can think of some way to convince Niathal and Daala to stop spooking the Imperials until we're finished here."

Leia was silent for a moment, then said, "Okay, maybe you have a point."

"It would seem so," Jag said. "We'll join you at Extraction Point Alpha and hope for the best."

A string of cannon bolts appeared out of empty space and came straight for the canopy. Han did not even check the tactical display to see where the attack had come from; he simply jerked the yoke up to the left—then, as their belly armor pinged with hits, cringed and wondered what was taking Luke so long to bring the backup shield generators online.

A pair of laser beams flashed past from *behind* the blastboat, so close to the canopy that Han felt their heat on his face. Then Fett's voice sounded over the comm speaker.

"*Right,* you crazy barve!" Another pair of beams flashed past from behind, this time not quite so close to the canopy. "Who goes left?"

Han jinked to the right, then saw two sets of twin circles flash past as Fett and his wingmate rushed ahead to engage the blastboat's attacker.

"I never did like having that guy on my tail." Han was juking and jinking so hard that he had not even noticed that the belly turrets had gone quiet. "Hey, Saba, you okay down there?"

"Okay? How can this one be *okay*?" She sounded more angry than hurt. "You are letting him steal our kill!"

"I wouldn't worry about it, Master Sebatyne," Leia said. "This looks like a pack hunt to me."

With Fett and his wingmate now taking the brunt of the attack, Han finally had a chance to glance down and see what had opened up on them. The tactical display showed a *Cutlass*-class corvette coming out to block their approach.

"Where'd *he* come from?" Han demanded.

"I believe he came from under the frigate," C-3PO said.

"There may be more Remnant vessels lurking back there—it might be wise to wait for support from Admirals Daala and Niathal."

"And let Buckethead beat us to the asteroid?" Han pushed the throttles to the overload stops, trying to keep up with the *Bes'uliike*. "No way."

Boiling puffs of color began to flower ahead as the corvette opened up with its entire bank of bantam turbolasers. Han swung the yoke hard left, easy right, then slammed it forward—diving straight toward a cloud of red flame that had blossomed a few centiseconds before.

"Captain Solo," C-3PO began, "have you forgotten that our shields—"

"*No.*" Han was already rolling away from the fireball. "And don't tell me the odds, either."

"There really wouldn't be a point," C-3PO replied. "Without functional shields, our chances of reaching the asteroid's surface are too small to calculate."

A triangle of turbolaser strikes blossomed ahead, and Han finally recognized the firing pattern as a RandoCluster Three. While it was impossible to guess where the next volley would erupt, the pattern was actually one of the easiest to penetrate. All you had to do was be lucky.

Han took them through the center of the fiery triangle and saw the white frown of a *Cutlass*-class prow pumping streaks of blazing color in their direction. Two pairs of blue disks—all that was visible of the two *Bes'uliike* Fett and his wingmate were flying—were swinging back and forth along the upper edge of the cockpit canopy, pouring dashes of blue light back toward the corvette.

"Hey, Luke—how about those shields?" Han called back.

There was no answer, and the shield lights on Han's status panel remained dead red.

"Luke?"

The only answer came from R2-D2, a confused whistle, followed by a long descending tweedle.

"Oh dear," C-3PO said. "It seems Master Skywalker is no longer with us."

"*What?*" Han's heart clenched so tight it seemed to stop beating, but he kept his gaze fixed on the rapidly growing corvette. "How? Our hull hasn't even been breached!"

The upper cannon turret fell silent, and Leia called down, "Not *dead,* Han. He's in a . . ." She paused, searching for the word, then finally explained, "I don't know how to explain it. Luke's just sort of . . . gone."

"*Sort* of gone?" Han echoed. He couldn't help himself—he had to look. "How can you be . . ."

Han let his sentence trail away, for Luke *was* sort of gone. His body remained strapped into his seat, with his hands resting on the systems console and his gaze fixed between the shield status display and the targeting screen. But it was like looking at one of those figures in the House of Plastex back on Coruscant. Luke wasn't breathing, he wasn't moving, he wasn't even blinking; he just wasn't *there.*

"Great." When Han looked forward again, it was to see that the corvette's beam-spewing arch had grown as long as his arm. He transferred missile control to the pilot's station and sent four concussion missiles streaming toward its bridge. "*Now* he decides to take some time for himself."

Caedus deactivated his crimson blade, leaving a blackened hole where the red helmet's eye plate had been just a moment before. The Strategic Planning Forum had fallen blissfully still. The Mandalorians were dead or close to it, the sniper had retreated into the projection booth to reload and regroup, and the Moffs were crouching in the seat rows, too shocked and confused to start bellowing orders that were sure to prove worse than useless.

Only the two Elite Guard stormtroopers who had survived the Mandalorian onslaught seemed to realize that the
battle had not ended. The pair were kneeling opposite each
other in the second row of seats, silently slipping thermal
detonators into the grenade launchers they had affixed to
their blaster muzzles. *This* sniper would not be killed so
easily, but in the time it would take to tell them that, they
would learn it for themselves.

Caedus started toward the Moffs, treading on armored
bodies and ruined seating with equal disregard. He could
see already that his plan had worked beautifully. Several of
the Moffs who had been speaking against him—including
those fools, young Voryam Bhao and flabby-necked Krom
Rethway—lay sprawled across the battle-chewed seats
with open eyes and smoking wounds. The rest were peering at Caedus with expressions ranging from awe to grati-
tude to shrewd comprehension.

As Caedus neared the bottom row of seats, the
stormtroopers raised their weapons and sent their detonators flying toward the sniper's hiding place with the charac-
teristic grenade launcher *whumpf*s. Their aim was true,
and both orbs shot straight into the booth's projection
aperture—then came flying back out toward the shocked
troopers and astonished Moffs.

Caedus was ready. He caught both detonators with the
Force . . . then had to close his eyes as two crackling balls of
white erupted above him. The air filled with the acrid stench
of disintegrated stone and vaporized durasteel, and the pop
and sizzle of electrical short circuits began to sputter through
a two-meter circle that had been melted through the booth
wall. Several Moffs turned and quickly opened fire into the
hole.

"No." Caedus used the Force to make himself heard
over the scream of their blasters. He motioned at the
stormtrooper survivors. "You two, secure the Moffs in the
anteroom. I'll handle the sniper personally."

"Personally?" Moff Westermal asked in his deep, refined voice. "Are you sure that's wise, Lord Caedus? You're already injured."

"Kosimo makes a good point," Lecersen added. "Let the Elite Guard deal with the sniper. The rest of the company will be here any moment."

"My injuries are of no concern," Caedus said, trying not to smile. They had called him *Lord* Caedus; a New Empire was at hand. "And the Elite Guard won't be arriving in time. I'm afraid the Mandalorians sealed this section of the command warren before their attack."

Caedus waved the Moffs up toward the anteroom, then turned back to the projection booth to see the muzzle of a pellet accelerator pushing through a makeshift firing port, which the sniper had cut through the projectionist's blaster-scorched viewing pane. He managed to raise the arm on his injured side in the weapon's general direction, then reached out with the Force and made a twisting motion with his hand. The barrel trembled for an instant, then started to bend against the edge of the firing port.

The sniper was not surprised. The weapon simply spun free as it was abruptly released, and the *snap-hiss* of an igniting lightsaber sounded from inside the projection booth. Despite the pellet wound his shoulder had suffered earlier, Caedus did not hesitate to activate his own blade. His pain would only fuel his power, and if he did not attack the sniper, he knew the sniper would attack *him*. He Force-leapt up through the hole into the smoky, flashing interior of the booth and pivoted around to block the fan of blue light that came slicing toward his neck even before he could sense who he was fighting.

Whoever it was, the enemy was *good*.

Caedus felt a boot slam into his ribs—an instant *before* he saw it coming with his Aing-Tii fighting-sight—and the breath left his lungs. He countered with a head-high backslash and brought his own foot up, landing a Force-enhanced snap-kick between the legs of the brown-robed blur attacking him. The blow drew a pained grunt but failed to even stagger his foe.

A bony elbow slammed up under his chin, rocking him onto his heels. Then, finally, Caedus felt a familiar tingle in the back of his mind, and he saw the image of a violet blade slashing at his vulnerable side. He swept his own lightsaber down across the front of his body in a desperate reverse block that barely caught the attack in time to prevent it from slicing him in two, then whirled into a spinning back kick that landed squarely in his foe's stomach and drove him back . . . a mere two steps.

It was enough.

Now Caedus could see who he was fighting, and he could not believe it. A gaunt-faced man with eyes as blue and cold as vardium steel, nostrils flaring red with anger and exertion, a thin-lipped snarl filled with confidence and disdain.

Luke Skywalker.

Just a few minutes earlier, Caedus had sensed his uncle's presence far above Nickel One, in the same blastboat as his mother, father, and Saba Sebatyne. And now here Luke was, *inside* the asteroid. Even Jedi Grand Masters could not be in two places at once—Caedus *knew* that—but he did not waste time being confused.

All that mattered was that Luke *was* here, somehow, and that he was the one swordsman in the galaxy whom Caedus did not dare fight one-armed. Even as Luke leapt forward weaving a basket of lightsaber slashes, Caedus sprang back out of the projection booth, launching himself into a high Force flip designed to put as much distance between himself and his attacker as possible.

Luke flew after him, not even bothering to try for the high position, simply coming up under him with a wild slash combination that was anything but subtle or deft or even tricky; just pure relentless ferocity. Caedus had to stretch himself out belly-down in midair to meet the attack, and even calling on the Force to bolster the strength in his good arm, it was all he could do to keep the powerful strikes from knocking his guard aside and leaving him wide open.

They started to drop, trading a trio of lightning-fast blows that left Caedus's hands stinging and his heart racing. The last time he had fought Luke, he had started with a painful kidney wound but two good arms—and barely managed to survive. Now, with a relatively bearable shoulder wound and a single good arm, he had to do more than survive, he had to prevail—because now there would be no mercy at the last minute. This time, his uncle would not care whether *he* survived as long as *Caedus* died, because now Luke knew the truth about who had killed his wife.

After the third exchange, Caedus and Luke came down in the seating area, two rows apart. Both landed on their feet, Luke more lightly than Caedus.

Caedus deactivated his lightsaber and flicked his hand downward, arming the dart thrower he had begun wearing beneath his sleeve after their last fight.

But Luke did something even more unexpected, removing one hand from his lightsaber and pushing the palm forward. An instant later, the unseen hammer of a Force blast caught Caedus in the sternum and drove him not over, but *through* the seats behind him.

He slammed into the next row and dropped to the floor foot-to-foot with the big Mandalorian he had killed earlier—the one in the black armor and red helmet. Caedus's head was spinning and his chest was more than aching—it was throbbing, burning, clenching so tightly he could hardly breathe.

But he still had his lightsaber—and he needed it. He

thumbed the activation switch and brought the weapon up just as Luke's blue blade came slicing down toward him. Caedus caught it on his own crimson blade, then straightened his arm, simultaneously parrying and pointing the dart thrower on his wrist into his attacker's face.

"Release!" he commanded.

A faint puff of air tickled Caedus's forearm as the thrower launched its darts, but Luke was already whirling out of the way. The slivers streaked past in a harmless black flash and vanished; then Luke was spinning into the row where Caedus lay, positioning himself above Caedus's head for the coup de grâce.

There was no time to leap up or loose a bolt of Force lightning, and the angle was particularly poor for blocking and parrying. Caedus's only hope lay at his feet, and he seized that hope with the Force, using it to pull the dead Mandalorian up over him, then hurling the corpse headlong into Luke.

Two bodies collided with the sharp crack of metal impacting bone. When Caedus did not die in the next instant, he realized he had finally driven his uncle onto the defensive. He rolled to a knee, his lightsaber ignited and raised between them.

Luke lay buried beneath the huge Mandalorian, blood pooling around his head and one motionless arm protruding beneath the fellow's side. By all appearances, Luke Skywalker was dead—or at least unconscious.

Caedus's heart began to pound not with fear, but with excitement. His visions of late had been filled with his uncle's face—Luke Skywalker attacking him here on Nickel One, Luke firing on him from one of Fett's *Bes'uliike*, Luke sitting on *Caedus's* throne, claiming the New Empire as his own. Had he—Lord Caedus—finally put an end to those visions—finally ruled out the possibility of those futures becoming *the* future?

Eager as he was to be rid of Luke, Caedus was also suspicious. His uncle had been using a new fighting style, one that he had never taught his students at the Jedi academy—one that he had never, as far as Caedus knew, used on anyone who had survived to describe it. The style was essentially conservative, brutal, and ruthless, designed to deal damage without suffering it—and not all that tricky.

Which meant *now* would be the perfect time to switch styles and trap an unwary opponent by playing dead. Using the Force to keep the Mandalorian pressed firmly down on Luke, Caedus retreated twenty paces to the body of a fallen stormtrooper, then deactivated his lightsaber and tucked it under his wounded arm. When Luke still did not move, he pulled a fragmentation grenade off the trooper's equipment belt. He thumbed the arming slide, then sent the grenade sailing toward his uncle and the dead Mandalorian.

Despite the ringing in her ears and the gauze in her head—despite her hugely aching skull and the big knot of *hurt* swelling on her brow—Jaina had never been so filled with the Force. She could feel it in every cell of her body, swirling through her like fire, burning more ferociously every moment. She had never felt so strong or so quick or so alert. She could drive her fist through a durasteel wall, or catch a blaster bolt between her fingers. Despite the red curtain of blood cascading from the gash where Vatok's helmet had split her forehead, she was aware of *everything*.

Including that grenade sailing toward her.

So Jaina reached out with the Force and sent it flying back toward her brother. An instant later, the weight pressing down on her grew lighter as Caedus's attention shifted to the grenade. She started to Force-hurl her friend's body off—then recalled how her brother had been anticipating her attacks. She grabbed the *beskad* hanging from Vatok's waist, *then* sent his body flying after the grenade.

The iron saber had barely cleared its scabbard before the

hammerfist of a grenade detonation jolted the forum. Vatok's body was silhouetted against the orange flash of the explosion. Jaina held him there, shielding herself from the fiery heat of the blast, and felt the searing bite of shrapnel only in her legs.

The detonation swept the last wisps of gauze from Jaina's mind. Not waiting to see if she had been seriously injured, she let her friend's body drop to the floor and leapt after her brother, lightsaber in one hand and Vatok's *beskad* in the other.

Caedus turned to meet her with his good arm forward and his wounded shoulder behind. Jaina struck high with the lightsaber and low with the *beskad*. Caedus slipped back, allowing both blades to pass, then sprang forward and counterthrust, trying to impale her with her own momentum.

Jaina was already spinning past his crimson blade, pivoting on a dead stormtrooper's chest plate as she brought Vatok's *beskad* around at neck height. But Caedus had anticipated her once again, leaning away to take the blow on his wounded shoulder rather than across his throat.

Jaina did not even feel the *beskad* cleaving bone. She simply heard a voice—*Jacen's* voice—cry out in shock and pain; then an arm landed on her boots. In the next instant Caedus was whirling away, screaming and flapping a red stump, and something hot and wet splashed across Jaina's face and throat and began to burn like acid.

A part of her—the part that had grown up with Jacen and trained with him on Yavin 4 and traded snowballs at Coruscant's polar playgrounds—was too horrified to act. That part wanted to stand paralyzed in shock, to pretend this was just some terrible nightmare from which she would shortly awaken. The other part—the part that had actually *asked* for this mission—knew what would happen if she let herself freeze.

Jaina launched herself after Caedus. The loss of an arm did not seem to faze him. He simply turned to meet her attack, his yellow eyes blazing with pain and fury, and their lightsabers met in a brilliant explosion of color. Jaina brought the *beskad* around again, striking low for his thigh . . . and knew she was in trouble when Caedus did not even try to block.

Caedus deactivated his lightsaber and let it drop between them. Jaina felt the *beskad* begin to bite, then her brother's palm sank deep into the pit of her stomach. In the next instant she was riding a bolt of Force lightning across the chamber, her muscles cramping, her teeth grinding, her ears roaring with the fiery sizzle of burning synapses.

A full second later, she slammed into a durasteel wall and felt a terrible popping in her ribs, then dropped to the floor, still holding her lightsaber and the *beskad*. The Force lightning had died away, but her muscles remained useless aching knots, and the stench of scorched flesh was so powerful she wanted to retch. Instead, she tried to rise—and succeeded only in sparking a dozen different kinds of pain.

Across the chamber, her brother was in little better shape. He sat slumped in a half-collapsed chair, his remaining hand clamped over the stump of his missing arm, his thigh wound dripping blood onto the floor. His yellow eyes were staring at Jaina more in confusion than rage, and his head was cocked as though he could not quite believe what he was seeing.

"*You?*" he gasped. "*Jaina?*"

Jaina managed to raise her throbbing head. It hurt— a lot—and her vision was starting to blur.

"I haven't changed *that* much, Jacen," she said. With her muscle control beginning to return, she pushed herself into a kneeling position. "And I hope you know how much this Sith nonsense is steaming Mom and Dad."

If Caedus heard her wisecrack, he did not show it. His yellow eyes began to dart around the chamber, searching for something Jaina did not understand—but maybe that was just because her head was throbbing so bad. The pain was beginning to muddle her thoughts.

Somehow, Caedus forced himself back to his feet. *That* would have been impressive—if it weren't so kriffing scary.

"Where's Luke?" he demanded.

"Right behind me," Jaina said, also standing. The effort sent pangs of anguish shooting through her lungs, and she realized she had a few broken ribs to go with the lightning scorch on her chest. She squinted in his direction, trying to keep him in focus so she could kill him. "Come over here, and I'll show you."

That brought Caedus's gaze snapping back toward her, and Jaina realized she might have overplayed her hand. She still had both arms, but the fact that her brother remained standing at all proved how much greater his Force powers were than her own. She tossed the *beskad* aside and summoned a fallen stormtrooper's power blaster to hand.

Then Jaina sensed someone watching her from the direction of the antechamber where the Moffs had fled. She looked up to find a pair of gray blurs dropping into firing positions in the doorways. She loosed a burst of suppression fire toward the two troopers, then Force-flipped up into the cover offered by the ruined projection booth, landing backward so she would be facing her enemy and in a position to defend herself.

Jaina's boots had not even touched the floor before the stormtroopers opened fire. She dropped the power blaster and used her lightsaber to deflect their bolts, angling them down toward her brother. If she kept him busy enough, he wouldn't be able to hurl another lightning attack her way. His lightsaber snapped to life and began to weave a crimson shield in front of him.

Then Jaina experienced an abrupt draining as her Force energies returned to their normal level. Suddenly she felt cold, tired, and in pain, and she barely had the strength to hold her lightsaber as it flicked back and forth, batting away blaster bolts. She retreated deeper into the projection booth, stumbling over combat debris that she normally would have sensed without any conscious thought. When she reached the wrecked control panel, she could finally drop behind cover.

Caedus's voice sounded out in the forum, still deep and booming and strong. "Not *her*! Skywalker is the dangerous one."

Skywalker?

Was Jaina beginning to hear things now, too? Or was Caedus beginning to imagine them?

The blasterfire shifted away from the projection booth and grew more erratic. Jaina poked her head up, peering over the scorched control panel through what remained of the projectionist's one-way viewport.

Her brother was limping up toward the anteroom, finally starting to look a little weak and dizzy himself. His good hand was still holding the stump of his severed arm. But his yellow eyes were round with fear and his brow was furrowed with anger, and he was looking toward the far corner of the chamber, which Jaina could not see from her vantage point.

"There, you fools!" he yelled. "Blast him!"

The two stormtroopers seemed to study the corner for a moment, then obediently opened fire again. Energy bolts quickly began to ricochet back into the seats, but whether they were being deflected by a lightsaber or merely bouncing off the walls was impossible to guess.

Jaina did not have the energy to investigate. She dropped back to her haunches and opened herself completely to the Force, drawing it into her exhausted, battered body from all sides. The muffled *crumph*s of door-breaker charges began to sound somewhere out in the forum as the rest of the Elite Guard began to blast their way into the battle area. She knew that her mission had just gone from difficult to impossible, but when was she ever going to get a better chance? Caedus was wounded and weak, and if she could just catch up to him, she might be able to finish him.

An urgent clatter began to build out in the forum as stormtroopers poured through the entrances they had just blasted open. Jaina rose and ignited her lightsaber, but before she could step back into the breach, she sensed a nervous insectoid presence studying her from the far end of the booth.

Jaina turned to look. The technician who had helped her earlier was poking his head through a melt hole in the rear wall.

"Jedi Solo, are you ready to depart?" the Verpine asked.

"Depart?" Jaina frowned; what a foolish idea. "Hardly. Caedus is still alive."

The Verpine nodded. "Yes, my hive mates report that he is being rushed to the infirmary," he said. "And *your* extraction team will meet you at SurfaceHatch TenCrater."

"Can't." Jaina shook her head, then nearly lost it as she tried to peer out into the forum and drew a volley of blasterfire. She whirled around and looked back toward the Verpine, who was crouching just outside the melt hole, trembling. "Can you get me into the infirmary?"

"*No!*" the Verpine replied. "You are too damaged to fight. I am worried you can't even make it to TenCrater on your own. I may have to carry you."

Jaina waved him off. She couldn't let Caedus regroup. She had already lost the advantage of surprise, and the one thing she knew for certain was that if she let him recover—

"Your extraction team is in a precarious position itself." The Verpine was having to yell to make himself heard above the blasterfire. "They insist you come *now.*"

Jaina felt her mother reaching out to her in the Force, calling her back. She could sense not only the fear her mother felt for her, but also the teeth-grinding terror of combat—and a certain sense of demand that carried with it the hard edge of an order.

Jaina sighed. She *had* promised the Council to obey orders. "Okay, okay." She made a dash—more of a stumble—for the exit. "Tell them we're coming!"

chapter ten

Ben could remember a time when his cell had been dark. That was how he knew his head was clearing. Most of the time, it seemed as though the illumination panel in the ceiling had always been on, that he had spent his whole life manacled to his durasteel bunk, that the only mental state he had ever experienced was a smoky delirium so nightmarish he never quite knew whether he was asleep or awake. He remembered blurry dreams in which he was visited by a glossy black droid—a tall, thin unit that looked like a scaled-down version of a YVH battle droid, with blue photoreceptors set in a gaunt, skull-like face. The droid—it had introduced itself as Double-Ex—was really curious, always asking questions about who had sent Ben, who had been with him, where he had come from.

The last question, Double-Ex had asked a lot. It wanted to know *that* more than anything, because it was desperate to discover the location of the secret Jedi base. And Ben was sure he never answered—not even with a lie—because the droid was always complaining about how stubborn Ben was, telling him that he was only hurting himself.

But it was Double-Ex who really did the hurting. The droid had an astonishing array of needles, probes, and electrodes hidden inside its fingers. Whenever Ben refused to answer, it would open one, jab him in the arm or thigh or bare chest with whatever tool was inside, then ask its question again, endlessly repeating the process with the eternal patience of a machine.

But how those sessions ended, Ben had no idea. He supposed he simply reached the limits of his physical tolerance and passed out. It would not have surprised him, though, to learn that Double-Ex simply depleted its batteries asking the same question over and over.

The one thing he knew for certain was that he had never revealed the location of the Jedi base. Jacen had taught him how to resist interrogation by placing a Force block inside his own mind, and that had been the first thing Ben had done when he awakened in a GAG cell. The rest of his captivity was a blur, but he remembered doing *that*.

The door hissed open, admitting a puff of air just warm enough to remind Ben how cold his cell was—especially lying manacled to his bunk wearing only his underclothes. He purposely did not raise his head or even turn to look; interrogator droids were programmed to identify the significance of such minor gestures, and he did not want to betray the hopefulness he felt now that he was alert.

But there was no hint of servomotor in the steps that approached his bunk, and the smell that came to his nose was too pleasant and feminine to be a droid's. Suddenly self-conscious about his near nakedness, Ben turned to look.

"Hello, Ben," Tahiri said.

She was dressed in the typical black GAG jumpsuit, but on her it somehow looked like so much *more*. It was tight in all the right places, with a satin sheen that highlighted the suppleness of her build. And she must have just come from a workout—or at least from somewhere a whole lot warmer than Ben's cell—because the front was open clear down to her solar plexus.

"How are you feeling?" she purred.

Ben quickly raised his gaze and saw that she looked far

healthier than she had when she had captured him. Her blond hair was full and silky, sweeping across her brow in a way that almost hid the three scars on her forehead, then dropping down to her shoulders in a wavy cascade. Her cheeks actually had some color in them, and her lips were full and red. Even her eyes, which had seemed so sunken and tired before, appeared larger and more animated.

When Ben failed to answer, Tahiri shot him a knowing half smile. "Sorry—I forgot. You're the man who tells us nothing."

She stepped over to his bunk, and Ben saw that she was carrying a canister of bacta salve in one hand—and a remote in the other.

"I actually admire that." She placed the bacta salve on the edge of his bunk, then displayed the remote. "I need to free one of your arms and legs so I can roll you on your side. You aren't going to make me use this, are you?"

Ben studied the remote and realized that it probably had an activator switch for the stun circuits in his manacles. "I guess that depends on what you do to me."

"He speaks." Tahiri smiled, then pressed a pair of buttons, and the locks on his left wrist and ankle clicked open. "Don't worry—it won't be anything you object to." She flicked her fingers at him. "On your side."

Ben rolled up on his side—and smothered a cry of pain as the pressure sores on his back pulled free of the bunk's sanisheet cover. The bunk settled as Tahiri sat on the edge and opened the canister of bacta salve, and he realized that there was a hint of musk to her odor—a *nice* hint, one that he found vaguely intoxicating, but not something he remembered smelling on her before. An instant later, he felt her fingertips on his shoulder, and ripples of warm relief began to radiate outward from where she was touching him.

"See?" Tahiri asked. "Not so bad."

"Except for the part where you caused them in the first

place," Ben said. He had to remind himself that she wasn't *really* being kind. "How long have you had me lying here?"

Tahiri moved to a different sore, then said, "I'll answer *your* question if you answer mine."

Ben sighed. "It was worth a try. Can you at least tell me if Captain Shevu is okay?"

"Same offer," Tahiri replied sweetly. "But I *am* sorry about these sores. They're not part of the program. We just can't afford to take chances with big, strong Jedi Knights." She ran her hand down his bare shoulder and biceps—and let it linger there. "I'm sure you understand."

"I guess." What Ben did not understand was what her hand was doing kneading the muscles on his arm. He didn't have any sores there—at least not that he could feel—but he didn't want her to stop, either. "You're making a mistake, you know."

Tahiri stopped kneading, and her fingers moved to a sore down near the middle of his back. "Oh?"

"You can't trust Jacen," he said. "He'll turn on you in the end—just like he turned on my parents and me."

Tahiri's touch grew a little more tense. "His name is Caedus now," she said. "*Darth* Caedus. And who says I trust him?"

"Then what are you doing with him?" Ben asked. "Don't tell me you think he's right?"

"What I think doesn't matter," Tahiri replied, "not any longer. We all make choices in our lives, Ben. You should have stuck with yours. You wouldn't be in the mess you're in—and this war might be over."

Her hand moved lower on Ben's back and began to work on a sore under the waistband of his shorts. He found her touch there a little disconcerting, but he didn't stop her. The sore did need to be dressed, after all.

Ben tried to focus on their conversation—on helping Tahiri see the mistake she was making. "Stick with the man who killed my mother? Have you been breathing coolant fumes?"

"Your mother *did* attack Lord Caedus first," Tahiri pointed out. "She threatened him in the lobby of the Senate."

"Because he's a *Sith*," Ben replied. "Because he was working with *Lumiya*."

"Whom your father murdered in cold blood," Tahiri replied. "I understand family loyalty, Ben—I even admire it. But you need to see that the Sith aren't necessarily the criminals here. Isn't that what a Jedi does? Weighs the facts objectively?"

"My father made a *mistake*," Ben protested. "You're twisting things around."

"Really?" Tahiri said. "Then why don't you enlighten me, Ben? I'm listening."

"Okay," Ben said. She sounded sincere, but he sensed a trap—and he *knew* that he wasn't going to persuade her on the basis of right and wrong. As far as he could tell, nobody in this war had any claim to the moral high ground. "Look, whatever it is you want—whatever it is that you think Jacen can give you—you're not going to get it."

"You're sure?" Tahiri asked. Her hand remained beneath the waistband of Ben's shorts, but began to drift up toward his hip. "What is it that I want, Ben?"

Now Ben was really beginning to have trouble concentrating. "Uh, Tahiri?"

Her hand reached his hip bone, and her fingers began to drift over. "Yes?"

"You wouldn't be trying to seduce me, would you?"

"Ben, that's a terrible thing to say." Tahiri's hand remained beneath the waistband of his shorts. "You're only fourteen. Still a boy, really." She lifted her finger, raising the waistband. "Aren't you?"

"I'm a Jedi Knight," Ben countered. He twisted his hip,

trying to pull it out from beneath her hand—and failing. "And I don't have any pressure sores up *there*."

"So you don't." Tahiri used a fingertip to trace a circle on his flesh. "Okay, let's say I *am* trying to seduce you. You have to admit it's a lot nicer way than torture to, um, *inquire* about the coordinates of the Jedi base."

"Yeah, I'd have to agree with *that*."

"So?" Tahiri slid her hand down his hip. "What do you think? Could it work?"

Ben closed his eyes. He truly *wanted* to say yes—and not just for the obvious reasons. He was really, *really* tired of being tortured, and he knew as well as anyone that all those truth drugs Double-Ex kept pumping into him were not doing his brain any good. There was every chance that, sooner or later, the droid would miscalculate a dose, or push an ear probe in a little too deep, or fail to notice the pool of sweat he was lying in when it jacked up the electroshocker, and he would die.

And the possibility that he wouldn't die—that he would remain rotting on his bunk until his body was one big pressure sore—was even worse. Faced with those choices, who wouldn't want to say yes to an attractive older woman? Who could resist, when he knew that this very well might be the only chance he was *ever* going to have to say yes?

There was just one little problem: Tahiri was a *Sith*. Saying yes meant betraying himself—embracing the very destiny that *Jacen* had tried to thrust upon him.

And Ben was not going to do that. Not ever. He opened his eyes and looked over his shoulder toward Tahiri.

"You're too nice to be a Sith," he said. "They *enjoy* torture."

Tahiri let out her breath. "I'm learning, Ben." She grabbed the waistband of his shorts and stretched it outward as far as it would go. "Just remember I *tried*. Whatever happens next, it's on you."

Tahiri let the band snap back—directly atop a pressure

sore on Ben's back. His mouth opened in pain, but he did not scream—he wouldn't give her that, either. He also resisted the temptation to whirl on her. Whatever she had wanted him to believe, he knew that she hadn't come alone—she would not have given him even that small chance of escape. So he remained facing the wall, waiting for the needle jab or electric shock or the blow to the head that would send him sinking back into oblivion.

Instead, the locks on Ben's remaining two manacles clicked open and a set of fluorescent green overalls came flying at him.

"Put that on," Tahiri ordered. "I'm tired of looking at those disgusting sores."

Ben rolled around and saw a pair of black-armored GAG troopers standing in his cell door, both wearing full face visors and pointing riot-class stun rifles in his direction. Tahiri was still beside him, standing now, her uniform closed to the throat and a lightsaber in her hand.

"You guys know this isn't going to work, don't you?" Ben asked, pushing his legs into the green suit. "If your torture droid couldn't crack me, *you* aren't going to."

The two guards glanced at each other, then one said, "Lieutenant, GAG doesn't *use* torture droids." Ben recognized his voice as that of Corporal Wyrlan, who had been on the raid with him when he had killed his first man. "You know that."

Ben frowned. He could sense through the Force that Wyrlan thought he was telling the truth, but his memories of Double-Ex were too consistent—and too detailed—to be hallucinations.

"The traitor is a prisoner, not a *lieutenant*," Tahiri said. As she spoke, she was careful to keep her attention fixed on Ben. "And guards do not discuss hallucinations, or anything else, with prisoners—especially *Jedi* prisoners. Is that clear?"

Wyrlan straightened. "Yes, ma'am. Sorry, ma'am."

"I don't need your apology," Tahiri said. "I'm telling you for your own good. The prisoner comes from a family of assassins and murderers. If you relax around him, he *will* kill you."

"I understand, ma'am," Wyrlan replied. "Thank you."

"My pleasure, Corporal." Tahiri smiled in his direction. "Lord Caedus can't afford to lose good men like you. GAG has too few as it is."

Tahiri waited for Ben to finish putting on his fluorescent green prisoner suit, then had Wyrlan secure him in shock shackles and stun cuffs. After testing her remote by dropping Ben to his knees with a powerful electric shock, she finally motioned him through the cell door.

Outside, Ben found himself standing on a mesh catwalk flanked by long rows of dimly lit cells with front walls of one-way transparisteel. Inside each cell, a single Bothan—shaved completely furless—sat or lay on a durasteel bunk, staring at the floor or ceiling or wall with an expression utterly devoid of hope. Many of the prisoners were missing body parts—mostly eyes, ears, and limbs—and some had fresh scars that suggested recent combat.

"The Bothan assassins," Tahiri explained. "They just keep coming—sometimes dozens a day. Darth Caedus had to open an entire wing just for them."

"You mean he doesn't just execute them?" Ben asked, surprised.

"Oh, he will," Tahiri said. "But he doesn't want to do anything that might detract from Admiral Bwua'tu's concentration right now. After we win the war, they'll all have a fair trial before the Special Tribunal on Bothan War Crimes. Then they'll all be properly sentenced to death."

Ben glanced around, awed by the immensity of the cellblock. It was easily two hundred meters long, with a cell every two meters. And when he looked through the mesh catwalks above and below him, he could see at least nine more levels.

"There must be a thousand units here," Ben said.

Tahiri nodded. "More—and Caedus has already ordered another wing to be prepared. But enough stalling. We have our own unpleasantness to attend to."

She took his arm—more to control than to guide him—and started down the catwalk toward the glowing white square of a security booth. Despite the pale glow coming from the cells, the prison was a silent and gloomy place. Every surface was coated in a gray, sound-absorbing synthalex, and the only illumination on the catwalk came from overhead glowstrips that automatically activated and deactivated as they passed.

Ben did not even consider trying to break free . . . yet. He still needed to find out what had happened to Lon Shevu, and Tahiri seemed to be moving him into a less secure area. So it seemed smarter to wait and learn as much about his situation as possible. They were probably somewhere deep in Coruscant's Galactic Justice Center, but in a part of the facility he had never visited before—a part, truth be told, that he had never even imagined existed.

They reached the security checkpoint at the end of the cellblock. Then they passed through a series of air locks and scanner chambers and entered a white-tiled processing tunnel so rife with disinfectant that Ben's eyes began to water. About a dozen Bothan assassins lay magclamped to hovergurneys, being scanned for evidence, sampled, shaved furless, and—finally—implanted with explosive locator chips that could be remotely detonated in the event of escape. All of this was being done under the watchful eye of a dozen YVH battle droids overseen by an equal number of heavily armed GAG guards.

When Tahiri noticed Ben's gaze lingering on the MD droid at the implanting station, she flipped her remote in front of his eyes—no doubt trying to prevent him from seeing *where* the chip was being inserted. Almost any Jedi would be able to locate and disable such a chip using little more than the Force and meditation—but knowing where to look would make the meditation unnecessary.

"Yes, you have one, too," Tahiri said. "So don't even think about trying to escape."

"Thanks for the warning." Ben shook the chains hanging from his manacles. "I was just getting ready to make a run for it."

"Funny boy." Tahiri thumbed a button on the remote, sending a jolt of electricity through Ben's ankle that dropped him to a knee. "Ha, ha."

Ben glanced behind Tahiri's knees and saw the MD withdrawing an injection hypo from beneath the Bothan's shoulder blade.

"I liked it better when you were trying to seduce the coordinates out of me," he said.

"Yes—pity *that* didn't work," Tahiri said. "Now we have to do it Lord Caedus's way."

She jerked him back to his feet. They went through another security checkpoint at the far end of the processing tunnel, then started down a long corridor. Along one side, a similar checkpoint was spaced every fifteen meters or so; along the other side ran a panel of waist-to-ceiling transparisteel. Through this viewing wall, Ben could see that the hall was actually a balcony. It overlooked a receiving area filled with special security bays, where guards were removing prisoners from GAG Doomsleds and sorting them into groups for final processing. Each bay had its own durasteel blast doors, which opened into a contained marshaling garage. In short, this looked like a pretty unlikely escape route to Ben.

As they approached the end of the corridor, Ben began to sense a lot of beings ahead—and beings in pain. No doubt he was being taken into a specialized torture wing. His mouth grew dry, and he began to think that maybe the receiving area wasn't such a bad place to try an escape after all—except that he still didn't know what had happened to Shevu.

Then a terrible thought occurred to him. He reached out into the Force and felt his friend's presence, no more than fifty meters inside the cellblock. Of course, that might be exactly what Tahiri wanted him to do—so that she could use Shevu as leverage against Ben. It didn't matter. Now Ben *had* to go in.

As they passed through the next checkpoint, Ben began to realize that something wasn't quite right with the picture he had been painting in his mind. The security here was not as tight as in the Bothan Wing, and he could sense through the Force that the booth guards were too relaxed for a high-security area. The scanning chambers were almost three meters square as well, as though they were used to transfer cargo or large loads.

When the final air lock opened, the atmosphere grew thick with the singular blend of stericlean and bodily infection, and Ben *knew*. He had smelled that particular combination too many times before, in too many infirmaries, after too many battles. He turned to Tahiri, his anger already rising into his throat.

"How long has he been in here?" he demanded. "His injuries weren't that bad."

"There were . . . complications," Tahiri said. She started them toward the ward where Shevu lay, staying close to the doors to avoid interrupting the steady stream of droid-orderlies ferrying medicines, supplies, and patients down the corridor. "But he stands a good chance of surviving, depending on you."

"Me?"

"Of course." They reached the doorway, and Tahiri turned to look at him. "I'm sorry—are you under the impression I brought you here because I'm too *nice* to be a Sith?"

Ben would have Force-hurled her into the nearest wall,

except he was pretty sure she would have blocked him and had the two guards stun him unconscious. Instead, he said, "You're learning."

Tahiri smiled and placed her thumb over the security pad on the wall. The doors hissed open, revealing a small four-unit ward. Three of the beds lay empty, with their lowered security panels forming a transparent apron around the base. The fourth bed was fully enclosed, with an ashen-faced man barely recognizable as Lon Shevu sleeping half naked inside. The blaster burns on his torso looked about half healed, but his arms and fingers were mottled with fresh bruises, scorch circles, and other signs of torture.

Ben was so astonished that he stopped halfway into the room and said, "There was no reason to do this. Shevu doesn't know anything about our operations."

Tahiri shrugged, closing and locking the door behind them. "It always pays to be thorough. Traitors are everywhere." She started toward the MD droid standing watch at Shevu's bedside, then stopped and turned back to Ben. "Of course, nobody knows that better than you."

Ben tore his gaze away from Shevu. "Eventually, we all betray something, Tahiri. It's what you stay true to that counts."

Tahiri's thumb started to slip toward the shock button on the remote—then she frowned and stopped, probably hearing Caedus's voice inside her head admonishing her to be the master of her emotions, not their servant. She turned without speaking and went over to the MD droid monitoring Shevu's vital signs.

"How's the prisoner?" she asked.

"Prisoner Nine-Zero-Three-Two-Bee-Tee is recovering as scheduled," the droid reported. "He should be ready to resume interrogation tomorrow morning, assuming his electrolytes stabilize."

"I'm afraid we'll have to move that up." Tahiri glanced

over at Ben, then added, "There have been some developments that require a more aggressive approach."

"I can't authorize that," the droid said. "With his electrolytes so far out of balance, a substantial physical stress of that kind is likely to induce myocardial infarction."

"You mean his heart might fail?" Tahiri turned to Ben. "What do you think, Ben? Do we need to risk a myocardial infarction?"

"There wouldn't be any use in it." Ben glanced around the room, looking for something he could use to disable Tahiri before she continued, but objects that could be hurled at a guard did not tend to be left lying around in prison infirmaries. He found only a large swinging panel labeled BIOWASTE PROCESSING, and even that would have to be ripped from its hinges first. "I won't tell you where our base is."

Tahiri sighed. "I was afraid you'd say that." She glanced at the guards behind him, and Ben's back began to prickle with danger sense. "It appears we'll have to do this the hard—"

Ben was already spinning to defend himself, but he never heard the final *way*. His body simply erupted into one huge cramp as both guards fired their stun rifles and Tahiri triggered his stun cuffs, and he felt himself falling into a white, electric fire.

When Ben finally stopped falling, he found himself chained into a heavy hoverchair—one of those he had seen the droid-orderlies using to move invalids through the corridor. Shevu was lying across from him, still strapped into his bed, but with the security panel lowered. The MD was standing at one corner of the bed. The droid's lack of attention to Shevu's monitor suggested it had been relieved of responsibility for the prisoner's welfare.

"Good," Tahiri said. "Now that we're all here and awake, perhaps you'd care to say hello to your spy, Ben?"

Shevu's eyes snapped open, and his head turned toward the center of the ward. "Ben?"

"Right here, Captain," Ben said. "I'm sorry—I didn't think they'd be watching you. Someone must have—"

"Ben, don't. We're soldiers." Shevu's gaze slid to Ben. His eyes were glassy with pain and confusion, but there was also something more—forgiveness, perhaps, and . . . could it be pride? "You haven't told them anything, have you?"

Ben shook his head. "Nothing."

Shevu's cracked lips formed a smile. "Good man." He glanced over at Tahiri. His expression changed to one of loathing, and the bed frame clanged harshly as his arm hit the end of its restraint. "Keep it that way. No matter what this little—"

"That's enough." Tahiri made a gesture with her finger, and Shevu's mouth clamped shut so hard that his teeth clacked. She patted him lightly on the cheek, then turned to Ben. "Let me tell you how this is going to work, Jedi Skywalker."

"It *isn't* going to work," Ben retorted. "I wouldn't betray the entire Order to save one man."

"No?" Tahiri shook her head, then reached into Shevu's bed and placed her thumb over his eye. "I can't tell you how much I hope you really don't mean that."

She began to push, and Shevu's mouth opened in an involuntary scream. His pulse rate shot up, and several of the waves crawling across the monitor above his bed oscillated wildly and erratically. Ben's guts began to tie themselves into cold, greasy knots, and he reached out with the Force, trying to pull Tahiri's hand away.

She fought him, at the same time depressing a button on the remote in her free hand. Four liquid jolts of pain shot through Ben's limbs and met in a burning collision inside his chest, and his concentration crumbled away in cinders. Shevu's arms and legs began to flutter against his restraints, and Tahiri said, "There's only one way you're going to stop this, Ben. How much pain are you willing to cause your friend?"

"A lot less than I'm willing to cause you," Ben replied.

Tahiri looked genuinely hurt. "I'm sorry to hear that."

Ben's stomach was clutching so hard that he thought he might throw up. He knew that he could not give Tahiri what she wanted—no matter *what* she did to Shevu. But how could he let her continue? She was doing more than just causing pain—she was blinding him.

And then Ben heard it, recognized that Shevu wasn't just screaming, that he was yelling one long word: *qquuuuieeeet!*

Ben clenched his jaw tight, then reached out again with the Force. This time, however, he was contacting not Tahiri but Shevu, pouring soothing energies toward him, touching his mind with soft suggestions of unconsciousness. As Shevu's screams grew a little less frenzied, Tahiri pulled her hand away and frowned at the MD droid. "What's wrong?" she asked. "You told me he was completely awake."

The droid studied Shevu's vital signs, which were oscillating more wildly than ever, then replied, "The prisoner is as conscious as medical stimulants can make him. He has simply grown accustomed to the pain you are inflicting on him. That's the only reasonable hypothesis."

"Not the *only* one," Tahiri said, looking to Ben.

Ben shook his head. "I don't know what you're talking about."

"You're lying, Ben." Tahiri raised her hand, and tiny forks of Force lightning began to dance on her fingertips. "I don't think your mother would have approved."

Before Ben could respond, she moved her hand over one of the half-healed blaster burns on Shevu's torso, then released a blue bolt of Force energy.

The monitor broke into an unreadable scribble of oscillating colors, and a long, hoarse rattle poured from Shevu's mouth. Half a dozen different alarms began to beep and chime from the monitor, then all the lines went flat.

The MD droid cocked its head, studying Shevu's vital signs for a moment, then announced, "Prisoner Nine-Zero-Three-Two-Bee-Tee has expired."

Tahiri stepped away from the bed looking as shocked and dismayed as Ben felt. "Do something!" she ordered the MD. "Revive him."

The droid obediently stepped to the bedside and extruded a long needle from its index finger, which it jabbed into Shevu's heart. When the lines on the monitor did not even blip, the droid clamped a breathing bag onto Shevu's face with one metal hand and pressed the other over the heart, then began mechanical efforts to keep both air and blood circulating.

But Ben already knew that the droid's efforts were going to fail. Tahiri couldn't use a dead man to coerce someone into telling her anything, and Ben knew his friend well enough to realize that Shevu would rather die than be used to help Darth Caedus secure his hold on power. So when Tahiri pushed things a little too far, Shevu simply let go of living.

"Stop it," Ben said. He couldn't bear to watch Shevu being abused any longer. "You can't bring him back. This is just beating up the body."

Tahiri glowered at him. "You can tell that from over there, Ben?"

The MD stopped working. "The prisoner is correct," it said. "Magnetic imaging confirms that Prisoner Nine-Zero-Three-Two-Bee-Tee suffered a stress rupture of the aorta."

Tahiri's jaw fell, and her Force-aura grew cold with horror, and that was when Ben knew she did not like what she was becoming, that she was serving Caedus for the same reasons Ben himself had followed Jacen so long—because she was confused and ashamed and desperate. She could not allow herself to see what a monster Caedus had become because that meant seeing what a monster *she* was becoming, too.

But none of that made any difference to Shevu now. And it was going to make even less difference to his wife, Shula, whom he had married just a couple of months earlier— then promptly sent home to Vaklin because he had *known* that something like this was going to happen.

"You should be proud, Tahiri. Now you're just like your Master." Ben was saying this not only because he was angry, but because it was true—and because if he could make Tahiri see just *how* true, then maybe she would come to her senses. "Jacen tortured Ailyn Vel to death, and now you've done it to Shevu. I guess you *are* a Sith."

To Ben's surprise, Tahiri did not whirl on him. She did not even seem to see him. She merely stepped back, staring at the MD's feet and slowly shaking her head.

"You're wrong. *I* didn't kill him."

"The prisoner was already in a weakened condition," the MD said, neatly dodging the question. It pointed a finger at the security pad on the side of Shevu's bed, and the limb restraints clicked open. "If you won't be needing the body, I'll send it down for processing."

"*Processing?*" Ben didn't know what he had expected, but the thought of his friend being sold to a bioparts dealer turned his stomach—and filled him with a sick, hollow feeling that was half anger, half guilt. "You can't—"

"I can't *what*?" As Tahiri whirled on him, the MD was lifting Shevu from the bed. "This is *your* doing, Ben. All you had to do was answer one simple question."

She depressed a row of buttons on the remote, and Ben's entire body clenched in electric agony.

"Where is the Jedi base?" She stepped closer, cocking her arm to backhand him. "Answer me!"

Ben glanced over at Shevu, who was being carried toward the processing chute, and shook his head. "Sorry."

Tahiri brought her hand down across Ben's face, striking him so hard that it rocked the hoverchair—and that was her mistake. Ben threw his weight in the direction of the tilt, tipping the hoverchair over on its side. Simultaneously, he was Force-hurling Tahiri into the two confused guards standing at his back.

By the time the trio crashed into one of the empty beds behind him, Ben was already reaching out with the Force, depressing keys on Tahiri's remote. His leg shackles snapped open instantly, but he managed to shock his arms senseless before he finally hit the proper key and released the stun cuffs.

Ben rolled out of the chair and spun around to find his captors rapidly disentangling themselves. Tahiri was already reaching for her lightsaber, and one guard was swinging his stun rifle around to fire. Ben gave the barrel a Force shove, pushing the muzzle toward Tahiri just as a white bolt of electricity shot out.

Tahiri gave a strangled cry, then her eyes rolled back and she dropped to the floor, twitching and shuddering. Ben summoned Tahiri's lightsaber to hand, barely activating it in time to bat a bolt from the second guard's stun rifle into the MD droid—which was holding Shevu's body in front of the processing chute, apparently waiting for the guards to bring the prisoner under control before proceeding.

The bolt struck the droid over its primary processing unit, and it stumbled back into the wall and dropped to the floor with Shevu's limp body in its arms. Ben used the Force to rip the stun rifle from the first guard's grasp, at the same time leaping at the second one. He deflected another stun bolt, then brought the lightsaber down on the weapon's barrel and quickly snapped the blade back up to within a centimeter of the trooper's chin.

"I'd really rather not have to kill you both," Ben said. "But it's your choice—and I don't have a lot of time for you to decide."

"Not k-k-killing is fine, L-L-Lieutenant," Wyrlan answered. His helmet turned toward the other guard. "Right, Garsi?"

"Fine with me," Garsi said, raising his arms. "Thanks for the choice."

"Don't make me regret it," Ben warned. He glanced up at the corners of the room and noted that the status lights on all four of the security cams were dark. "How come those monitors aren't active?"

Wyrlan and Garsi turned their helmets toward each other, then Garsi said, "You saw what was going on in here. Would *you* want someone sneaking a holo of that to HNE?"

Ben considered this, recalling how Tahiri had locked the door behind them, and realized there was a very good chance that central security did not know he had just freed himself.

"I see your point." He motioned at the processing chute. "Would someone alive survive a trip through there?"

"Sure," Wyrlan said. "It's just a repulsor track that carries bodies down to the collection docks."

"But they have escape safeguards," Garsi warned. "It wouldn't be smart to try leaving that way."

"And *I* won't be," Ben said. He motioned at Tahiri. "Put her in the stun cuffs and drop her down the chute."

The two troopers obeyed, then Wyrlan motioned at Shevu's body. "What about him?"

"He's leaving with me," Ben said. "Take off your armor."

A LONG TIME AGO . . .

Jaina Solo and her brother Jacen are wandering through the shadowy halls beneath the Jedi academy on Yavin 4, keeping to the musty subterranean passages where no one else ever goes. They are fourteen, and they are walking because their friend Tenel Ka has just lost her arm in a lightsaber accident, and they have to do something, even if walking is all they can do. They are in pain, and they wish it could be the same pain their friend is feeling. Maybe if they could share it with her, it wouldn't seem so horrible. Maybe it would feel like things hadn't changed so much after all.

But Jaina knows that can't be true, because Uncle Luke has promised to call when Tenel Ka is ready to see her friends, and they have been walking for hours. Still, there has been no summons. They can only keep wandering, alone together, trying not to be overwhelmed by their shock and despair. And Jaina senses through their twin bond that Jacen has other, more painful emotions. He is filled with shame and self-loathing because it was his lightsaber that removed Tenel Ka's arm—because he was so intent on proving himself to her that he failed to notice when her blade blurred with static, and half a second later her arm was lying on the ground.

So Jacen has lost something, too. And all Jaina can do is walk with him, to let him know through their twin bond how she sees him: a kind, thoughtful young Jedi who would never hurt a friend deliberately—a brave, resourceful brother whom she would rather have at her side than anyone . . .

chapter eleven

What time is it when an Imperial walker steps on your chrono?
Time to get a new chrono!

—Jacen Solo, age 14

The stain ran across Jaina's jaw and neck down to her shoulder, a line of crimson ovals where she had been splattered by her brother's blood. She had tried to wash it off with soap and water, with surgical sanitizer, even with the enzobleach Hapan orderlies used to keep the *Loyal Dragon*'s infirmary spotless. Now she was using a Relephonian sarsestone, literally trying to scour the spots away—but she might as well have been trying to rub off a blaster scar. Her efforts only seemed to make the stain brighter and redder.

A soft hiss sounded behind Jaina, and in the mirror above her sink, she saw the privacy partition at the front of her convalescence bay sliding aside. Before she could put the sarsestone down, her mother was coming through the opening, her thin brows arching in surprise.

"What are you doing up?" Leia demanded. Her mouth was frowning with reproach, but her brown eyes were sparkling with relief. "You should be in a healing trance."

"I *have* been." Jaina set the sarsestone on the sink and began to rinse the grit off her hands. "For a week now, I think."

"Yeah, well you need another one—and maybe a whole

lot more," her father said, following Leia into the cramped bay. "Luke didn't look this bad after the wampa tried to eat him."

"Gee, thanks, Dad." Jaina shifted her gaze to her father's reflection and didn't think he looked much better. The lines in his brow had grown so deep that his face had gone from ruggedly handsome to haggard; the bags beneath his eyes were so big they belonged on a Yuuzhan Vong warrior, not Han Solo. "That's just what a woman standing in front of a mirror wants to hear."

"I'm your father." He slid the partition closed behind him. "It's my job to be honest."

"Okay, but do you have to be so good at it?"

Jaina smiled at his reflection, then wet a cloth and began to wipe the sarse grit off her neck. She couldn't remember much about her extraction—or the last half of the fight—because that big ugly split above her right eye had come with a nasty concussion. She had hazy memories of a long aching run on legs so filled with shrapnel they rattled, of always being short of breath because it was impossible to fully expand her lungs with four broken ribs.

The next thing she remembered was stumbling into the hangar with a company of stormtroopers on her tail, then Jag, Zekk, her mother, and about half a dozen other Jedi—okay, Jag wasn't a Jedi, but he had *fought* like one—coming out of nowhere to drive them off. And she recalled her uncle warning the others about her injuries as they rushed to help her, how he had seemed to know every blow she had taken without having to even glance in her direction.

But the thing she remembered most was the fear in her father's face as they loaded her aboard his blastboat, how his head had somehow seemed to turn around 180 degrees to look over the back of his seat—how the color had drained from his face at the sight of the blood oozing from her red-soaked robes.

"Sweetheart, you can't wash them off," Leia said. She had come to the sink without Jaina realizing it, and now she was standing at her side, reaching for the cloth. "They're burns."

"No." Jaina studied the little ovals in the mirror again. She could see why her mother might mistake them for spatter burns—they were certainly bright enough, and the edges were distinct—but her mother hadn't been there. She hadn't seen how those spots were made. "It'll come off. It's a bloodstain. *His* blood."

Jaina felt the bottom sink out of the Force, and her mother pulled the cloth away.

"Jaina, they'll fade as soon as we can get you into a bacta tank," Leia said, turning her back toward her bed. "And if they don't, we'll have the skin repaired."

"Mom, I'm *not* in battle shock," Jaina insisted. "It's blood! I got splattered when I cut off Ja—er, Caedus's arm."

"Okay, take it easy—we believe you." Han came around the bed, then took her arm and started her back toward it. "But it's not coming off. I'll ask Luke if he's got any special Sith-blood solvent."

"Sith-blood solvent?" Jaina allowed him to sit her on the bed. "Dad, please. I'm not inventing this. I *remember* getting splashed."

"Really?" This from her mother, whose doubtful tone suggested she was at least going to treat Jaina like a not-too-brain-addled adult. "It's interesting how you remember *that,* but not much else about the fight."

Jaina frowned. "You think he brain-rubbed me?"

Leia shook her head, then pointed at the wound on Jaina's throbbing brow. "I think *that* brain-rubbed you. It scrambled your memories, and you may not be remembering things exactly the way they happened."

"Like what?" Jaina asked.

Leia didn't even need to think before she answered. "Well, do you remember what happened with Jag and Zekk?"

Han bit his lip to keep from smiling, which only made Jaina frown harder.

"They helped with the extraction," Jaina said. "They both fought very well. I remember that."

"We're talking about later," her father said. "As they were loading you into the blastboat."

"I, uh . . ." Jaina paused, trying to grab hold of a hazy image floating at the edges of her memory—one of Zekk's big snowy smile, and Jag's durasteel eyes doing something they hardly ever did—widening in surprise. "I thanked them?"

"I guess you could call it that," her father said. He pulled a chair out from the wall beside her bed and dropped into it smirking. "You asked them to bunk with you."

"*Bunk* with me?" Jaina asked. "Both of them?"

"Well, what you really proposed was taking quarters together," Leia corrected. "All three of you."

Jaina caught the twinkle in their eyes and realized what they were trying to do. "Very funny, guys, but I'm serious." She tapped her throat. "These aren't burns."

"You think we're making this up?" her father asked.

"Of course," Jaina said. "You're running a classic Zeltron Shift—embarrass the spoilsport."

"We *could* be, except we're not," her mother said, chuckling. "See-Threepio filed the whole conversation in his memory. Do you want to hear it? He's right outside."

"That *won't* be necessary," Jaina said. Her parents were both great bluffers—which meant they never tried to pull one when calling it would be easy. She swung around and leaned against the headboard, then asked, "So . . . did they say yes?"

Her father's brow shot up, then he shook his head and

ran a hand down his chin. "You're not ready for that," he said. "You don't have the patience."

Jaina laughed and ran a finger over the spots on her neck. "If these are burns, how come they're not sore? And why isn't my skin dry?"

Her father closed his eyes in exasperation, but her mother said, "You *have* been in a healing trance, Jaina."

"Which means they would be healed by now," Jaina replied, "*if* they were burns."

Her father opened his eyes, then reached up and took her hand. "Look, it was a tough fight," he said. "And Luke's pretty sure you're remembering right about the arm. It's natural to feel a little guilty."

"I *don't* feel guilty," Jaina objected. She felt her mother's gaze on her, then realized she wasn't being entirely honest. "Not much, anyway—not enough to make me imagine things."

"Okay, we'll ask Cilghal to take a look," Leia said. "There could be another explanation."

"There is." Jaina could tell that her mother didn't believe another explanation was needed, but her reply was utterly reasonable—the kind designed to cut an unnecessary argument short. "The Force might be trying to tell me something."

Her father fidgeted and began to look more uncomfortable than ever. Her mother nodded as though she believed that were a possibility, then sat on the foot of her bed.

"Okay," Leia said. "Any ideas what that would be?"

"Maybe." Jaina didn't know how her parents were going to take this next part, because she wasn't sure how she felt about it herself—whether she was just looking for an easy way out of a dirty job she had left undone, or whether she had given up on her brother too soon when she decided to kill him. "I can't be sure that I'm remembering this right, but I wasn't the only one who was confused at the end of the fight. After I cut off his arm, Caedus seemed surprised that it was me."

"What?" Han asked. "He didn't think a girl could do it?"

"That's not what I mean," Jaina said. "He didn't seem to realize he had been fighting *me* until after we stopped—and when he did, he stopped attacking."

"Well, he *was* missing an arm," Leia pointed out.

"But there were a couple of stormtroopers trying to blast me," Jaina explained. "He ordered them to redirect their fire."

Her parents looked at each other for a moment, then Leia asked, "And you think that has something to do with those marks on your neck?"

"I think it might." Jaina took a breath, then said, "What if we're wrong? What if Jacen is still in there somewhere?"

Her father's face grew hard. "He *isn't*."

"But he let me go."

"That's not the way it looked when you entered the hangar with all those stormtroopers behind you," her mother said. "As for what happened after you cut off his arm—he was probably in shock. You said yourself that he seemed as confused as you were."

"That's true," Jaina agreed. "And my memory *isn't* clear. But these stains—"

"Could mean anything—even if they *are* stains," her father interrupted. "And if Caedus *did* let you go, it's not because he felt bad about getting into a fight with his sister."

"Your father's right," Leia said. "You're about the only one in the family he *hasn't* been trying to kill. It would be a mistake to assume that's anything more than an accident of circumstance."

Jaina knew they were right, of course. Even if Caedus *had* hesitated, it didn't excuse what he had done in the past—and it didn't mean he would hesitate again. But he *had* directed fire away from her. A part of Jaina wanted to believe that meant there was some hope of redeeming Jacen. The other part remembered that Caedus had been grievously wounded at the time, and he had thought he was seeing Luke somewhere else. That had made no sense to her at the time—it still didn't—but what made more sense? That a Sith Lord had suddenly turned soft, or that he had been making a tactical choice based on a shock-induced hallucination?

"Okay," Jaina said, nodding. "Let's just figure out what these marks are, because they're *not* burns."

Her mother nodded. "We'll have Cilghal take a look as soon as we get back to Shedu Maad."

Jaina frowned. "We're going back?" she asked. "But Caedus is on *Nickel One*."

"Surrounded by three fleets of his own and about six from the Confederation and our coalition," her father explained. "The Corellians and Bothans have jumped into the action, and the Roche system is turning into a firestorm."

"Luke thinks *our* fight is going to move away from the Roche system," Leia said. "And you need some time to heal."

Before Jaina could ask exactly *where* Luke thought the fight was going to move, the privacy partition slid open and C-3PO's golden form appeared in the opening.

"Excuse me for interrupting," the droid said. "*Mand'alor* Fett is requesting a few words with Jaina."

"Fett?" Han was instantly on his feet. "No way. Tell him she's—"

"I won't stay long," Fett said, pushing past C-3PO. He was wearing his new green *beskar'gam* with no helmet—a concession, no doubt, to the stubborn efficiency of Hapan Security forces, who tended to frown on masked strangers wandering around their Battle Dragons. His dead brown eyes did not betray the anger Jaina sensed in him through the Force. "I just need a quick post-action briefing."

"Sorry," her father said, stepping forward. Jaina knew that it was not the first time Han Solo had seen Boba Fett without a helmet on, but her father's gaze still seemed riveted to Fett's swarthy, square face. "She's in no condition—"

"Dad," Jaina interrupted. "It's okay. He deserves to hear what happened—what I can remember of it, anyway."

Her father looked at her and scowled, then turned back to Fett and scowled more. "Keep it short. She's been through a lot."

Fett nodded. "Haven't we all."

For a moment, the two men stood looking at each other, Fett waiting for Jaina's parents to leave, her father letting him know that wasn't going to happen. Outside the bay, Jaina glimpsed another Mandalorian in full armor standing behind C-3PO. She couldn't see him well enough to identify, but judging by his size and the way he was keeping an eye on Fett's back, she guessed it was Fett's de facto second in command, Beviin.

It was Leia who finally broke the standoff. "We're not going anywhere, *Mand'alor.*" Unlike Han, she was careful to address Fett by his title. "If you've got something to ask, go ahead. Otherwise, Han is right—Jaina needs to rest."

Fett's gaze shifted to Leia, a narglatch sizing up a mother shenbit. He gave a barely perceptible nod, then turned to Jaina.

"I know Mirta and her team connected with you at the FlakBlaster emplacement," he said. "What I don't know is how they did."

Jaina closed her eyes. *Those* memories—the memories of what had happened to Mirta and the first couple of Mandalorians—were all too clear.

"They only got a handful of Moffs—maybe half a dozen," she said. "I don't know which ones, because the

Moffs weren't my target—and the last part of the battle is still pretty hazy for me."

"How hazy?" Fett demanded.

Jaina opened her eyes and saw him studying the wound on her forehead, no doubt hoping that she had missed the part of the battle where his commandos finished off the rest of the Moffs and escaped.

"Not *that* hazy." She concentrated for a moment, trying to recall what she had seen in those last few minutes of fighting. "Your team had trouble getting through the body-guards, then Caedus arrived."

"And?"

"And he rescued the rest of the Moffs," Jaina said. "I don't think you should have sent in the team after their *Tra'kads* got hit. All you did was strengthen Caedus's hand."

Fett's eyes flashed with irritation. "Caedus wasn't sup-posed to *have* a hand," he said. "You were supposed to take him out."

Jaina resisted the urge to tell him that it was Mirta who had spoiled the plan. There was no point in adding to the pain he was already feeling—and it might even be danger-ous.

Her father, unfortunately, lacked Jaina's self-restraint. "You can't blame Jaina for that," he said. "The way I heard it, she would have had him if Mandalorians could follow orders."

Fett's eyes flashed. "Mandalorians don't follow *Jedi* or-ders," he said, speaking through clenched teeth. "We know how they treated the clones."

"Probably because they had a sense of who the clones were *really* serving," Leia countered. "Blind obedience de-serves even less respect than mercenary—"

"I think we've all said enough about that," Jaina inter-rupted. She shot a warning glance first at her parents, then at Fett. "Unless you three are *trying* to start another war?"

All three fell silent and stared at one another.

"I'll take that as a no," Jaina said. "Mirta chose her moment without knowing where Caedus was—I remember that pretty clearly—but I doubt we were *ever* going to know where he was. Caedus was one step ahead of us all the way."

Fett tore his gaze away from Leia, and turned to Jaina. "Thanks," he said. "What about Mirta?"

Jaina's stomach grew hollow, and she was suddenly unsure whether he was asking how she died or whether she had survived. Unfortunately, the answer was the same either way.

"She was the first to go," Jaina said. She saw the blood drain from Fett's face, but there was no hint of surprise. He might not have heard about Mirta's fate, but he *had* known. "I'm sorry, Boba."

Fett dipped his head absentmindedly, then asked, "You're sure?"

Jaina nodded. "It happened a long time before this—" she gestured at the split above her eye. "So I've got a pretty clear memory of it. Caedus threw her into a high corner, and she came down on her head."

"Not what I meant, Jedi," Fett said. "You're sure she was dead? Not moving?"

"I don't . . . let me think." Jaina closed her eyes, trying to recall if there had been time to stretch her Force awareness toward Mirta, if there had even been time to glance in that direction. She saw nothing; she had no memories of Mirta after that at all. "I don't remember—I don't even know if there was time to look."

"So you don't *know* that she's dead, do you?" Fett asked. There was as much hope as blame in his voice. "For all you know, she could be alive. You left without checking."

Jaina considered the accusation, recalling how frenzied the battle had been—and began to feel very guilty.

"I probably *did*," she admitted. "But I don't want to give you false hope. It was a long fall, and I know Mirta. If she'd been able to move, she would have been fighting."

"Of course. She's a Mandalorian." What Fett left unsaid—but Jaina knew he was thinking—was that Mandalorians didn't abandon fallen comrades, wounded *or* dead. "But she wouldn't have been moving if she was just—"

"Mirta wasn't our concern." The pronouncement came from the entrance to the convalescence bay, where Luke had just arrived in his customary dark robe. He stepped inside and went to stand face-to-face with Fett. "You have no right to come here and blame Jaina for anything. You inserted yourselves into our mission thinking we would serve as your shields."

"And you made sure we paid the price." There was more pain in Fett's voice than Jaina would have thought him capable of showing. She suddenly understood why he had *really* come here—and it had less to do with discovering the truth than with finding someone to blame for it. He flicked a thumb in her direction, then continued, "She might have got him if you had stuck to your plan, Jedi."

"Or if you had offered to work *with* us instead of trying to use us," Luke replied calmly. "And the first option, by the way, is still open."

"Not for us," Fett shot back. He turned to Jaina. "Thanks for the briefing, Jedi."

Fett spoke in a tone that suggested he really meant *thanks for nothing,* and Jaina decided that not only could she not abide serving as his scapegoat any longer—but it might be dangerous to do so. As he turned to go, she stretched a hand toward him.

"Wait."

Fett stopped and turned his head toward her without pivoting his body. "You remember something else, Jedi?"

"As a matter of fact, I do," Jaina said. "I don't know what happened to Mirta, and I'm sorry for that. But you're the one who chose to go after the Moffs under Caedus's nose."

"Mandalore has a treaty to honor," Fett said simply. "I had to do something."

"There were a lot of things you could have done," Jaina retorted. "But you *wanted* Caedus to know you were behind all this, and now you've dragged Mandalore into the middle of the war in a big way. And for what? Your personal vendetta."

Fett's eyes narrowed. "You sure this is any of your business?"

"You made it my business when you sent Mirta to Nickel One," Jaina said. "She wasn't there because of what *I* wanted. Did you really think that baiting Caedus wouldn't cost you? That he wouldn't tear off a piece of you—and that he's not going to *keep* tearing off pieces?"

"I *thought* I had trained someone to take him down," Fett retorted.

"And I will," Jaina said. "But this is war, not an assassination, and in a war, *everybody* takes casualties."

Fett studied her for a moment, the anger in his eyes slowly turning to enigma. When she did not continue, he finally asked, "You done, Jedi?"

Jaina nodded. "Pretty much." She did not bother wondering whether she had gotten through to him. Boba Fett had always been a creature of bitterness and revenge, and she supposed he was too old to change now. "Shoot straight and run fast, Boba."

Fett actually smiled. "Thanks for the advice, Jedi," he said. "Die proud."

He stepped around Luke and left the convalescence bay, leaving both of Jaina's parents scowling after his back.

"Don't blast him, guys," she said, chuckling. "That's Mando for 'good luck.' "

Her father's frown only deepened. "Weird language," he said, looking back toward her. "You don't really expect him to take any of that advice, do you?"

"I'm afraid it wouldn't matter if he did," Luke said. "What's left of the Fifth Fleet is already on its way to bombard Mandalore."

Han whistled. "That's going to be a mess."

"A big mess," Luke agreed. "But it's going to keep the Mandalorian *Bes'uliike* tied up defending their home planet—when they *could* be out here tipping the balance of power back out of Caedus's favor."

Leia cocked a brow. "*Back* out of his favor?" she asked. "Does that mean you've seen something decisive?"

Luke nodded. "Indeed I have." He smiled and produced a piece of flimsiplast from inside his robe. "According to Hapan Intelligence, Bwua'tu is on his way to take over operations in the Roche system."

Jaina did not like the implications of that. As Caedus's most competent and trusted admiral, Bwua'tu was usually placed in charge of war theaters where her brother *wasn't*.

"So Caedus is going back to Coruscant?" she asked. Jaina did not like *that* possibility at all; without Shevu, it would be nearly impossible to pinpoint an opportunity when they stood a reasonable chance of actually getting to Caedus. "That's going to complicate things."

"Actually, it won't," Luke said. "I don't think Caedus *will* be returning to Coruscant."

Han cocked his brow. "You think it's a trick?"

"Not the way you're thinking," Luke said. "But I have a feeling that finding Caedus won't be a problem."

Leia's eyes narrowed. "You've seen something, haven't you?" She pointed at the intelligence report in his hand.

"And I'm not talking about something on a piece of flimsi-plast."

"No, it's not an intelligence report." Luke stepped to Jaina's bed, his eyes fixed on the crimson stains running across her throat. "It's a lot more certain than that."

chapter twelve

What does an Imperial Star Destroyer wear to a formal occasion?
A bow TIE!

—Jacen Solo, age 14

In a galaxy whirling madly out of control, where the war erupted in another system every day and whole cities could be blasted away by simple fiat of the GA Chief of State, nobody much cared when a young human walked into the seedy cantina of the Nova Station refueling depot and took a seat at the bar. The other patrons—a motley assortment of humans and nonhumans—simply looked over long enough to see that he appeared harmless. The red-skinned Twi'lek bartender paid him even less attention; he just glanced up from the newsflimsi he had been reading, then turned his attention back to his reading.

So Ben did not understand why he had that prickly feeling all over . . . the feeling that almost always meant he was being watched. Before beginning his journey back to the secret Jedi base on Shedu Maad, he had taken all the proper precautions to ensure that he wasn't being followed. He had Force-zapped the locator chip under his shoulder blade even before leaving the GAG prison, then traveled around Coruscant changing transportation at random and altering his appearance multiple times. He had even taken Tahiri's lightsaber apart and inspected it for tracking devices, then slipped into a hospital and used the Force to convince a friendly technician to run him through an electromagnetic pulser to disable any bugs he *hadn't* found. And still, he kept having these prickly feelings, as though someone had actually followed him to Nova Station—and might be capable of following him all the way back to the secret Jedi base on Shedu Maad.

When Ben did not take the hint and leave, the bartender reluctantly tore himself away from the newsflimsi and came over. He tossed a plastoid coaster on the grimy counter—it stuck where it landed—then curled a lip, showing the sharp yellow teeth on one side of his mouth.

"What will it be, my friend?" he asked.

"A Sapphire Fogblaster—spun, not mixed," Ben said, naming the drink his instructions had specified to order. "And a menu—I'm starved."

"The menu is there." The Twi'lek pointed at a display above the dispenser island behind the bar. The sole entry read NELAB STEW: 10 CREDITS. "A *spun* Fogblaster is eight credits."

"Okay," Ben said. "What's nelab stew?"

"You don't want to know—especially if you're going to eat it. Me, I'd rather stay hungry." The Twi'lek remained in front of Ben, studying him with open suspicion. "You even have the credits for the Fogblaster?"

Ben started to object to the rudeness, then realized it was probably a fair question. He had worn his stolen GAG armor only long enough to intimidate a spaceport cargo manager into quietly shipping Shevu's body to Shula on Vaklin as a "service to the Guard." After that, he had begun a series of Force-influenced clothing trades that had inevitably resulted in a long chain of downgrades. At present, he was drowning in an oversized tunic-and-tabard combination that a portly pedway chronovendor had hesitantly exchanged for a shimmersilk cloak, which Ben had obtained an hour earlier from a spaceport juggler. The clothes had been barely presentable when they were acquired, and now they were rumpled, dirty, and foul smelling.

"Sorry," Ben said, pulling a twenty-credit chit out of his pocket. "I must look like a stowaway."

"It makes no difference to me how you came." The Twi'lek snatched the chit from Ben's hand. "As long as you have credits."

He went to make the Fogblaster. Ben had never tasted a Fogblaster—or any other recreational intoxicant—and he wouldn't have known the difference between one that had been spun and one that had been mixed if his life depended on it. But he was almost tempted to see if it would dull the aching rawness of his emotions. He still felt sick about what Tahiri had done to Shevu—and his friend's death had reawakened other, even more painful feelings. He kept suffering flashes of the same grief and despair he had experienced after his mother had died, and sometimes it was so bad that he had to reach out to his father for support.

Surprisingly, what Ben did *not* feel was rage. He didn't hate Tahiri for what she had done, he didn't even dislike her. The truth was, he mostly felt pity for her. He had been where she was, had done things that were nearly as terrible because Jacen had convinced him he was serving the galaxy. Now Ben really didn't want to punish Tahiri—he wanted to *save* her.

The bartender returned, carrying an icy, long-stemmed glass the size of a soup bowl. He placed it on the coaster with both hands, as though he was afraid to spill, then stepped back and waited.

When Ben did not immediately reach for the drink, he asked, "Something wrong?"

Ben studied the drink warily. Inside the glass was a dark, bubbling concoction that steamed blue vapor into the air—and smelled like something a ronto would leave in the street.

"No—it looks fine, I guess," Ben said. "Maybe I better have a glass of water, too."

The Twi'lek's head-tails shivered—a sign that he had been insulted—then he said, "Water costs extra."

"Fine," Ben said. "Take it out of that chit I gave you."

The Twi'lek eyed Ben just as warily as Ben was eyeing the Fogblaster, then produced an empty pail from under the counter and sat it down next to the drink.

"If you have a problem, my friend . . ." He pointed at the pail.

"Uh, thanks," Ben said, putting any thought of actually *trying* the Fogblaster out of his mind. "Could you make that water a large?"

The Twi'lek rolled his eyes and went to retrieve another glass. Ben took a straw from a holder on the counter and stuck it into the drink, then pretended to sip. His rescue instructions—relayed over a "borrowed" comlink by an anonymous Hapan Intelligence operative on Coruscant—had been to proceed to the Big Boom cantina in Nova Station, located in the Carida system. There, he was to order a Sapphire Fogblaster—spun, not mixed—and wait for "someone he recognized" to approach him. It was all very mysterious, but then agent-recovery operations usually were. Ben just wished he had been able to order something to eat.

As he waited, Ben swiveled around to watch the all-Bith band on the stage. They were playing some sort of flighty, outdated rill-music that his mom had loved but always made *him* wince, and now he found himself actually growing fond of it as he scanned the cantina's other customers. He still had that feeling of being watched. With any luck, the watcher would be his contact, scrutinizing him from one of the cantina's darker corners to make certain Ben hadn't been followed.

Ben was still looking when the bartender returned.

"Here's your *water*," he said, clunking the glass down. "Don't get any in the Fogblaster—it'll explode."

"Thanks." Ben turned to find a glass about a third the size of the Fogblaster sitting on the bar in front of him, along with four credits—his change from the twenty, he assumed. "How much *was* that water?"

"It's good water," the Twi'lek replied, turning away without really answering the question. "Let me know if you want a refill."

Ben scowled and was considering dumping it into the Fogblaster when he sensed two beings approaching from behind. He turned on his stool and saw a pair of red-haired women whom he *sort* of recognized. They were obviously Hapan. He could tell that much by their striking beauty and the stylish synthatex flight suits—one gold, one maroon—that they wore. The pair were obviously twins, with broad full-lipped grins and high, sharp cheekbones.

What made Ben's jaw drop, though—what made him *stare*—were their long straight noses and thin arcing eyebrows. Those he recognized perfectly, because they could have been on Tenel Ka's face. The first woman—Gold Suit—noticed him staring and smiled. The second—Maroon Suit—simply rolled her eyes, then took the stool next to Ben's and reached for the Fogblaster.

"Finally," Maroon said, taking a long pull on the straw. "You have no idea how *long* I've been looking forward to this."

"Eight days?" Ben asked. That was how long ago he had received his instructions from the operative on Coruscant. He offered his hand. "Sorry to keep you—"

"Eight *days*? Are you kidding?" asked the other sister, the one in gold. She took a straw from the container and inserted it in the glass, then began to drink along with Maroon. "Try eight *hours,* handsome."

"Uh, okay," Ben said. He was pretty sure these were his contacts, because he sort of recognized them and they certainly seemed to think he was the one they were looking for. He extended his hand to Gold. "I'm Ben—"

"We *know* who you are," said Maroon. Like Gold, she looked to be about ten years younger than Tenel Ka—though it was always difficult to tell with Hapan women. "I'm Trista. That's Taryn."

Taryn batted her eyelashes at him. "We've come to take you home." She took another long sip of the still-bubbling Fogblaster. "Isn't that just *luminous?*"

"Yeah . . . about that." Ben glanced around the cantina again and saw that most eyes—especially human, *male* eyes—were openly staring in their direction. "I think we're being watched."

Trista rolled her eyes again. "*Of course* we are. If you're going to travel with us, you'd better get used to it."

"That's not the kind of watching I mean, Trista," Ben said. As the son of the most famous Jedi in the galaxy, he was no stranger to public attention himself. "I mean *watched*, as in being spied on."

"Oh, *that*." Taryn leaned in close to his ear, filling it with warm breath as she whispered. "That's just our security team. We're Tenel Ka's cousins."

Ben scowled, instantly growing suspicious. "I didn't know she *had* cousins."

"Nobody knows. That's what makes us so useful." Trista flicked a finger toward Ben's water. "You going to drink that or not? They have nice water here."

Ben left the water untouched—he was not about to drink *anything* around these two until he was certain of their credentials. "Prince Isolder is an only child."

This caused both sisters to break into giggles.

"Pleaaase!" said Taryn. "Do you really believe Ta'a Chume accepted a male heir *willingly*? Isolder is the only *surviving* legitimate son, but you can be sure that if one of his half brothers had turned out to be a half sister, *she* would have been the heir."

Ben had to admit they had a point—and they *did* look an awful lot like Tenel Ka. Taryn used her sister's distraction to finish the Fogblaster, then put her arm through Ben's and rose.

"Come on, handsome," she said, pulling him up. "Let me show you our skiff."

Trista scowled at the empty glass, then rose and joined them, wrinkling her nose at Ben's tunic. "And let's get you into some fresh clothes. Where have you been riding? The garbage hold?"

Ben raised his brow. "How did you—"

"I never should have asked." Trista started toward the exit, speaking over her shoulder. "Would it have been too much trouble to steal a fresh set of clothes *before* you came to the Big Boom?"

Ben allowed them to lead him out of the cantina and down a long corridor lined by viewing ports. Outside the transparisteel hung wispy curtains of crimson gas, the still-cooling ejecta of the supernova that had flash-boiled the blood of billions of Caridans nearly two decades before Ben was born.

Recalling that the explosion had been a deliberate act of reprisal directed at the home of the Imperial military academy, Ben found himself wondering whether *any* war ever accomplished anything, whether all of sentient history was just a long chain of one sentient-made cataclysm after another. Certainly he had known far more war than peace during his fourteen years of life, and that was even more true for his cousins than it was for him. Ultimately, he thought, *that* was what had driven Jacen mad—not the lust for power, but the fear that nothing he did mattered, the sad conclusion that the only way to achieve total peace was through total control.

By the time they entered the private hangar bay where Taryn and Trista had docked their skiff, the prickling feeling was stronger than ever. Ben still had not seen any sign of the sisters' security team—but then, if it was a good team and keeping a low profile, he *wouldn't* have. Still, he stopped just inside the door, eyeing the sleek blue lines of a Batag needle ship and reaching out in the Force, searching for the source of his uneasiness.

"Don't be shy," Taryn said, pulling him toward the little skiff. "There's plenty of room for three."

"And it has a sanisteam," Trista added.

"Give me a second," Ben said, stopping three paces from the hatch. The docking bay was a typical mini hangar, a steel cavern with a small jungle of feed hoses hanging from the ceiling, and there weren't many places to hide—even if he *had* felt any living presences inside. "Has your security team cleared this hangar?"

"Of course," Trista said. "That's what security teams *do*."

Ben ignored her sarcasm. "And they're watching us now?"

"They'd better be," Taryn said. "But I promise no one will peek at your sanisteam, if that's what you're so worried about."

"Uh, thanks." It hadn't even occurred to Ben that someone *might* peek. "Can you ask them to stand down for a couple of seconds?"

Trista frowned. "Why?"

"Jedi stuff," Ben said. "I need to check something out."

Trista looked to Taryn, who simply shrugged. "The prince seems to trust him."

"The prince?" Ben asked. "Isolder?"

Taryn shook her head in disbelief. "There's only *one* prince right now, Ben," she said. "And he's the only one Her Majesty would trust to return you to the secret Jedi base."

"All I need is to borrow a decent craft," Ben said, bristling at the idea that he needed to be *returned* anywhere. "I *can* get there on my own."

"*Of course* you can," Taryn said. "But Her Majesty didn't know what condition you'd be in."

"Oh—I guess that makes sense," Ben said, feeling a little foolish for being defensive. He turned to Trista. "What about your security team?"

Trista sighed, then fished a comlink from a utility pocket and opened a channel. "Gentlemen, we need you to turn your backs for a minute."

No acknowledgment came, and Ben continued to feel as though they were being watched.

Both sisters frowned, and Taryn asked, "Bad signal?"

"Bad *something*," Trista answered. Into the comlink, she said, "Acknowledge!"

A moment later, a static-scrambled voice said, "Sorry . . . in a . . . zone."

Taryn and Trista exchanged puzzled glances, then Taryn said, "That explains it . . . sort of."

Trista nodded. "We'll be careful," she said, reaching into a utility pocket. "Let's get our package inside."

She pulled a remote out and pointed it at the skiff. Ben did not sense any danger, but he signaled her to wait and reached for the lightsaber he had taken from Tahiri.

"Let me check it out first," he said.

The sisters looked at each other, then snorted in amusement.

"You check out *that* skiff and we'll deliver you to the prince on a stretcher," Trista said. She depressed one of the remote's controls, and blue forks of current began to dance over the hull. "If anyone had touched the *Blue Slipper*, they'd be lying on the deck beside it."

"It's the *latest* in antitheft systems," Taryn added. "Not even on the market yet. It makes those time-consuming entanglements with local law enforcement *so* not necessary."

Ben flushed, feeling a little foolish for trying to play the gallant. Hapan women knew how to take care of themselves, and they were accustomed to being the ones in charge—and that would be even more true for intelligence operatives. He shrugged and followed them toward the *Blue Slipper*.

Even if there *was* a problem with the security team, the skiff itself seemed safe enough. The interior was tidy, spotless, and elegantly snug. It had gray leather lounge seating arranged around a level-float table that could be height-adjusted for any occasion or stowed out of the way on the ceiling. To the aft was a sleeping cabin with a deluxe refresher unit. But it was what lay forward that interested Ben the most—a small galley with an AgiMuud processing unit and over a thousand items on the menu.

Trista saw him eyeing the galley. "*After* your sanisteam," she said, shooing him toward the refresher compartment. "You'll find fresh undergarments and a clean robe in the sleeping cabin."

"Compliments of Her Majesty herself," Taryn added, smiling. "She seems quite fond of you."

"The feeling is mutual," Ben assured her. "I've admired Tenel Ka—er, *Her Majesty* pretty much my whole life."

"She'll be happy to hear that in our report," Trista said. "It will be awhile before we depart. I want to do a complete sweep and systems check before launch."

Taryn cringed. "Looks like *I'll* be needing the sanisteam next." She followed Ben aft and pulled a pair of grease-stained utilities from the sleeping cabin closet, then started forward to change in the lounge area. "No peeking, Ben."

"I wouldn't think of it." Ben was starting to see her flirtatious humor for what it was—a way to put others both at ease and a bit off-guard. Clearly, the sisters were the *best* kind of intelligence operatives . . . the kind that nobody would suspect. He reached for the door, then added, "On my own, anyway. Thanks for the idea!"

Taryn's jaw dropped.

Ben smiled and closed the door, then undressed and stepped into the sanisteam. As he washed, he kept Tahiri's lightsaber at hand and his Force senses vigilant, alert for any presences in the hangar that might explain his uneasy feelings—or the communication problems with the security team. The only beings he detected were Trista and Taryn, busy doing their checks and inspections, and a few droids.

Ben was better at detecting droids than most Jedi, but his awareness of them was never very distinct. In this case, he just sensed concentrations of electrical energy that seemed to be moving around on their own. Droids, in other words. But there was nothing unusual about their presence inside a space hangar.

What worried Ben far more was the likelihood that Tahiri had learned how to hide her presence in the Force. If she had, she might have caught up to him on Coruscant and been tracking him ever since. And *that* would explain why it was so hard to pinpoint the source of his uneasiness. But that would also mean it had been a mistake to spare Tahiri's life, and Ben did not want to believe that. Preemptive killing was a GAG practice, the way of the dark side. Ben had no intention of backsliding toward either one.

Ben sighed and eyed the lightsaber. Unfortunately, doing the right thing was no guarantee that your actions weren't going to haunt you later. Sparing a foe's life did not mean that she was going to become your friend; likely as not, it just meant she would be back later, trying another attack. Nobody ever said the light side was easy—it definitely required a lot of patience.

By the time Ben had finished his sanisteam, Trista was warming the engines for departure. He wrapped a towel around his waist and slipped out of the refresher compartment—then noticed that the door to the main cabin was slightly ajar.

"Sorry!" Taryn called. "I don't know *how* that was left open!"

"Must have been a stowaway," Ben answered with a sly smile.

He knew she hadn't actually peeked—he would have sensed *that* in the Force—but he liked the way she talked to him. She treated him like an adult instead of a boy. He could imagine her joking the same way with Zekk . . . but definitely *not* Jag. Jag was too full of himself for joking around. Ben honestly couldn't understand how Jaina could stand his *I'm a big ace pilot* routine. Maybe it was just because Jag was the first eligible man Jaina had met who was nearly the pilot her father was.

As Ben slipped into the clothes Taryn had left out for him, the mouthwatering aroma of nerf steak and yobas began to fill his nose. He quickly pulled on his boots and stepped into the lounge to find a meal steaming on the table.

"I took a guess," Taryn said, placing a glass of golden goff-milk next to the plate. "I hope you don't mind."

"*Mind?*" Ben dropped into a seat. "I think I'm in love!"

"Silly man—royal cousins don't *do* love." Taryn chuckled. She motioned at the fork and knife. "I'm afraid you'll have to eat fast. It won't take us long to reach the prince's starcutter."

Trista announced their departure over the intercom, then the skiff slipped from its moorings with a small downward jolt. It was the slightest of bumps, barely perceptible, but it caused Taryn to raise her brow and look toward the flight deck.

"And she won't let *me* do the flying." She leaned closer to Ben and asked, "Why does being born five minutes earlier make *her* the senior team member?"

"I heard that," Trista said over the intercom.

"Heard *what?*" Taryn asked innocently. "We were talking about the Cheruban glach races." She gave Ben a conspiratorial wink. "Isn't that right, Jedi Skywalker?"

Ben didn't answer. The prickle that said he was being

watched had returned, and this time it was stronger than ever. He reached out in the Force and—to his relief—did *not* sense nothing. There was a concentration of electrical energy on the upper hull of the skiff—a concentration that was slowly moving back toward the tail fins, where it would be able to take cover from an unexpected visual inspection.

Ben returned his unused fork and knife to the table. "There's no reason an auxiliary droid should be crawling around on your outer hull, is there?"

"There's a *droid* on the hull?" Trista's voice was sharp enough that Ben would have heard her even without the intercom. "What kind?"

"The kind that shouldn't be there," Taryn replied. "Hit the hull scrubber."

A soft warning chime sounded, then the lights dimmed and the ambient whirring of the ventilation fans slowed to a near stop. An instant later a melodic crackling sang through the hull as the *Blue Slipper*'s antitheft system was activated. Ben concentrated on the droid's presence—and sensed no difference.

"Didn't work," he reported. "It's probably pulse-shielded."

"*Pulse-shielded?*" Trista echoed over the intercom. "What *is* it, a battle droid?"

"Yeah, probably." Ben rose and turned to Taryn. "Where's your EV locker?"

Taryn raised thin brows. "No way you're going out there, Ben. Our orders are to deliver you to the prince safe and sound."

A loud clanging echoed from the stern as the droid went to work on the hull with a tool or weapon—Ben could not tell which.

He looked toward the noise, then said, "Well, *someone* has to go out there. And since I'm the only one who can

Force-stick himself to the exterior of a hull, it should probably be me."

Trista's voice came over the intercom. "He may have a point, Taryn. The droid just sent a message back to Nova Station, and something in the docking bays just made an S-thread transmission."

No one bothered to state the obvious: the droid's message had been relayed to something waiting outside the Carida Nebula.

"Fine." Taryn led the way forward and opened a hidden locker that served as a combination emergency equipment closet and air lock. "Just don't get yourself killed. Her Majesty would hold it against us."

Ben smiled. "I'll do my best," he said. "Keep me posted on our tactical situation."

"Any idea who we're expecting?" Trista asked.

"No, but it was calling *someone*," Ben said, climbing into one of the EV suits. He was glad to see that the suit was one of the best available, with self-adjusting body gloves and a tough eletrotex shell that not even a blaster bolt could penetrate. He glanced toward the clanging again. "And it seems pretty clear that the droid would rather have me dead than let me escape."

Once Taryn had removed the rest of the EV suits from the locker, Ben stepped inside and began to evacuate the air. By the time the procedure was finished, Trista was reporting over the helmet comm that the prince's starcutter, the *Beam Racer,* had appeared on the tactical display and was dispatching its squadron of Miy'tils to support them. She also warned him to be careful leaving the air lock because the banging sounds had stopped—but Ben had known that much already. He could sense the droid lurking on the hull above the air lock, a ball of hot, quivering energy.

Ben opened the hatch but stayed inside, borrowed

lightsaber in hand, as blasterfire split the wispy red curtain of nova gas.

Less than a second later the flurry of bolts died away and a droid hand—a *black,* skeletal droid hand—shot down from the upper edge of the hatch and opened fire with a standard blaster pistol. Ben activated Tahiri's lightsaber and began to bat blaster bolts back out into space, but his mouth had suddenly gone dry, and he felt an irrational panic rising inside.

He recognized that hand—could *never* forget that particular hand. Inside those fingertips were a dozen different anguishes—electrodes, needles, tiny torches, acid pads, and so much more. It was all he could do to keep analyzing the droid's firing patterns—to just keep batting bolts aside and not lash out with his borrowed lightsaber—because he was *terrified* of that hand on a level far below thought, on a level so deep he associated the mere sight of it with suffering the way a ronto associates its driver's face with food.

Trista's voice came over Ben's helmet speaker. "Jedi Skywalker, are you *always* this much trouble?" she asked. "A Star Destroyer just came out of hyperspace between us and the *Beam Racer.*"

An instant later another voice came over Ben's helmet comm—this one thin and raspy, the voice of his nightmares in prison. "Did you really think you could escape *me,* Ben?"

"D-Double-Ex?" Ben didn't have to work very hard to sound scared.

"Who else, Ben?"

Double-Ex continued to pour fire into the air lock. Ben dropped into a corner where the droid's firing pattern did not seem able to reach, deliberately landing with a heavy thud. Then he let Tahiri's lightsaber roll from his hand, still activated, and tumble through the open hatch out into space.

The blasterfire stopped, and an instant later the glossy

black figure of a thin droid with a skull-like face and blazing blue photoreceptors came swinging through the hatchway.

Ben was waiting with his hand already outstretched. "Hello, Double-Ex," he said.

With only comm waves to carry the sound, the droid had no idea where the words were coming from, and its head swiveled toward the opposite corner of the air lock.

"Good-bye, Double-Ex."

Ben hit the droid with the hardest Force shove he could manage. Double-Ex let out a comm squawk of surprise, then flew out of the air lock backward. It instantly began to pour blasterfire back through the hatch, but only a moment passed before the difference between its momentum and that of the *Blue Slipper* made the angle impossible.

Ben stuck his head around the edge of the hatch and was relieved to see a helix of bright dashes still pouring from the blaster pistol as the droid tumbled into the blood-colored gauze of the Carida Nebula.

Then he noticed the matte-black hull of the *Anakin Solo* sliding past in the distance, the cloaking cone and gravity generator dome leaving no doubt about its identity. To his surprise, the hulking Star Destroyer seemed to be turning away from them, pouring ion cannon fire toward a target he could not see. The squadron of Miy'tils that had been sent to escort the *Blue Slipper* were flittering around its exhaust ports, no doubt trying to land a lucky missile and disable the *Solo* before it captured its target.

"*Fierfek!*" Ben cursed. "Are they going after the *Beam Racer*?"

"I wouldn't say going *after*," answered Trista. "Their tractor beam already has a lock."

"So they're going to capture Prince Isolder?" Ben gasped.

"They already *have*," Taryn replied. "There's only one escape now, and I truly hope he doesn't take it. Isolder has always been a good uncle to us."

As the *Solo* drifted out of sight behind the *Slipper*'s tail, it finally dawned on Ben that they were turning *away* from the confrontation.

"What are you doing?" Ben asked. He pulled the air lock's exterior hatch closed and sealed it. "Maybe I can help him."

"You Jedi," Taryn said, "always thinking you can do the impossible. No wonder you get in so much trouble."

Ben scowled and started to cycle air back into the lock. "But—"

"Not a chance," Trista said. "Her Majesty is going to be angry enough about losing her father."

chapter thirteen

I heard two droids talking the other day. The first one asked, "Did you beat the Wookiee at sabacc?" And the second said, "Yes, but it cost me an arm and a leg."

—Jacen Solo, age 14

"Isn't medicine miraculous today?" Caedus asked. No one answered, of course. It was a rhetorical question. "A being is more likely to die of a meteor strike than of old age or disease."

Little more than a standard week after losing his arm, Caedus was pacing—actually *pacing*—back and forth across the ward room. With his good arm, he was waving a hypo filled with a special preparation of protocells and neural growth stimulants. His mind was alert, focused, and filled with an energizing optimism that he had not experienced since his days at the Jedi academy on Yavin 4.

"Today's too-onebee droids can replace a blaster-shattered kneecap with an ilinium prosthetic more durable than the original." Caedus stopped next to the only occupied bed in the ward and gestured at the stump of his severed arm, which still showed the white fusing scar where the skin had been closed over the bone. "They could have reattached my natural arm, had I been willing to lie around in one of *these* for a couple of months."

Caedus intentionally slammed his prosthetic kneecap into the bed frame, rocking it so hard that the occupant— a young sinewy woman with curly brown hair and dark eyes—flinched. He smiled and held the hypo over the bed, easily within her reach . . . had she been able to move her arms.

"Yes, today's medicine can even rebuild the nerves in a ruptured spinal cord. One little injection"—Caedus looked at the needle, which was nearly as long as his finger, then continued—"well, maybe not so little—is all it takes to start the process."

The woman's dark eyes began to grow glassy, and she looked away.

"Come now, Mirta," Caedus said. "This war will be over soon, and you'll be released with all of the Alliance's prisoners. There's no reason you need to be strapped into a hoverchair when that happens."

So far, the woman had not said a word, not even to acknowledge her identity. But even if GAG's terrorist-recognition technology had not identified her, Caedus would have known her. She had her mother's mouth and her grandfather's cold, dead eyes, after all. More importantly, he could feel her hatred burning in the Force, and *that* was what identified her most clearly—her obsession with avenging the death of Ailyn Vel.

"But we must start the process soon—before the damage grows irreversible," Caedus said. "How many Jedi accompanied your team?"

Mirta continued to look away, but her face blanched and a small, pained voice croaked, "Go . . . get . . . borked."

"Ah . . . she speaks. Progress at last."

Caedus's smile was sincere. A response—any response—meant he had found a vulnerable spot in her armor.

Then the ward room door hissed open, and Mirta's face hardened as she recovered her composure and looked to see who had arrived. Caedus spun on his heel, already summoning the Force shock he would use to rebuke the fool who had ignored his order for privacy—then saw who it was and realized why he hadn't sensed her coming. After learning how to conceal herself in the Force, Tahiri had begun to employ the technique—like Caedus himself—as a matter of course.

"Ah, Tahiri. You're just in time." Caedus motioned her into the room, then turned back to the bed. "Mirta was about to tell us who cut off my arm."

Tahiri remained silent for a moment, then said, "I'd think you would *know* that, my lord."

"Appearances can be deceiving," Caedus said. "Isn't that so, Mirta?"

Mirta only glared at him in silence.

"We're back to that, are we?" Caedus sighed and looked sadly at the hypo, then turned back around to Tahiri. "It seems our prisoner is determined to live the rest of her life strapped to a board. I assume you've come to report. You may proceed."

Tahiri frowned. *"Here?"*

"There's no need to worry about betraying our secrets." He glanced over his shoulder. "Does the prisoner *look* like an escape risk?"

Mirta's rage came boiling through the Force like a turbolaser strike, blasting Caedus so fiercely it felt almost physical. He allowed himself a smirk—more to signal his intentions to Tahiri than to congratulate himself, of course—and began to plot how he was going to turn that rage to his own ends, to redirect it at someone who had been making a real nuisance of himself lately.

Tahiri looked past Caedus toward the bed, apparently debating whether her news should be relayed in front of even an incapacitated enemy, then finally said, "I'm afraid I have a failure to report, my lord."

"Your plan to discover the location of the secret Jedi base has failed," Caedus surmised. Actually, the broad outlines of the plan had been *his,* but the failure was obviously in the details—and those had been mapped out by Tahiri. "Ben slipped free of your surveillance."

"*Slipped* isn't quite accurate," Tahiri said. "He discovered our, um, *agent* trailing him and took measures."

Caedus frowned—though not because Tahiri had lost track of Ben. He had foreseen that possibility in his visions and taken other measures. He just didn't like the idea of losing his secret security droid. As irritating as SD-XX could be, lately it had seemed to him that the droid was the only one who truly understood him.

"What about the . . . agent?" he asked. Tahiri had been wise to avoid mentioning SD-XX in front of Mirta. Caedus had every intention of sending her back to Boba Fett in one fully functional piece, and he preferred to keep private the existence of his security droid. "Is he still functional?"

"I don't know," Tahiri replied. "We weren't able to recover him."

Caedus fought to keep his anger from rising. He had already made the mistake of letting his emotions control him, and that blunder had cost him so much more than Fondor and the deserters the traitor Niathal had stolen. It had cost him his daughter's love—it had cost him Allana.

When he felt certain of sounding merely annoyed rather than enraged, Caedus asked, "Why not?"

Tahiri's eyes began to sparkle. "We were otherwise occupied, my lord," she said. "I saw another opportunity to learn the location of the secret Jedi base, and I seized it."

When Tahiri did not elaborate, Caedus frowned and inquired, "Do you *really* intend to make me ask?"

Tahiri smiled, and he knew that it was something big. "I think so, yes."

The joy she felt in her triumph was contagious; Caedus actually found himself grinning. "Very well," he said. "Exactly *what* did you seize?"

"The *Beam Racer*," Tahiri reported. "And the prince was aboard."

Caedus's brow shot up. "You captured *Isolder*?"

Tahiri nodded. "I did."

"And he revealed the location of the Jedi base?"

"Not yet," she said. "But before losing contact, our agent reported a conversation in which it was said that Tenel Ka wouldn't trust anyone else with the location of the Jedi base."

Tahiri's face grew clouded, then she added, "I thought you might want to perform the interrogation yourself. I—I *killed* the last subject I worked on."

Caedus's heart went out to her. He remembered how *he* had felt when his first suspect died under interrogation: horrified and frustrated and ashamed all at once, but mostly afraid of what he was becoming. He would have laid a comforting hand on her shoulder, except the only one he had left was holding a hypo with a very long needle.

Instead, he said, "It's not your fault, Tahiri. The suspect holds his own life in his hands. If he won't cooperate, we can't be blamed for the consequences."

"I know," Tahiri said. "But I was angry—"

"We all make mistakes," Caedus interrupted, growing impatient with her self-examination. He had absolved her of guilt—what more did she require? "Where's Isolder now?"

A flash of pain shot through Tahiri's eyes, but she quickly collected herself. "The prince is secure in the *Anakin Solo*'s brig, with the rest of the *Racer*'s crew," she said. "I offered to confine him in one of the VIP cabins, but he refused to guarantee his behavior."

"He's an honorable man," Caedus said, nodding. He thought of how many times—going as far back as his student days on Yavin 4—he had imagined having Isolder as his father-in-law, and a pang of sorrow shot through his breast. "I'm glad it won't be necessary to interrogate him—at least not harshly."

Tahiri frowned in confusion. "He didn't strike me as the kind of man who'll be easy to break."

"He wouldn't be," Caedus agreed. "But I've already learned the location of the Jedi base."

Tahiri's mouth dropped, but she seemed too astonished to actually voice the question.

Caedus closed his eyes and turned in the direction of Hapan space. "In the Transitory Mists, on this side of the Consortium, somewhere between Roqoo Depot and Terephon, I would say." He opened his eyes and turned to Tahiri. "I'll grow more precise when we get closer."

Tahiri's brow shot up so high that the scars on her forehead laid at an angle. She looked like she wanted to ask a dozen different questions, but all she seemed able to manage was *"How?"*

Caedus smiled. "It's in my blood, Tahiri."

He left it at that—this was neither the time nor the place to explain how a Nightsister blood trail worked. The fighting around the Roche system was growing fiercer by the hour, but he could not leave—did not *dare* leave—until he understood what had happened to him in the Tactical Planning Forum. He had been fighting Luke one moment, Jaina the next, and then they had *both* been there—not just illusions of them, but presences real enough to bat blaster bolts back at the stormtroopers attacking them.

"Come here," Caedus said, motioning Tahiri to Mirta's bedside. "*You're* a woman—perhaps you can find a way to make her discuss the Jedi on her strike team."

Tahiri obediently came to stand beside the bed, but Caedus could see in the way she averted her eyes that she had lost her stomach for harsh interrogation. Of course, that only meant it was more important than ever to push her back into it—to remind her that a Sith never allowed personal feelings to interfere with the mission.

"The subject has no sensation below her shoulders, so our options are limited," Caedus noted, adopting an impersonal tone that he hoped would make it easier for Tahiri to begin. "And I suspect she wants to die anyway, so death threats won't work, either."

"When do death threats *ever* work?" Tahiri's gaze began to roam over Mirta's sheet-covered body, and Caedus could see that his strategy was effective—that she was starting to focus on the problem instead of herself. "But she's part Mandalorian, right?"

"Maybe even completely," Caedus said. "The way their culture works, what you *say* you are is more important than what spills out of your veins. The file says she even married a Mandalorian recently. Why?"

"Mandalorians are way too proud," Tahiri said. "Smug, even. It's the biggest weakness I've seen in every one I've met."

Caedus considered this for a moment, then asked, "You're thinking humiliation?"

Tahiri nodded. "But we have to take it further. The subject's a decent-looking woman for her line of work, and that has to make her vain."

Caedus glanced over Mirta's face and knew by the rush of fear he felt in the Force that Tahiri had struck a chord. "So, disfigurement," he said. "I *hate* that."

"Who doesn't?" Tahiri asked. "But she's a member of Fett's family, right? Compared with the emotional stuff she must be carrying around already, a little humiliation is nothing. If we want to break her, we have to maim her so badly that people will pity her. Then, if she *still* doesn't give us what we want, we send her back to Mandalore."

That inspired Mirta to raise her head. "Go ahead, you dung-sucking dark side slut! See what happens."

"So disfigurement would be a problem for you?" Caedus asked. He glanced over at Tahiri with a look of admiration. "It sounds like you've found your inner Yuuzhan Vong. Congratulations."

"Thanks." Tahiri's pride was genuine, her attention now

completely focused on the task at hand. "Call me whatever you like, Mirta, but the choice is yours. We're only the instrument of *your* decision."

"Go drown in a cesspool," Mirta shot back. "I'm looking at a dead woman."

"Mirta, there's no reason to be angry with *Tahiri*." As Caedus spoke, he began to put the power of the Force behind his words, using its energies to plant them deep in her mind. "She isn't the one who sent you on this mission."

Mirta's gaze flashed over to Caedus. "I *volunteered*."

"Of course you did," Caedus said in a reasonable tone. "You're Boba Fett's granddaughter. What else *could* you do?"

He saw the shock of recognition in her eyes and knew that she realized what he was trying to do. No matter. He had time and the Force on his side. With those two for allies, the only question was how long it would take to implant the conviction that her suffering was her grandfather's fault, that Fett had sent her on the mission *knowing* it would fail. And once Caedus had done that, all he would have to do was stand back and let Mandalorian nature take its usual course.

When no further foulness spilled from Mirta's mouth, Caedus shrugged and turned to Tahiri.

"The threat alone will never work on this subject," he said. "I'll have someone bring a mirrpanel so she can see what we're doing to her."

He stepped over to the wall and used a knuckle to depress the call button. When the door to the ward slid open an instant later, he was surprised to see that his black-clad GAG guard was accompanied by a white-uniformed medic with a Remnant insignia on her collar. In her slender hands, the medic held a blood-collection kit.

Before his guard could explain the woman's presence, Caedus turned to her directly. "Is there something you require here, Lieutenant?"

The woman paled, but clicked her heels and inclined her head. "Lord Caedus, the Moffs request a sample of the prisoner's blood for their genetic databank."

"Later," Caedus said. He was willing to accommodate the Moffs, but not in the middle of his interrogation—not when he was just starting to make progress. "You can wait outside until we're done, or leave your comlink identifier with one of the guards."

"Yes, Lord Caedus." The woman looked so relieved that Caedus had to wonder if the rumors of his harsh treatment of Lieutenant Tebut had already crossed navies; it was just another reminder of the costly mistakes he had made by letting his emotions get so out of hand. "Thank you, Lord Caedus."

She began to back out of the chamber until Tahiri said, "Wait."

Caedus glanced down his shoulder at her. "You have a good reason for countermanding my command?"

"Uh, if you don't mind, my lord," Tahiri said. "I'd like to know the purpose of the sample. Does it have something to do with the Empire's nanokiller?"

Before answering, the lieutenant looked to Caedus for permission.

"Go ahead," Caedus said. "An order from my apprentice is an order from me."

"Thank you, my lord," the lieutenant said. She turned to Tahiri. "That's correct, ma'am. Since the prisoner is a granddaughter to Boba Fett, the Moffs thought it might be wise to develop a strain targeting him."

"That *is* a good idea," Caedus said. Mirta's fear was a boiling cloud in the Force—and with good reason. A sample of her blood would accomplish in a needleprick what he had expected to spend days—perhaps even weeks—working on. "And how long will it take to develop that strain?"

"Their close family relationship will make it fairly easy,"

she reported. "No more than three days. It might be as fast as one, if we're allowed unlimited access to the prisoner."

Caedus half turned, looking back at Mirta's horrified face. "I think we can arrange that," he said. "Would you like me to hold her head so she doesn't try to bite you?"

"That would be very kind, Lord Caedus." The lieutenant started forward, already removing the sterile cover from her collection kit. "Thank you."

"Wait!" This time, the countermand came from Mirta. "I'll tell you who was on my team."

Caedus raised his hand to stop the lieutenant. "I *thought* you might have a change of heart." He began to put the power of the Force behind his words again. "How touching. You're actually trying to *protect* the man who sent you into this mess."

Mirta ignored his sarcasm. "No samples." She pointed her chin at the hypo in his hand. "And I get my injection. Agreed?"

"And you really believe that I'll keep my word?" Caedus asked. The question wasn't an idle one. He was actually interested in how the rest of the galaxy perceived him. "Or do you have some proposal to guarantee that I do?"

"Not that I have any other choice, but I'll trust your promise," Mirta said. "If you'd lie to a woman in this condition, you really are a supreme sleemo."

The insult made Caedus's stomach clench in anger, but he recalled what had happened the last time he hadn't controlled his anger and nodded.

"You keep your part of the bargain, and I'll keep mine," he said. "Who was with you?"

"There was only one Jedi," Mirta said. "Your sister, Jaina."

"My *sister*?" Caedus roared despite himself. "You expect me to believe that?" He waved the stump of his arm at her. "That Jaina did *this*?"

"I don't know *who* did that, but Jaina was the only Jedi

I saw." Mirta seemed completely unimpressed by his anger. "And don't look so surprised. She's been training with Mandalorians."

"Then why didn't she share their disposal barge?" Caedus demanded. He turned to the lieutenant. "Take your sample."

"*What?*" Mirta seemed genuinely shocked. "You're a Jedi! Can't you tell I'm not lying?"

"I'm a *Sith*," Caedus corrected. "And I don't need the Force to know you're lying. There were two Jedi there. I fought them both."

Mirta did a good job of appearing completely confused—even in the Force. "I don't know about that, but the only one who came with *us* was Jaina."

"Then how did *Luke* get in?" Caedus demanded. He whirled on the lieutenant. "What are you waiting for? I gave you an order."

"Of c-course." The frightened lieutenant stepped to the foot of the bed—where the prisoner could not even attempt to bite her—and pulled the sheet off Mirta's feet. "Sorry, my lord."

Mirta watched in horror as the lieutenant raised a vein, then, just before the needle was inserted, said, "Okay, Luke was with us."

The lieutenant looked to Caedus for instructions.

Caedus ignored her. "I know *that*. How did he get into the planning forum?"

"With us." Mirta's answer sounded more like a question than an answer, and Caedus realized she was *still* lying to him—he could even sense it in the Force. "We had control of the Nickel One security system and help from the Verpine—"

"Yes, I know all that, too," Caedus said. "I'm interested in Luke—in how he *really* slipped into the asteroid. This is your last chance."

Mirta's eyes grew desperate. "I *told* you," she said. "We

came in through a gun emplacement, then blew a reactor core to cover our breach point."

Incredibly, Mirta was still lying about something. Caedus could sense it in her desperate Force aura—that she was being mostly truthful but misleading him about something crucial.

"At least *something* you said is true," he said. He passed the hypo to the lieutenant. "Take your sample—and give her this injection. She told half the truth, so I'll keep half my word."

Mirta began to curse him again, and Caedus knew he had made all the progress he was going to that day. He motioned Tahiri to follow him, then left the room and started down the corridor toward his quarters, deep in thought as he puzzled over how Luke had really gotten into the room.

It *always* came down to Luke. It had been Luke's eyes into which he had been looking when his arm was taken, it was Luke's face that haunted his dreams, it was Luke who he saw in his visions. Sometimes Luke was chasing him through a desert landscape filled with spires and arches, sometimes Luke was driving a crimson lightsaber through his heart . . . sometimes Luke was wearing Caedus's black robes, sitting on *his* dark throne, ruling *his* Sith Empire.

"That was a lot of trouble," Tahiri said, finally tearing Caedus out of his thoughts. "If you were going to betray your promise, why bother justifying it? It's not like anyone there was going to talk about it."

Caedus stopped in the middle of the corridor. "I *didn't* betray my promise," he said. "Mirta was lying about *something.*"

"Sure, after you started pressing her," Tahiri said. "But I didn't sense the lie the first time. If Luke was there, she didn't know how he got there."

"Luke *was* there," Caedus insisted.

"Sorry," Tahiri said, not quite cringing. "I didn't mean to suggest—"

"No—forgive *me*," Caedus said, finally realizing what he had overlooked—what the Force must have been telling him all along. "I was just coming to a decision."

Tahiri remained silent, waiting for his pronouncement.

"Have Mirta transferred to the *Anakin Solo*, and inform the Moffs that I would like them to place their assets at my disposal and select a command committee to accompany us."

"Very well," Tahiri said. "Shall I inform them of our objective?"

"My uncle." Caedus began to walk again. "I've been growing more and more convinced that killing Luke Skywalker is the key to winning this war—and I'm *sure* of it now."

chapter fourteen

What's the difference between a lightsaber and a glowrod? About two thousand degrees!

—Jacen Solo, age 15

It felt great to sweat again. The outdoor sparring session wasn't the only exercise Jaina had performed since returning to the secret base at Shedu Maad—since she'd *limped* back after failing to kill Caedus on Nickel One. But today was the first time Cilghal had allowed her to really let go— to prove to Luke and everyone else that she was ready to attack again.

Jaina sprang at Zekk, doubling him over with a powerful thrust kick to the gut, then dropped to her haunches— and realized *why* when an electrostaff came swinging through where her neck had been a split second earlier. She immediately spun into a squatting leg-wheel, hooking her heel behind a furry stump of a leg and sweeping it forward.

Lowbacca roared in surprise and tried to transfer his balance to his other leg, but Jaina was already coming up on his flank, driving her shoulder into him and sending him tumbling. The electrostaff came down across Zekk's shoulder, emitting a sharp crackle as it discharged its immobilizing shock. Jaina slapped the flexible "blade" of her own staff across Lowbacca's back, then heard Jag rushing in behind her and sent him flying with a back kick to the belly.

Tesar was on her like a rancor, driving her back with a flurry of scaly-footed kicks and cane strikes, his dark Barabel eyes bulging with the joy of the fight. Jaina parried a head strike, blocked a gut kick by driving an elbow into his instep, then hook-trapped a blazing-fast head slap and hung off his enormous arm as she swung up, wrapping her legs around his waist and shocking him three times in the ribs before his reptilian neural system registered the incapacitating jolts and finally dropped him to the grass in a heap of quivering scales.

Jaina rolled over her shoulder and came up ready to face her last unzapped opponent, but Jag was still sitting on the far side of the courtyard. He was trying to catch the wind that had been knocked out of him and rubbing a red welt where he had apparently struck his forearm with his own electrostaff.

"You didn't have to shock *yourself*," Jaina teased. She deactivated her electrostaff. "You could have just said stop."

Jag didn't smile, but a twinkle did come to his durasteel gaze. "I'm not so sure," he said. "You had that wild look in your eye again."

Jaina did not need to ask *what* look. She knew the one he meant; it was the one she had learned in Keldabe, when Beviin taught her the art of losing herself to the fight. She looked around at her four opponents, who were all still resting on the grass, trying to catch their breath and let their neural systems recover from the jolts they had received.

"You four want to go again?" She looked around the courtyard perimeter, where her parents, uncle, and several Masters stood watching the workout session. Behind them loomed one of the amber-stained mine buildings the Jedi were now calling home, with the billowing crowns of a few dozen kolg trees showing above the structure's corrugated roof. "Maybe we could get Master Durron to help out."

If *that* didn't prove to them that she was ready to go after Caedus again, nothing would.

"No more sparring today, Jedi Solo," said Cilghal. The Mon Calamari Master stepped into the practice area, holding a large bioscanner in her flipper-like hands. "Even if your injuries no longer trouble you, they are not healed."

"They're healed enough," Jaina countered. "*Caedus* is recuperating, too, you know."

"Then perhapz someone else should harry the prey a bit while you recover," Tesar said, still sitting on the mat. "This one would love to take over the hunt."

Jaina glanced over. "No offense, Tesar," she said, cocking her brow. "But if *I'm* not ready, how come *you're* the one on the ground?"

Tesar's pebbly lips drew back in reptilian surprise, then he slapped his tail on the grass and began to siss almost uncontrollably.

"*No offensse!*" He slapped his tail down again. "Truly funny!"

Lowbacca chuffed in puzzlement, then looked over at Tesar and shook his head. Barabel humor remained inscrutable—at least to Wookiees.

Zekk rose, looking a little embarrassed, and stepped over to Jaina. "Okay, maybe you've got a point," he said. "But if you reinjure yourself training, where will you be then? Caedus will have healed, and you won't."

Jaina considered this, then sighed. "You *would* have to be the voice of reason." She raised her arms so Cilghal could run the bioscanner over her ribs. "All right. Let's grab a set of shatter panels."

"*Panels?*" Jag started toward her. "Jaina, listen to Zekk. You've got to—"

"Shatterpoint is a Force technique, Jag, not a physical one," Luke said, speaking from the edge of the courtyard.

"And Jaina does need to practice. It shouldn't aggravate her injuries." He turned to Cilghal. "Right?"

Cilghal studied the bioscanner for a moment, then nodded. "As long as you don't twist your body too violently, Jedi Solo."

"Thanks," Jaina said. "I won't."

As Zekk and the others fetched a set of panels from the edge of the practice mat, Jaina closed her eyes and began a breathing exercise to clear her mind. During one of her debriefings with Luke, she had described how Jacen had used shatterpoint to destroy Roegr's *beskar'gam*. Luke had surprised her by suggesting that he teach it to her.

Jaina should not have been surprised that her uncle had mastered the technique himself—but she was. So she had foolishly blurted out something about it being a lost art, and that hardly anyone could master it. Luke had simply smiled and replied that an art was not lost just because it could be wielded only by a handful, and that if her twin brother was one of the few capable of learning it, so was she.

By the time Jaina had cleared her mind, her four sparring partners stood around her in a semicircle. Each was holding a small panel in front of him, his legs braced and his elbows locked so the panel would not move when it was struck.

Jaina did not take any time to study her targets or be certain of her strike. She simply looked at the panel in Jag's hands—a homogoni slab five centimeters thick. She actually *saw* how the Force bound its cells together, how they were organized into long lines that gave the wood its grain, and exactly where that grain could be split. Then she simply let her hand slide out and do it, let her fingertips touch the place she had seen. At once, she felt the Force shooting through her hand as it rushed into that weak spot, shattering the bonds that had held the slab together.

The homogoni did not just split, it shattered, and Jag was left holding two tiny fragments with a pile of slivers at his feet.

"Nice job," he said.

Jaina had already turned to the panel in Zekk's hands, a plastoid breastplate that had been taken from a captured stormtrooper. She saw the plastoid as she had seen the homogoni, but now there was no true grain, just layer after layer of polymers crossing in every conceivable direction, with one spot where the layers were particularly thin. She let her hand slide out again. The breastplate fragmented into a dozen pieces and clattered to the grass at Zekk's feet. Next, Jaina turned to Tesar and let her hand slide out to touch the small square of hfredium hull plate he was holding. The square parted into triangles and fluttered out of the Barabel's hands.

Finally, she turned to Lowbacca, who was holding a disk of raw *beskar*. Luke had arranged to buy the disk from one of the arms dealers that the Mandalorians were now quite freely supplying with the stuff. She almost hesitated, but forced herself *not* to think, to just see and do, and before she knew it her hand was shooting out toward the heart of a spiral of carefully worked metal crystals.

And the disk crumbled, just as Roegr's breastplate had when Caedus had tapped it with the pommel of his lightsaber.

Behind her, Jaina's father let out a loud, embarrassing whoop. "Who needs a lightsaber?" Han exclaimed. "I haven't seen anything that impressive since your mother wrapped a chain around Jabba's throat."

"Han, you didn't see that," her mother said. "Freeze-blind, remember?"

Jaina turned to find her mother tapping her temple near her eyes, and her father still pumping his fist into the air. But it was the doorway a dozen meters behind them that caught her interest. Emerging from it was a handsome young man with reddish hair and his father's blue eyes, with a pair of well-dressed Hapan women following close behind.

"*Ben?*" Jaina spread her arms and rushed across the grass to greet him. "You're back!"

She wrapped him in a tight embrace and whirled him back and forth, ignoring for the moment whether he wished to speak himself—or even needed to breathe.

"Don't you *ever* do that again!" she ordered.

Ben managed to disengage himself. "Do *what*?"

"Move away from your backup!" Jaina said. "What were you thinking?"

She finally began to notice the women accompanying Ben—and grew so distracted she did not hear Ben's reply. They were definitely identical twins and definitely Hapan nobility, with the fine clothes and haughty bearing typical of women of that class. But they were more than that. With their long straight noses, thin arcing eyebrows, and silky red hair, they were obviously relatives of Tenel Ka—and fairly close relatives, at that.

". . . not to get *you* and Aunt Leia captured, too," Ben was saying. "That's the protocol for a situation like the one we were in at Monument Plaza, and it was the right thing to do."

"Yes, it was," Leia agreed, joining them. "Welcome back. And please forgive Jaina. She was just worried about you. We all were."

"Thanks, Aunt Leia." Ben smiled at her briefly, then looked back to Jaina and frowned. "I'm a *Jedi*, Jaina, with a job to do, just like you. If we're going to keep working together, you're going to have to remember that—okay?"

Jaina lifted her brow. "Yeah, sure, Ben. Sorry." She looked to the two women accompanying him. "What have you two been feeding him?"

The two women looked at each other, then the one on the right said, "Don't blame *us* if you can't handle your men. All we did was deliver him to Her Majesty, as ordered."

Ben just shook his head, then turned to his father, who was standing quietly beside Leia.

"Good to see you, Dad," he said. "At least *you're* not treating me like a kid anymore. Thanks."

"You're welcome, Ben," Luke said. "But there's no need to thank me. All I did was give you a mission, and you performed brilliantly. Without you, we wouldn't have known where to look for Caedus—and we wouldn't have known what he was up to in the Roche system."

Ben beamed for a second, then hugged his father. Jaina was surprised to see that he had already grown almost as tall as Luke. In a year, he might even be taller.

"I guess I had a good teacher, Dad." After a moment, Ben freed himself and stepped back, his expression growing serious again. "But there was a problem with my escape—a big one."

"There always is, kid," Han said. "What's this one?"

Ben hesitated. "Maybe I'd better let Tenel Ka explain it. She has the intelligence reports."

"Tenel Ka is *here*?" Zekk gasped.

Ben looked at Zekk as though he had just asked a very foolish question. "Of course she's here," he said. "You didn't think the *Dragon Queen* came all this way just to deliver *me*, did you?"

Jaina frowned and looked to her mother, who did not seem surprised at all. "What did I miss?"

"Sorry," Luke said. "I didn't want to interrupt your sparring. The *Dragon Queen* arrived an hour ago with most of the Hapan Home Fleet."

Now Jaina was *really* confused—as were Jag, Zekk, and the others. Moving an entire fleet to a secret base wasn't a very good way to keep it secret.

"What's the Home Fleet doing *here*?" Zekk asked.

"Her Majesty will explain all that shortly," said one of the women with Ben. She stepped to Zekk's side and looped a hand through his arm. "In the meantime, why don't you show me around, handsome? My name's Taryn."

Zekk looked somewhere between confused and shocked; then his expression softened.

"Maybe we can do that later . . . Taryn." He nodded toward the door, where a large Hapan security detail was escorting Tenel Ka and Allana into the courtyard. "Right now, I'd like to hear what Her Majesty has to say."

Taryn looked annoyed—but only for a moment. "Later is good, too," she said. "But don't disappoint me. We have a date."

"Uh, sure." Zekk was clearly reeling from the straight-forward manner of Hapan women; he flushed and glanced over at Jaina. "I mean, if *you* don't mind."

Taryn turned to Jaina, her expression more appraising than apologetic. "He's yours?"

"Well, n-no," Jaina said. Zekk looked even more un-comfortable, and through the Force, she could feel Jag smirking at her dilemma. "Of course he's not *mine*. We don't—"

"Well, then," Taryn interrupted. She smiled and squeezed Zekk's biceps. "Lucky me."

Taryn's twin sister rolled her eyes. "We're supposed to be on duty, Taryn."

"Don't be such a Dug, Trista," Taryn replied. "I can have fun *and* do my duty."

Trista stifled her reply as Tenel Ka emerged from the building, holding the hand of a beautiful little girl with her mother's red hair and a cute button nose. Jaina's heart broke. It was the first time she had ever seen her niece, and Allana's resemblance to Jacen at that age was striking. She could not understand how her brother could have intro-

duced so much evil into the galaxy when he had such inno-
cence to protect. Nearly everything else Caedus had done
might have been forgivable, but how could he have taken
his own daughter hostage?

As Tenel Ka and Allana arrived, the group made a place
for them to stand, but there were no big Solo hugs for Allana. Her paternity was known by only a few, and for
Allana's sake, Tenel Ka and the Solos wanted to keep it that
way.

"Your Majesty," Luke said. "Thank you for visiting us
here on Shedu Maad. We're honored."

Tenel Ka smiled and impatiently motioned for everyone
to stop bowing. "There is no need for formalities when we
are alone, my friends," she said. "Nor do we have the time.
I'm afraid I've come with some alarming news."

Luke nodded. "We suspected as much when you arrived
with your fleet. What is it?"

"As Ben may have told you," she said, "my father was
captured and taken aboard the *Anakin Solo*."

Ben *hadn't* told them, of course, which certainly explained the dead silence that greeted her announcement.

After a moment of quiet, Ben said, "It was my fault. I
thought I was clean, but—"

"It wasn't your fault, Jedi Skywalker," said Trista. "You
told us we were being watched."

Leia stepped over and took Tenel Ka's hand. "I'm so
sorry, Your Majesty. If there's anything we can do—"

"Perhaps later, Princess Leia," Tenel Ka interrupted.
"But Prince Isolder knew the location of this base. Appar-
ently, Darth Caedus forced him to reveal it, because the
Anakin Solo has broken out of the Roche system with
the Remnant assault fleet. They were last seen entering the
Transitory Mists near Roqoo Station."

"Caedus is coming to *us*?" asked Saba Sebatyne, looking
entirely too happy about it. "You are certain?"

Tenel Ka nodded. "And there may not be time to evacuate. The Mist Patrol informs me that with the right charts, Caedus could be assaulting the Maad system within twelve hours."

"What are the chances he has the right charts?" Han asked.

"Even if he doesn't, the Force will guide him," Luke said. He turned to Tenel Ka. "But I doubt your father revealed our location. I think Caedus may have found us another way."

"What other way?" Tenel Ka asked. "Only a handful of people know the location of this base."

Luke motioned Jaina forward, then pointed at the stains that Jaina still had not been able to scrub off her face and neck. "Do you recognize this?"

Tenel Ka's jaw dropped. "Those are not burns?" Before Luke or anyone else could answer, she leaned in closer to Jaina. "That's Caedus's blood?"

"I *knew* it," Jaina said, growing uneasy. "It's from his arm, and it won't come off—"

"Because it's a blood trail," Tenel Ka explained. "Some of the Nightsisters used the technique to mark their slaves—so they could always track them down."

Jaina's heart sank. "So *I* led him here." She turned to Luke. "And you knew? Why did you let me stay?"

"I knew Caedus would be coming," Luke corrected. "For *me*."

Jaina frowned. "But he *saw* me cut off his arm," she said. "He must know that I'm the one hunting him."

"He knowz you are the Sword," Saba corrected. "Does one win a battle by breaking the Sword, or the warrior who wieldz it?"

Luke turned to Tenel Ka. "Thank you for the warning. I don't mean to be an ungracious host, but we have to prepare, and we may not have long. Perhaps you and Allana should leave while there's still time."

"We are staying, as is my fleet," Tenel Ka said. "If the Jedi fall, so does my throne. Better to defend it here among friends than on Hapes, with more enemies at my back than in front of me."

"It will be an honor, Jedi Majesty," Saba said. "This one will be proud to hunt at your side."

As Luke and the others began to make plans for the coming onslaught, Jaina was still struggling to grasp how her brother had taken advantage of her. She did not understand exactly how Nightsister blood trails worked, but she assumed the Force-user somehow maintained a connection to the blood he had shed, and employed that to keep track of his living property.

If Jaina had had any lingering doubts about whether there might be any trace of Jacen left inside Darth Caedus, they were gone now. Caedus had known *exactly* what he was doing when he ordered those stormtroopers to redirect their fire. And his cold calculation in the face of such an injury scared her even more than seeing him stand up after losing his arm. He hadn't wanted Jaina killed *then*, because he needed her to lead him to the Jedi *now*.

When Jaina returned her attention to the others, it was to find her father studying her with sad, sympathetic eyes.

"It finally happened, didn't it?" he asked.

"Yeah," Jaina said. "I think it did."

Ben frowned. "*What* happened?"

"Her last hope died," Leia said. "She realized that Jacen is totally gone. There's nothing left to bring back into the light."

Jaina nodded. "That's pretty much it," she said. "I started to wonder again when he ordered those stormtroopers to redirect their fire. But whatever I thought I saw—it was in *my* eyes, not his."

Ben contemplated this for a moment, then asked, "But

how *do* you know when someone can be brought back toward the light?"

"First, they must *want* to be redeemed," Tenel Ka said. "All Caedus wants is to control everything he sees. There is no use wishing otherwise, Ben."

"*I* did some pretty terrible things," Ben pointed out. "And no one gave up on *me*."

"*You* got a little confused, kid," Han said. "That happens. But you didn't go around killing family members and burning planets."

Jaina glanced over at Luke. He was studying Ben not with shock or disbelief over his son's naïveté, but with pride. Luke understood his son much better than they did, she realized. Whatever Ben was working through, it had nothing to do with Jacen . . . *or* Caedus.

"Ben?" Jaina asked. "Are you talking about Tahiri?"

Ben looked uncomfortable. "I'm just asking a question. How else am I going to know?"

"But you must have a reason for asking," Leia prompted. "What is it?"

Ben looked at the ground and exhaled, trying to gather his thoughts—or his courage. Finally, he said, "I think Tahiri hated what she did."

"Killing Shevu?" asked Leia.

"Right. And torturing me. She almost—" Ben stopped there, cringing at some memory he didn't care to share. "Tahiri tried everything she could to avoid hurting me. And when Shevu died, she felt horrible. She's not like Caedus. Not yet."

The reply came from an unexpected source, a little voice down by Tenel Ka's thigh. "Jedi Jacen *likes* hurting people," Allana said. "He scares me."

Jaina shuddered. Now Caedus's own daughter feared him. The Jacen Solo she had grown up with would never have wanted such a thing.

She crouched in front of her niece and took Allana's tiny hands in her own. "He'll never scare you again, Allana. I promise."

Allana looked doubtful. "You *really* promise?"

"Sure," Jaina said. "I really promise."

chapter fifteen

Why was the Jedi Master cross-eyed? Because he couldn't control his pupils!

—Jacen Solo, age 15

An approaching battle fleet crept into view, a distant crescent of blue pinpoints shining bright against the shadowy depths of the Transitory Mists. To one side of the formation hung the nebulous smudge of the gravity well the fleet was skirting, a barely glowing protostar so deeply purple it was almost black. To the other side lay a hazard even more dangerous, a Mist-cloaked field of icy monoliths that had once been the third gas giant in an unstable triple-world cluster.

Jaina glanced down at the StealthX's tactical display and, as she expected, saw only static. The Mists in this part of the Maad system were so thick that an object had to be nearly recognizable before it could be scanned or signaled. That was one of the reasons Luke and Tenel Ka had selected this spot for the ambush. The other reason was—of course—the natural abundance of navigational hazards. Caedus's fleet would be forced to make a long realspace approach through a narrow "safe" channel, with barely detectable gravity wells and moon-sized ice chunks hiding in the Mists to every side. All Jaina had to do was to lure him in—and make him believe this was the route to the secret Jedi base.

It was a simple plan, really—at least in theory.

So far, she seemed to be doing a good job. Caedus had followed the blood trail this far, anyway. Her position was just across the midsystem void from Shedu Maad—more or less in line with it, and close enough that he was unlikely to have noticed her shift from the real base. At least, that's what Luke had told her, and he obviously knew more about blood trails. Her next task was to head back down "the Throat"—Saba's name for the channel where Tenel Ka would ambush Caedus. Jaina had to make it look like she was rushing back to base to sound the alarm.

At that point, the Jedi would launch an assault on the *Anakin Solo,* covering her so that she could board and hunt down her brother. She tried not to think about that last part of her job. If she let her thoughts rush too far ahead of the actual events, she might not get there at all.

Jaina began to bring up the systems she had left dormant to conserve her batteries, then realized she had not sensed any sharpening in her wingmate's Force aura. She glanced over to the other StealthX and found Zekk's helmet turned toward the other side of his canopy, facing the amber-striped disks of Qogo and Uluq—the twin gas giants locked in a mutual orbit at the base of the Throat. He was so lost in thought that he didn't even sense Jaina looking in his direction, and she was surprised to discover that made her feel a little sad.

They had been so close for so many years, Jaina had simply taken for granted that they would always be the ideal mission partners, in Force contact on an almost unconscious level, able to read each other's thoughts and intentions almost to the same degree as her parents. But that wasn't really true anymore. Something had changed while Jaina was away training with the Mandalorians. She had returned to discover that sometimes it took a conscious effort to maintain her connection with Zekk, almost as though she had to keep reminding him that she was there.

Jaina had tried to tell herself that the change was due to

her current mission, because she had to confront Caedus alone. But she knew better. The truth was, Zekk had probably just grown weary of waiting for her to sort out her personal life. Or maybe the time apart had helped him realize he didn't need to be anything more than her wingmate. That probably shouldn't have made her sad, but it did.

Jaina reached out and gave Zekk a Force nudge. His helmet swung toward her a little too quickly, and a tinge of embarrassment came to his Force aura. She frowned, wondering if he had been thinking of those Hapan intelligence agents, and immediately one of the names—*Taryn*—popped into her mind. Jaina shook her head in disbelief.

Careful, Zekk, she thought. *That one will twist you up.*

A ripple of confusion rolled through the Force. Jaina grinned behind her breath mask—wistfully, but it *was* a grin—and pointed up the Throat toward the protostar.

Caedus's fleet had already changed from a crescent of blue pinpoints to a snaking ribbon. A handful of faint, tiny specks were moving ahead of the ribbon and fanning out in all directions—scouting craft, on their way to map hazards and check for ambushes. They were going to find both, Jaina knew, but it didn't matter. The Masters had foreseen that possibility, and squadrons of Miy'tils were hiding at key points to ensure that none of the reconnaissance skiffs survived to report their discoveries.

Zekk quickly brought up his own systems, then they accelerated out into the Throat and turned straight for Uroro Station—an abandoned transfer facility floating in the gravitic equilibrium point between Qogo and Uluq. Luke and most of the Jedi were there, along with a select group of younglings and academy staff. If it was going to be an effective decoy, it would have to feel like the real thing when Caedus reached out to it through the Force.

Jaina made no attempt to hide her presence in the Force, since the whole idea was to *let* Caedus sense them returning to Uroro Station. And it would have been pointless anyway, since Zekk hadn't been taught the technique yet.

They had been traveling down the Throat for about two minutes when Jaina felt a prickle of danger sense. Not only had they been spotted, she realized, but they were about to be fired upon. She reached out to warn Zekk, but he was focused on her and the mission now, and he had already picked up on her panic. They banked hard to starboard—and felt space jump as a turbolaser strike erupted behind them.

Jaina dived and Zekk climbed—that almost *never* happened—and a sheet of fire boiled past her canopy. She feared for a moment that Zekk had been hit, but then she felt him worrying about her and knew that he was okay. It took nearly a minute of dodging and barrel-rolling before there was enough of a lull in the barrage to chance forming up again, and by that time Jaina's flight gloves were soaked with sweat. It felt like the Throat was vomiting fire.

This was something the Masters hadn't anticipated, and it was going to complicate things. If she and Zekk returned to Uroro Station under fire, Caedus would sense the trap— it would look like they were *trying* to lead him right to their "secret" base. So they would have to dodge into the ice field and make it look like they were attempting to lead Caedus away from the station.

Right . . . but they couldn't dodge too soon. The thought came to Jaina without her quite understanding *why* she had realized it. Apparently, Zekk was trying to tell her something through the Force—but he couldn't be too obvious, because Caedus might be monitoring their meld. She checked her tactical display and still didn't see anything on the screen except the conspicuous disks of the two gas giants. Then she noticed the distances to the pair and understood.

Jaina and Zekk were still two minutes away from the

place where Tenel Ka was hiding with her fleet. If they left the Throat now, and Caedus followed, the Hapans wouldn't be in position to attack.

Jaina smiled and brought her StealthX in a little behind Zekk's, allowing him to take the lead. It was good to be flying with him again—even if it *was* going to be nearly impossible to survive the next two minutes.

And Jaina had a hunch he felt the same way.

From the observation deck of Uroro Station, the Throat suddenly looked like a long, dark tunnel with an atomic furnace at the other end. Han could see nothing inside but a boiling ball of turbolaser fire, slowly expanding as it drew nearer to their position. Saba and the other Masters stood waiting in rapt silence, already dressed in their combat-rated vac suits in anticipation of boarding the *Anakin Solo* to rescue Prince Isolder. Han would have bet they were as scared as he was, had there been anyone in the chamber who looked willing to take such a sucker bet.

Luke must have noticed something in Han's demeanor— maybe the way he was biting his lip, or his fingernails digging into his palms—because he clapped a hand on Han's shoulder.

"They're doing fine, Han," he said quietly. "They don't even seem frightened."

"I'm glad *someone's* not." Han did not want to keep looking out the viewport, but he couldn't tear his eyes away. "What made us think he'd just follow her?" he growled. "He's been trying to kill everyone *else* in the family."

Saba glanced over, her bulging eyes so far open that they looked like they might fall out of their scaly sockets. "Who sayz we *didn't*?" she asked. "But we had to make it look like *someone* was on patrol, and Jaina is the best one to whet Caedus'z appetite."

"Oh, that makes sense," Han said sarcastically. He turned to Leia, who seemed only marginally less worried than he was. "Our next kids are *not* going to be Jedi."

"Sure, Han, whatever you say." Leia's eyes did not leave the viewport. "But I don't think you have to worry about having more kids."

"Hey, *I'm* still young," Han said. "And *you're* a Jedi."

Before Leia could utter a comeback, Corran Horn's voice rang out from the portable control panel at the back of the deck, where C-3PO and R2-D2 were working. The two droids were tweeting and sniping at each other as they helped assimilate data streaming in from a dozen different sources.

"We're starting to receive relays from the Hapan observation posts," Corran said. "I'll put it up."

All eyes shifted to the portable wall display that had been affixed along one side of the deck. It was not a true tactical display. Instead, a simple graphic represented all the data being relayed from the Hapan observation posts via line-of-sight transmissions, visual flash codes, and even droid couriers. The Throat was depicted as a white ribbon snaking down the center of the screen toward a spoked wheel labeled URORO STATION. Coming down the center of this ribbon was a collection of simple designator codes identifying the vessels in Caedus's fleet. From what Han could see, it included the handful of Remnant Star Destroyers that had escaped destruction in the Roche system, along with a sizable support flotilla of heavy cruisers, pocket destroyers, and frigates.

But it was what lay in the heart of the fleet that made Han's stomach sink. Floating alongside the *Anakin Solo* was a designator reading MEGADOR, with a question mark. Han glanced back at the red ball boiling down the Throat and began to feel queasy. The *Megador* was a *Super*-class Star Destroyer. It carried more than five times the firepower of a typical Imperial II like the *Anakin Solo*. And there had

been rumors of a weapons upgrade that included three batteries of new long-range turbolasers. If *that* was after Jaina
and Zekk, he didn't know how long they could last.

"I don't think we'll be giving anything away by launching our defenses now, Master Horn," Luke said. "Give the
order."

"About time," Han muttered.

He glanced over to see that Luke had also turned away
from the display. But instead of staring out the viewport
toward the approaching fleet, Luke was standing with his
hands clasped behind his back and his head down, his eyes
closed as though lost in his thoughts . . . or his memories . . .
or some kind of Jedi trance.

Corran acknowledged the order and relayed the command. The Jedi fighters did not begin to automatically
stream from the station's dilapidated hangars, however. To
avoid any possibility of making Caedus suspect an ambush
by reacting a little *too* quickly, Luke had insisted that the
pilots remain in the ready rooms with their helmets off and
flight suits open.

Han spent the next thirty seconds looking from the viewport to the wall display, trying to guess when Jaina and
Zekk would finally be out of danger. The Hapan Home
Fleet could be seen clustered together along one edge of the
display, a mass of designator symbols packed tightly
among the craggy blue blotches representing the field of ice
chunks. It seemed all too likely that Jaina and Zekk would
not try to escape the barrage until they were well past the
Hapan position. And he admired their courage, he really
did. He just wished that *he* could have been out there instead.

At long last, lines of starfighters began to stream away
from the station. There was a squadron of Wookiee-piloted
Owools, and another squadron of the new blastboats
piloted by Alliance deserters who had chosen to seek out
the Jedi instead of heeding Niathal's call to join her. Then

came the StealthX wing, a black tide of cruciform shadows that remained silhouetted against the firelit depths of the Throat for only a moment before winking out of sight.

The fighters had been gone for a full minute when Leia reached over and grabbed Han's hand, *hard*. His heart stopped beating—probably because it had gotten stuck in his throat—and he knew she was about to tell him she had just felt something in the Force.

"What is it?" he asked, steeling himself for the worst. "Are they—"

"Not under fire anymore," Leia said. "I don't know how, I don't know where, but they're safe."

Han let out a long breath of relief. "Why wouldn't they be?" he asked. "Jaina's got my luck."

Leia smiled. "That, and the Force," she said.

Han would have argued the Force comment, except that the firestorm in the Throat suddenly seemed to be dying away. He checked the wall display and saw that Caedus's fleet was slowing down. Unfortunately, it was still short of the area where the Hapans were lying in ambush.

"Uh-oh," he said, more to himself than anyone else. "It looks like they're getting careful."

Saba hissed, and the rest of the Masters in the room began to whisper about Caedus's battle powers and his ability to read the future. Luke said nothing; he just stood in front of the viewport, his hands folded behind his back and his gaze fixed on the deck between his feet.

"Hey, Luke?" Han asked. "You okay?"

"He is gone again," Saba said. "Why does he keep doing that when we need him most?"

The twinkle in the Barabel's bulbous eye suggested she knew *exactly* why Luke kept doing it, but that wasn't much comfort to Han. Right now, the young Jedi kids and support staff brought along to act as decoys were waiting in the docks on the bottom level of the station, packed into transports and ready to evacuate when Luke gave the order. The idea had been that the kids would leave before the attack on the station came. But with those long-range turbolasers, Caedus was almost close enough *now* to open fire—and it was beginning to look like he intended to stand off and do just that.

"Uh, maybe we'd better handle this order ourselves," Han said. That was the trouble with wars—the enemy always had a way of doing something unexpected that ruined your carefully made plans. "The *Megador* is getting close enough to open up on us, and this place isn't exactly well shielded."

Saba studied Luke for a moment, then said, "I will ask my fellow Masterz."

She turned to consult with Kyp, Cilghal, and the others.

"Great," Han muttered. "They ought to reach a decision about the time the battle's over."

"Don't be so cynical," Leia chided. "They're Masters—they can hear you."

Han winced and glanced over his shoulder at the circle. No one seemed to be looking in his direction, but Kyp did wag a finger at him.

The finger had not yet stopped when C-3PO announced, "The observation posts are reporting that the *Anakin Solo* and *Megador* have both launched their starfighter complements."

That news brought the Masters' debate to an early halt. Saba and the others stopped to glance over at the wall display, which showed the enemy starfighters as a stream of flickering dots streaming out to meet the Owools and blastboats.

"He's not buying our act," Han said. "We need to give him a reason to keep coming down the Throat—and clear out while we still can."

Saba nodded her agreement, then turned to the other Masters—who also nodded, almost as one.

Saba turned back to Han. "Okay," she said. "The Masterz agree. You can give the order."

"Me?" Han asked. "But I'm not—"

"It was *your* idea," Saba interrupted, tilting her head at him. "Do you not think it is a good one?"

"Don't have a doubt," Han said. He snapped the comlink from his pocket and opened a channel to the convoy commander. "Time to get out of here, Ben—but don't send everyone at once. We've got to make it look good."

"Okay." Ben's voice sounded uncertain. "Uh, this is Uncle Han, right?"

"Yeah," Han said. "You got a problem with that?"

"No," Ben said. "But Dad—er, Master Skywalker—said to wait for *his* order."

Han glanced over at Luke, who was still staring at the floor with nothing in his eyes but his pupils, then looked at the wall display again. Caedus's fleet had *slowed*, but it hadn't stopped, and it would be only a couple of minutes before it could start firing on Uroro Station.

"Your dad's busy right now," Han said. "And the *Megador* is probably going to open up with her long-range turbolasers real soon. I kind of thought you'd want to be gone when that happens."

"Oh," Ben said. "I guess that makes sense. Initiating decoy operation at once."

A few seconds later, a motley assortment of light transports began to shoot away from the station. The first part of their trajectory carried them directly up the Throat toward Caedus's fleet. But within a minute or so, they started to arc around the bulge of Qogo's amber-striped sphere, heading for the ice field where the Hapans lay in hiding. If all went according to plan, Caedus would pursue, Tenel Ka would ambush him, and the assault fleet would be destroyed.

But battles never went according to plan. As it grew more apparent that the transports were fleeing, the Remnant fleet *did* begin to accelerate down the Throat again, moving to pursue them into the ice field just as Luke and Tenel Ka had hoped. But the *Solo* and the *Megador* remained behind with a handful of escorts, moving down the Throat to fire on Uroro Station.

"That's not good," Leia observed.

"It could be worse," Han said reassuringly. "I'm not sure how, but it *could* be."

Of course, *that* was when the life returned to Luke's eyes. He shook his head and frowned out the viewport for a moment, then turned to study the situation on the wall display. The last of the transports was passing through the ice field, heading for a Mist passage that would carry it back to the Hapan ground forces Tenel Ka had left to defend Shedu Maad.

"Strange," Luke said. "I don't *recall* telling Ben to evacuate."

"Guess you were talking in your sleep again," Han said. "But it was time. Trust me."

Luke chuckled. "It seems I have no other choice—as usual," he said. "But Caedus's caution does throw a hydrospanner in our plan. I don't suppose you came up with a brilliant alternative plan while I was 'sleeping'?"

"Actually, I have," Han said. "First, we all get the kark off this heap before they start blowing it apart."

"I must say, that certainly seems like a brilliant plan to me," C-3PO offered, turning away from the control panel. "I only hope the next step is equally clever."

"I'm working on that," Han said, starting for the exit. "But button up your vac suits, everybody. If I know my Jaina, she's going to board the *Anakin Solo* one way or another—and we're going to be right there behind her."

Like the little brother it was named for, the *Anakin Solo* hung in the shadow of the mighty *Megador*. The *Megador* was pounding away with its long-range turbolasers, pouring a river of crimson beams down the Throat toward Uroro Station. With its own long-range battery still out of commission after the sabotage at Kashyyyk, the *Anakin Solo* was concentrating on perimeter protection, using its normal turbolasers and point-defense arrays to build a shell of anti-starcraft fire around both vessels.

Jaina glanced over at the scorched ruin of a StealthX floating next to her own pock-holed wreck. Zekk was leaning down in the cockpit, trying to splice together a wire beneath the control panel. She knew it was nothing critical because, incredibly, both StealthXs were still flyable. But she thought about urging him to head back to Shedu Maad. Trouble was, she was pretty sure he wouldn't go unless she came, too, and that wasn't going to happen.

So Jaina reached out to him through their combat-meld, urging him to be ready. His helmet popped back into view, looking toward his tail first, then his flanks, and finally turning forward. When he finally seemed to realize there was no immediate threat, Jaina had the distinct impression that he thought she was crazy.

He was probably right. Neither of their starfighters was in any condition for a fight. Jaina's shields were only a fond memory, and three of Zekk's laser cannons had drooping tips. Both starfighters were low on fuel, leaking coolant, and had been forced to revert to vac suit life support. Any squadron commander in any navy in the galaxy would have ordered them to return to base.

But they didn't have a squadron commander, and Jaina and Zekk were hanging on the edge of the ice field, directly between the Remnant assault fleet and the two Alliance Star Destroyers. When the Hapans sprang their ambush, the *Anakin Solo* and the *Megador* would rush to support the assault—and when they did, the *Anakin Solo* would be turning straight into the two StealthXs.

Jaina knew it was crazy. But they both had a full load of

shadow bombs, and there was no sense carrying them all the way back to Shedu Maad.

A tiny ball of orange blossomed between Qogo and Uluq as one of the *Megador*'s turbolaser strikes found its target, and a spray of tiny specks began to fly toward both planets. When the flames died away, Jaina could see that the massive station was still spinning, despite the loss of about a sixth of its outer wheel. But now that the gunners had confirmed their range and targeting, it would not be long before the rest of Uroro Station disappeared. She only hoped the evacuation had been completed in time.

The *Megador* continued to spit crimson beams down the Throat, striking the target half a dozen times in as many seconds. Uroro Station started to come apart in chunks large enough to identify, and Jaina began to see sections of spokes and wheels tumbling toward the amber-striped faces of the twin gas giants.

Then the Force shuddered with the surprise of thousands of beings, and the Mists began to flash and flicker with a never-ending cascade of turbolaser fire.

"Time to arm the shadow bombs, Sneaky," Jaina said to her astromech droid.

A tweedle sounded in Jaina's helmet earphone, and the droid scrolled a question across her status display.

"All of them," Jaina replied. "And when I give the launch order, send them—"

Sneaky chirped in indignation, then inquired whether she was under the impression that his logic circuits had been damaged during their recent brush with incineration. If she wanted to arm them *all*, of course she wanted to launch them *all*.

"Thanks," Jaina said, wondering if his personality module had suffered some heat damage. R9 units were usually a little heavy on self-preservation routines, not self-awareness. "Didn't mean to doubt you."

Sneaky accepted the apology, then suggested that *now*

might be a good time to dump the shadow bombs and run for the safety of the base. Jaina didn't have the heart to explain they wouldn't *be* returning to Shedu Maad. If they were going to land anywhere, it would be aboard the matte-black Star Destroyer in front of them.

The *Anakin Solo* fired its ion engines and began to accelerate, starting to bank toward them almost immediately. The *Megador* lagged behind, its huge mass requiring more energy to move, and its big engines more time to reach peak efficiency. Through the gap between the two, the starfighter battle raging in the Throat was just visible, a color-laced mesh of streaking lights and sudden eruptions. Jaina could already make out the sickle-nosed dots of a few Wookiee Owools and the sleek cylinders of about half a dozen Skipray blastboats, along with the tiny cruciform shapes of the XJ7s swarming them.

What truly surprised her, however, were the blocky silhouettes of the StealthX flight already coming up toward the *Anakin Solo*'s belly. They were moving too fast and erratically for her to get an accurate count—even silhouetted against the amber disk of Qogo's striped face—but she guessed there were about three dozen of them. They were rolling and dodging and sliding away from the *Solo*'s defensive fire as though their pilots knew where it would blossom before it arrived.

Leading the pack was the charcoal wedge of a Mandalorian *Bes'uliik*—large and somewhat ungainly, but still fast and powerful. It was taking more fire than the StealthXs, since it was leaving a long stream of bright blue efflux in its wake and its sensor-negation technologies weren't as efficient. But it hardly mattered, because it was being flown by the best starfighter pilot Jaina had ever seen—Luke Skywalker, of course—and it was weaving through the firestorm coming its way like a holovid stunt pilot running a special-effects course.

Jaina fired her own ion engines, then looked over to find

Zekk giving her the thumbs-up signal. She nodded, then they hit their thrusters and shot forward, angling toward the shield generator domes on top of the *Anakin Solo*'s bridge.

The first thirty seconds of their approach went as smoothly as could be expected. Jaina lost one of her engines when a faulty feed pump developed a vacuum lock, and the green glow faded from Zekk's cockpit when his spliced wire came apart and the instrument panel went dark. But nobody fired at them, or sent a fighter to investigate the pair of dark blurs coming the *Anakin Solo*'s way, and they were well within laser cannon range when a prickle of danger sense raced down Jaina's spine.

A blast of alarm flooded the battle-meld as Zekk felt the same thing. Whether it had been the stains on her neck that finally gave them away, or the combat-meld, Jaina could not say—and it hardly mattered. The fact was, Caedus had sensed them through the Force. He knew they were coming, and he knew where they were right now.

An image of a generator dome—the one on the far end of the *Solo*'s bridge—flashed through Jaina's mind. Zekk was letting her know which dome he was targeting. She pointed the nose of her StealthX at the other one.

"Launch, Sneaky!" she ordered into her throat mike. "Launch, launch, launch!"

A soft clunk reverberated through the cockpit floor as the torpedo tubes opened. At that same moment, space turned white as the *Solo* opened up with every point-defense weapon on Jaina and Zekk's side of the hull. The gun crews didn't waste time trying to find their attackers; they just put up a tightly laced cage of cannon fire and hoped the enemy would fly into it.

Unable to see through the wall of energy, Jaina turned her hands over to instinct and closed her eyes, picturing the generator dome in her mind and using the Force to hurl the shadow bombs toward it. She felt the cockpit rock as can-

non bolts tore through her StealthX's unshielded wings . . .
then Sneaky let out a static-filled overload screech and
went silent.

Jaina felt herself sinking into her seat as the StealthX
banked, and she opened her eyes to find the *Solo*'s bridge
sliding past her starfighter's belly, with balls of flame erupting at the far end as Zekk's shadow bombs blasted their
way through the shields to the generator dome.

An instant later, Jaina's StealthX began to buck hard,
and everything below her went orange as her own bombs
hit. The orange brightened and golden forks of dissipation
energy began to dance all around the starfighter, and then
the color turned so luminous and fiery that even the flash-
tinting in her helmet visor could not prevent Jaina's eyes
from aching.

A shock wave caught her from behind and sent the
StealthX spinning. The cockpit began to shake and shudder as pieces of starfighter began to fly off the craft—
cannons, sensor cones, hull armor. The inertial compensator gave out, and her helmet-heavy head began to whirl
around on her shoulders. She pressed back against the neck
rest, trying to brace, and fought not to vomit. Everything
hurt—her eyes, ears, gut, joints. She was coming apart just
like her starfighter, Jaina knew, and there was nothing she
could do about it.

But she did something anyway.

Jaina felt her feet working the rudders, her hand fighting
to bring the stick back, her arm stretching toward the
throttles. And slowly, the spinning stopped. The *Anakin
Solo* drifted into view and stayed there, hanging outside
her canopy a little below starboard, and she found herself
more or less in one piece.

Actually, it was less, because Zekk wasn't there anymore. Jaina couldn't feel him in the Force—couldn't even
find the combat-meld. She hadn't felt him die, hadn't experienced a sudden shock of fear and pain, could not even re-

member a wistful pang of regret or farewell. He was just . . . *gone*.

After bringing her StealthX fully under control—and making a quick systems check to see if anything was about to explode—Jaina began to expand her Force awareness, searching for his presence. Instead of Zekk, she found the familiar tingle of her danger sense—with the blazing flash of a turbolaser bolt following close behind.

The strike blossomed a kilometer short of her StealthX, but Jaina knew the next one would not miss. There was only one way the gunners could have known where to direct their fire—that there was even something to direct fire *at*.

Caedus.

Jaina slammed her throttles forward and was relieved to feel the StealthX steal forward on two still-functioning engines. Deciding she had nothing to lose by making it as difficult for her brother to find her as possible, she began to hide her presence in the Force again. To her relief, the next turbolaser strike erupted even farther away than had the first, and the next few were little better than stabs in the dark. The gunners knew generally where she was, but not her exact location. Blood trails, it seemed, were not all that precise—at least, she *hoped* that was true. Jaina circled back toward the fight.

The *Anakin Solo* was only about the length of her arm from this distance, but she could see that both ends of the bridge were gone, along with the generator domes that had once been attached to them. Luke and his wing were just beginning their run, popping up over the *Anakin Solo*'s nose while the *Megador* dropped down behind them, sweeping space with cannon and turbolaser in a desperate attempt to keep the StealthXs off its companion ship. The *Anakin Solo* itself was pouring turbolaser fire into the ice field, trying just as desperately to drive Tenel Ka's Home Fleet away from the Remnant's assault fleet.

It was a doomed effort. As Jaina accelerated back toward the fight, the Jedi StealthXs began to loose their shadow bombs. Geysers of flame shot up all along the *Anakin Solo*'s unshielded hull, traveling down its spine in long rows, leaving in their wake jagged, star-shaped breaches ringed by red-hot durasteel. Bodies, equipment, and atmosphere began to rise from the ruptures in long plumes of steam and flotsam. It grew difficult for Jaina to see the sweeping expanse of the ship's dark hull—much less pick her target.

The *Bes'uliik* held its fire, weaving through the stabbing flashes of laserfire toward the bridge. Jaina thought for a moment that Luke meant to crash his fighter into the bridge, but at the last instant he opened up with all systems, pouring cannon bolts and concussion missiles into the thick blast shielding. A circle of durasteel turned white and started to bleed away in glowing bubbles of metal, then Luke pulled up and vanished over the *Anakin Solo*'s stern with the rest of the Jedi wing.

The *Megador* was right behind him, dropping down over the *Anakin Solo* like a mother velker over her chick. Still, the StealthX wing tried to come around for another pass, wheeling up behind the *Anakin Solo*'s bridge in a dark curving swarm . . . that was quickly shredded by the *Megador*'s sweeping turbolasers.

By this time, Jaina was almost on top of the *Anakin Solo*'s vast plain of black durasteel—close enough to see half a dozen StealthXs explode and several more disintegrate from near-miss shock waves, and suddenly there were EV beacons and pieces of StealthXs tumbling everywhere.

Luke's *Bes'uliik* dodged through a flurry of bolts and beams, then came around, starting to lead the survivors back for another run through the teeth of the *Megador*'s batteries. Seeing that they would never make it—and that even if they did, they would never survive—Jaina opened herself to the Force again and reached out to Luke with all the strength she could muster, urging him not to waste himself and his Jedi like that.

Don't! She dropped the nose of her own StealthX toward the cloaking cone on the *Anakin Solo*'s upper hull. *Go!*

Luke continued on course for an instant, until a trio of cannon bolts hammered some sense into him by bouncing off the *Bes'uliik*'s *beskar* nose. Jaina felt him reach out to her, telling her to trust in the Force, then he dipped a wing and led the remaining Jedi away from the *Anakin Solo*. She would have to do it all herself now—save Isolder *and* kill her brother.

No sooner had Jaina thought this than she felt her brother's attention turning her way again. An instant later cannon bolts began to stream up from all directions. The StealthX bucked half a dozen times as it took hits, then something popped, and the cockpit went red with fire-warning lights.

It didn't matter. Jaina could not have pulled up if she wanted to—and she didn't want to. She blew the canopy and ejected, then watched, enthralled, as her flaming StealthX crashed through the thin shell of the cloaking cone and exploded through the decks below.

Get ready, Caedus. Jaina activated her suit thrusters, then concealed her Force presence again and started down into the fuming ruins of the cloaking cone. *Here I come.*

chapter sixteen

Do Bothan politicians ever tell the truth? Sure—they'll do anything to win an election!

—Jacen Solo, age 15

Victory was within his grasp.

On the Commander's Deck of the *Anakin Solo,* air was whistling away through a web of hairline cracks in the blast shield. Caedus's day cabin was gone, and a concave blowout cup was forming in what used to be an interior wall. Lockdown alarms were blaring in every cabin on the bridge, and the entire command staff was running for the hatchways.

But Caedus stood calmly in the Tactical Salon, his gaze fixed on the holodisplay as though he were trying to make sense of the disjointed battle depicted there. He already *knew* what had happened, of course. The Jedi had used the blood trail to lure him into an ambush, then Luke had led a desperate attack on the *Anakin Solo* in an attempt to take him out.

And Caedus had *survived*. When the Jedi had begun their attack, he had been in his observation bubble, using his battle meditation to see, through the Force, what the fleet's sensors could not. He had been forced to watch the whole thing in his mind's eye, issuing useless orders and futile warnings as his sister and Zekk took out the shields. A moment later, the StealthXs had rolled onto the *Anakin*

Solo's upper hull, their Jedi-guided shadow bombs blasting holes four decks deep.

Then Caedus had spotted the *Bes'uliik*. When he realized Luke was flying it, his intestines had filled with ice. Knowing that Luke was coming for *him*—just as Caedus had seen in his visions—he had leapt from his meditation chair and rushed into the Tactical Salon, barely sealing the hatch before Luke launched his bombs.

The hatch had held, and it was still holding. And now here Caedus was, staring at the holodisplay but seeing a throne—a white throne in a brightly lit chamber. There was no one on it, but it was surrounded by a hundred beings regal enough to belong in the seat. They were beings of all species—Bothans and Hutts, Ishi Tib and Mon Calamari, even humans and Squibs—and they all had the easy, amicable bearing of old friends.

But what held Caedus there—what kept him staring at the vision with no regard for the screaming alarm sirens or the flimsiplast fluttering past on escaping air—was the tall, red-headed woman at the center of the crowd. She had her mother's thin arcing brows and full-lipped mouth, but her nose was her grandmother's—small and not too long, with just a hint of a button at the end.

"Lord Caedus!" Tahiri's voice had grown as shrill as the lockdown alarms, and she was tugging his arm, trying in vain to move him away from the holodisplay. "What's wrong with you?"

"Wrong? Nothing—nothing at all."

Caedus kept himself rooted to the deck, continuing to stare at his grown-up Allana until a piece of flimsiplast blew through the holograph. Then the white throne and the regal friends all faded away, and the face of his beautiful daughter twisted into the angry, hateful visage of his sister Jaina.

Get ready, Caedus, she was warning him. *Here I come.*

Caedus laughed. "I *am* ready, Jaina." He turned his back on the vision, finally allowing Tahiri to pull him away. "And I've already won."

"I'm sorry, my lord." Tahiri continued to hold his arm, literally dragging him out the hatch at the rear of the salon. "I don't understand."

"Jaina is coming for me," Caedus explained, still laughing. "*Luke Skywalker* couldn't kill me. What does *she* expect to do?"

"I honestly don't know," Tahiri said. She sealed the hatch, and the whistle of escaping air grew inaudible. "But it wouldn't do to get careless. You're still recovering, and she's—"

"Practically dead already," Caedus said, starting toward the turbolift. "My sister is nothing to be concerned with. We've won. I've *seen* it."

Tahiri looked more worried than convinced. But rather than argue the point, she seemed content just to pull him into the turbolift. As they descended toward the Auxiliary Command Center hidden deep in the well-protected bowels of the vessel, she took a moment to straighten her own robes, then stepped around in front of him and began to tug his robes into place.

"The Moffs are in a bad state," she warned him. "They're scared—"

"Of course they're scared," Caedus said. "They think only of themselves, and they fear only for their own lives."

Tahiri folded back the lapel of his outer cloak. "Actually, they're just as worried about their assault fleet," she explained. "They're afraid we're going to lose the war."

"*Lose?*" Caedus scoffed. "Haven't they been viewing the intelligence briefings?"

"They're more concerned about our situation here," she said. "Actually, so am I."

Caedus's temper began to rise. Bwua'tu had already

wiped out Niathal's traitors and trapped *both* the Bothan and Corellian fleets at Carbos Thirteen. Admiral Atoko was neutralizing the Mandalorian nuisance by inflicting some sorely needed urban renewal on Keldabe—with just the *remains* of the Fifth Fleet. And yet, the Moffs were worried because they had run into some relatively minor resistance here. Did they really expect *Jedi* to be defeated as easily as Mandalorians and Corellians?

But Caedus did not let his anger take control of him. That would do nothing but divert his attention, and he could not afford to lose his focus now—not with Jaina on the loose, not when he was so close to victory that he had actually *seen* it.

"I appreciate the warning, Tahiri," Caedus said. "I'll be sure to reassure them."

"That might prove difficult, my lord," Tahiri said. "Even for you."

She looked down at her feet, and Caedus could feel her gathering her courage.

"Tahiri, how long have we known each other?" he asked. "Tell me."

Tahiri nodded, then met his gaze. "There's something they're keeping from us. I can feel it when I'm around them."

Caedus smiled. "*Of course* they're keeping something from us," he said. "They're Moffs."

Tahiri would not be put off by his jokes. "They don't trust your abilities yet—not really," she said. "It might be better if we had never been ambushed."

"It's hard to argue against that," Caedus said. "But I don't see what it has to do with our situation."

"*Fix* it," Tahiri said. "I think that's what it's going to take to keep their faith."

"Fix it how?" Caedus asked. "Are you under the impression I can change the past?"

Tahiri looked confused. "Well . . . yeah," she admitted. "You did it for me."

Now Caedus understood. "The kiss, you mean."

"What else?" she asked. "You flow-walked me back to the battle on *Baanu Rass,* and I kissed Anakin. If you could do *that,* why not flow-walk back and warn someone about the ambush?"

The turbolift reached the auxiliary command center and stopped. Before the door could open, Caedus reached out and depressed the HOLD control. He knew why Tahiri believed he could do such a thing: because he had *allowed* her to believe it. Her obsession with Anakin had been a convenient tool for him; she had wanted—*still* wanted—to bring Anakin back so badly that Caedus had not even needed to imply the possibility. Tahiri had simply seized on the hope, and he'd used that to bend her to his will. But the time had come to disabuse her of that notion. With victory at hand, he needed to move Tahiri to the next stage, to help her develop into a true Sith Lady with aspirations of her own—and the cold ruthlessness to achieve them.

Caedus placed a caring hand on her shoulder. "Tahiri, I'm about to tell you something that's going to make you very angry. I want you to feed on its power, because you're going to need it before this last battle is over. But if you let it take control, you'll be lost. You'll never be any good to me again. Can you handle that?"

Tahiri's confusion turned to distress. "What is it?" she demanded. "Are you telling me it wasn't real? That when we flow-walked back to see Anakin, we were just—"

"The flow-walking was real," Caedus interrupted. "We did return to the battle at *Baanu Rass,* and you *did* kiss Anakin. But the past didn't change. It *can't.*"

Tahiri's eyes started to burn with denial. "That makes no sense," she said. "If I really kissed him, then we changed the past."

Caedus shook his head. "When you drop a pebble into a river, what happens? There's a splash, and then the splash disappears. The splash is real, but the river doesn't change. It continues on just the same."

"But it *does* change," Tahiri objected. "Maybe you can't see it, but the pebble is still there, rolling along the bottom."

"And the kiss is still there, too," Caedus said. He reached out and gently tapped Tahiri's temple. "In there. That's where the bottom of the flow is."

"In my *mind*?"

"In the way you *perceive* the past," Caedus said. He was not surprised by the anger and disbelief in Tahiri's voice. When the Aing-Tii monks had explained why he couldn't stop Anakin from dying, he had reacted the same way. "We went back to the battle on *Baanu Rass,* and you kissed Anakin. What changed? The past—or your *memory* of the past?"

Tahiri shook her head, still not ready to let go. "What about Tekli and the rest of the strike team? You were worried about them seeing us."

"About *remembering* that they had seen us," Caedus corrected. "Just like Raynar remembered seeing me when he crawled out of the *Tachyon Flier.* But I wasn't *there.* I was on Coruscant, being tortured by Vergere. What Raynar remembered is the splash."

Caedus could tell by Tahiri's crestfallen expression that she was beginning to understand—but she wasn't quite ready to give up.

"What about being harmed?" she said. "If we're just splashes, how come we had to be so careful about reacting to the past? A *splash* can't be harmed."

Caedus shook his head. "Tahiri, you *know* the answer. The mind is a powerful weapon—especially for Force-users. If we started to *remember* being harmed . . ." He released the HOLD control, and the door slid open. "I'm sure you understand."

For a moment, Tahiri was speechless, her face red with fury, her eyes damp. She stepped out of the turbolift. "Oh, I understand, Lord Caedus. You're the slime under a Hutt's tail. Feed on *that*."

Caedus smiled and calmly stepped into the vestibule, where two squads of black-armored GAG sentries stood at slack-jawed attention. Across from them, spilling down a long corridor servicing the *Anakin Solo*'s auxiliary intelligence and control cabins, was a platoon of gray-armored Elite Guard stormtroopers who served as the Moffs' collective bodyguard.

Caedus stopped in front of the battle-seasoned GAG sergeant and gave a sigh of feigned exasperation.

"Apprentices," he said. "They can be so touchy about criticism sometimes."

The sergeant nodded sagely, and Caedus felt the tension drain from the Force as guards from both groups decided that the trouble between the two Sith was nothing they needed to worry about.

"It's the same with all subordinates, my lord." The sergeant glanced at a flat-faced Gotal with gray sensory cones and spotty cheek fuzz, then leaned closer and added, "Sometimes I feel like killing them myself."

"It might be better if you let the enemy do that for us," Caedus said, giving an appreciative chuckle. "Are you still in contact with Commander Berit?"

The sergeant's expression turned grim. "Not since we were hit, my lord," he said. "There hasn't been any contact at all from Dark Deck. Our entire comm net has gone dead. So has surveillance."

"I was afraid of that." Caedus nodded, making the same assumption the sergeant obviously had: that Dark Deck— the nickname for Ship Security Headquarters—had been destroyed in the StealthX attack. "My sister has boarded the *Anakin Solo*. I need you to organize a search."

"As you wish, my lord," the sergeant said. "Do you have any, um, special insight as to where we should start?"

Caedus shook his head. "She's hiding in the Force, so I can't actually feel her presence." Realizing the seasoned sergeant would be too disciplined to ask the logical follow-up question, he glanced at the ceiling and added, "It's more like a *smell*, Sergeant . . . a smell that permeates everything."

The sergeant received this with the calm composure of a man who had spent a lifetime accepting orders he didn't understand. "Very well," he said. "And when we find her?"

"Alert me," Caedus said. "I'll have to address this personally. Trying to handle her yourself will just get you and your people killed."

"Thank you for your consideration." The sergeant sounded more relieved than he should have, and a little surprised. "Then you think the *Anakin Solo* is going to survive this?"

The question caught Caedus off-guard—it had never occurred to him that the *Anakin Solo* might *not* survive. He considered his answer for a moment, expanding his Force awareness to all corners of the Star Destroyer, and was surprised by the amount of pain, confusion, and fear that he felt. But there was also the determination and focus of a crew well accustomed to desperate battles, of beings who understood that their best hope of survival lay in keeping their heads and performing their duties.

Caedus looked back to the sergeant. "It's too early to know for certain—but I'll share a secret with you." He laid his hand on the sergeant's shoulder. "It really doesn't matter. We've *already* won."

A touch of doubt and disappointment flashed through

the sergeant's eyes, and his expression quickly grew guarded and neutral. "That's good to hear, my lord."

Caedus shot him a knowing half smile. "It's unwise to doubt me, Sergeant," he said. "We *have* won. I've seen it."

Caedus left the sergeant to his unspoken skepticism and entered the Auxiliary Command Center, where the personnel looked anything *but* confident of victory. The ship's officers were sitting at their consoles at the far end, shouting into their mikes or at one another as they struggled to determine the extent of the *Anakin Solo*'s damage. The command staff were clustered around a mostly blank holodisplay near the chamber entrance, looking less harried, but worrying more—with so little reliable data to analyze, they had nothing else to do.

Tahiri stood off to one side before a bank of unoccupied assimilation stations. She was surrounded by a mob of thoughtfully frowning Moffs, speaking with their de facto leader—gray-haired, combat-trim Lecersen—in the concerned tones of someone facing a sad, unpleasant truth.

As Caedus approached, Lecersen abruptly stopped speaking and turned to face him. "Lord Caedus, how good to see you well," he said. "I was just explaining to Lady Veila how worried we were about your welfare."

"That's true," Tahiri said. "The Moffs seem *quite* concerned about your sanity."

The Force boiled with shock and dismay, and several Moffs began to sputter denials, their eyes growing wide and afraid. Only Lecersen seemed unsurprised by Tahiri's bold betrayal of their confidence; he watched her with equal parts hatred and admiration. Caedus allowed himself a small smile of pride; as angry as Tahiri was with him, she had clearly decided she was not going to be *anyone's* tool.

After allowing the Moffs to sputter their denials for a moment, Tahiri turned to Caedus. With ice in her voice, she added, "I *tried* to tell them you're just Hutt spawn, but for some reason they don't seem to believe me."

That Tahiri would speak to him this way seemed to shock even Lecersen. A dead silence fell over the group, and Caedus knew that how he handled the insult would determine not only how much authority he retained over *her*, but how the Moffs viewed him, as well. After glaring at Tahiri for a moment, he decided the best tactic was to exploit her outburst.

"Yes, well you know me so much better than they do." He shifted his gaze to the Moffs. "The Moffs will learn, I'm sure."

Lecersen and several others gave a nervous, testing laugh—which Caedus silenced with a scowl.

"Moff Lecersen, you'll be kind enough to fill me in on the discussion you were having with my apprentice." Caedus made it an order, deliberately pushing his authority to test the Moff's willingness to challenge him. "Leave out the part where you suggest I'm insane. I really have no interest in your opinion regarding that."

Lecersen started to deny he had made such a suggestion, then seemed to remember how difficult it was to lie to a Force-user and nodded.

"As you wish, my lord," he said. "I was simply expressing our concern over the tactical situation and suggesting a course of action to change the tide of battle."

"Suggestions are always welcome," Caedus said. "In the future, bring them directly to me. There's no need to trouble my apprentice with them."

Lecersen inclined his head. "As you wish, Lord Caedus," he said. "I was suggesting to Lady Veila that we might be able to save the Remnant assault fleet by disrupting the Hapan command structure at its highest levels. We do *that* with an attack on the *Dragon Queen*."

Caedus couldn't read Lecersen's thoughts quite clearly enough to determine what kind of attack the Moff was suggesting. But he had no doubt about the real target. The

Dragon Queen was Tenel Ka's personal flagship. If the Moffs were talking about going after it, they were talking about going after Tenel Ka herself.

And Caedus wouldn't have a problem with that, except that he had sensed another familiar presence aboard the *Dragon Queen* during his battle meditation. Just before the ambush, he had noticed *both* mother and daughter, hanging on the far side of the Hapan fleet.

At first, Caedus had been confused by the discovery, believing that Tenel Ka would never endanger their daughter by bringing her into battle. But then he had put himself in Tenel Ka's place and realized she had no other choice. He had taken Allana once, and Tenel Ka was not the type of woman to let that happen twice. She was the kind of woman who would keep her daughter close at all times, even in battle. That way, she could be sure that if Caedus tried to abduct their daughter again, he would have to go through Tenel Ka first.

After taking a moment to compose himself—and to make certain his alarm wasn't showing on his face—Caedus tucked his hand behind his back and nodded.

"An interesting thought," he said. "Go on."

Lecersen looked vaguely—but pleasantly—surprised. "You're aware of how our nanokiller works?"

Caedus nodded, remembering the blood sample the Remnant medic had taken from Mirta Gev. "You can tailor it to attack specific targets, based on their genetic markers," he said. "All you need is a sample of the target's DNA."

"Exactly," Lecersen said. "But it doesn't have to be *their* DNA. It can come from a close relative. We were able to develop a strain for Boba Fett using his granddaughter's DNA, for example. And with Prince Isolder being held captive—"

"Of course," Caedus said. He could see where this was

going, and he didn't like it—not with Allana aboard the *Dragon Queen*. But he couldn't allow the Moffs to see his alarm. If they learned of his weakness, they would not hesitate to exploit it. "How *is* the Fett project going, by the way?"

Lecersen smirked. "It's complete, my lord," he said. "Admiral Atoko confirmed a successful delivery shortly before we left Nickel One."

Caedus allowed his joy to show in his face. "So there's a nanokiller waiting for Fett in Keldabe?"

"Not just Keldabe," Lecersen corrected. "It was air-dispersed. By now it's spread across half of Mandalore. Once Fett finally tires of playing starfighter ace and returns to the surface, it's just a matter of time before he comes into contact with it."

"What about the safe date?" Tahiri asked. "I thought you designed the nanokiller so that it stopped being a threat after a few days."

"That's for the weapons strains," Lecersen explained. "The assassin strains—like the one we sent after Fett—can last forever. As long as they absorb a little light every three or four days, they never die."

"Well done," Caedus said. "Thank you." He expanded his gaze to include the rest of the Moffs, too. "All of you."

Lecersen clicked his heels and inclined his head. "A pleasure to be of service, my lord," he said. "But it was for us, too—payback for that attack on Nickel One."

"Even better," Caedus said. "Fett should be taught that he's the smallest rancor in the pit."

"Quite," Lecersen said. "Let's hope the lesson kills him."

"Let's—but I don't see how a nanokiller can help us now," Caedus said, trying to dismiss the idea without seeming afraid of it. "The battle will be over by the time your strain is ready."

"Not necessarily, my lord," Lecersen said. "The difficulty in developing the strain comes in *excluding* genetic markers from the target pool. If that's not a concern, the process can be accelerated. We could have a sample ready in as little as . . ."

Lecersen paused and looked to Moff Rezer for an answer.

"One hour," Rezer said. Like Lecersen, he was a hard-eyed man with a grim mouth and a military bearing. "Two at the most."

Caedus raised his brow. "That *might* be fast enough," he admitted, growing more worried. "But deploying the weapon is still a problem. Even if we knew the *Dragon Queen*'s location, it would take the whole assault fleet to support a boarding action."

"Actually, we have reports of the *Dragon Queen* standing off on the far edge of the battle," Rezer reported. "So slipping a party of commandos aboard shouldn't be a problem—especially if they look like the crew of a crippled missile boat."

Tahiri nodded. "It just might work," she said, turning to Caedus. "You know how Hapan royalty is. Half the officers aboard the *Dragon Queen* are probably related to Tenel Ka somehow."

"It *is* an intriguing possibility," Caedus said. He had never told Tahiri about Allana's paternity, so it seemed likely that she was supporting the Moffs' suggestion because she believed it was a good one—not because she wanted to punish Caedus for exploiting her obsession with Anakin. Still, it *did* mean he was going to have to dismiss the plan a little more forcefully. "But a nanokiller won't be necessary. We've already won."

"Forgive me, but it hardly *feels* like we're winning," Lecersen said, looking as surprised as he did doubtful. "And the few reports we *have* received from the field—"

"Moff Lecersen," Caedus interrupted, "I see things ordinary beings cannot. Victory is ours already. There will be *no* nanoattack against the *Dragon Queen* or any other vessel. Is that clear?"

Lecersen's jaw clenched, but he dipped his head in acknowledgment. "As you wish, Lord Caedus," he said. "I was only trying to save lives—*Imperial* lives."

"Then do exactly as I say," Caedus replied. "You will save a lot of lives—*yours* among them."

Lecersen's eyes flashed at the threat, but he knew better than to test Caedus's patience. "You have my complete faith," he said. "I look forward to your victory."

Caedus could feel that the Moff was lying, but it was impossible to tell about *what,* exactly. Did the fool think he could actually steal a sample of Isolder's blood from beneath Caedus's nose?

"*Our* victory, Moff Lecersen," Caedus replied. An explosion rumbled down from somewhere above, and he glanced up. "We're all in this together, wouldn't you say?"

Lecersen's smile was more of a sneer. "How kind of you to say so, my lord," he said. "I was beginning to think you were more interested in our fleet than our advice."

"Nothing could be farther from the truth," Caedus said. "Now, if you'll excuse me, I really must go find my sister—before she finds *us.*"

The blood drained from the faces of all the Moffs, and Lecersen said, "By all means, my lord. We'll make the necessary preparations for transferring the flag to the *Megador.*"

"I'm afraid there won't be time for that," Caedus said. "The *Megador* will be busy saving your fleet."

This drew a murmur of surprise from the Moffs, and Rezer said, "But that will leave the *Anakin Solo* exposed to another StealthX attack."

"Which is why we'll be following the *Megador* into battle," Caedus said. "You can't win wars without risking lives, gentlemen. This is where we risk *ours*."

Caedus motioned Tahiri to follow, then inquired of the captain of the *Anakin Solo* about the Star Destroyer's condition. After learning that the shields were the only critical system that would not be repaired within minutes, he congratulated the captain and the crew on their good work—then issued his commands. If the captain was alarmed by the prospect of following the *Megador* into battle without any shields, he had the good sense not to show it. He simply acknowledged his orders and turned to execute them.

Caedus nodded his approval, then started toward the door, speaking to Tahiri as he walked.

"The true Jedi base can't be far from here," he said. "I need you to take a StealthX and find the transports that just fled Uroro Station. They'll show you the way."

"And that will matter because . . . ?" Tahiri asked.

"Because it won't take long for the *Megador* to break the Hapan ambush," Caedus explained. "And then we'll be right behind you."

"Okay," Tahiri said. "But letting me believe we could bring Anakin back was a terrible way to use me. I still haven't forgiven you."

"And I doubt you ever will," Caedus said. "That was kind of the point."

They left the Auxiliary Command Center and came to the turbolift. Caedus motioned Tahiri in first.

"You go on up," he said. Caedus thought about kissing her on her scarred forehead and wishing her good luck, and perhaps there had been a time when the gesture would have been welcome. But no longer; he had taught her an important lesson about trust, one that he knew would stay with her forever. "I have something I need to take care of."

"Isolder," Tahiri said, nodding. "Too bad. I kind of liked him."

"Me, too," Caedus said. He could not help wondering if

Tahiri knew about Allana's paternity after all. Perhaps she had chanced on him whispering the name in his sleep, or overheard something while he had Allana aboard the *Anakin Solo*. "But I'm not going to take a chance—not with this."

chapter seventeen

What do you call sleet storms on Hoth? Summer!
                                    —Jacen Solo, age 15

The *Anakin Solo*'s Prison Hold proved to be everything Jaina had imagined it would be. A cavernous vault of durasteel, it was filled with catwalks, checkpoints, and identity scanners. The detention cells were arrayed to the right side of the Primary Access Tunnel, stacked five-high in three long rows. There had to be a thousand units, and the volume of yellow light pouring through the transparisteel doors suggested that most were occupied. Locating Isolder's cell was going to be a problem, and Jaina did not have time for problems. If she expected to have any chance of killing her brother, she had to find Caedus before he found her—and he had half the security teams on the *Anakin Solo* already searching for her.

The *clank-clank* of boot heels on deck steel echoed up the corridor. A pair of guards rounded a corner about twenty meters ahead, emerging from a short side hall labeled INFIRMARY CHECKPOINT. Jaina pulled her prisoner—a female security officer now wearing Jaina's own StealthX flight suit—across to her side, opposite the guards.

"There's no brave option here, CeeCee." Jaina spoke in a low voice, addressing the woman by the first and middle initials on the GAG utilities that Jaina had taken from her.

"If you even meet their eyes, I'll kill you all, and *still* do what I came to do. Understand?"

"If I wanted to do something stupid, I would have done it in the processing center," CeeCee replied. "I'd rather live."

"Good," Jaina said. "I'd rather let you."

CeeCee was a couple of centimeters shorter than Jaina, and a little smaller, too. So Jaina's flight suit was a tad baggy on her—but only an experienced pilot would notice the poor fit. CeeCee's GAG uniform, on the other hand, was so tight on Jaina that it felt like something Alema Rar would have worn—a full size too small, and snug in all the wrong places for a woman trying to avoid attention.

As the guards drew nearer to Jaina and her prisoner, the stomach-dropping *thuboom* of a hull-hit reverberated through the ship. The lights flickered and blinked out, then blinked on again, out one more time, and finally returned to normal. The guards cast a nervous glance at the ceiling, then seemed to shiver off their anxiety and started down the corridor again. It would have been an exaggeration to say that the crew had become inured to the sound of turbo-laser strikes impacting their Star Destroyer, but they were certainly growing accustomed to it. There had been a lull in the explosions for about half an hour after Jaina boarded, but then the *Anakin Solo* had followed the *Megador* forward and begun to take a steady trickle of hits. Whatever else he was, Caedus was certainly no coward.

When the distance had closed to within a couple of meters, the guards pulled their shoulders back and stopped. Jaina began to draw on the Force, using it to reinforce the impression in the two men's minds that she was a familiar face—someone they ran into every now and again. It was a calculated trade-off. If her brother sensed her calling on the Force, it might give him a hint about her location. But if a suspicious guard reported a stranger wandering around the

Prison Hold, it would bring him running—probably with an entire platoon of GAG troopers to back him up.

"Good day, Captain," said the tallest guard, a sandy-haired man with a heavy, square jaw that reminded Jaina of Zekk's strong features. "May we see the prisoner's cell assignment chit?"

"If you *must*," Jaina said, reinforcing her image as just another imperious GAG officer. She reached into a thigh pocket and produced the chit she had been given at the processing center a few minutes before. "Be fast about it. I don't have much time."

The guard glanced at the chit, then said, "In that case, you're lucky you ran into us." He pointed back down the corridor toward an intersection Jaina had just passed. "The women's block is back there. We'll escort you."

"I don't need an escort. I *know* where the women's block is." Jaina used a dismissing wave of her hand to draw the guard's attention away from the suggestive tone of her voice. "I'm taking the prisoner to the infirmary first. She needs to be examined."

The guard turned to his companion. "The prisoner needs to be examined first," he said. "We'll escort the captain to the infirmary."

Jaina swallowed her frustration. "I don't need an escort." This time, she distracted the pair by pointing at the hall from which the two had emerged. "I can *see* where the infirmary is."

The two guards frowned, then the shorter one—he had hair that was one shade lighter than black—said, "She can see where the infirmary is, Dex."

Dex sighed, then passed back the chit. "Thank you, ma'am. Do be careful." He pointed at a silver dome hanging from the ceiling. "The surveillance system is out."

"Thanks for the warning." An idea occurred to Jaina, and she added, "So was the prisoner index. Can you tell me what cell the Hapan prince is in?"

Both guards frowned, and Dex asked, "Why would you need to know *that*?"

"Because . . ." Jaina let her explanation trail off there, trying to make the best of her tight uniform by flashing a coy smile. Playing the flirt had worked pretty well for her *mother* on Coruscant, so Jaina saw no reason it shouldn't work for *her* here. She raised her brows. "I hear he's worth looking at."

Dex shook his head in annoyance. "I don't think I can help you with that, Captain."

The two guards marched off without awaiting a proper dismissal, leaving Jaina to stand there wondering what her sixty-year-old mother had that she didn't.

"*That* was smooth," CeeCee observed. "You should probably just stick to the Force tricks."

"I got rid of them, didn't I?" Jaina started forward again, dragging her prisoner across the tunnel toward the infirmary checkpoint in case the guards looked back. "And how do you know that *wasn't* a Force trick?"

"If it was, it needs work," CeeCee answered.

"Careful," Jaina warned. "It's not too late to kill you."

CeeCee laughed at the threat, then asked, "Is that *really* what this is about? Isolder?"

"Of course." Jaina stopped at the entrance to the short corridor leading to the infirmary checkpoint and pretended to be checking CeeCee's wrist restraints. "You think Jedi go around breaking into prisons for fun?"

"No, I *thought* you were here for the Mandalorian," CeeCee said. "I heard she was working with a Jedi when Caedus captured her."

"*Her?*" Jaina asked. "Was this on Nickel One?" When CeeCee hesitated, Jaina added, "There are a *lot* of ways a Jedi can hurt you—most of them so bad that you can't even scream."

"Okay—you're right. She came from Nickel One. She's

supposed to be related to Boba Fett." CeeCee pointed her chin toward the checkpoint, where a suspicious-looking guard sat inside his control booth, studying them through a transparisteel viewing panel. "In there. I hear Caedus is handling her interrogations personally."

Jaina was suddenly filled with so much guilt and anger that she felt as though she would burst. Mirta had *survived*. And Jaina had abandoned her—just as Fett had implied when he visited Jaina in the hospital. It didn't matter that it had seemed inconceivable that Mirta was alive, or that Jaina had been so wounded and dazed herself she could not think straight, or that any retrieval attempt would almost certainly have cost Jaina her own life.

Jaina had left a wounded comrade behind. To a Mandalorian commando, that was all that would matter—and to Fett, all that would matter was that it had been Mirta.

"Kriffing Mandalorians!" Jaina slammed her palm against the tunnel wall, drawing a disapproving glower from the guard inside the checkpoint control booth. "I don't have *time* for this!"

"Uh, sorry I brought it up, then," CeeCee said, sounding genuinely frightened. "But if you're going after Isolder, my thumbprint won't help you. He's in Block C—maximum security—so you're going to have to fight your way in. Maybe you could dump me in my cell first."

"Maybe I *could*," Jaina said. She shoved CeeCee down the corridor toward the infirmary checkpoint. "If you're not lying about the Mandalorian."

The smart thing would have been to forget that CeeCee had ever mentioned a Mandalorian prisoner. That was what Fett would have done in her place, maybe even Mirta herself. But Jaina was a Jedi, not an assassin. She couldn't just turn her back on an ally—even a *quasi*-ally.

Kriffing Mandalorians. They were like Hutts—once they got their claws into you, they never let go.

At the checkpoint, Jaina spun her prisoner around backward and stepped over to the security pad, reaching for the thumb scanner with the same hand that held CeeCee's arm. With the Force and a little sleight of hand, she prevented the guard from seeing whose thumb it was that actually touched the pad, and his suspicions seemed to subside as the scanning booth slid open.

Once they were inside, he activated an intercom and asked, "Authorization?"

"Don't have one," Jaina said. "I just need to get her checked for ejection injuries before we interrogate her."

The guard nodded and initiated the scan—wincing only slightly as the boom of another, smaller hull-hit rang through the ship. None of the items in Jaina's equipment belt seemed to trouble him, but he frowned and pointed at the thigh pocket where she had stowed her lightsaber.

"What's that?"

"High-power glow rod." Jaina pulled the lightsaber from its pocket and stuck the emitter nozzle against the transparisteel in front of his eyes. "Want me to show you?"

"No." Not wanting to be blinded by the powerful light, the guard quickly looked away and reached for a button on his panel. "Please proceed, Captain. You know where the exam rooms are."

The far door slid open, and Jaina led CeeCee into the prison's infirmary wing. Like the other side of the Primary Access Tunnel, it was a cavernous durasteel vault with five stories of catwalks ascending into the murky heights above. But each level seemed to have its own purpose.

The lowest level, about three meters below the balcony where Jaina and CeeCee had emerged, seemed to be a combination morgue and waste disposal area. A single black, four-armed droid with a skeletal frame and green-glowing photoreceptors was working in the pit, pulling medical waste off a conveyer belt and feeding it into a white-mouthed fusion incinerator. On the wall across from the incinerator was a line of a dozen meter-square body drawers, all closed and presumably full, as there were a pair of corpses resting on gurneys along the wall.

The main level was lined with examination rooms, while the next story up had too many attendants pushing hovergurneys along the catwalk to be anything but diagnostics or surgery. Jaina led her prisoner over to a lift tube and found two possibilities on the control panel: PATIENT CELLS on level four, and AUTHORIZED ACCESS ONLY on level five.

Jaina was still pondering her choices when CeeCee said, "Patient cells. They don't allow regular medical staff on the interrogation level, and your friend needs attention. She won't be hard to find."

Detecting no hint of deception in CeeCee's Force aura, Jaina pressed PATIENT CELLS, and they ascended to level four. The catwalk was modestly busy, with a handful of nurses and medical droids bustling in and out of the cells, usually alone but sometimes in the company of an escort carrying a stun stick. At the far end of the catwalk, a pair of GAG guards stood in front of a closed door holding blaster rifles.

Guessing they would be guarding Mirta's cell, Jaina started forward, pushing her prisoner ahead of her. They passed several open cells where nurses or droids were stooping over the lowered access panel of a blocky gray containment bed, tending to their patients. A couple of times, they passed guard-escorts leaning against doorways, swinging their stun sticks and looking bored.

No one gave Jaina a second look as she passed with her prisoner—in part because it had been nearly five minutes since a hull-hit had boomed through the ship. Either the battle was turning in Caedus's favor, or the *Anakin Solo* had become so battered that it wasn't even worth firing at anymore. Jaina wasn't betting on the latter possibility.

By the time they were three-quarters of the way down the catwalk, she felt certain no one was paying any attention to them. She stretched her Force awareness out toward the cell and found an angry, disheartened presence lying inside.

Though Jaina could not actually sense the bed that Mirta was lying on, she knew it had to be there. She visualized a blocky gray containment bed similar to the one she had seen in other cells, then grasped it in the Force and jerked hard.

A muffled cry of surprise sounded through Mirta's door, and the puzzled guards looked from the door to each other. Jaina grasped the bed in the Force again, this time lifting the bottom end off the floor and letting it drop. A sharp bang came through the door, followed by another cry of surprise.

The closer guard pressed his thumb to the security pad then stepped into the cell while the door was still sliding open. The other one frowned at Jaina and CeeCee, who were within a few meters of the cell door and still approaching.

He stepped forward, moving to block their approach. "Ma'am, I'm sorry, but—"

Jaina Force-hurled him through the door and shoved CeeCee into the cell after him, then followed and slapped the interior door control. The startled guards were just picking themselves up, spinning around to bring up their blaster rifles. Jaina flicked her fingers, and the nearer guard's weapon flew from his hands and smashed butt-first into the farther one's temple. She followed up that attack with a snap-kick to the closest guard's jaw, and both men collapsed in unconscious heaps.

CeeCee had slipped behind her and was moving toward the door. Jaina swung her arm back, pointing at the woman, and warned, *"Don't."*

She turned to find CeeCee standing a meter behind her, one arm half stretched toward a control panel on the wall. There were pads labeled INTERCOM, LIGHTS, PATIENT EMERGENCY, and ALARM.

Even before Jaina stepped toward her, CeeCee lowered her arm and said, "This is going to leave a bruise, isn't it?"

"Probably."

Jaina smashed a hammerfist into the hinge of CeeCee's jaw, then caught her when her eyes rolled back and her knees buckled.

"The noble *jetiise*," a muffled voice said behind her. "Gracious even in victory."

Jaina laid CeeCee on the floor next to the cell's empty second bed, then turned to see Mirta Gev watching her through the transparisteel access panel on the first. She hardly looked like the same woman Jaina had met on Mandalore. Her eyes were sunken and rimmed in purple, her skin was ashen, and her curly brown hair lay straight, flat, and dirty on her head.

"Hello, Mirta," Jaina said. As she spoke, she collected the weapons and comlinks from the two guards she had knocked unconscious. "It's good to see you. I'm glad you're alive."

Mirta snorted and looked away. "If you want to call it that."

Jaina scowled at the bitterness in Mirta's voice. Still holding the weapons and comlinks she had taken off the guards, she stepped over to the bed and kneed the access control. As the panel slid down, she saw that Mirta lay beneath a thin blanket, her legs extended straight out and her right arm resting motionless at her side. Her left arm was slightly bent, and Jaina could see the outline of a heavy restraining cuff around her wrist.

Jaina laid the weapons and comlinks on the foot of Mirta's bed, at the same time saying, "Look, I'm sorry about what happened on Nickel One." She pulled the blanket back and unbuckled the restraining cuff. "But I thought you were dead."

"It might have been nice if you'd checked," Mirta said. "You could've put a bolt through my head and spared me this."

Mirta raised her hand and gestured at her motionless body, and then Jaina understood why only one hand had been restrained. Her heart sank.

"Ah . . . Mirta. I'm so sorry." Jaina shook her head. She was so sad she could barely bring herself to meet Mirta's gaze, and so frustrated she wanted to blast someone. "I can't get you out of here."

Mirta nodded. "I know who you came for," she said. "The only thing I can't figure out is what you're doing in *here*."

"I might have gotten played." Jaina hooked a thumb at CeeCee, wondering whether the GAG captain had known all along that Mirta could not be rescued and had just been trying to eat up time Jaina did not have. She pulled the rest of the restraints from the storage bin under Mirta's bed and began to buckle the unconscious guards to the empty bed. "If I make it, I'll try to come back for you."

"If you make it, I'll be so happy I won't care," Mirta said, her head turned so she could watch Jaina work. "But there *is* something you should know. It may help you with Caedus."

"Thanks," Jaina said. She pulled CeeCee over next to the guards and used the restraints from the empty bed to secure her in place with them. "I'll take all the help I can."

Mirta did not continue, and Jaina looked to find the Mandalorian studying her.

"You have to do some things for me," Mirta said. "If you survive, I mean. You have to promise."

"Maybe," Jaina said cautiously. She knew better than to

make a blind agreement with a Mandalorian. "What do you have in mind?"

"You have to warn *Ba'buir*," Mirta said, using the *Mando'a* word for her grandfather. "The Moffs took some of my blood—they've designed a nanokiller for him."

Jaina nodded. "I can do that."

Mirta's eyes grew as dead and cold as Fett's. "And you have to . . ." Her voice grew strained and cracked, and Jaina could tell that she was fighting some sort of internal battle. "You have to tell him he deserves it. That he did this . . . to me."

Jaina frowned. "Okay, I can do that, too, Mirta," she said. "But you're not sounding like yourself. Are you sure you want me to do that?"

Mirta shook her head. "No—but I can't help . . . I just have this anger . . . because your brother is right about one thing, at least. He did this to me!"

"Caedus did this to you?" Jaina asked. She did not understand what her brother had done to Mirta, but she *could* tell that it was ugly. "Or Fett?"

"*Ba'buir.*" Mirta looked away, and it grew obvious there was no use reasoning with her. "It . . . He sent us on a death mission. Promise!"

"Okay, if I make it," Jaina said. Fett would want to know the truth, anyway, and she could always soften it by telling him of her suspicions. "I promise."

"Good." When Mirta looked back toward Jaina, a certain sad peace had returned to her face, but she did not look grateful. Far from it. She raised the one arm she could move, pointing it at one of the blaster rifles Jaina had laid on the foot of her bed. "And the last thing. It's easy."

Jaina looked at the blaster rifle and knew she could not make the deal. "No, Mirta, I'm not going to do that," she said. "Even if I don't make it, I don't think your grandfather really believes—"

"Jaina, it's not for *that*." Mirta pointed at the three prisoners Jaina had tied to the bed. "When they wake up, I'm going to need a way to keep them quiet for you."

Jaina breathed a sigh of relief, then placed the blaster rifles and comlinks on the bed where Mirta could reach them. "Good point. Thanks."

"You're welcome," Mirta said. "Now, the thing you need to know about your brother . . . he underestimates you."

"That's not really news, Mirta," Jaina said. "Maybe not even true. He's magnitudes stronger than me in the Force. All I've got on him is five weeks of Mandalorian commando training."

"And that's enough to get the job done." Mirta's tone was reprimanding, like a parent scolding a child for wanting a third bowl of frezgel. "But I mean, his weakness is more delusional. He's convinced *you* couldn't have taken his arm—at least not alone. He thinks Luke was with us."

Jaina paused, recalling Caedus's confusion at the end of the battle. She also recalled her own condition, how the strange surge in her Force powers had suddenly faded just before Caedus had redirected the stormtroopers' fire. "Maybe Luke *was* there."

Mirta shook her head. "He wasn't. I was conscious most of the time—and I didn't see him." She waved the blaster muzzle at the door. "Now get out of here. You've only got an hour before my next meds are due—and no offense, but I don't want you as a roommate."

"No problem. We'd probably kill each other." Jaina patted Mirta on the arm, then turned toward the door. "May the Force be with you, Mirta."

"Yeah, sure, Jedi," Mirta said. "Shoot straight and run fast."

Jaina slipped out of the cell and closed the door behind her. She used her fingernail to scratch up the security console thumbprint reader, then started down the catwalk toward the turbolift.

Jaina hadn't taken even three steps when the muffled zing of a blaster discharge sounded from inside Mirta's cell. She stopped, her heart dropping with shock and disbelief— then heard two more discharges and realized it wasn't Mirta she should have been worried about.

Kriffing Mandalorians.

Seen through the egalitarian lens of a detention cell's one-way transparisteel, the acclaimed Prince Isolder did not look so different from other men. He was a bit taller, perhaps, with squarer shoulders and straighter teeth. And there was something in his upright bearing, even sitting alone in a cramped durasteel cell, that hinted at his unshakable sense of self—at the quiet dignity that seemed to give him strength in even the most desperate and trying of circumstances.

This was a man who had married for love in a culture that laughed at love, a father who had raised a Jedi daughter in a society that scorned Jedi, a prince who had always served his subjects first and his vanity last. He was a man, in short, of the best sort, a man with the wisdom to follow his own heart, and a heart large enough to make the journey worthwhile.

And Caedus would have liked to believe that those were the reasons he found himself so reluctant to kill the man . . . but he knew better. The reason he was hesitating was because he was not certain that it was the right thing to do.

The logical course was to let Lecersen and the Moffs have their fun with their nanokiller. Eliminating Tenel Ka and Allana was certainly not going to *hurt* the Alliance's chances of winning the battle, and it might even help. But how could Caedus sacrifice his own child so that all the *other* children in the galaxy would grow up in safety? The way of the Sith was the way of pain, he knew that, but he did not see how he could let the Moffs kill his daughter without becoming a monster even worse than Palpatine or Exar Kun.

Could Allana's life be the price the Force demanded for peace? For making his vision of the white throne a reality?

No, Caedus realized. Allana had been one of the beings in the vision. Without her, there would *be* no white throne.

The knot of fear that had been binding Caedus's insides slackened, and, with a new clarity, he saw what he had to do. He had to stop the Moffs' plan at any cost. If he wanted to bring peace to the galaxy, he had to save Allana—not sacrifice her.

The stomach-dropping *thuboom* of a hull-hit reverberated through the ship. The lights flickered and blinked out, then blinked on, out one more time, and finally returned to normal. Inside his cell, Isolder cast a nervous glance at the ceiling, then seemed to shrug off his anxiety and leaned back against the wall again.

Caedus opened the cell door, but remained standing outside. Isolder glanced over, his eyes betraying none of the surprise that Caedus sensed in the Force.

"Jacen Solo," Isolder said, pointedly not rising. "I've been wondering why I haven't been interrogated yet. Obviously, you've been saving the fun for yourself."

"It's Caedus now, Prince Isolder," Caedus said. "*Darth* Caedus. And the reason you haven't been interrogated has nothing to do with fun. We have other means of locating the Jedi base, so I saw no need to impinge on your dignity."

Now Isolder *did* allow his surprise to show in his eyes. "How very considerate of you," he said. "I wouldn't have expected that from child-stealing scum such as yourself."

Caedus winced at the insult. "We all make mistakes," he said, biting back his anger. There was nothing to be gained by retaliation, and Isolder deserved no punishment for speaking the truth as he saw it. "I'm sure you'll come to appreciate that in good time. Now, if you'll please come with me."

"I don't think so," Isolder said. "Whatever you—"

"I wasn't asking." Caedus used the Force to pull Isolder off his bunk, then drew him stumbling through the door. "Please don't consider my respect a weakness, Prince Isolder. That would be one of those mistakes I just mentioned."

"Of course," Isolder answered, recovering his dignity along with his footing. "It seems I'm entirely at your disposal. May I inquire where you're taking me?"

"To join your crew aboard the *Beam Racer*," Caedus said. "I'm afraid you'll have to depart in the middle of a battle, but we've almost broken though. Once you're clear of us, you should be safe enough."

Isolder stopped and turned around. "You're *releasing* me? Why?"

"Because my only other choice is to kill you," Caedus said. "And I'd really rather not."

Isolder looked more than skeptical—he looked flat-out distrustful. "So I can lead you to the Jedi base."

"We already *know* where the base is," Caedus said. "We'll be jumping to Shedu Maad as soon as we break free of your daughter's fleet."

Isolder's face betrayed nothing, but Caedus could tell by the disappointment in the prince's Force aura that his analysts had guessed correctly about the destination of the transports that had fled Uroro Station.

"You'll be free to go anywhere you wish, as long as you don't allow yourself to be captured again," Caedus continued. "It's only fair to warn you that the *Racer* will explode at the first brush of a tractor beam."

Isolder frowned, obviously trying to figure out what Caedus was doing, then abruptly said, "This is about the nanokiller, isn't it?"

Caedus was actually surprised. "Very good, Prince. I'm afraid the Moffs are rather keen on using it against Tenel Ka."

Isolder glared at him with narrowed eyes, and Caedus could feel a murderous intent gathering in the Force.

"You're not as clever as you think, *Jacen.*" Isolder spat in Caedus's eyes. "I'd rather die than fall for your ploy."

Caedus sighed and wiped the saliva away, wondering whether there was any way to convince the prince that this *wasn't* a ploy. Clearly, Isolder believed Caedus was trying to trick him into inadvertently carrying the nanokiller onto the *Dragon Queen*—and it was certainly a reasonable assumption. The question was, could Caedus convince him of the truth? And was it worth the effort—especially when he had so much else to do, a battle to win, his sister to deal with . . . *Luke* to kill.

The answer was regrettably obvious.

"I was *afraid* you'd say that." As Caedus spoke, he was grasping Isolder in the Force. "And death is certainly an option."

Caedus made a twisting motion with his hand, snapping Isolder's head around backward. There was a loud pop that made Caedus feel a little sick to his stomach, and the prince collapsed at his feet, dead before he hit the catwalk.

Caedus sighed again, then removed the comlink from his chest pocket and managed to get a scratchy channel to his aide, Orlopp.

"I'm afraid Prince Isolder won't be joining his crew aboard the *Beam Racer,*" he said. "Tell them they'll have to depart without him."

". . . sure they will," came the patchy reply. "They're . . . loyal."

Of course they wouldn't. Isolder had been a great man, a good leader. No decent crew in the galaxy would abandon him.

"Then you'll have to blow the ship in her berth." Caedus used the Force to levitate Isolder's body, then started down the catwalk toward the infirmary and its fusion incinerator. "And void the hangar when it's done. We can't afford to take any chances with this."

chapter eighteen

What do you get when you cross an Ewok with an astromech droid? A short circuit!

—Jacen Solo, age 15

As Jaina hurried toward the lift tube, she noticed that the catwalk was gradually emptying ahead of her. No one seemed to be panicking to get out of her way, or even paying her much attention. But while there were plenty of nurses and orderlies entering patient cells, none was emerging. Only the droids seemed to be going about their normal business, wheeling medicine carts from door to door or popping into and out of cells with electronic chartpads in their hands.

Jaina feared for a moment that someone had heard Mirta's blaster shots—or noticed the absence of her guards—and triggered a security alarm. But the mood seemed to be more nervous than frightened, and when she passed an open door, those inside did not look away or pretend to be busy. They simply watched her pass with vague interest, as though they were wondering who *she* was that she didn't feel the need to take shelter from the coming storm.

And that was just what she was sensing, Jaina realized—the fear of approaching turmoil. A general hush had fallen over the entire wing, and the Force had gone electric with anxiety. She glanced through the safety mesh and saw that even the main deck of the infirmary, where the waiting area for the busy exam rooms was located, was gradually emptying.

Jaina stopped at the next open door and poked her head into the cell. Inside, a female Falleen was working under the watchful eye of two black-armored escorts, changing the bandages of a Bothan male missing both arms and a leg. Judging by the smoothly scorched stump that the nurse was currently disinfecting, it appeared that he had lost the three limbs to lightsaber strikes.

"Another assassin," said a guard, noticing the object of Jaina's gaze. "Don't know why the Bothans keep sending them. Caedus just cuts 'em up and sends them down here."

"Something we can do for you, Captain?" asked the other, the older of the two.

"Yes, thanks." Jaina tore her gaze away from the Bothan, wondering if that was how *she* was going to end up. "Can you tell me why everything is getting so quiet? Is the *Anakin Solo* in trouble?"

"The *Anakin Solo*'s doing fine, ma'am," the guard said. "The last I heard, the *Megador* had those Hapan scolds on the run, and we were getting ready to jump with the rest of the fleet."

"You must not do much duty in the infirmary," the young guard added. "It always gets like this when Darth Maniac is around."

"Darth Maniac?" Jaina's pulse began to pound in her ears. "Caedus is here—in the infirmary?"

"Yes, ma'am." The older guard scowled at his young companion, no doubt misinterpreting Jaina's surprise as disapproval of the nickname. "Word is, he's in the scanning booth."

"Coming up *here*?" Jaina asked, thinking of Mirta and the obvious attention Caedus had been paying her. "In the middle of a battle?"

The guard shrugged. "Maybe not this time. They say

he's got a body with him, so he could be headed to the disposal pit."

A body. In the prison hold.

Jaina thought of Isolder and made the most likely assumption, and her heart sank. She backed out of the cell without thanking the guards, then started down the catwalk as fast as she could move and still be walking. She tried not to imagine what had happened, but the answer was too obvious to ignore. After the blood trail went dead at Uroro Station, Caedus had no doubt resorted to his favorite trick and tortured the information out of Isolder. Now the prince was dead and the fleet was preparing to jump to Shedu Maad. Truly, there was no low to which her brother would not sink.

As Jaina walked, she concentrated on vanishing into the Force and stayed near the inner side of the catwalk. She didn't know quite how Caedus's blood trail worked, but she suspected it would be stronger when they drew near to each other. And if his danger sense began to tingle because she was focusing on him too intently, he would know she was closing in.

Once Jaina reached the lift tube, however, she allowed herself a quick glance down to the main deck. Five dark figures were escorting a hovergurney around the disposal pit toward a cargo lift at the far end. Four of the figures were armored, and the fifth was raising his hand, signaling the others to stop while he craned his neck back to look around.

Jaina pulled away and focused her mind on Zekk, on the hope that he was still alive because she hadn't felt him die, on how much she was going to miss him if he had. And she thought, also, of the terrible likelihood that she would *never* know what had happened to him—that he had managed to go EV before his StealthX was destroyed, then been swallowed up by the Mists. Even with an active rescue beacon, he would be nearly impossible to locate with normal equipment; the Mists would simply devour the sensor waves. If Zekk—or his body—was going to be found, it would be by a Jedi.

Hoping she would live long enough to help with the search, Jaina stepped into the lift tube and began her descent. She had no idea whether focusing on Zekk had worked. Maybe Caedus had dismissed whatever he had felt as the glare of an unhappy subordinate. Or maybe he would be waiting, lightsaber in hand, as the lift door opened. Jaina only knew that if he had felt even that brief glance, she could not risk another.

She emerged from the lift with her lightsaber semihidden behind her forearm. To her relief, the only thing waiting was an MD droid about to step into the tube.

"Lord Caedus and his escorts, did you see them going toward the disposal pit?"

"Why yes, Captain," the droid replied politely. "They had a body with them, Prisoner Ay-Ess-Two-Three-Oh-Fifty-two-Ar, I believe."

"Would that be Prince Isolder?" Jaina asked.

"I believe that was his name, yes," the droid replied. "The poor man—it looked like Lord Caedus had snapped three of his cervical vertebrae."

"Thanks." Jaina started across the deck toward the cargo lift, her anger boiling in her stomach—then something the droid had said caught her attention, and she spun around to ask, "The prisoner's neck—how do you know it was Lord Caedus who snapped it?"

The droid stopped inside the lift and turned to face her. "It always *is,* Captain."

The MD droid pressed a control button and ascended out of sight.

As Jaina started toward the morgue lift, a stern female voice suddenly echoed across the main deck.

"Your attention: all Prison Hold surveillance and communications systems have been restored. Maintain Lockdown Level Two. We'll be jumping to final objective in five minutes. Repeat, five minutes. This will be your final announcement."

The *final objective* would be Shedu Maad, Jaina knew. She couldn't say whether killing Caedus would prevent the assault on their base—she kind of doubted it, as a matter of fact—but it might confuse things enough to give the Jedi a fighting chance.

Recalling the surge of Force power she had experienced when she fought Caedus the first time, Jaina wondered if she should reach out to her uncle Luke when the fight began. Perhaps he would be able to bolster her strength as he had on Nickel One. But then she recalled Mirta's comment about her brother underestimating her, and she realized that calling on Luke would be a mistake. From what Mirta had said—and what she had observed herself on Nickel One—Caedus was obsessed with their uncle. He would be ready for Luke's strength, prepared to see through Luke's illusions as he had not been the first time. If Jaina expected to win this fight, she would have to fight in a different way—her *own* way.

She stepped into the cargo lift and descended. There was a growing stench of disinfectant and hot metal, and the air grew warm and still. When she reached the morgue level, she was tempted to use the Force to probe for the location of Caedus's guards. She resisted. Either the guards were waiting for her or they weren't—and if they weren't, she would only be giving Caedus a warning he did not need or deserve.

The door opened into a rectangular corridor, wider than it was tall, with gray durasteel walls and a long row of hatches running down one side. The four guards were standing about ten meters away, in front of a single hatch on the opposite side, looking back toward the cargo lift. There was no sign of Caedus; presumably, he had gone through the hatch behind the guards.

Jaina hurled herself onto the floor, rolling toward the four and shrieking softly but shrilly. They swung their blasters around, letting out curses of surprise and confusion. Jaina rolled to a knee about three meters in front of them and pointed back toward the lift.

"B-b-bothans!" she stammered.

That was all it took. The guards raced past her, bringing their blaster rifles up to fire. Jaina sprang up behind them and ignited her lightsaber, then used a single stroke to cut all four men in half.

The fight had begun.

The Biodisposal Pit was just what the name suggested, a sweltering, foul-smelling durasteel hole into which poured all of the dirty bandages, used scalpels, excised organs, dead bodies, and other hazardous waste from not only the infirmary but the *Anakin Solo*'s entire Prison Hold as well. As might be expected, it was a relatively quiet and lonely place, half cloaked in shadow by the overhanging expanse of the main deck, and half illuminated by the harsh brilliance spilling from the open mouth of the fusion incinerator.

Having left his guards on the other side of the hatch where they would not witness the gross violation of prison procedure he was about to commit, Caedus was left to pull Isolder by himself. As he dragged the hovergurney toward the fusion incinerator, an overqualified GP-2 medical droid rushed out of the shadows, holding a dripping scalpel in one hand and waving the other in a frantic gesture to capture his attention.

"No, no, no!" the droid said. "That corpse hasn't been identified yet."

The droid pointed its scalpel into the shadows, but before it could explain what it wanted, the stern voice of a female security guard came over the public address system.

"Your attention: all Prison Hold surveillance and communications systems have been restored. Maintain Lock-down Level Two. We'll be jumping to final objective in five minutes. Repeat, five minutes. This will be your final announcement."

The GP-2 continued to point until the announcement was over, then said, "Put it there until I can collect a tissue sample and verify the identity."

"That won't be necessary in this case." Caedus started to continue toward the incinerator—then felt the skin-blistering heat pouring from its mouth and pushed the gurney toward the droid. "This one goes directly to the incinerator."

The droid accepted the gurney. "I'm afraid that isn't procedure," it said, retreating into the shadows with the gurney. "Thank you for the delivery."

Cursing the slavish devotion to procedure of mechanical minds, Caedus followed the droid and was temporarily blinded as his eyes struggled to adjust to the darkness.

"In this case, procedure doesn't apply," Caedus said. "It's overridden."

Something hard brushed past him, then the droid demanded, "On whose authority?"

"Mine." Caedus turned, following the voice, and found himself squinting as he watched the droid's silhouette pull a flimsiplast carton off the conveyor belt, inspect the contents, and thrust it into the incinerator's mouth. "Lord Caedus."

"Lord Caedus?" The droid returned, moving from bright light to deep shadow as effortlessly as only machines could. It fixed its photoreceptors on his face for a moment, then said, "Identity confirmed. Prisoner Ay-Ess-Two-Three-Oh-Fifty-two-Ar will be disposed of without identity verification or tissue sample collection."

The GP-2 returned to the gurney it had been working at and jabbed a ten-centimeter needle into the half-bald corpse of an emaciated Wookiee. "Thank you for the delivery."

Caedus gritted his teeth. Maybe he should have just used the Force to feed the prince's body into the incinerator himself—except the droid would probably have rushed over and pulled it out half burned.

After a moment, he said, "This matter takes priority over all others. I need to witness the disposal myself. *Now.*"

The droid's head snapped around. "Is there a contagion concern? Because if there is, the collection of tissue samples cannot be overridden, even by—"

"It's a security matter," Caedus said. "Do it *now.*"

"Very well."

The droid set its syringe down on the Wookiee's gurney, then went over to Isolder and began to cut the clothes off the body. Caedus did not object, suspecting it would take longer to argue the matter than to simply let it happen.

After a moment, the droid paused to study Isolder's arms.

"Oh, I see," it said. "The tissue samples have *already* been collected."

"*What?*" Caedus went over to the gurney. "Show me."

The droid turned both of the prince's hands up, revealing half a dozen bruises and needle marks on the interior of the forearms. There was a muffled scream in the corridor outside, but Caedus could barely hear it over the fiery roaring in his ears. He did not need to ask what the marks meant, because he had seen similar marks on Mirta's arms after the Remnant medic collected her samples for the nanokiller.

The marks meant that Lecersen and the Moffs had betrayed him . . . and his vision. They meant that Allana's nanokiller was probably *already* on its way to the *Dragon Queen*.

Caedus pulled his comlink and opened a channel to his

aide, Orlopp. "Have a hold placed on all launches from the *Anakin Solo*," he ordered, turning toward the door. "And find out if we've launched any missile boats recently— especially missile boats carrying Remnant forces."

There was an uncomfortable pause, then Orlopp asked, "Did you say missile boats?"

Caedus's stomach went cold. "Tell me."

"A missile boat just launched from this hangar," Orlopp reported. "I had to wait for it to clear the containment field before I blew the *Beam Racer*."

"What about the crew?" Caedus asked. "Were they ours?"

"They were in Alliance uniforms," Orlopp reported. "*New* uniforms . . . and a Remnant colonel saw them off. Shall I have a recall order issued?"

"It's worth a try, but they won't obey." Caedus came to the door and, lacking a second hand to reach for the control pad, stopped to finish his order. "Have my StealthX prepped for immediate . . ."

He let the sentence trail off as the door opened on its own, revealing a dark-uniformed woman with an athletic build and brown, furious eyes.

"Jaina?"

A lightsaber *snap-hissed* to life, and suddenly Caedus felt as though he were going to vomit fire.

The invisible fist of a Force blast slammed Jaina in the chest and sent her flying back, her breath groaning from her lungs and her lightsaber hissing free of Caedus's stomach. From the fight on Nickel One, she had learned the dangers of letting her head snap back on impact. She tucked her chin, then fought to hold it there as she struck the durasteel wall on the far side of the corridor.

Jaina almost wished that she *had* been knocked unconscious. Stinging needle-thrusts of pain zippered down her spine as her vertebrae rocked beneath the impact, and the synthmesh supporting her half-healed ribs came apart in a single agonizing pop. She dropped to the floor, fighting to keep her pain from carrying her down into numb oblivion, gazing back to where she had surprised Caedus . . . where Caedus still stood in the doorway, his mouth gaping in surprise, with a thumb-sized scorch hole just below his ribs. *But he was still standing.*

Jaina's pain-clouded mind did not understand how he could take a lightsaber through the gut and *do* that. Why didn't Caedus just lie down and die like most people? Didn't he understand she was trying to do him a favor?

Apparently not, because as soon as she began to gasp for breath, his hand shot up, the fingers splayed and pointed in her direction. Jaina barely brought her lightsaber around in time to absorb the forks of blue lightning that came dancing toward her chest.

Then Caedus stepped forward, the Force lightning still shooting from his fingertips. Jaina could not believe what she was seeing. With *that* wound, he was coming after her. She feinted an attempt to roll to her knees. When Caedus shifted the lightning to block her, she brought her free hand up and gestured toward his shoulder, using the Force to hurl him back through the door. A loud, thudding crash sounded from deep in the shadows, and the voice of an annoyed droid began to complain about the mess.

Jaina was instantly on her feet, springing through the door. But Caedus was just as quick, forgoing his Force lightning in favor of his lightsaber. She saw a fan of crimson light arcing toward her out of the dark side of the pit and spun toward it, blocking and kicking in the same move. Caedus grunted as her boot caught him somewhere above the waist, but behind his crimson blade, he was no more than a gray blur, and it was impossible to tell where the kick had landed.

A black boot heel came shooting under Jaina's guard, driving hard into her sore ribs. She stifled a cry and circled into the shadows, trying to acclimate her eyes to the darkness because it was impossible to sense Caedus in the Force. He fought to keep his advantage, dancing back and forth behind his crimson blade, anticipating her every move—and making her pay for each step with a painful kick or elbow strike.

Knowing that sooner or later one of Caedus's blows could be fatal, Jaina risked a quick look around, searching for something she could Force-hurl. The dark side of the pit was black; she could see nothing in there. And the bright side of the pit was so glaring that she could see only the white, glaring mouth of the fusion incinerator and the conveyor belt that fed it.

Caedus made her pay for the survey in blood, landing a pommel across her cheek that split the flesh and smashed the bone. Jaina countered with a driving knee to the thigh, then a downward slash that Caedus barely turned in time to save his hand.

A flimsiplast crate emerged from the conveyor belt chute beside them. It wasn't much—certainly not heavy enough to do damage—but it was all Jaina had. She gave a little ground, allowing Caedus to force her toward the door so she could let the crate move past him and bring it flying into him from behind.

Then the dark shape of the pit droid came clanking out of the shadows. "Excuse me, please," it said. "I must inspect—"

That was as much as it said before Jaina grasped it in the Force and drew it, stumbling, into Caedus's flank.

The droid was more than heavy enough to send Caedus staggering. He whirled instantly, bringing his blade around at shoulder height. By then Jaina had slipped into the shadows and was lunging forward, her shoulders back but her boot heel driving in under his lightsaber.

Once again, Caedus anticipated her. He spun around, leaning away to protect his vulnerable midsection and bringing his leg up to counterkick. Jaina Force-launched herself into him anyway, whipping her lightsaber around in a down guard to keep his blade at bay. His counterkick landed first, driving into her stomach with a deep sharp ache. Her stomp caught him on the hip and sent him falling onto the conveyor belt.

The flimsicrate burst at the seams as Caedus's shoulder and head came down on top of it. Jaina leapt in to press the attack—and was stunned by how quickly he popped back up. There were more than a dozen used syringes hanging from his shoulder and face. He barely seemed to notice. Letting his lightsaber deactivate and drop to the floor, he reached toward her, making a twisting motion with his hand.

Jaina felt her chin twisting around and went with it, using the Force to accelerate her whole body into a spin, still leaping toward Caedus, bringing her lightsaber around in a clearing arc. She felt the blade meet metal, and the droid's ebony head popped into the air. Then she was on Caedus, slashing at his head with her lightsaber, bringing her boot toe up under his chin when he grew predictable and ducked.

The kick snapped Caedus's head back and sent him tumbling over the conveyor belt. Thinking she had just won the advantage, Jaina dropped her free hand toward the lightsaber he had let fall—then barely saved her arm when the crimson blade *snap-hissed* to life and went spinning past.

Caedus's hand shot up on the other side of the conveyor belt and caught the hilt; then the rest of his body slowly rose into view. His flesh was bulging around the scorch hole in his abdomen, and there were half a dozen syringes planted in his face almost to the barrels. He was in obvious pain—and he was feeding on it. His eyes were bulging and maniacal, his nostrils red and flaring, his lips drawn back so far it almost appeared that he didn't have any.

Jaina brought her lightsaber to high guard and braced her feet, ready for Caedus's attack.

Instead, he deactivated his blade.

"Jaina, listen to me." There was a throaty, gurgling quality to Caedus's voice, and it seemed obvious that the only thing keeping him on his feet was Force energy—a *lot* of it. "You need to get out of my way. I'm trying to save Tenel Ka and Allana."

"Sure you are," Jaina scoffed. As she spoke, she extended her Force awareness in all directions, trying to figure out why Caedus was stalling when his body was running out of time. "Just like you saved Isolder."

"Isolder would have made the same choice. In fact, he *did*." Caedus clipped his lightsaber to his belt, a trust-building gesture that might have had some meaning, had he not been a lying Sith murderer. "Jaina, we don't have *time* for this."

"So die already."

Jaina launched herself into a Force flip, tumbling over the conveyor belt head-down so that she could strike before Caedus had time to unclip and ignite his lightsaber.

Caedus didn't even try. He simply glanced toward the open mouth of the fusion incinerator. In the next instant Jaina felt herself rushing toward its searing heat, and it took all her Force strength to pull herself aside the half meter that saved her life.

But the durasteel into which she slammed was still scorching, and the pain of impact was nothing compared to the sizzling shock of merely contacting the furnace exterior. She dropped to the floor screaming in rage and anguish, her nostrils filled with the stench of singed hair and charred skin, the black GAG utilities still burning on her back.

Then Jaina opened herself fully to the Force, drawing it in through the power of her emotions—not through her anger or pain, as a Sith might, but through her love of what her brother *had* been . . . the teenage jokester who could always find hope in a desperate situation, the questioning warrior who had bested the Yuuzhan Vong warmaster in personal combat, the reluctant champion who had shown a galaxy the way to compassionate victory.

The Force came pouring in from all sides, saturating Jaina and devouring her, filling her with a roaring maelstrom of power, carrying away her pain and leaving in its place the strength not only to survive, but to rise and fight.

Caedus was already on the far side of the conveyor belt, pulling the syringes from his face and shoulder while he staggered toward the exit. Jaina used the Force to depress the control pad, and the door closed in his face.

Caedus whirled with fury in his eyes, but Jaina was already bounding over the conveyor belt, her hair still trailing smoke. He splayed his fingers and sprayed Force lightning at her. Jaina caught it on her lightsaber and whirled past, bringing her blade down where Caedus had been an instant before and leaving a long gouge in the door.

Caedus's blade snapped to life beside her, a crimson fan whirling toward her shoulders. She dropped to her haunches and used her free arm to block the Force-driven snap-kick she knew he would launch at her throat.

Ankle met arm with a sharp crack. What looked like an extra joint appeared in the middle of her forearm, then her wrist flopped over Caedus's leg, a useless throbbing thing no longer under her control.

It didn't matter. Jaina was a dead woman if she didn't win this—maybe even if she *did* win. She whipped her lightsaber around in a high block and deflected the reverse slash Caedus was bringing down toward her neck.

Then she dived forward, whipping her violet lightsaber at his other foot. Caedus sprang away backward, trying to draw both feet out of harm's way at once, and countered by flipping his own weapon around, bringing it up beneath her belly.

Neither blade cut deep, but both did damage. Jaina felt a searing pain across her abdomen, then felt a terrible uncoiling inside her as something she didn't want to think about bulged into the void left by the slashed muscle.

Jaina's blade tapped Caedus behind the boot, touching just long enough to sever the crucial tendon running up the back of the ankle. He landed in an awkward stagger, nearly falling as his foot flapped and flopped without any control.

Jaina came to a knee facing him and knew Caedus was about to die. He had one arm and one good leg, and they were not even on the same side of the body. He could not pivot and he could not retreat. All she needed was to get past his lightsaber and attack the armless side of his body— before she collapsed herself, or he recovered enough to kill her with one last Force blast.

Jaina sprang.

Caedus tried to turn to meet her, but only staggered, his lightsaber falling to his side as though it were a cane. It wasn't, of course, and his momentum kept him stumbling back toward the bright side of the pit, his eyes filled with rage and exhaustion and despair.

Jaina feinted at his head, then began to whirl toward his armless side, bringing her lightsaber around in a flat, high slash that he could not hope to block. It was a sure kill, one that would land even if she died first—which she thought she might, since the attack would leave her completely open to an avenging counterstrike.

But Caedus seemed to know that Jaina had already killed him, and whatever he had in mind, it was not vengeance. When her blade came around, his lightsaber was still hanging at his side. He was staring up toward the ceiling, his gaze fixed somewhere far beyond the murk overhead, and the only attempt he made to save himself was to take one step back into the light spilling from the furnace.

It would not be enough, Jaina knew. She closed her eyes

and felt the lightsaber sink in, felt it slicing through his ribs into his chest. And Jaina felt something in the Force, too—something that made her pulse stop and her chest sink and her blood freeze in her veins. Her brother was reaching out to Tenel Ka, *screaming* at her through the Force, warning her there was danger, urging her to take Allana and . . .

Then the blade reached Caedus's heart, and he dropped at her feet, and Jaina felt nothing at all.

chapter nineteen

*What's the difference between a Jedi Knight and a Jedi Master?
Ask me in twenty years!*

—Jacen Solo, age 15

Stars had finally come to Shedu Maad's black skies. Ben could see a thousand of them chasing one another across the night. They were flinging tiny slivers of light back and forth, erupting into orange novae and silver supernovae, falling from the sky trailing long ribbons of flame. About a hundred were descending in wild unpredictable helixes, trying to evade a pursuing torrent of streaks and flashes. Most failed—then blossomed into a spray of color and finished their descent in the form of dozens of brightly glowing specks.

But all too often, the shooting stars swelled rapidly into the fiery-nosed lozenges of Remnant drop ships. They made a long sweeping curve toward the abandoned mining complex the Jedi had been using as a base, then began to trade cannon fire with the Hapan gun emplacements hidden in the surrounding terrain. Some would make a single pass over the central compound, loosing a flurry of missiles into the already flaming buildings, then wheel around and drop into the trees.

It did not seem to matter to the Imperials that most of the buildings were empty—just as they had been before the Jedi arrived. Nor did it seem to matter that much of the fire they were encountering was coming from the enormous strip and pit mines adjacent to the compound. They had been given an objective to capture, and capture it they would, no matter how worthless it was, or how many stormtrooper lives it cost. Once they had succeeded, Ben and the rest of the base's inhabitants would retreat even deeper into the labyrinth of tunnels, shafts, and open pits that was the mining world of Shedu Maad. The Imperial commanders would analyze the situation and assign their stormtroopers another objective, and so it would continue until one side made a mistake or simply wore down their adversaries.

"We're going to hold out," Ben said. He was standing on an old strip-mining terrace, studying the battle from inside a thicket of the gummy maboo cane that somehow thrived on this particular variety of mine-ravaged ground. "They're not getting enough troops down to box us in."

"Well, that's a relief," said Trista, now wearing night-vision goggles and the self-camouflaging body armor of a major in Her Majesty's Select Commandos. "Here I was worrying that we'd actually have to *fight* this thing out."

"Be nice, Trista," Taryn chided. She was also wearing night-vision goggles and commando armor with an officer's insignia on the shoulders, but Ben had his doubts about whether either sister was actually *in* the military. While none of their fellow Hapans—even General Livette—seemed to question their right to wear the uniforms, they never saluted anyone, and no one ever saluted them. "How's Ben supposed to know you're superstitious?"

"I'm not superstitious," Trista countered. "I'm just saying it's better not to make predictions. Nothing ever goes the way you think it will."

Taryn shook her head. "That's always been your problem. You worry too much." She cringed as a drop ship circled low overhead, a StealthX close behind pumping cannon bolts into its tail, then added, "Still, I wish it was

Zekk telling me that." She turned her goggles in Ben's direction. "No offense, handsome."

"None taken," Ben said. "Zekk's got a better chance of keeping up with you, anyway."

Taryn gave him a sly grin, then cocked her brow. "How good a chance?"

"Uh, pretty good," Ben said. "I guess. I can't believe you're thinking about that right now."

"I can think about a *lot* of things at the same time," Taryn purred. "It's the sign of a healthy mind."

Ben felt the heat rising to his cheeks and started to turn away—until he felt a sudden jolt of shock and despair in Trista's Force aura. He looked over and found her pressing her finger to her comlink earpiece, quietly murmuring into her throat-mike, asking questions like, "Do we know if she survived?" and "Who's heard about this? Anyone moving yet?"

Ben glanced back to Taryn and found her also holding a finger to her comlink earpiece, listening intently but not speaking. She saw him studying her and motioned him close.

"There's been an attack aboard the *Dragon Queen,*" she whispered. "Almost everyone with royal blood is dead."

Ben's heart dropped so far he'd have to pick it off the ground. "Tenel Ka?"

Taryn shook her head. "Don't know yet."

"Allana?"

Taryn shook her head again and did not answer.

The two sisters listened for another moment, then Trista clicked off. She pulled her blaster rifle from its holster and checked its power charge.

"We're going to hold out," she said, quoting him. "You had to say it, didn't you?"

Ben frowned, struggling to make the connection between what had just happened on the *Dragon Queen* and the battle on Shedu Maad. "You're saying I *jinxed* us?"

"It's not your fault. This is a Hapan thing." Taryn checked her own blaster rifle, then pointed at the lightsaber still hanging from his belt. "You *do* know how to use that, right?"

"Uh, sure." Ben snapped the lightsaber off his belt. "If I have a good . . ."

He did not bother finishing the sentence, since both sisters had already retreated from the maboo thicket and were heading toward an old mine adit that entered the hillside at the back of the terrace. The two guards stationed at the mouth of the tunnel took one glance at the blasters in the sisters' hands and looked away, obviously taking pains not to see the pair.

Once they had entered the cool mustiness of the adit, Ben asked, "What was *that* all about?"

"The *Megador* still has most of the Home Fleet bottled up at Uroro Station." Trista removed her night-vision goggles and led the way down the passage, following a line of hastily strung ceiling lights toward the Hapans' command center. "So it's just the *Dragon Queen* and a few of Ducha Requud's Battle Dragons up there. Since the attack on the Queen Mother, SigTel has been picking up a lot of comm traffic between the *Anakin Solo* and the *Deserving Gem*."

"I guess that explains things . . . sort of," Ben said. SigTel was the Hapans' Signals Intelligence unit. Apparently, they suspected the Moffs were trying to strike a deal with Ducha Requud to take Tenel Ka's place. "But I was actually asking why the guards pretended not to see us."

"Oh, *that*." Taryn's voice turned teasing, and Ben knew he was not going to get a straight answer. "We sort of turn invisible sometimes. Don't Jedi?"

"It's different for us," Ben answered. "We actually have to sneak."

The lights ended a thousand meters later, next to an old repair chamber cut into one side of the adit. Once again, the guards stationed at the door looked aside as Trista and

Taryn approached, and Ben followed the sisters into General Livette's makeshift command center.

About a dozen senior officers—all women, of course—were gathered around a large holotable that displayed Shedu Maad's strange topography. In the center lay the main mining pit, a vine-draped abyss more than ten kilometers wide, with a gray-green lake filling the bottom. It was surrounded by uniformly terraced hillsides cloaked in maboo cane, and enormous flats covered with kolg forest—old strip mines and tailings ponds slowly being reclaimed by nature. The display also showed a patchy web of red lines beneath the surface terrain; these represented what little the mapping crews had learned about the network of underground tunnels and shafts that honeycombed the area.

As the officers noticed Ben and the sisters, the urgent drone that had filled the chamber quickly faded, and they turned to face the trio with expressions ranging from irritation to fear. Trista went left and Taryn went right, leaving Ben to wonder what they wanted *him* to do. Deciding it would be safer to stay where he could block the door, Ben stopped at the base of the table and held the hilt of his lightsaber in plain sight.

Taryn stopped about halfway down the table, positioning herself behind the officers and shaking a warning finger when one of them started to turn around. Trista marched straight to General Livette, a stern-jawed woman who did not bother with the usual Hapan vanities, leaving her hair gray and the old blaster burn across her cheek unaltered.

Livette scowled at Trista. "You had better have a good reason for interrupting us *now*—especially with blasters in your hands."

"Don't pretend you haven't heard," Trista said, pointing the blaster at Livette's head. "It makes you look complicit."

Livette's expression went from haughty to resigned, and

feelings of guilt tainted her Force aura. "Of course, I've heard of the unfortunate attacks aboard the *Dragon Queen*," she said. "The news is all over the fleet."

Trista used her free hand to point at Livette's comlink. "Open a channel to *Deserving Gem*," she ordered. "Have the comm officer put you through to Ducha Requud and tell us what you hear."

Livette obeyed, then suddenly looked a little ill and held the comlink out so everyone could hear. It was a woman's voice, screaming in terror and begging for her life.

"There *aren't* going to be any deals with the Moffs," Trista said. "I hope that's clear."

"Ab—absolutely." Livette fell silent as she contemplated something, then she smiled to herself and said, "As a matter of fact, I was just about to ask for you. We've had reports of a female Jedi penetrating our perimeter with a squad of Elite Guard stormtroopers."

"A *Jedi*?" Trista asked. "With the Imperials?"

"That's not a Jedi," Ben said, stepping to the edge of the table. He was pretty certain that General Livette had actually *authorized* the penetration, but he wasn't going to argue the point if Trista and Taryn didn't. "Where are they?"

Before answering, Livette looked to Trista. "I hope you realize that nobody in this chamber was aware of Ducha Requud's betrayal." She was hardly smooth; Ben didn't even need the Force to tell that she was lying. "Our loyalties lie strictly with the *legitimate* successor to Her Majesty Tenel Ka . . . assuming there *is* a need for a successor, of course."

"Did we *say* something to make you believe we doubted you, General?" Taryn asked coolly. "As long as we win the battle, there won't be any reason to suspect the loyalty of anyone in this room."

"I'm glad we all agree." Livette turned to one of her officers, then said, "Show them."

The officer tapped the keys of a data remote. A blue star appeared in the holo, about a kilometer down the terrace from the headquarters—but only a few hundred meters from the underground hangar that the Jedi starfighters were using to refuel and rearm.

"We believe this may be their target," the officer said, pointing at the hangar. "There are reports of a hidden shaft here"—she pointed at the blue star—"that provides access to the hangar."

Trista looked to Taryn. "Take Ben. I'll stay here to protect General Livette in case you run into problems." She turned to the general again. "But I certainly hope that doesn't happen. We wouldn't want a repeat of Ducha Requud's unfortunate accident, would we?"

Livette finally paled. "It might be wise to take a squad of Her Majesty's Commandos along," she said. "They'll be waiting for you outside."

Ben allowed Taryn to lead the way out into the adit, then stepped to her side and asked, "What happened on the *Dragon Queen?*"

"It sounds like a nanokiller," Taryn answered. "The *Queen* took some prisoners aboard. Half an hour later, puffs of silver mist started coming out of the ventilation system and taking down anyone with royal blood."

"But everyone else is okay?" Ben asked.

Taryn looked over. "There was a *lot* of royal blood on the *Queen,* Ben."

"I know," Ben answered. "But *someone's* got to be alive—not everyone aboard had royal blood. So how come no one's telling us what happened to Tenel Ka? If she's dead, they ought to know it for sure."

"You think Her Majesty survived," Taryn surmised. "Allana, too."

"I think they could have," Ben said hopefully. "Tenel Ka would have sensed trouble coming, and she's been keeping Allana very close to her."

The mouth of the tunnel appeared ahead, a black arch where the ceiling lights simply ended, and Taryn looked away.

"It's the way we do things," Taryn said. "When a Queen Mother dies, we like to keep things uncertain for a while. It gives us a chance to tighten up security around potential successors—and to see which one seems a little *too* prepared to take her place."

"Like Ducha Requud," Ben said. He could reach out in the Force to see if Tenel Ka was alive, but it would serve nothing except his curiosity—and it might be a distraction Tenel Ka did not need, if she *was* alive. "I guess that makes sense. But who's *we,* exactly?"

Taryn did not look over. "Who do you think, Ben?"

"I have no idea."

"Good," Taryn said, putting her night-vision goggles back on. "It would have been a shame to kill you."

For once, she did not sound like she was joking. Ben put on his own goggles and followed her out into the night, where they met a dozen male commandos and started down the terrace toward their intercept point. It was a difficult trip through thick stands of maboo, especially since they had to travel quietly over broken ground. Taryn surprised Ben by setting a brutal pace in near silence, and he had to draw on the Force to match her.

The commandos were quiet but not quite silent, and when they drew within two hundred meters of the objective, Taryn signaled them to slow down and move more carefully. She took Ben and continued forward, then crept into a cane thicket at the edge of the terrace and peered down into the forest.

Even with the night-vision goggles, it was difficult to see much through the billowing crowns of the kolg trees. About seventy meters from the base of their terrace, a troop of mangy-furred rat-monkeys were huddled together on a high branch, their infrared silhouettes cowering in fear at the constant roar of Jedi starfighters entering and departing the nearby hangar.

Something about the monkeys struck Ben as odd. If they were so frightened of the noise and light of the starfighters, why were they cowering in the *top* of the kolg tree? He began a systematic search of the nearby forest canopy, and soon spotted another troop of rat-monkeys climbing into the treetops.

"There," he whispered, pointing. "Coming toward us."

Taryn ran her gaze down his arm toward the trees, then said, "Ben, we're not looking for . . ."

She let her sentence trail off as she realized the significance of what he was pointing out, then glanced back into the maboo thicket. The commandos were not yet in sight.

"What's taking them so long?" she hissed.

An unpleasant thought occurred to Ben. "You don't think they were loyal to—"

"No, they're just *men*." She swung her goggles in Ben's direction. "No offense, handsome."

Taryn slipped out of the thicket and angled down toward the point where they expected to intercept the enemy, which Ben guessed would be about where the forest met the slope. The ground was still muddy enough that he and Taryn were leaving an easy trail to follow. But the maboo cane wasn't as thick on the embankment as it was on the flat part of the terrace, so there was a risk of being spotted on the way down.

By the time Ben and Taryn reached the bottom of the slope, he could hear the soft whisper of leaves and branches rubbing against plastoid armor. He dropped behind a fallen kolg tree next to Taryn and peered out through the underbrush, hiding his presence in the Force. It was only a matter of time before Tahiri felt Taryn and the commandos, but at least she would not realize that they were accompanied by a Jedi.

Fortunately, Tahiri seemed to be concentrating on other

things for the moment. She emerged from the forest at the head of the column, an infrared silhouette with one hand outstretched, her palm turned downward as though feeling something rising from the ground. Behind her came a line of about a dozen stormtroopers, the four in the middle carrying a litter with a metal cone resting in the center.

Ben thought the cone might be a canister full of Remnant nanokiller—until he saw a set of colored lights blinking in a three-red-two-yellow-one-green pattern that he had been trained to recognize early in his days as a GAG antiterrorist operative: a baradium warhead.

Ben touched Taryn's forearm and directed her attention to the warhead . . . and felt her muscles tense beneath his grasp. Even a small baradium warhead would be powerful enough to blow the top off the entire ridge—and a warhead that required four men to carry it *wasn't* small.

Tahiri stopped about fifteen meters away, in the center of a treeless circle of underbrush, and motioned the stormtrooper behind her to stop.

"I think this is it," she said. "Bring up the penetration charges. But keep that warhead back. We don't want to detonate it just *trying* to get into the tunnels."

The troopers carrying the warhead backed away, but the rest came forward. One of them removed his backpack and pulled a set of hollow, telescoping rods from the interior, which he extended and passed to his fellows. In the meantime, Tahiri began to wander the perimeter of the treeless circle, probing it with the Force and directing the stormtroopers to drive their rods into the sandy soil about every three meters.

As Ben watched them work, he slowly grew more outraged by the depth of the betrayal General Livette had nearly committed. Not only had she agreed to let a Remnant strike team destroy the Jedi hangar, she had obviously provided them with very precise intelligence about a buried access tunnel—and what they would need to open it. Even

more amazingly, nobody seemed surprised—or even particularly upset—by the treachery. They just expected and
dealt with such behavior from their "loyal" nobles. It was
almost enough to make a sane man wonder if Caedus
could be right about the galaxy needing an iron fist—
almost.

After watching the stormtroopers work for a few moments, Taryn dropped to her belly and slowly began to
work her blaster rifle into a gap under the kolg tree. Realizing she intended to take a shot at Tahiri, Ben caught her
arm and shook his head. He wasn't being softhearted. The
second Taryn set the sight on her target—maybe even
sooner—Tahiri's danger sense would kick in. And Ben
really didn't like the idea of starting a firefight outnumbered more than six to one.

Taryn scowled and tried to pull her arm free, but re-
lented when Ben shook his head and refused to let go.

Once the stormtroopers had finished driving their poles,
a second man opened his pack and began to arm and pass
out the penetration charges, which his fellows inserted
down the hollow rods they had driven into the sandy soil.
When that was finished, the demolitions man passed a
small detonator to Tahiri. She motioned for the squad to
retreat, following a few steps behind.

The last man had just stepped out of the circle of rods
when Tahiri suddenly spun around, looking not toward
Ben and Taryn, but toward the slope down which they had
come a few minutes earlier.

"There's someone coming," Tahiri said, pointing.

Taryn was already rising to a knee, laying the barrel of
the blaster rifle across the kolg trunk. "*Now* can I blast
her?" she whispered.

"Who's stopping you?" Ben whispered back.

"*Men.*"

A blue bolt screeched away from the barrel of her
blaster, but Tahiri was already diving into the trees. She

brought the detonator around beneath her body, pointing it toward the circle of penetration charges.

Ben felt the gut-punch shock wave of an all-too-close detonation, then his goggles went momentarily dark as the optics were overwhelmed by the blast flash. He cowered behind the kolg trunk with Taryn as it was pelted by falling sand and brush.

In the next instant the forest erupted into screaming bolts of blasterfire. Ben poked his head up over the tree and saw a column of sand dropping back toward the ground—and *into* it, where an enormous sinkhole was draining into the tunnel or shaft or whatever it was that Tahiri and her men had just opened.

To the left of the sinkhole, a dozen of Tenel Ka's Select Commandos were charging through the trees, exchanging blasterfire with the startled Imperials. Behind it, two troopers were dragging the litter with the big baradium warhead toward the hole, defended by the whirling blade of Tahiri's lightsaber.

"I'll take the troopers out," Taryn said, thrusting her blaster rifle into Ben's hands. "You keep the Jedi busy."

"She's not a . . ."

Ben let the sentence trail off as Taryn plucked a trio of fragmentation grenades off her equipment harness and thumbed the arming switch on the first one. He propped the barrel on the tree and opened fire on Tahiri, switching from one corner of her body to another so she would have to move her blade across the greatest distance to defend herself.

But Tahiri was as quick as she was precise, batting Ben's first bolts back into the tree behind which they were hiding, then deflecting them up toward the grenade that Taryn had just sent arcing her way. The third bolt she deflected struck home, and the grenade detonated harmlessly above the newly reopened mine shaft.

Taryn thumbed the arming switches on her last two grenades. "I *said* keep the Jedi busy!"

Ben jumped up and began to fire—not at Tahiri, but at the baradium warhead, forcing her to dive into position to protect the bomb. Taryn sent both grenades flying across the shaft just as Tahiri dropped into a cartwheel. The Hapan whooped in delight as the maneuver carried Tahiri past the warhead—and out of position to defend the troopers dragging it forward.

The grenades detonated to either side of the litter, shredding the stormtroopers' armor and hurling their torn bodies aside. Tahiri was caught by the shock wave and hurled out of sight into the trees. The warhead dropped to the ground unharmed.

"Good job." Taryn took her blaster rifle back and clambered over the log. "Now let's go finish—"

She let the sentence drop and opened fire into the woods. Ben snatched up his lightsaber and jumped over the log, then saw Tahiri charging back out of the trees, bloody and battered but still swatting Taryn's blaster bolts back at her. He activated his own lightsaber and stepped forward to defend the Hapan—then watched in amazement as Tahiri deactivated her lightsaber and launched herself in a high arc toward the shaft, one hand stretching toward the warhead.

"Uh-oh." Ben opened himself to the Force and reached out for the warhead, grasping for it with his mind . . . saw it rising off its broken litter, starting to float toward the shaft. *"Blast!"*

He raced forward, gathering himself to spring, and heard Taryn calling behind him.

"Ben? Ben, wait. *No!*"

But Ben was already somersaulting after Tahiri, dropping down into the shaft above her. As they fell, she whirled around and brought her blade up, slashing at his neck—but not quickly enough to prevent him from blocking. He countered with a snap-kick to the spine that drew a pained grunt and sent her sailing into the wall.

Still falling, she came tumbling back at him, double-slashing at his midsection, then planting a boot in his ribs that drove the wind from his lungs and sent *him* slamming into the rocky wall. He tumbled out of control for an instant, plummeting through the darkness, then used the Force to bring himself under control.

How deep *was* this hole?

Tahiri's blade came weaving at him out of the murk, and Ben realized he had lost his night-vision goggles. He blocked, blocked again, then realized he had left his stomach wide open . . . and still managed to get his blade down a split second before Tahiri pressed her advantage.

Gasping in relief—she'd *had* him, but she had been too slow again—he kicked off her hip and hit the wall behind him, then used the Force to stick himself against it, *hard*. It was a hot, painful way to slow his descent, but it was better than the alternative.

Ben saw a glow above him and looked up to see Tahiri doing the same thing on the opposite side of the shaft, a dark figure behind a bright blade, glaring down at him with bright eyes. He pressed harder, slowing his descent more so she would not have the altitude advantage—then heard a loud splash below as the warhead reached the bottom.

Water. *Great.*

Tahiri pushed away from the wall, dropping toward him behind a wild cyclone of kicking boots and slashing blade.

It was a foolish attack. All Ben had to do was guard high, then parry and take her legs off at the knees. He raised his blade to do just that—then finally realized what he was seeing and parried without countering.

Tahiri dropped past, her face not showing relief, but screwed into a mask of surprise and rage, and Ben realized that she really didn't want to kill him. Maybe she didn't even want to survive.

She splashed into the water, then screamed and went silent.

Ben hit half a second later, letting out his own scream as his knees were driven up to his chin. Cold, dark water poured over his head and began to rush down his throat. He coughed into the water, sucked in more water, and finally regained control of his reflexes and closed his mouth.

There was water in his ears, and he could feel his hair swirling around him, but he had no idea how far under he was. He looked up and saw steam rising past the tip of his lightsaber, so he knew he couldn't be that deep. So why wasn't he rising to the surface?

Ben tried to kick himself up—and immediately realized the problem. All that sandy soil that he had seen dropping into the sinkhole had to go somewhere, and now he was buried to the waist in it. Still fighting not to cough and gulp down more water, he grabbed the slick rock beside him, wiggling his legs and trying to drag himself forward, slowly opening a cavity around his hips.

After a few seconds, Ben managed to pull himself free and half scramble, half float to the surface—where it took him a few more seconds to realize that only about half of the gasping and coughing he heard was his own. He turned and found the silhouette of Tahiri's head and shoulders about three meters away, her lightsaber between them but not attacking, her free hand stretched toward a line of lights blinking in the distinctive three-red-two-yellow-one-green pattern of the baradium warhead.

"Tahiri, you don't want to do that." Ben tried to stand and immediately sank back to his knees in the wet tailings. "I *know* you don't, because you're no better suited to being a Sith apprentice than I was."

Tahiri glanced over, but kept her hand stretched toward the warhead. "Stay out of it, Ben." Her face was plunged into shadow, but he could still see her hair and eyes, both gleaming silver in the blade light reflecting off the water. "You don't have to get hurt."

"See? That's what I mean." Ben gave up trying to stand and simply knelt, using his shins to spread his weight across the wet pile. "If you were Sith material, you wouldn't *care* whether I got hurt. You wouldn't have gotten so mad when you killed Shevu."

"I don't *like* killing anyone, Ben," Tahiri said. She switched her free hand to her lightsaber, so that now she was holding it in a powerful two-handed grip. "That doesn't mean I ever hesitate."

Ben snorted. "You're not even a good liar." He started to knee-walk toward the warhead. "I'd have thought Caedus would have taught you *that* much."

Tahiri held her blade in front of Ben's chest. "I'm not lying, Ben."

"Then you'll have to prove it," Ben said. He brought his own blade up and pressed it against Tahiri's, forcing it aside. "I'm going to go over there to take the detonator charge out of that warhead. There's only one way to stop me—and you won't do it."

Tahiri switched off her lightsaber—then switched it back on so fast that Ben barely had time to lean out of the way before the blade extended where his throat had been a moment before. But the follow-through never came, and Ben's head remained firmly attached to his shoulders.

"Close—I'll give you that." The way Ben's heart was hammering, he felt like he might die of fear even if Tahiri *didn't* kill him—but he was willing to take that chance. He leaned around the blade and started knee-walking toward the warhead again. "But not close enough. When you come back to the Order, we'll get Uncle Han to teach you a few things about bluffing."

Tahiri sighed, then switched off her blade. "I'm *not* coming back to the Order, Ben."

The tension left Ben's body so fast that his hands began to shake uncontrollably. She was giving up.

"No? Then what are you going to do? Become some kind of bounty hunter?" Ben reached the warhead and began to dig it out. "Because you *know* Caedus isn't going to take you back."

"Yeah, but I'm done with him," she said bitterly. "I'm done with *all* Solos."

Tahiri hung her lightsaber on her belt, then removed a glow rod and shined it up the water-filled tunnel. "Is anybody going to be looking for me down here? I'd rather not get killed trying to sneak away."

"You won't, if you help me with this," Ben said, grunting as he struggled to turn the warhead so that he could reach the access panel. "They forgave *me*."

"Yeah? Well, you were just a kid. And you still are." Tahiri knelt in the water next to Ben, then used the Force to spin the warhead so the access panel was facing them. "It'll be different for me."

"Probably," Ben allowed. "It'll take time, and you'll have to answer for your actions. But they *will* forgive you—I promise."

"I'm not sure that promise is yours to make," Tahiri said.

Before Ben could answer, a loud splash sounded nearby, and Ben looked over to see a rope dancing next to him.

"If you're going to run, you better do it now," Ben said. "I'll tell them you drowned and floated away or something."

Tahiri's brow rose. "You'd *lie* for mc?"

"If you want me to," Ben said. "And don't worry—I'm a lot better at it than you are. That's one thing Jacen taught me that I haven't forgotten yet."

Tahiri turned on the glow rod again. Her face was solemn but resolute. "I think it's time to leave the lies behind," she said. "It's time to leave a lot of things behind."

For a moment, Ben wasn't sure whether she meant to come back with him—or just to get herself killed.

Then a bright light began to shine down on them, and Taryn's voice echoed down from above.

"Move, and you're a dead woman," she warned. "Ben, get away from her."

Ben looked up to see the Hapan rappelling swiftly down the shaft, holding the rope in one hand and her blaster rifle in the other.

"It's okay," he called up. "She's with us."

A LONG TIME AGO . . .

It is during the truce at the Battle of Ithor, and Jaina is an X-wing pilot with the legendary Rogue Squadron. She is lying on her bunk aboard the Ralroost, *trying to get some much-needed rest before the Yuuzhan Vong renew their attack. But the bunk on the other side of the cabin is empty, and sleep won't come because of that. She has just lost her friend and wingmate Anni Capstan, and she cannot close her eyes without seeing Anni's face.*

Jaina is filled with emotions she does not know how to control, and all she wants is to make them go away. The strongest is guilt—guilt that she survived when Anni did not, guilt that when Colonel Darklighter asked her to record a message for Anni's family, she did not even know their names. They had been flying together and bunking together for months without talking about their lives back home. Now it is too late for Jaina to ask, and that makes her feel more guilty than anything.

Then the place in Jaina's heart that belongs to her brother Jacen begins to warm, and she knows he is standing outside her cabin. She doesn't wait for him to knock.

She simply opens the door and crawls back into her bunk and says nothing.

Jacen comes and sits on the edge of her bed. He doesn't need to ask what's wrong, because he knows—because he is her twin, and he feels it, too.

So Jacen just strokes her hair until she starts to hurt a little less and finally falls asleep. He stays with her through the night because he knows that if he leaves, she'll wake and won't be able to sleep again.

And Jaina hears him whispering to her in her dreams, telling her that no one you love really ever has to die—not if you don't want them to . . . All you have to do is hold a place for them in your heart.

chapter twenty

What's the difference between an Ewok and a Wookiee? About two hundred kilos!

—Jacen Solo, age 15

If you were a GAG commando posted to the *Anakin Solo,* the last thing you wanted to see right now was a wing of Jedi StealthXs storming the already battle-torn hangar you were assigned to defend. Han was pretty certain of that. And he was *absolutely* certain you didn't want to see the *Millennium Falcon* following them in—not after the announcement Tenel Ka had just made . . . not when some of the mudcrutches you were protecting were Imperial Moffs.

With the StealthX wing cannons blasting away and GAG defenders returning fire from every hatchway and corner, the hangar was already one big eruption. But that didn't keep Han from firing a rackful of concussion missiles into the control booth, or stop Leia from turning the *Falcon*'s blaster cannon on anything wearing a black uniform.

The conflagration quickly faded as Han and the Jedi eliminated the defenders' heavy weapons. As one, the StealthXs dropped to the deck and popped their canopies. Out came a dozen Jedi Masters leading fifty Jedi Knights, all leaping and whirling as their lightsabers batted a hail of blaster bolts back toward their attackers. Han kept the *Falcon* up high so that Leia and their two cannon gunners—

Jagged Fel and a senior apprentice named Derek—could provide covering fire.

Luke and the other Masters led the way toward the back of the hangar. The driving tip of the Jedi wedge, they were Force-hurling and Force-blasting any GAG trooper foolish enough to send a bolt their way. A squad of sharpshooters began to lay fire from the smoking ruins of the control booth; Saba Sebatyne raked a taloned hand through the air, and they came flying down to the deck headfirst. A late-arriving E-Web opened fire from inside a ventilation grate; Kyp Durron made a tapping motion with his finger, and the barrel sagged, causing the weapon to misfire and explode. A platoon of black-armored GAG commandos rushed through a hatchway, streaming fire from T-21 repeating blasters; Luke glanced at a nearby shuttle and sent it tumbling into their line.

Behind the Masters followed the much larger body of Jedi Knights, fanning out in teams of two and three, securing hatchways, disarming—sometimes literally—tenacious fighters who refused to surrender, seizing control of vital components including the containment field and ventilation system. Within moments the Jedi controlled the hangar, and the few GAG commandos who had not already died or surrendered were either fleeing or tossing their weapons aside.

Han set the *Falcon* down, then unbuckled and turned to Leia. Her eyes were already fixed out the forward viewport, focused somewhere *beyond,* and she had The Look. Han's heart dropped—his entire *being* dropped. He had seen that look only twice before, once when Anakin had died and once when she had thought Luke was dead, and he had spent every minute of Jaina's hunt terrified that he was going to see it again. And he didn't know if they could stand it—if even he and Leia were strong enough to handle the loss of their last child.

Unable to sit still, and unable to bring himself to ask

Leia, Han turned to his missile control panel and began to enter a new set of specifications.

"Threepio, go load the baradium missile."

"The baradium missile, Captain Solo?" C-3PO asked from the navigator's station behind him. "I don't believe Master Skywalker's plan calls for a baradium missile."

"It doesn't," Han said. "You heard Tenel Ka's announcement. They killed *Allana*. If Jaina is gone, too, *nobody* who was a part of it is leaving this . . ."

Han felt Leia's hand on his arm and let his sentence trail off, but he didn't look over. He was just too afraid.

"Han, we need to hurry." A click sounded from the co-pilot's seat as she unbuckled her crash webbing. "Jaina's still alive."

Han's throat tightened. *"Still?"*

He didn't know whether to let his breath out or hold it until his heart started to beat again, but he rose to leave—and that was when he saw that Leia still had The Look.

"Leia?" he asked. "What—"

"It's Jacen." Her voice cracked, and her hand slid down his arm to grab his. "Jaina got him."

When the disposal pit door opened, Jaina was sitting on the floor where shadow became light, holding Jacen's head in her lap and whispering that he wasn't really dead—that he would always have a place in her heart, now that she could finally feel their twin bond again.

Except that Jaina wasn't actually whispering the words. She wasn't even thinking them, really. *Imagining* might have been a better way to describe it, or *experiencing*. She was more a witness to her thoughts than their author, lost in that hazy netherworld of anguish that existed only in the narrow margin between wakefulness and death.

So when Jagged Fel rushed into the disposal pit and began yelling that he'd found her, that they needed to *hurry,* she wasn't quite sure what she was seeing. She thought maybe he had come to join her and Jacen, and that made her a little sad, though she couldn't quite figure out why.

Then Jag knelt at her side and tried to pull Jacen away, and that made her *angry*. She Force-hurled Jag away, yelling what she had meant to be *Don't touch him*, but what came out as "Doonguchem."

Nothing if not brave, Jag picked himself up and returned, moving more slowly now. This time, he didn't try to take Jacen away from her. He simply knelt at her side and gave her a stim-shot, then took hold of her hand.

"Help's on the way, Jaina," he said. "You're going to be fine."

Jaina wasn't sure she believed him, but she squeezed his hand anyway. As the stim-shot took hold and her head slowly cleared, she began to remember the things she would be leaving unfinished if she didn't make it—and probably even if she did.

"Do something . . . for me?" she asked.

"You're going to make it," Jag said. "I promise."

"You *can't* promise." Jaina would have smiled, but her flayed-open cheek hurt too much, and her mouth—no, her entire face—didn't really seem to be working right. "And I still . . . need you to . . ."

"Of course," Jag said. "Anything."

"Find . . . Zekk."

Jag's face fell. "Okay," he said. "As soon as the medics get here, I'll go tell him—"

"*No,*" Jaina gasped. "He's *missing*. Hit during the StealthX raid."

"Oh." Jag looked even more distressed, and Jaina loved him for that. "We'll find him. Don't worry."

"*Have* to worry."

"I'll make sure Master Skywalker knows, too," Jag assured her. "We *will* find him."

If he can be found, Jaina thought, silently adding the unspoken condition of search-and-rescue missions. She squeezed his hand again. "Thanks."

"Thanks aren't necessary," Jag said. "Zekk is a good man."

"Not for . . . Zekk." Jaina shook her head—and wished she hadn't as her neck erupted into scalding pain. "For getting here first. Glad it was . . . you."

"Me, too." Jag looked more worried than pleased. "But hold on. Help is coming."

Jaina nodded, but said, "Second thing . . . Mirta Gev."

Jag's brow rose. "Yes?"

"Upstairs." Even with the stim-shot, Jaina found it an effort to talk, and her thoughts were beginning to grow hazy again. "Alive. Get her . . . out."

Jag nodded. "I'll make sure."

"Not someone slow," Jaina warned. "She has . . . blaster rifles."

"No surprise there," said a familiar, cocky voice. "She's Mandalorian, right?"

Jaina looked up to see her parents rushing over. Their eyes were rimmed with red and their faces were pale, but her father was doing his best to look smug and confident, while her mother was trying—and failing—to hide her alarm behind a calm veneer.

As they drew nearer and saw Jacen's head resting in Jaina's lap, they finally exhausted their last reserves of composure. Her father's lip began to tremble and her mother's brown eyes turned liquid with sadness. They knelt beside her, trying not to look at their son's body but unable not to, and seemed helpless to speak around the lumps in their throats.

After a couple of seconds, her mother pulled an airsplint from the medpac in her hands and immobilized Jaina's broken arm, while her father found a canister of sterinumb and gingerly sprayed her burns. The tasks seemed to help them focus their thoughts, and they began to give her unscorched shoulder and unbroken arm tentative squeezes of affection.

On some level, Jaina knew, they were probably trying to reassure her, to let her know that nothing had changed between them. But that was impossible, of course. Jaina had become the Sword of the Jedi, with everything that meant.

Always you shall be in the front rank, a burning brand to your enemies, a brilliant fire to your friends. Yours is a restless life, and never shall you know peace, though you shall be blessed for the peace that you bring others. Take comfort in the fact that, though you stand tall and alone, others will take shelter in the shadow that you cast.

So Luke had spoken when he made Jaina a Jedi Knight, and so Jaina had become. It wasn't a destiny she would have chosen—but who ever *truly* chooses? She doubted that her brother had envisioned his destiny to end *here*, with him lying dead in his sister's lap.

Once her back was coated with sterinumb, her father finally seemed to find the strength to speak. "How are you doing, kid?"

"How . . . I look," Jaina replied. "And not just . . . the outside."

Her father nodded. "Yeah, me, too." He looked back toward the door, where Cilghal had just arrived, leading a pair of young Jedi Knights with a hovergurney. "But you've got to pull through, okay? I don't know if we can make it without you."

"*I* do." Jaina looked to her mother, then added, "You together . . . nothing can break . . . that."

Her mother smiled sadly. "Maybe not," she said, stepping back so Cilghal and her assistants could start to work. "But I'm really tired of having that tested. So you listen to your father."

*   *   *

The Elite Guard stormtroopers probably knew that one platoon could not stand against so many Jedi Masters. But they had been ordered to hold the *Anakin Solo*'s Auxiliary Command Center at any cost, and brave men were born under every flag. So they tried.

And they died.

When it was done, the smoke hung in the corridor so thick that Han could barely see to pick his way over the body parts. His eyes were watering and his hands trembling, though that had more to do with the anger he felt than the acrid stench of melted armor and charred flesh. He did not need to look beneath any helmets to know that the men strewn across the deck had been in the prime of their lives, some of them just a little older than Anakin had been when he fell to the Yuuzhan Vong, many of them younger than Jaina . . . and Jacen.

Han came to the end of the corridor, where Luke, Saba, Kyle, and the other Masters now stood before an enormous blast door. He stopped beside Jag Fel and ran a hand over his face. Leia had left the ship, heading to a Battle Dragon healing center with Jaina and Cilghal. So it was up to Han to calm himself. Once Cilghal had pronounced Jaina stable enough to move, he had insisted on staying with Luke to confront the men responsible for his granddaughter's death.

But Han was beginning to question that decision now. He was closer than usual to being dangerously out of control, and—despite Cilghal's assurances that Jaina was no longer in any immediate danger—he could not keep his thoughts off her. He closed his eyes and tried to calm himself with that Jedi breathing technique Leia had taught him.

It didn't work. His hands continued to tremble, and his eyes watered more than ever.

Finally, he gave up and said, "This makes me sick."

Jag looked over, then pulled a small squeeze tube from a

pouch on his equipment belt. "I have some stink-mask, if that would help."

"Not the smell." Han waved a hand at the carpet of dead troopers behind them. "*This*. What's the point? It's not like there was anybody left to come save them."

Jag surveyed the carnage, contemplating. The ground assault on Shedu Maad had failed with Tahiri's surrender to Ben, and the elements of the *Anakin Solo*'s crew that had not defected to the Jedi in the last half an hour were either dead or on their way to dirtside detention chambers. The Moffs did not even have a realistic chance of reinforcement from outside the ship; with Battle Dragons reverting to realspace every couple of minutes as they managed to disengage from the *Megador,* the space battle itself was clearly shifting in favor of the Jedi coalition.

Finally, Jag nodded and said, "My father said it was easier to get a Moff to spend lives than money. That appears to be as true for the Remnant as it was for the Empire."

A series of tremendous bangs sounded from deep within the blast door. Han looked over to see Luke holding a hand out and the door slowly creeping open. Protruding up from the sill was the stub of one of the thirty-centimeter locking pins that had been holding the heavy door in place.

"Unbelievable," Jag gasped.

"Yeah," Han agreed. "Now you know who to call if you need a mountain moved."

As soon as the door had slid open far enough to permit entrance, Saba dived through, with Kyp, Kyle, Corran, and the other Masters close behind. There followed a short flurry of blaster screeches and surprised cries, and by the time Han and Jag's turn came, all had fallen silent inside.

To Han's disappointment, he did not find the Moffs lying dead in a row as he entered the chamber. They were all seated around a tactical display that currently showed nothing but Mist static. Some were holding their hands over scorch wounds on their shoulders, but most were star-

ing at their laps with expressions ranging from fear to outrage. One—a young man with a black goatee and a shaved
head—lay on the floor in two still-smoking parts.

Saba, Kyp, and Kyle were standing around the table behind the Moffs, lightsabers in hand but not ignited. The
rest of the Masters were busy taking Caedus's command
staff into custody. Han found himself squeezing his blaster
grip so hard that he thought it might crack, but he resisted
the temptation to raise his hand and start shooting. With
all those Masters standing there, his bolts would just get
batted away anyhow.

Finally, Luke entered the room and went to the head of
the table. "As I'm sure you've heard by now, Darth Caedus
is dead."

The Moffs gave an affirming murmur; some looked worried, but none appeared sad.

"Good. That leaves you with two choices," Luke said.
"The first is this: you become Hapan prisoners of war and
face a war crimes trial for your nanokiller attack against
the royal family."

Several Moffs paled visibly, but one—a grim-faced man
with short, steel-gray hair, actually looked relieved.

"That doesn't sound like a very attractive option," he
said. "What is your other proposal?"

Luke turned and studied the man for a moment, then
said, "Frankly, Moff Lecersen, my other *proposal* sickens
me. But we need the Remnant's support—and its fleets—to
end this war. The easiest way to achieve that is to invite the
Moff Council to join us in reestablishing the Galactic Alliance."

A murmur of relief rounded the table, but now Lecersen
looked worried, his eyes narrowing in suspicion.

"That seems more than generous, Master Skywalker,"
he said. "What's the drawback?"

Luke waved Jag forward, then pushed him toward the
front of the table. "Him," he said. "I can hand you over to

the Hapans, or I can hand you over to someone who will let you live—as long as you stay in line."

Most of the Moffs frowned in confusion, but Lecersen leaned forward and studied Jag's face for a moment. "Aren't you one of Soontir Fel's sons?"

"That's correct," Jag said. "I'm Jagged Fel."

"I see." Lecersen leaned back, contemplating Luke, then contemplating Jag. Finally, he asked, "Do you think you're up to it, son?"

Jag frowned. "Up to what, sir?"

It was Luke who answered. "Taking Pellaeon's place," he said. "Administering the Moff Council, at least until the current crisis is resolved."

"You'd be doing us a favor, Commander Fel. You have good Imperial blood, and the alternative is . . ."—Lecersen paused and glanced around the table, directing the rest of his comment to his fellow Moffs—". . . well, most likely a long unpleasant incarceration, followed by an even more unpleasant death."

A light seemed to come on in the eyes of several of the other Moffs, and they began to nod their enthusiastic agreement. But Jag seemed to be as stunned by the whole thing as Han, and he simply stood at the table frowning, trying to sort through the implications of what Luke was proposing.

Finally, he turned to Luke. "Why are you springing this on me now?" he asked. "It would have been good to have some time to think it over."

"For you," Luke said, nodding. "But I wanted it to be clear to the Moffs that this isn't something *you* arranged—that you're doing them a service, not making a power play."

"*And* doing the galaxy a service, as well," added a round-faced Moff with beady eyes and two chins. "Without *our* support, the Jedi coalition will have a difficult time convincing Bwua'tu and his fellow admirals that they've rejoined the Galactic Alliance."

"And with our fleets, the Alliance will have the power it needs to force the Confederation to the bargaining table," another Moff added. "You could end the war, Commander Fel."

Jag sighed, and Han's insides began to twist into an angry knot.

"Seen in that light," Jag said, his voice strong but lacking enthusiasm, "I really have no choice."

Lecersen smiled, then stood and started to offer his hand to Jag, and this was too much for Han. He quickly stepped between them, then whirled around to face Luke.

"That's *it*?" he demanded. "You're just going to let them change sides?"

"It's the best thing for the galaxy, Han," Luke said. While there was a hint of sorrow in his eyes, his face remained composed. "But if there's something you want addressed—"

"You're blasted right there's something I want addressed." Han turned toward the table, blaster still in hand. "Whose idea was it to sneak the nanokiller aboard Tenel Ka's flagship?"

Most of the Moffs' faces went from shocked or frightened to relieved. But one, a square-jawed Moff with a military bearing and cold blue eyes, began to look worried—especially when the others nodded toward him.

Han stepped to the table and pressed his blaster barrel to the man's head.

"What's your name?" Han didn't know why he cared. Maybe he was just stalling because he didn't want to blast a man—even a child-murderer—in cold blood, or maybe because he didn't want to sidetrack the peace deal for his personal vengeance. But how could he let this man—or *any* of the Moffs—get away with what they had done to Allana? "Was it your idea?"

"Why do you care?" Considering that there was a very angry man holding a blaster to his head, the Moff was surprisingly calm. "My 'friends' have appointed me to take the blame. So go ahead—if you must."

Han thumbed the safety off. When no one tried to stop him from pulling the trigger, he glanced around the table at the Masters, who all stood watching him with folded hands.

"What's wrong?" he demanded. "Are you just going to let me blast this guy?"

"It is your choice," Saba said. "This one does not think it will interfere with our peace deal. We have plenty of Moffz. Blast two."

Han began to feel more foolish than angry. He looked over at Luke. "You, too?"

Luke shrugged. "Nobody is going to miss one Moff, not after all the killing that has happened here already," he said. "So do it—if it's going to make you feel better."

That was just the trouble, of course. It *wouldn't* make him feel better. It wasn't one Moff who was guilty of sending the nanokiller after Tenel Ka, it was *all* of them. And the soldiers who had sneaked it aboard the *Dragon Queen*. And the scientists who had developed the blasted stuff in the first place.

Han contemplated this for a moment, then looked back to Luke. "I don't think one is going to do it for me," he said. "How many can you let me have?"

That caused an uneasy stirring around the table—especially when Luke considered the question for a moment, then asked, "Well, how many do you think it would *take*?"

Han saw by the twinkle that came to the eyes of Saba, Kyle, and Kyp that they knew as well as he did that Luke wasn't going to let him blast any of the Moffs—that they had known all along he wasn't going to kill anyone and had just been giving him the room to reach that conclusion himself.

Han let the Moffs squirm a little longer, then finally lowered the blaster. "Probably more than you can spare." He turned to Jag. "But they've got to pay for what they did. Maybe set up a mission to help out worlds in poverty or something—a real generous mission."

Lecersen scowled. "I don't know if we have the resources for—"

"I think that's an excellent idea," interrupted the Moff whom Han had been threatening. "And I hope you'll join me in being one of the largest contributors, Moff Lecersen—considering that you're the one who suggested the delivery method."

Lecersen's face paled. "You make a persuasive argument."

"Good," a familiar voice said from the doorway. "I'm sure Allana would be honored to have such a mission undertaken in her memory."

Along with everyone else, Han turned to find Tenel Ka striding into the room. She was dressed as a warrior queen, wearing an opalescent eletrotex flight suit and carrying a lightsaber in her hand. There was a barely contained fury in her that even Han could sense, but she seemed to have her emotions under far better control than he did.

Tenel Ka stopped at Han's side and acknowledged the bows she received from everyone—except the Moffs—then said, "Thank you, Captain Solo, for suggesting it—and for not spoiling a rare chance to end this war."

Han's eyes widened in shock. "You're okay with letting them off?"

"No, I am not 'okay' with their treachery, and I never will be. But I am a queen. I cannot put the desire for personal vengeance before my duty to end this war." Tenel Ka turned an icy glare on the Moffs. "And that, gentlemen, is the only reason you will be permitted to live. I suggest you *never* test my forbearance again."

The Moffs all nodded their understanding, and Lecersen

even bowed. "We won't, Your Majesty," he said. "The council sincerely apologizes for its indiscretion."

"It was *not* an indiscretion, Moff," Tenel Ka said. "And if anything like that ever happens again, it won't be the *council* we come hunting."

Tenel Ka spun on her heel, her face still clouded with anger, and started toward the door.

"Come with me, Captain Solo," she said, motioning for him to follow. "There is something I really must tell you."

epilogue

*How did the Empire capture Gamorr without firing a cannon bolt?
They landed backward, and the Gamorreans thought they were retreating!*

—Jacen Solo, age 15

The crimson stains left by her brother's blood had finally
faded from Jaina's face and throat, but perhaps not from
her heart. Why hadn't she believed him when he said he
was trying to save Tenel Ka and Allana? She should have
sensed that he was telling the truth, or at least realized that
he would know better than to ask for quarter to save *himself*. They had, after all, been twins, and had she only been
willing to look for the little goodness that remained in
him—the little bit of Jacen that had not died—she would
have found it.

Jaina wasn't foolish enough to believe it would have
been enough to bring her brother back into the light. He
had gone too far into darkness for *that*. But if she had just
believed him, had not been so sure it was just a Sith trick,
she might have given him the two seconds he needed to explain.

And Allana might still be alive.

A soft hiss sounded from the entrance to Jaina's private
convalescence suite. She glanced away from the ceiling mirror and saw her parents coming through the door, their
eyes bright with joy and relief.

"Hey, kid," her father said. "Good to see you up."

"This isn't really 'up,' Dad." Jaina was floating in a sterile hoverest cabinet, suspended in midair with a nurturing bacta mist swirling over her burned flesh and an opaque modesty curtain draped over—but not touching—her bare skin. "Unless you're comparing it with what'll happen if there's a power failure."

"At least you're out of the tank," her mother said, entering the cabin behind him. "Now we can actually *talk* instead of just smiling and waving."

"Smiling and waving wasn't so bad. It was good to know you were out there." Jaina grew quiet, then said, "But I *do* have a lot of questions."

Her father's face turned somber. "Zekk?"

Jaina nodded. "For starters. Any word?"

"Nothing," he said. "They've found a few StealthX pieces floating around, but there were several lost, so it's impossible to know whether any of it came off his."

"What about his rescue beacon?"

"There's no sign that it was triggered," her mother said. Unlike the rescue beacons of most starfighters, the StealthX beacon wasn't automatic; it had to be activated by the pilot or his astromech when he went EV. "But the Mists *are* pretty thick around there."

"And no sign of him in the Force, of course," Jaina surmised. That was actually the most likely way someone would find him—but only if he was conscious enough to reach out. "I sure haven't felt anything."

"Luke said they're going to keep looking." Her mother stepped over next to the hoverest and looked as though she wanted to touch Jaina, but that was strictly forbidden, of course. "But Mirta Gev sends her thanks."

"She made it back to Mandalore okay, then?" Jaina asked.

"Not exactly," her father said. "She's safe—"

"And healing nicely," her mother added. "So is her husband . . . Ghes Orade, I believe."

"Just not on Mandalore," her father added. "Turns out Fett can't go back there—ever. Neither can his granddaughter."

"*What?*" Jaina couldn't imagine the force that would prevent either of the two from returning to their home. "Why not?"

"The Moffs," her father explained. "They were pretty mad about that commando raid on Nickel One, so they made a special strain of nanokiller just for Fett and dropped a few tons of it into Mandalore's atmosphere. If he or Mirta ever go back there, it's just a matter of time before it gets them."

"That's terrible." Jaina thought of Mirta and her plans with Ghes, and she *felt* terrible. "Are you sure?"

"Unfortunately, yes," her mother said. "Tahiri reported it during her first questioning, and the Moffs confirmed it."

"They claim there's no way to fix it," Han said. "A *Mand'alor* who can never set foot on Mandalore—kind of poetic justice, isn't it?"

"It might be justice, but I wouldn't call it poetic," Jaina said. "It's just sad . . . especially for Mirta."

A silence fell over the room just long enough for her mother to shoot her father a "be careful" look, then Leia said, "Well, we *do* have some good news."

"Jag is coming to see me?"

"As soon as he can," her father promised. "He's pretty busy with the peace conference right now. The Moffs seem to keep getting the idea that *they're* the ones who won this war."

"*Won?*" Jaina raised her brow. "The war is over? *Completely?*"

Her mother nodded. "They're having the ceremony now." She retrieved the remote from its storage pocket in Jaina's hoverest cabinet and pointed it at a vidscreen suspended near the ceiling. "We might be able to catch the last part."

As the screen activated, it showed the image of a large dais that had been erected in the vast main hangar of a Star Destroyer. At the front of the dais stood a podium and high table bearing a single sheet of flimsiplast covered in scrawls that appeared to be the signatures of the long row of dignitaries seated at the rear of the platform.

A tall, regal-looking woman in a white admiral's uniform, with green eyes and long copper hair going to gray, was taking the podium to tremendous applause, and a caption at the bottom of the screen read NEW ALLIANCE CHIEF OF STATE DAALA.

"Daala?" Jaina gasped. She stared at the screen in disbelief for a moment, then finally snorted and looked back to her parents. "Very funny, guys, but I'm not really in the mood for practical jokes."

Her parents glanced nervously at each other, then her father said, "No joke, kid. That's the only hitch with the peace deal. Bwua'tu wouldn't take the job—he said he's an admiral, not a liar—"

"What he actually said was that he didn't think he was cunning enough to last in the job," her mother interrupted. "And then he recommended Admiral Daala instead."

"I think the old goat's got a thing for her," her father said.

Her mother shot him a scowl of exasperation. "The admiral's feelings are speculation, of course," she said. "But Daala turned out to be the only universally acceptable choice."

"Universally?" Jaina asked. *"Really?"*

"Well, some of the Moffs squirmed a bit," her father admitted. "But then Jag worked out a deal where Daala promised to let bygones be bygones—as long as half of the new Moffs are female."

Jaina's head was spinning. Female Moffs. Daala in charge of the Alliance. That wasn't going to be good for the

Jedi. But maybe it didn't need to be, if it meant an end to the war.

"Daala might not be *that* bad," her father said. "Give her a chance."

"Okay." Jaina turned her gaze back to the vidscreen, where the admiral was at the podium, waiting for the applause to fade. "Let's hear what she has to say."

Jaina's mother turned up the volume. After a moment, Daala began to speak in a deep, cultured voice.

"What can I add that has not already been said here today?" she began. "If this war has taught us anything, it is that we *all* lose when we fight. My friends, the time has come to try a new way—"

Here, she had to stop and wait for the applause to die down again—and it took nearly a minute.

When she was finally able to continue, she said, "The way of cooperation, so that we can all win *together.*"

More thunderous applause.

Daala motioned for quiet, then continued, "My friends, it is my promise to you here today that sometime in the not-too-distant future, we will live in a galaxy where our space navies exist to *better* our societies, not defend them—where we won't *need* Jedi to sort out our differences and mete out justice, because we will be living under a government that *is* just."

The crowd rose to its feet, roaring and cheering, and Jaina realized with a cold shudder that Jacen had not failed. He had sacrificed everything—his name, his family, his reputation, his life—to unite the galaxy. And now here Jaina was, watching the birth of a galaxywide league of worlds dedicated to working together in peace.

Had Jacen *won* after all?

"Hey, take it easy, kid." Her father stepped in front of the vidscreen. "Daala's not *that* scary."

"Sorry, Dad," Jaina said, glad to be looking at his face instead of Daala's. "It's not Daala. I was just thinking of . . .

of what Caedus sacrificed. At the end, there was a second when he just stopped fighting so he could warn Tenel Ka."

Jaina could not bring herself to look at her parents when she told them this next part, but she *had* to tell. They deserved to know.

"I think he became Jacen again for a second before I . . . before I killed him."

"Jaina, it's okay." Her mother started to reach for her arm again, then barely caught herself. "If you had hesitated, *you* would be the dead one."

Jaina shook her head. "I could have given him a second," she said. "If I had, maybe he could have made Tenel Ka understand in time to save Allana."

Jaina forced herself to look back to her parents and was amazed to see that they didn't appear all that upset. In fact, they looked a little bit guilty.

"Yeah, about that," her father said. "There's something we haven't been able to tell you yet."

Jaina frowned. "What?"

Her mother went the door and opened it, then said, "Amelia, would you come in here for a minute?"

Jaina looked to her father. "Amelia?"

"A war orphan," he said. "Turns out the kid's Force-sensitive. Your mother and I are going to be acting as guardians while she's at the Jedi academy."

Jaina began to grow very suspicious. "An *orphan*?"

"That's how it was explained to us," her mother said. "But it's possible the mother just felt the Jedi academy would be a safer environment than she was able to provide."

She ushered a nervous-looking child of about four or five into the room. The girl had a swarthy complexion and short-cropped black hair, and for a minute, it actually fooled Jaina. But the button nose was a bit of a giveaway— as was the familiar hint of her brother and Tenel Ka in the girl's Force presence.

"Hello, Jaina," Allana's small voice said. "They tell me we're going to be sisters now."

Jaina smiled, her heart suddenly filling with a joy she had not thought imaginable just ten seconds earlier. "I guess we are, Amelia. Welcome to the family."

THE STORY CONTINUES...

**With the end of the brief but
brutal reign of Darth Caedus
comes a period of unexpected
stability. Under the strong hand
of former Imperial Admiral
Daala, star systems set aside
their differences in the hope
of forging a lasting peace.**

But for the Jedi, many of whom had once looked to Jacen Solo for inspiration, the transition has been anything but smooth, as Luke Skywalker strives to chart a new course for the Order, and gropes for an understanding of what ultimately drove his nephew to embrace the dark teachings of the evil Sith Lords.

The road to reconciliation has been harder still for Han and Leia Solo, who have now lost both their sons. Some measure of solace comes in the form of Allana, Jacen's Force-sensitive daughter, whom the Solos have adopted at the request of the girl's mother, Queen Tenel Ka of Hapes. But Han, especially, craves the distraction of action, and so he, Leia, and Allana embark on an investigation into the origin of the *Millennium Falcon,* the charmed starship that has seen Han through so many years of adventure.

By all indications, their quest should be safe, innocent: something to keep them interested and busy. But as they piece together the clues of the past, hints of a more profound mystery begin to reveal themselves, and a faceless threat lies in wait—one that has already launched a tentative assault not only on the Jedi Order, but on the Force itself.

STAR WARS: MILLENNIUM FALCON

THE FUTURE AWAITS . . .

It has been two years since the death of Darth Caedus. Chief of State Natasi Daala has ushered the Galactic Alliance into a time of unprecedented calm, and now the entire galaxy stands poised to freely embrace the same enduring peace that Jacen Solo once sought to impose as a Sith Lord.

In this new era, Luke Skywalker finds himself battling for control of the very order he founded. After Jacen's fall to the dark side, much of the galaxy sees Jedi Knights as rogue soldiers too dangerous and unstable to leave unfettered. It is a view shared by Chief Daala, who has sworn to bring the Order under government control—or disband it entirely.

But the greatest threat to the Jedi remains unseen, a faceless menace even more lethal and insidious than the Sith who have plagued the Jedi for millennia. Awakened by Jacen Solo during his five-year odyssey, this hidden peril is reaching out from the darkest corner of the galaxy, assaulting Jedi Knights in ways that even Luke has yet to perceive—but which he must quickly thwart if he is to have any hope of redeeming the New Jedi Order.

Don't miss the further adventures of
Luke Skywalker, Leia Organa Solo, and Han Solo
in the brand-new epic series,
Star Wars: Fate of the Jedi,
beginning with *Outcast*, by Aaron Allston,
in bookstores April 2009!